BESS LINNET

Three Before Nine

A Story of a Childhood

First edition

ISBN: 978-1-9163729-3-1

Editing by Monica Byles
Cover art by Jean Mackey Lebleu
Cover art by Ben Gilbey

This book was professionally typeset on Reedsy.
Find out more at reedsy.com

for the children

So many words unspoken,
That tear apart the soul and hold you
Chained to yesterday

— MAISIE JOHNSON
THE DARK LYRICS © MAISIE JOHNSON

1

Leaves in Vermont

The leaves, in autumn in Vermont, are every shade of fire. In the woods behind our rented ranch house on a newly developed cul de sac, the sun hit the foliage from above, setting the trees ablaze with colour. Even the all-powerful sun had to fight to reach the earth, the leaves were so dense; only shafts of light, alive with dancing motes, touched the forest floor.

'Look at this one, Beth Anne,' my mother said. 'Look how big it is – and so red! But see how it's not only red? Do you see the veins of yellow? Isn't it beautiful!'

My feet swooshed through the fallen leaves as we made our way among the trees, searching. I picked up a bright leaf and presented it wordlessly to my mom.

'That one is so orange, it reminds me of a pumpkin!' Mom exclaimed in delight. 'Speaking of pumpkins, Pumpkin, this might be the first Halloween you go out trick or treating – you're a big girl now, aren't you, big enough to be brave?'

I nodded enthusiastically. Mom kept my leaf and added it to the others in the bag she had brought along for that very purpose.

Mom knelt down briefly. 'There's the tower – do you see it?' she asked, pointing towards a clearing in the woods. 'Do you think you'll manage to climb all those stairs?'

I nodded again. Mom rose and walked briskly ahead. I trotted along just behind her, eager to reach the forty-foot tall brick structure. I remembered the ache that would come over my legs – recovering, as they still were, from the correction of the clubfoot I had been born with – but there was no way I would tell my mom that my body was tired. I knew better, even at four, than to sabotage this rare outing. I knew, even then, that my mother was like a bird: you had to keep very still when she was with you, so you could wonder at her for as long as possible before she flew away.

My excitement grew as the tower, crowned by its curious set of rectangular teeth of brick, came closer and closer, but so did my anticipation of disappointment. Would the tower be closed? Would my mom have a change of heart and turn us back, saving the tower for another day?

'This is the first time we've been here since your sister was born, isn't it?' Mom asked, as we neared the base of the tower, which – thankfully – was open to visitors that day. 'There's the plaque about Bennington. Do you know, your birthday is actually on Bennington Battle Day!' Mom threw her head back and laughed. I laughed too. I had no idea why it was funny to be born on Bennington Battle Day, but if it made Mom happy, I was all in favour. 'If we hadn't moved to Vermont, I never would have known that your birthday was a holiday. And Alice was born on Flag Day. Andrew wasn't born on any holiday, but his birthday is close to Veteran's Day. How appropriate.'

The sky remained cloudless, but a shadow passed over my mom's features; I was still beside her, but she was gone.

I held my breath. I itched to scramble up the tower stairs, to arrive out of breath at the small square platform with the flagpost dead centre and hold on to the iron railings between the brick teeth to behold the beauty laid out for me in every direction.

Mom returned – not all of her, but enough. 'Come on then, your turn to lead the way,' she said, as if we'd been playing 'It' and it was my turn to tag.

I pelted up the stairs, then ran from railing to railing at the top, eyes wide as I took in the explosion of colour below.

'I forget every time how terrifying this is,' Mom muttered when she reached the top seconds after me. She grabbed my shoulder to keep me from leaning over the guard rail. 'You certainly didn't inherit my fear of heights, did you, Beth Anne?'

When we got home, my mom turned on the iron.

'What we'll do,' Mom told me, 'is we'll pick the most amazing leaves from our collection, and we'll stick them between two sheets of wax paper. We'll use the iron to melt the wax – that will stop the leaf from decomposing any further. We'll be able to hang the wax paper leaves in the windows, so we'll have colour all through the winter months, even when the trees are bare. That'll cheer us up when there's snow on the ground, won't it?'

We sorted through our spoils. I puffed up with pride when Mom let me choose all the winning leaves. When Andy toddled into the room, Mom sent him straight out again. 'You can't be in here, Andrew,' Mom told my freckled brother. 'The iron is on. It's too dangerous.' By now I was walking on air with the favour bestowed upon me.

I was permitted to stay in the room, but I wasn't allowed to handle the iron. I watched Mom's deft movements as she slipped a leaf into a waxed paper sandwich bag then pressed the iron down on top. An acrid smell filled my nostrils and made my throat tickle; I resisted the impulse to pinch my nose shut.

Mom seemed to know instinctively how long to keep the leaf, in its wax-paper sleeve, pinned under the shiny metal of the iron. When the wax had melted, but not burned, Mom removed the iron and lifted the finished product gingerly between her right thumb and index finger.

There it was, a volcano of red and yellow in the shape of a maple leaf, trapped forever by my mother's magic.

'Isn't that gorgeous?' Mom said.

I clapped my hands together in delight.

2

Fly

I was standing – not by accident, but by design – in the middle of the road when I saw him. I stood waiting because I knew he would materialise at some point – I could bank on it – but I wasn't sure exactly when. I heard him coming first. Soon he was close enough for me to feel the thumps as the sound of the motorcycle hit my chest. When he turned the corner into our cul-de-sac, I was bowled over. There was my dad, like some sort of swarthy astronaut cowboy, astride a gleaming, barely controlled beast of a machine. My instinct told me to run, screaming, back into the house, but I held my ground, right there in the middle of our road. Dad would have to pass me to turn into our driveway.

He didn't pass me. Instead he pulled up – close, but not too close – and put his feet down. The sound of the motorcycle continued to reverberate through my four-year-old torso as the engine idled.

'What do you think of my wheels, Beth Anne?' Dad asked. Even in that short sentence I heard the remnants of his Georgian drawl. 'I'll make you a deal – you let me past, and I'll run in and tell your mother I'm taking you for a little spin.'

My mouth opened involuntarily into a huge 'O' and I jumped to the right to make way. Dad parked the motorcycle, dismounted, and disappeared into the house. I stayed next to the bike, admiring the golden angel wings of the logo on the gas tank. I reached out to lay my hands on the wings; the tank was still warm from the residual warmth of the engine.

Dad caught me off guard when he came out. 'Don't touch the motorcycle when I'm not around, Beth Anne,' he admonished. 'It's a big piece of machinery, and it's plenty dangerous if you don't understand it. Before we go for our quick ride, I'll just explain the basics of how the motorcycle works to you.'

Dad began pointing to various parts of the bike. He said words I had never heard before – ignition, pistons, internal combustion. I hadn't the foggiest notion what he was on about, but I nodded respectfully, and if he touched any part of the machine, I followed suit, tentatively placing my fingers exactly where my dad had.

'Now for the safety talk. We don't have a helmet for you, but I won't go too fast, and we won't go very far. You've got to make me one promise though,' Dad said. He knelt down so as to look me straight in the eye, but I could only meet his sea-green gaze briefly before the intensity made me lower my eyes. Instead I watched in fascination as the hairs of Dad's moustache moved in time with his mouth forming words.

'You have to promise to hold on,' Dad said. 'You can't let go at all, not even for one second, because motorcycles aren't like cars. So you're going to sit behind me, right here,' Dad motioned to the black leather seat, 'And you're going to keep your arms around me without letting go. OK?'

My heart jumped in my throat. I raised my eyes to meet Dad's again and I nodded.

Dad was not satisfied with a nod. 'Don't just nod – tell me you promise to hold on,' he specified.

I glanced again at the golden wings sparkling on the gas tank.

'I promise,' I said.

Dad swung me off the ground and placed me on the black leather seat. My feet dangled far above the ground. Dad knitted his substantial brow. 'I hadn't thought about where you'd rest your feet,' he muttered. 'Tell you what, just keep your feet pulled in tight – don't stick them straight out or anything.'

I nodded again. Dad tossed his leg over and started the engine. 'Just grab on,' he shouted to me above the din. I did as I was told, clutching my dad's sides so tightly I noticed the pressure of every fingernail. We sped off.

The wind whooshed across my cheeks and sent my long hair flying like a straw-coloured flag behind me. The road, which normally seemed so distant from my vantage point in the back seat of our car, now rushed to meet me at a million miles per hour. Dad turned out of our somnolent cul-de-sac and onto a less familiar street; houses of varied shapes and sizes flashed by in rapid-fire while the trees behind them became a single green blur. I resisted the strong urge to clap, remembering my promise to under no circumstances relinquish my hold on my father.

My parents, when inspecting me upon my arrival in the delivery room, would have noticed immediately that I had not been born unscathed. I was born with congenital talipes equinovarus, or clubfoot, particularly on my left side but also, to a lesser degree, on my right side. Clubfoot can be treated more or less invasively, depending on factors such as the severity of the deformation and the doctors' assessment of the patient. When I was born in 1967, my parents were encouraged to put me in a brace and special shoes; this method avoided surgery, but demanded parental involvement on a day-to-day basis and regular check-ups with doctors. Mom, who had come within spitting distance of completing a nursing degree, must have understood exactly what was wrong with my jaunty feet. When the doctors, satisfied with my progress, declared me recovered enough to lose the brace and the orthopaedic shoes, they advised my parents to let me walk and run as much as possible, ideally barefoot, to maintain proper rotation.

Mom listened to the doctors. By four I was intimately acquainted with the many surfaces my bare feet might encounter when walking or running outdoors: the tickle of blades of grass between my toes, the near-burn of sun-hot asphalt on the ball of my foot, the almost unbearable pain of sharp gravel under my heel, the refreshing squelch of mud, even the shocking cold of snow. Mom's diligence paid off; my leg and foot gained greater and greater strength and range of movement. By four, only specialists would have noticed the particular gait of a corrected clubfoot.

Success came, however, at a price. I learned, by four, that my body was not to be trusted; it did not always obey my wishes, and worse yet, it sometimes worked against me, circumscribing my movement. Already my body was a traitor to my spirit.

As the world whizzed past my dad's motorcycle with thrilling velocity, the trials and limitations of my body became irrelevant. All that mattered, that late afternoon in Burlington, was the throb and hum of this machine whose golden wings had offered me freedom. I didn't need to drag my leg along in a brace, clomp around in orthopaedic shoes or even walk barefoot – I could just fly.

3

American Pie

I was playing with my orange Matchbox dune buggy in the sand box underneath the enormous spruce tree that had given the street of our new home its name when Mom came to fetch me.

'It's getting dark, Beth Anne,' Mom told me. 'Time to leave your toy here until tomorrow.'

I formed a fist around the weathered car – was it mine, or had I appropriated it from Andy? – and stepped out of the sandbox.

'Pumpkin, I don't want that car in the house. It's an outside toy – it has sand all over it. Just leave it in the sandbox – it'll be just where you left it in the morning. The cicadas won't fly away with your Matchbox, I promise,' Mom joked.

I stretched my hand out over the sandbox and released my favourite toy. It landed on the golden dunes with a discreet thud.

'Come say hello to Fred and Rachel,' Mom said, leading me into the house and towards the living room where my dad's business partner and his wife were ensconced in the deep sofa, Fred with a cigarette in his right hand, Rachel with a drink in her left, their remaining hands entwined just above the deep crack between the overstuffed cushions. My dad stood balancing an LP on the stacking spindle of the record player; as I made my way towards Fred, Dad swung the turntable arm over and returned to his seat nearest the speaker.

'What a sight for sore eyes! Give your Uncle Fred a big hug, sweetheart,' Fred exclaimed, resting his cigarette in the intricately carved ashtray on top of the wooden side table inlaid with mother-of-pearl. The elephants on the surface of the table weren't bothered, and I was accustomed to the smoky fog.

As Fred enveloped me in his ample embrace and Rachel patted my hair maternally, the record dropped; Don McLean began to sing in his sweet, clear tenor.

'Show Fred and Rachel what you can do, Beth Anne,' my mother prompted me.

I staged bashfulness.

'I'll help you get started,' Dad offered, and he began to sing along with the voice coming through the speakers in the rich baritone that earned him a welcome in any choir.

I joined in with the first chorus and Fred and Rachel cheered. That was all the encouragement I needed; I jumped off the sofa, spun around the room, opened my voice full throttle and sang every word of 'American Pie' while the adults clapped in time.

'How did she learn that party trick?' Rachel asked my mom, as I tumbled back into the sofa.

'She's been reading for a few months now,' Mom said. 'It's actually causing trouble at kindergarten – they don't know quite what to do with her.'

'They make me go read with the second-graders,' I told Rachel.

'Isn't that good though?' asked Rachel, who hadn't yet had children of her own. 'That you get to be in a group at your level, instead of being held back with the ones who can't manage *See Spot Run*?'

I snuck a glance at my mom – did she want me to tell Rachel the truth, or did she want me to pretend that I liked the long lonely walk through the empty hallway, the timid knock on the door, and the sullen stares of thirty enormous second-graders who hated me for showing them up?

Mom nodded at me. 'Rachel's our friend, Beth Anne. You can say what you want.'

'I don't like reading with the second-graders,' I confessed, as I snuggled up next to Rachel. 'They're scary.'

'Oh, you probably just don't want to stick out. But how could you not stick out? You're like a little angel – an angel who can read.' Rachel gave me a squeeze.

'I'm not so sure she'll be acting like an angel when I tell her it's bedtime,' Mom said.

I burrowed further into Rachel's side. 'I love you, Beth Anne, but if your mama says it's bedtime, then bedtime it is. Fly away, angel – I'll see you again soon. Give Auntie Rachel a big smooch before you go though,' Rachel instructed me, bending her left cheek towards me. I obliged, planted a kiss, then scrambled off the sofa and trailed my mother out of the living room.

'Hey,' I heard my dad call out, 'I think you forgot something, there, Tiger.'

I skipped back and kissed my dad's stubbly cheek. 'That's better,' Dad said. 'Sleep tight.'

Mom turned back the covers and patted my bed to show me where I belonged. I burrowed in and pulled the blankets all the way up to my chin, not because it was cold, but because it was safer that way.

'What about the closet?' I asked Mom.

Mom bristled ever so slightly. 'There's nothing in the closet except clothes, Beth Anne. The only thing you have to fear in this room is nausea from too much pink,' she added.

I pursed my lips. I had helped pick out the colours for my room at the paint and decorating store Dad and Fred both owned and ran together. The roses spilling all over my wallpaper were pink, my lampshade was pink, and best of all, the yarn of the thick shag carpet under my always-bare feet was not just pink, but vivid magenta, with a helping of burned orange thrown in for good measure.

Mom was jolly from the wine with dinner, but she was still paying attention. 'There could never be too much pink in the world for you though, isn't that right, Sunshine?'

I pressed my advantage. 'I think there might be something in the closet,' I said.

'I don't think I was scared of monsters in the bedroom when I was your age,' Mom said with a sigh of resignation, as she crossed to the closet door, opened it, waved her hands at the contents with a flourish – handmade dresses in calico fabrics, handknit woollen jumpers stacked on shelves, even handsewn corduroy trousers with elastic waistbands – then closed the door firmly. 'That came later,' Mom added.

Mom had demonstrated unequivocally that no physical monsters were present in my walk-in closet – but I knew Mom had seen something in there, something that I couldn't yet see because it was visible to her alone, and because of that, the gesture intended to comfort me left me more uncertain than before. To ask for any further reassurance would be pushing my luck, so when Mom leaned over to kiss me goodnight, I smiled up at her.

'Good night, Sunshine,' she said. 'See you in the morning.'

4

Elgar

The good times, like the evening with Fred and Rachel, didn't last. More and more often in the evenings – when Andy and Alice had been asleep in their shared room for hours, but I remained awake and vigilant in my own rosy room – other sounds would waft up the stairs and slip under the door. There was only the slightest of cracks between my door and the hall, but the noises were masters of contortion, and they found their way in, unbidden and unwanted: only the tone at first, as if there had been a key change from major to minor, then the raised voices, and finally the crying. All of these I could manage. I lay there, in my bed fit for a princess, and willed the sounds equally to stop and to carry on: to stop because I hated them, to carry on because the silence when they ended was what I truly couldn't bear. The silence could be broken three ways: by the creak of the stairs if my parents made up and retired, by the resumption of the argument, or most terrifying of all, by the rev of a car engine. When I heard the growl of the motor, when the artificially white beam of the headlights poured in through my windows and across my damask chenille bedspread, that meant that Mom was not only leaving in spirit, but leaving corporeally as well, and the house would fall into a state of forced silence as both my father downstairs, and I upstairs, awaited her return.

The first few times it happened I stayed in my room, in a state of suspended animation, rolling the pompoms of my bedspread repetitively between my fingers and fending off sleep. If I stayed awake long enough, I might be rewarded by the reappearance of the strong white beams of the headlights, followed by the now much quieter hum of the engine as Mom pulled remorsefully back into the driveway. The soft click of the front door would follow, and then, if I could force myself to resist exhaustion for just a little while longer, I would hear subdued voices from downstairs, then the footsteps of both of my parents as they ascended the wooden staircase on their way to the master bedroom. I would feign sleep when they passed my room, because sometimes Mom would gently turn the doorknob and a sliver of warm yellow light from the hall would fall across my face as she gazed at me where I lay, ostensibly dreaming.

But then came the night when, unusually, my mother opened my door before rather than after her departure. The noise was amplified that night – the shouting was punctuated by the muffled report of porcelain shattering – and then Mom ran upstairs. She rushed to the master bedroom, and for a moment I thought the evening had reached a new sort of conclusion, one that I vastly preferred, because it meant Mom was still in the house. Every nerve ending in my body tingled as I listened.

The door to my bedroom opened. I was so surprised that I forgot to fake sleep. I turned wide-eyed towards my mother, whose face was ravaged by recent tears and whose right hand clutched a small case.

'What are you doing still awake, Sunshine?' Mom asked me without expecting an answer. She tiptoed in and perched on the edge of my bed. 'I'm going away for a few days, Beth Anne,' Mom said. I heard the tremor as she fought back more tears. 'I want you to be a good girl and look after your little brother and sister, OK?'

My insides began to resemble the rags I had watched Mom twist and twist, squeezing out every drop of excess water, when she was cleaning, but I kept my tears inside like a good girl and nodded solemnly.

'Cooperate with your father,' Mom added.

'When will you be back?' I asked. I wasn't sure that I'd be able to keep track of the time, as the blending of hours into days, let alone days into weeks, remained mysterious, but I hoped her answer would help me classify the interim as 'short' or 'long'.

Fresh tears glistened on Mom's cheeks. 'I'm not sure, Sunshine, but you'll be fine here,' she said, then reconsidered. 'You'll be better off here. Now you get some sleep – you've got school in the morning.'

Mom kissed me on the top of my head, then stood up and walked out, closing the door fully behind her. Only when I heard the car pull out of the driveway did I permit myself to cry, and even then, my sobs were muffled, so as not to wake Andy and Alice in the room next door. But sleep refused to come to me, and because I had not heard my father's deliberate steps on the wooden staircase, I guessed that I was not the only one awake. My suspicion was confirmed when something other than light seeped into my room; he had the volume low, but Dad was playing music downstairs.

I did something I hadn't done before. Gathering all my courage, I crawled out from under my covers, left my bedroom, then – holding tightly to the banister – walked tentatively down the stairs, testing each stair with my toes before going on to the next one, to where Dad was sitting alone in the darkened living room. He was in his usual chair, right next to the record player and one of the enormous speakers, just like he had been the evening I sang for Fred and Rachel, but Dad wasn't laughing tonight.

'Did the music wake you?' Dad asked, as I walked towards him.

I shook my head. 'Mom woke me when she came in to tell me she was going away,' I said, doing my best to display no emotion.

The cello took the melody. I listened as its strings moaned and pleaded, only to be answered by the thrilling response of the upper strings, then the cello again, then the entire orchestra, back and forth, back and forth, as the music swirled undeterred towards resolution.

'That's right,' Dad said. 'Your mother needs some time to herself. I'm sure she'll be home soon. And in the meantime, I'm still here and I'm going to give you a hug, let you listen to a few more minutes of Elgar, then carry you upstairs and put you right back in bed, where you belong at this hour of the night.'

Dad did as he promised, but instead of just a hug, he let me sit next to him, as the cello sang its plaintive song, until my eyes grew heavy and the room began to blur.

When the door of my room next clicked shut, I didn't even hear it because I was already fast asleep.

5

Moustache

I entered a state of suspended animation. Each night after Dad tucked me in, I lay awake, hoping to hear Mom's car pulling into the driveway. Each night I fell asleep accidentally, still hoping.

Occasional get-togethers with Fred and Rachel provided welcome respite from the gloom that hung over our altered, reduced family. Sometimes they came to our house on Spruce Street bearing casseroles and wine; sometimes Dad bundled the three of us into the car and took us over to Fred and Rachel's.

Fred and Rachel lived in a house very unlike ours on one of the most sought-after hills of Burlington. Our house was New England; theirs was New York, skilfully transplanted to New England. While Fred and Rachel remained childless, they were flanked on each side by neighbours with children. The children in the house with the black car in the driveway were older; they had no interest in playing with random visitors. The boy in the house with the red car though, Kevin, was an only child hungry for playmates. Kevin's strongest asset, in my eyes, was his Big Wheel. Everything about the Big Wheel was enticing – from the low-slung blue seat to the size of the front wheel, detailed to resemble spokes – but it was the streamers that made Kevin's plastic trike irresistible.

That Saturday afternoon Rachel came down the porch stairs to the driveway to meet us.

'Would you look at Alice – hasn't she grown!' Rachel cooed, as she opened the door to the back seat of our car. Alice recognised Rachel and raised her arms to be picked up. 'Oh, Mark, look at her – she knows me,' Rachel said to my dad.

Dad, who had correctly anticipated that Rachel would be the one to carry Alice from the car to the house, muttered, 'She sees a lot more of you than she does of her mother,' as he held Andy's hand for the walk up the porch stairs to the front door.

'Is Kevin home?' I asked Rachel.

'I think so,' Rachel said, as she cradled Alice. 'Why don't you go knock on his door, Beth Anne?'

At home Alice often cried. Rachel's skill at soothing Alice, a skill I hadn't mastered, lifted the burden of keeping my promise to my mother to look after my little sister. I understood already, at five, that Rachel couldn't marry Dad because of Fred, which was a shame, but I liked Fred's bear hugs, so I forgave him for blocking that path. I bounded over to Kevin's house. It was Kevin himself who opened the door; he'd put his shoes on as soon as he'd heard us talking in the driveway.

'Hi,' Kevin said.

I studied Kevin's nose to see if any new freckles had sprouted since the last time we'd played together: no, Andy still won.

'Hi,' I said. 'Where's your Big Wheel?'

'It's in the garage,' Kevin said. 'I'll go get it.'

Kevin stepped back over the threshold of his front door.

'Close the door, Kevin,' I heard Kevin's mother shout. 'You're letting the flies in.'

Kevin did as he was told, then went to fetch his trike. The red, white and blue streamers glittered in the spring sunshine. I hoped Kevin would let me have the first go, but he took his rightful turn as the trike's owner and sat down at the wheel.

To propel oneself uphill on a Big Wheel was no easy task, so I stood behind Kevin and with my hands on the back of the blue plastic seat ran as fast as I could, pushing with all the strength I could muster. Finally we reached the top of the hill, where the grunt work would pay off.

'Can I go down first?' I asked. 'Because I did the pushing?'

Kevin was an easy sell. 'Only if I go next,' he stipulated, climbing out of the driver's seat.

I contorted myself into the trike. The black asphalt of the hill beckoned. I grabbed hold of the handlebars and put my feet on the blue pedals.

'Are you ready?' Kevin asked from behind.

'I'm ready . . . set . . .'

'Go!' we both shouted. My feet went round faster and faster as I pedalled like mad and Kevin sped me up further by pushing from the back. As the incline increased, the Big Wheel gained speed. Soon Kevin could no longer keep up. He let go of the seat rest and began running along behind me, hollering all the while.

When the trike achieved maximum velocity, I raised my feet off the pedals and let gravity take over. It wasn't my dad's motorcycle, and it wasn't even my own trike, but for a few thrilling seconds, I was as invincible as any charioteer.

Kevin caught up with me at the foot of the hill when the Big Wheel had run out of steam and my heart rate had slowed.

'That was the best ride ever!' I announced.

'My turn!' Kevin answered.

* * *

Mom called us on the telephone sometimes. If I saw a cloud pass over my father's face after he'd picked up the phone and said hello, I began to prepare myself, steeling myself to chat happily, willing myself to convince Mom that I was being not just a good girl, but such a good girl that she should definitely come home.

The sound of Mom's voice through the clunky black telephone receiver gave me a queasy feeling in the pit of my stomach. I hungered not only to hear her, but to see her, to touch her. I pressed the heavy receiver as tightly as I could against my ear, grabbing every word Mom said with a ravenous appetite until she asked me to hand the phone back to Dad, or, if she had heard him babbling in the background, to Andy. Alice was years away from understanding telephones; to hear Mom's disassociated voice would have done her more harm than good.

One Thursday, when the teacher had once again exiled me from the classroom because of my advanced reading, my yearning to see my mother overwhelmed me. I decided there and then that if Mom wouldn't come back to me, then I would go to her.

Instead of walking to the second-grade classroom as I had been told to do by my kindergarten teacher, I brazenly walked right out of school. I had formed a hypothesis in my head that Mom was at the pool. Mom had taken me to the pool several times. I remembered how Mom smiled when she held me gently in the water, how she had convinced me, against my better judgement, to let go of the side of the pool that I was clutching, how she had assured me that she'd been a lifeguard, so she wouldn't let me go under. When I reluctantly took my hands from safety, began to paddle, and moved forward through the water, swimming for the first time, Mom cheered. When she let go of me entirely and I stayed afloat, she clapped her hands.

'You're swimming, Beth Anne! You're swimming!'

The pool was not far from my school; I would meet her there. I somehow managed to cross the busy main street in one piece, but then I became confused. I didn't know which building the pool was hidden inside. None of the exteriors looked familiar. Maybe I should just go home; maybe Mom would be there, sitting at the kitchen table smoking a cigarette, feeding Alice lunch. But where was home? How would I get there?

I began to sob. Tears that I had held back for too long burst out of me, and I stood there on the bustling sidewalk paralysed, a five-year-old truant howling with grief, until a passing woman stopped to help.

'Are you lost?' the woman asked me. 'Where's your mother?'

I tried to explain to the woman that my mother was at the pool. The woman looked at me quizzically. 'I don't think she'd be at the pool without you, dear,' the woman said. 'Aren't you old enough to be at school?'

I cried even harder when I confessed that yes, I was indeed old enough to be at school. The woman kindly escorted me back across the street and straight to the principal's office, where I was told that I must never again, under any circumstances, leave the school without permission, and where I was made to wait until my father was able to leave work to collect me early as I was too distraught to return to class.

I didn't find her at the pool, but shortly after I walked out of school I came home one day to discover that Mom was, indeed, sitting in the kitchen smoking a cigarette. Mom opened her arms wide when she saw me.

'I've missed you, Sunshine,' Mom said, and her voice was even more beautiful in person than it had been when it had come to me through the twisty black phone cord.

I rushed into her embrace, soaking in her presence. 'I love you,' I murmured into her body; Mom didn't hear me.

My parents didn't speak to each other at dinner that night. My dad's jaw, when he wasn't talking to me or Andy, was clenched shut. The cloud, previously reserved for my mother's phone calls, had become a storm front.

When Dad left for work the next morning, he was carrying a suitcase. Dad didn't come home that night, or the next night, or the night after that.

Several days later, I was in the sandbox under the spruce tree, pretending my orange Matchbox dune buggy was Kevin's Big Wheel and making it speed down the hill I had carefully built up out of damp sand, when Mom called me inside.

'Your father's on the phone, Beth Anne,' she said, with an edge of hostility. 'Hurry up inside.'

I left my toy in the sandbox and made my way to the kitchen. After a few pleasantries, my dad cut to the chase.

'I have to ask you something, Beth Anne,' Dad said.

I waited. I missed being able to watch Dad's moustache when he spoke to me. I tried to envision it – all the black hairs moving in synchronicity with his words – but it was already becoming fuzzy in my memory.

'Beth Anne,' Dad asked, after clearing his throat, 'I have a very important question to ask you. Do you want to come and live with me, or do you want to stay where you are, with your mom?'

My mind reeled, but I said nothing. I heard the faint echo of my own breathing as I stared through the kitchen doorway to where Alice was doing her utmost best to walk independently. The phone line crackled.

'Did you hear me, Beth Anne?' Dad asked.

Alice toppled over, but that didn't deter her; she had caught sight of me, and now she had a plan. Alice stretched out her chubby baby arms, raised herself, held on to the edge of the table, then let go and took a few steps in my direction before landing again on her padded bottom.

'I want to stay here,' I said to my father, waving to Alice with my free hand.

6

Amber Wave

Sunlight poured through the enormous windows onto the bed where Dad was propped up reading the Sunday *Burlington Free Press*. Andy and Alice were snuggled up next to Dad, one child on each side. Dad's coffee mug was sitting at least somewhat out of harm's way on the bedside table; Dad had ignored it for so long that the coffee had gone cold. I was doing somersaults across the foot of the bed when I caught sight of Dad's chest hair poking out from the V of his bathrobe.

'Andy, look at Dad – he is so hairy!' I told my little brother.

Andy lifted his head and peered at Dad's chest. 'Hairy!'

'That's just the front of me,' Dad said. 'You should see the back. I'm like an ape man,' he continued, beating his chest and making gorilla noises for effect. Alice gurgled, Andy laughed, and both imitated him as best they could.

Monkeys didn't strike me as a suitably impressive comparison. 'Not like an ape man,' I countered, 'like a bear.'

'Ooh, a bear, I love it,' Dad said. 'Like a grizzly bear. And watch out, because this grizzly bear is on the prowl, and what he likes to eat most of all, better than anything else, is . . .' Here Dad raised his outstretched arms and adopted his most ferocious expression, then growled, 'Girls who do somersaults!'

Dad lunged from his half-sitting position, leaving Andy and Alice to fall into the many cushions at the head of the bed, and seized me gently by the ankle.

I screamed in mock terror. Dad let go immediately, leaned back into his previous position, and resettled Andy and Alice. I resumed my somersaults. I liked the bed in the flat Dad had moved to after leaving our house on Spruce Street because we were allowed to play on it. The bed in the master bedroom on Spruce Street that had been my parents', and was now my mom's, was still off limits as it always had been. Mom's nearly completed nursing degree had left her with a strong drive to maintain hospital corners with which somersaults were incompatible.

Later that day, when Andy and Alice were napping after lunch, I played with Dad's new labyrinth game while Dad strummed his guitar absent-mindedly while watching some sort of sporting event on his black-and-white TV the size of an album cover. The labyrinth was a wooden box, about a foot square, with wooden wheels at the side and front to control the tilt of the maze itself. A path through the sixty numbered holes, each delineated by wooden barriers, was printed on the maze; the goal was to direct the steel ball bearing to the highest-numbered hole possible. When the ball did eventually fall through a hole, it then rolled along the floor of the box beneath the maze to a mouse-hole exit with a tiny ball dock. Once there, the ball could be picked up and set back in its starting position to resume play.

Try as I might, I never managed to get the ball further than about the twelfth hole in the lower left-hand corner of the maze plate. No matter what combination of tilts I attempted with the directional knobs, as soon as the ball's intended direction was away rather than towards me, the ball would disappear into a hole, usually hole thirteen or fourteen.

Dad was keeping one eye on the TV and one eye on my progress. When he heard the light thunk of the ball bearing hitting the floor of the game, he placed his guitar on the sofa next to him and came over to the table.

'You're still not having much luck, hey?'

I shook my head. 'Show me how you do it?' I begged.

Dad had completed an engineering degree before becoming a small business owner; playing the angles came naturally to him.

'Watch carefully,' Dad said. His green eyes tracked the ball as he steered it past each new danger. All was going to plan until hole forty-four. 'Oh, sugar,' Dad said. I had overheard Dad swearing a couple of times when he thought I wasn't listening, but he never, ever swore in front of me, Andy or Alice.

Dad plucked the ball from the mouse-hole dock and started over. This time he made no wrong moves, and when the ball had safely completed the course, Dad held his right hand up for me to high five.

'That's how it's done, Beth Anne,' Dad said, 'Easy as pie.'

* * *

Dad moved to the farm in Shelburne from his flat in town to save money. Instead of an entire apartment to himself, at the farm Dad had only a room, but he shared the entire communal living space with Annie, Stanley and their two children, Melinda and Brian.

The first thing I noticed about Dad's new home was that it was further away. Dad's apartment in town had been within walking distance of the house on Spruce Street. I had never left school to find Dad, but it comforted me to think that if I ever really needed to find him, I just might be able to. Not so with the farm. Even if I borrowed Kevin's Big Wheel, there was no way I could transport myself that far from downtown. The next thing I noticed was that Annie, Stanley, Melinda and Brian were a family. I wondered if Dad would become an adopted part of their family; if so, by extension, we would too.

'Melinda is a year younger than you, but a year older than Andy,' Annie told me when she welcomed me to the farm for our first visit. 'And Brian is right between Andy and Alice. Isn't that funny? Your ages slot together perfectly!'

I smiled. I was excited to play with Annie's daughter Melinda – to play with someone other than Kevin, to play with a girl nearly my age. At the farm, playing usually included dancing. Annie and Stanley had a stereo built into a wooden chest as long as I was tall. Once a record started, if I closed the lid of the chest, I could sit on top; if the music was loud enough, I could feel the vibrations coming through the integrated speakers and buzzing against the backs of my bare legs. I never sat down for long, because as soon as I made myself comfortable, Mindy would spin over, take my hands and pull me down onto the varnished wooden dance floor, which was really just the floor. The varnish made the floor particularly slippery, and on it Mindy had learned how to do a pirouette that wouldn't have gained her points in a ballet exam but definitely gave her star status in my eyes. I spent whole songs copying that pirouette, until I fell down or became too dizzy to carry on, whichever came first.

The kids – all five of us – drank milk, and the adults – all three of them – drank wine with dinner at the farm in Shelburne. When Mom had wine with dinner at home on Spruce Street, she grew more and more distant. Sometimes, even at dinner, she cried. I didn't know what to do when she cried, so I would just sit there, eating my dinner although my appetite had vanished, because Mom was a big believer in finishing plates. If Andy's or Alice's lips began to quiver when they saw Mom crying, I'd shoot them an admonishing look, a look that said, 'I'm your big sister, and if I look at you like this, it means you'd better stop what you're doing right now or else.' That usually worked. Sometimes Mom pulled herself together; sometimes she didn't.

When Annie, Stanley, and Dad drank, none of them shed tears. Mostly they talked, and sometimes they laughed. Annie had a nasal laugh which, particularly when combined with her twinkly blue eyes and her pixie face, led me to believe she could be partly elf. I had seen several Christmas specials on TV, so I was well informed about elf characteristics. Stanley, however, was physically quite unlike Santa Claus: he was clean-shaven, unlike my permanently moustachioed dad, and he had not the slightest trace of a tummy. Temperamentally, though, Stanley – who worked as a teacher – paid attention when kids spoke to him, just like Santa Claus. I was fond of Stanley, but I could tell that Stanley wasn't too fond of my dad.

Dancing was not the only thing Mindy and I did at the farm. Sometimes we played in the toy room, a magical room designed to act as the receptacle for all of Mindy and Brian's many enviable toys. The best part of the toy room was that the adults didn't care at all whether or not the room was tidy; perhaps as a result, it never was. Sometimes we enlisted Andy and Brian as participants and went out into the gigantic yard to play tag; Alice was still too little to join in.

One June weekend when we went to visit Dad at the farm, just before school ended for the summer, Stanley was gone. No one said anything about Stanley at dinner, and I guessed that, like Mom once had, Stanley had needed some time to himself.

I asked Dad about Stanley in the car on the way home to Burlington. Dad kept his eyes on the road straight ahead of him, but cleared his throat in a way that meant my question had disrupted his usual equilibrium.

'I wanted to talk to you about that actually, Beth Anne,' Dad began in the voice he reserved for imparting important information. 'Things have changed at the farm. Annie and I have fallen in love, and Stanley moved out last week.'

'Did he move to your apartment?' I asked. I was thinking I might be able to go and see Stanley; I had missed him over the weekend.

Dad laughed awkwardly. 'No, Stanley didn't move to my apartment. He moved in with some friends. I haven't told your mother about this yet. She may not be too happy. I think it's best if I tell her tonight, in person, instead of over the phone.'

I didn't hear Dad's discussion with Mom about Stanley. Forewarned and forearmed, as soon as we arrived back home I ran to the sandbox to check on my dune buggy.

The evening before the last day of kindergarten, Mom told me to say a special goodbye to any friends I had made at school, because I wouldn't be returning to Redmond Elementary in September; we were moving in August to Duxbury, to a house we would share with someone named Michael. I didn't need to say any special goodbyes at school.

Burlington, Vermont, is far enough north that darkness in July falls late in the evening and even then, only after a substantial period of dusk. Because of my inability to go to sleep in anything other than optimal conditions unless exhausted, Vermont summer evenings often found me awake until night had well and truly fallen, sometime after nine o'clock. This particular July night, it was late enough that Mom had to rouse me from a deep sleep. I opened my eyes, expecting daylight, but the sky outside my windows was pitch black.

'Your father's store is burning,' Mom said, shaking my shoulder gently with her hand. 'Get up. I'm taking you and Andrew over. Alice can stay in her cot.'

I had already learned, during the months that Mom and Dad had been apart, to speak as little as I could about Dad, but the thought of Dad stuck in his store in a fire was too much for me to bear without comment.

'But . . . but . . . Dad?'

'Oh, don't worry, your father is fine. The fire started at night after everyone had gone home for the day. His insurance company will probably cover the damage so he won't lose much, just what the deductible won't cover. Now out of bed. You don't even need to put clothes on, it's warm outside. Just get your socks and shoes on. I'm going to go get Andrew. I'll meet you downstairs.'

Andy was so dazed when he came downstairs, still rubbing his eyes, that it made me giggle. I hit his bicep to wake him up.

'Ouch!' Andy winced. 'Why'd you do that?'

'To keep you from going to sleep standing up.'

'I'm not asleep,' Andy protested.

'Kids, hurry up, get your shoes on,' Mom ordered.

The smoke was the first sign. I gasped and covered my nose with my hand; Andy followed suit. Mom didn't take any notice of our nascent respiratory distress; she carried on walking briskly towards Dad's store. Except only the black skeleton of Dad's store was there now, engulfed by flames. A living wall of fire was decimating the building that had stood tall only hours before; I could hear the tongues of the flames hissing and cackling over the noise of the enormous crowd that had gathered to witness the spectacle, over the shouts of the firemen, over the roar of the water from the hoses.

'Why hasn't the water stopped the fire?' I asked Mom. My face felt hot. Even at this distance the fire was throwing off huge amounts of heat.

'The fire spread too fast for them to control it,' Mom explained. The reflection of the flames flickered on her skin, giving her a waxen appearance. I thought about the paint colour cards in Dad's interior decorating store with their fanciful names: Azure Blue, Amber Wave, Chartreuse. I liked to flick through the colour cards, searching for the best names, just like I did with our 64-pack of Crayola crayons. The carpet samples, hanging in thick books from metal rings, were even more fun; the names – stated at the top of the smooth labels sewn on to the lower right-hand corner of each square – were equally evocative, but the samples did the paint swatches one better by providing tactile as well as visual information. I said my silent goodbyes to the paint cards, the carpet books, and the rest of Dad and Fred's store. I clutched Andy's hand tightly, but Andy didn't reciprocate. Andy didn't seem upset at the loss of the store and everything in it – on the contrary, Andy's mouth hung open in frank admiration of the blaze.

'Andy,' I said into my brother's ear. Mom's head was three feet above me; there was no way she would overhear given all the background noise. 'It's *Dad's* store that's burning. Don't you care?'

Andy's eyes widened in horror. 'Dad?'

I huffed in annoyance. Why couldn't Andy keep up? Hadn't he been paying attention when Mom told us Dad was safe? 'No, not Dad himself, Dad himself is fine. Everybody is fine, but not the store. The store has burned down, Andy, so no more touching the numbers on the cash register.'

As long as Dad wasn't burning, Andy wasn't bothered about the cash register. 'Five fire engines,' Andy informed me, pointing.

I counted. Andy was right: there were five fire engines.

When we got home to Spruce Street, Mom held the front door open for us. 'Remember, be as quiet as mice. I will not have you waking Alice at this hour,' Mom said in a stage whisper.

I did as I was told, tiptoeing into the house and upstairs as though one false move would blow my cover. Andy, to my pleasant surprise, did the same; I was proud of him. Mom slipped into my room to tuck me in and kiss me goodnight. Her face was still shining, as if sparks from the fire had taken root inside her and she was now lit from within. When I closed my eyes, expecting sleep – for once – to come instantly, all I saw was the wrecking ball of flames demolishing my father's store, over and over.

7

Milkweed

The red wooden house in Duxbury stood by itself at the top of a hill. It would take a whole minute of running full tilt across first the substantial yard, then a field, and finally another yard to reach the nearest neighbouring house – a modern house in natural wood with sliding glass doors and an elevated deck. Mom said that that house belonged to out-of-staters. We had been out-of-staters too when we first moved to Vermont, but Mom considered us nearly native now because Alice had been born in Burlington. Alice had the distinction of being not just the only Vermonter, but also the only civilian; Andy and I were Air Force brats, but Alice was not. Many years later, when I was working a summer job as an ice cream scooper for the tourists at the Ben & Jerry's factory in Waterbury, I slipped and called myself a Vermonter when asked about my provenance.

'You're not a Vermonter,' my questioner replied, face crinkled in disgust. 'You can't tell me your parents were born here.'

'No,' I admitted, blushing in embarrassment. 'They were born in Pennsylvania and Georgia.'

'I bet you weren't even born here, were you?'

I looked down at my hands, one idle, one holding the silver metal

ice cream scoop poised above the mint chocolate chip, which was –
to the disappointment of many children – white, rather than sickly
green.

'No, you're right. I was born in Illinois,' I mumbled.

'I thought so,' my interrogator crowed, vindicated. 'You can't
call yourself a Vermonter unless you, your parents, and even your
grandparents were born here, alright? I'm a Vermonter – my great-
grandparents were both born merely a stone's throw from where I
live now. You're not a Vermonter, and neither are Ben and Jerry. They
make good ice cream though,' my customer added, grudgingly.

I never made the same mistake again. I had *grown up* in Vermont,
but I was not *a Vermonter*.

At six, however, if Mom said I was no longer an out-of-stater, then
it was so. I was a Vermonter, now living in the foothills of Vermont's
most charismatic mountain, Camel's Hump.

There was a path very close to our house that led upwards. One
sunny August morning, before school had started but after most of
our boxes were unpacked, Mom prepared a picnic lunch and told us
we were going for a hike.

'We'll bring the wagon,' Mom said. 'We can put the picnic basket in
it, and when Alice gets tired of walking, we'll be able to pop her in
too.'

I felt a twinge of jealousy. Our wagon was not just any wagon, it
was a red Radio Flyer, with the distinctive white italic lettering on
the side and the long metal handle. It wasn't as much fun as Kevin's
Big Wheel; Andy, although he did his best, wasn't capable of dragging
me far in the wagon, and try as I might, I couldn't work out a way to
both push and ride in the wagon myself. I had experimented with
pulling the wagon at a running start, then pivoting and jumping in, in
the hopes that the wagon would continue to roll at speed – this had
failed. Still, pulling the wagon was an honour – only a very strong

girl could transport her little sister that way – and maybe, after I had put in my time with helping, Mom would let me ride with Alice, even if only for a minute.

Alice's toddling gait determined our pace, but Mom was prepared for that. 'Keep your eyes open for blackberries,' she said. 'I've brought a container along; we can pick as we go. I'll make a blackberry and apple pie when we get home. Or maybe a crumble – that'd be easier. Be careful of the thorns though.'

I scanned the side of the path. When I spotted a bush, I thrust my hand toward the berry prize. Thorns scraped my forearm; when I drew my hand back in pain, I saw the white tracks the thorns had left on the outside of my forearm, otherwise brown from all my time outdoors. On the inside of my forearm, the scratch was the same colour as my skin, but I could see the tiny furrows where my skin had been ripped. I held the damaged arm with the good arm and stopped walking.

Mom had been watching. 'If you pick slowly, Beth Anne, you should be able to avoid the thorns. Like this,' she said, steering her hand towards a juicy blackberry as long as one of Alice's fingers. She plucked it, held it up for me to admire, then dropped it into the container.

I followed Mom's example, weaving my hand past the thorns towards the next blackberry with surgical accuracy. The berry was sun-hot. I popped it into my mouth. It was like eating summer. I picked and ate five more.

'You can eat a few, but not every berry you pick,' Mom cautioned. 'Remember we need them for the crumble.'

Caught out, I vowed to overfill the container to make up for my greediness. I sprinted ahead, so I would reach the next bush before Andy, who was picking methodically; his mouth and fingers were stained purple from the share of blackberries he had already claimed for himself. I ran past a stand of tall plants with flowers a lighter shade of purple than Andy's mouth. As I did, several feeding butterflies took to the air in an eruption of orange. I heard Alice squeal with joy behind me.

'Those are monarch butterflies, Beth Anne,' Mom called out to me. 'Aren't they beautiful? They're about to fly to Mexico – it's too cold for them in Vermont in the wintertime. They're a bit like me – they need sunshine and heat.'

'Mexico?' I said, incredulous. I had, even by then, learned enough about geography to know that Mexico was not in the United States. Surely Mom was pulling my leg. But Dad was the josher, not Mom.

'All the way to Mexico,' Mom confirmed. 'Thousands of miles. They're stocking up on milkweed nectar for the journey – that's what those flowers are. Milkweed is a fascinating plant. When it's finished flowering, it forms a pod, and in the fall, if you break the pod open, there are hundreds of milkweed seeds inside. The seeds hang from feathery tops – that's what catches the wind. Each seed is like a tiny parachute; each one wants to become a new milkweed plant. We'll go for another walk in a couple of months and you can see for yourself.'

'Why *milk* weed? Are the butterflies drinking milk?'

Mom smiled, but didn't laugh at me. 'I guess you could say the nectar is like milk for them, but that's not how the plant got its name. No, it's called milkweed because the sap that runs through the stalk is thick and creamy, like milk. I'll show you,' Mom said, as she came alongside me with Alice ambling after her. Mom grabbed a stalk that ended in the light purple flowers and yanked it unceremoniously apart. She held the bleeding end of the stalk up for me to observe. 'See that white liquid? That's the sap.'

I touched the proffered liquid with my index finger. It was sticky. I rubbed the sap onto the back of my other hand; it formed a shiny film.

'We'll come back in a couple of months,' Mom promised again, 'so you can see the seed pods.'

Michael, our new dad, wasn't with us on that walk towards Camel's Hump. Maybe he was working, or maybe he was hang-gliding. Mom had driven us all the way to New Hampshire once so we could watch Michael fly. Mom herself had a debilitating fear of heights. Michael could ask until he was blue in the face, but there was no way Mom was going to join him in the sky. Had Michael offered, I would have jumped at the chance to soar like a butterfly.

School started after Labor Day. I was enrolled in the one-form elementary school at the foot of our hill. My teacher, Miss Ray, was kind and pretty, but she couldn't be by my side all the time, and she couldn't protect me from the other children, some of whom were horrible. I had caught the papilloma virus and a large wart had grown on my writing hand; my bloodthirsty tormentors seized on this anomaly.

'Witch!' they shouted at me on the playground during recess. 'Don't touch us! Only witches have warts!'

Home was preferable to school during the day, but in the evening, after the three of us kids had been put to bed, the arguments between the adults started. Unlike Dad, who had never raised his voice even under duress, Michael didn't hesitate to shout back if Mom shouted first. The car began to leave at night again; I wasn't sure which adult remained behind. Was it Michael who got fed up with arguing and drove away, or was it Mom? I tried peering out of my window when I heard the car start, but night-time in rural Vermont is inscrutable, and it was impossible for me to reach a conclusion based on my furtive glances. Mom was working as a waitress at the Holiday Inn in nearby Waterbury; sometimes her shifts explained the – for me – unpredictable comings and goings of the car, but there was no way for me to know for sure who was home and who wasn't unless I ventured out of bed. I admired Michael for his ability to soar like a bird with man-made wings in primary colours, but I didn't really know him, and I was loath to risk leaving the comparative safety of my room only to happen upon Michael alone downstairs rather than Mom.

Mom kept her word about taking us back to the mountain path. After school started, but before it snowed, Mom bundled us into our warm coats and hats and led us back to the track towards Camel's Hump. With every passing month Alice was gaining stability; soon she would be able to keep up – at least with Andy – and this freed Mom to flit between the three of us, tailoring her commentary. Mom asked me about school. I must have – unusually – confessed to being lonely, because Mom suggested we could host a party and invite some of the other first-graders round. We had a big house, after all, and she could bake cookies. I wasn't sure that was a good idea, but I didn't want to disappoint her, so I kept my mouth shut.

'There's some milkweed,' Mom said, after we had trudged up the hill for several minutes. 'Go pick one of the seed pods, Beth Anne, and I'll show you what the floss is like.'

I snapped a brown husk off the tall plant at the side of the path, now unadorned by monarch butterflies, and handed it to my mom. The husk was lighter in weight than I had expected; the skin was buckled and tan, like the shell of a walnut, but the shape was like that of an avocado seed.

Mom cracked the pod open. The inside was jam-packed with downy filaments. Mom handed the open pod back to me. 'Now take those seeds and spread them to the winds,' Mom said. 'Hopefully some of them will take root, and if they do, they could grow into new milkweed plants. Here Andrew, here's one for you, and one for you too, Alice – Alice, don't eat the seeds. Throw them, like this,' Mom said, demonstrating with a pod of her own, flinging the delicate white parachutes with their precious cargo of deep brown seeds in every direction. Andy and I copied Mom, tossing the milkweed floss with as much force as we could. We knew without saying that we were competing with one another, but we were also having enormous fun, the sort of fun we were most likely to have on sunny days outside when Mom was both enthusiastic and tethered, like she was that day. Mom was the same way in the garden she was cultivating in the yard opposite the driveway of our new house; it was as though Mom grew roots of her own when in proximity to plants.

Mom must have decided that Halloween would be a good excuse to invite children from my first-grade class to a party. Mom had never liked Halloween, but she understood that children did, and the holiday would lend a theme to the party: there would be apple-bobbing, there would be candy, there would be costumes. Mom felt that a ghost costume was perfectly adequate for me. First she draped a white sheet over me, poked my face gently with her fingers, and marked out where the eye holes should be, then she took up a fold of the excess sheet on the ground, pinned the length she thought I would be able to manage without tripping, and whisked the sheet off for cutting.

I was terribly excited about the party, but when the first children arrived, accompanied by their parents, I started to panic. What if the kids started calling me a witch again, even though I was clearly a ghost? What if they didn't talk to me, just like they didn't at school?

I couldn't bear the thought of either eventuality. I cast off my ghost costume, let myself out of the side door, and sprinted towards the milkweed path. I ran as fast as I could, willing myself up the mountain; maybe, unencumbered by Andy and Alice, I would even reach the sleeping lion itself, the summit of Camel's Hump that Mom had taught me to recognise.

I didn't get very far before guilt first slowed then stopped me. I couldn't run away from my own party. Mom had picked out a huge pot for apple-bobbing. She had eschewed candy – suspicious as she was of anything she hadn't made herself – but had baked sheet upon sheet of chocolate chip cookies. She had seen to it that I would be a comfortable and convincing ghost. I tucked my tail between my legs and slunk back to the house.

'There you are!' Mom exclaimed when I reappeared. 'I was looking for you! I sent Andrew out to find you. Did he bring you back?'

'No,' I said. 'I came back on my own.'

'Hmm, I wonder where Andrew's gone then,' Mom said. She had a glass of wine in her hand and was standing next to the mother of one of my classmates. 'Well, I'm sure he'll turn up. Marsha here was just telling me that her daughter Missy really likes dogs, just like you do! Do you play with Missy sometimes?'

I nodded. Missy didn't call me a witch, and she certainly wouldn't call me a witch when I had again donned my ghost costume. I went to look for her.

* * *

I don't know what Andy could possibly have done, at his tender age, to warrant punishment a few weeks after the party, and I don't know how I could have been considered innocent when he was deemed guilty. Whatever Andy's transgression, sentencing him to the woodshed where Michael waited with his belt was not right. Alice and I followed Andy on his dead man's walk from the house to the woodshed. Time froze when I heard the repeated thwack of Michael's belt against skin. Andy was silent, save for the involuntary escape of breath after each hit, but Alice was not; as soon as Alice began to wail, the air around me became viscous, silencing my mouth so I couldn't scream like my sister, petrifying my limbs so I couldn't run into the shed punching and kicking, blocking the neurons in my normally agile brain from firing so I was unable to formulate a plan to save my brother.

I hated Michael at that moment, hang-glider or no hang-glider, and I carried on hating him when the moment passed. I thought – with the omnipotence of a six-year-old – that if I could hate him hard enough, maybe he would leave.

Mom took me to the doctor to have the wart on my hand surgically removed. She explained to me that they would not be cutting the wart out, but freezing it, and I would have to go back again to complete the freezing process. It hurt, but not like I expected it to hurt, and the cold reminded me pleasantly of the numbness that came after too much time playing with snow in wet mittens.

Hand triumphantly smooth, I went to school prepared to be instantly accepted by the classmates who had previously persecuted me.

At lunchtime, however, the usual children taunted me. 'You're a witch! Witch!'

'I am not,' I shouted, holding up my hand with pride. 'Look! The wart is gone!'

The kids came over to inspect. I waited for them to admit defeat.

'Doesn't matter,' said the leader. 'You're still a witch.'

Miss Ray, who must have known what was happening on the playground, gave me the chance to practise real witchcraft at the end of the school year by casting me in a starring role as a mouse in the first-grade production. Miss Ray encouraged me to approach my role as a method actor might, by incorporating all I knew about mouse behaviour – thanks to our cats, I did indeed know a fair amount about how mice behave, especially under chase – into my portrayal.

It was not Shakespeare, but it was performance, and I embraced my character so fully that during the show Beth Anne Evans ceased to exist, replaced temporarily by a four-foot tall mouse.

Parents were invited in as audience. After the show, Mom spoke to Miss Ray.

'Thanks so much for all your hard work this year,' Mom said.

Miss Ray brushed off Mom's praise. 'It hasn't really been work. They're so sweet at this age,' Miss Ray said to Mom, and then she turned to me. 'You were an amazing mouse! Very convincing!'

I blushed. 'Thank you,' I said to my feet.

'We'll see what we can get you to play next year,' Miss Ray said.

'I'm afraid Beth Anne won't be here next year. We're moving when school gets out – we're off to Waterbury,' Mom said.

Miss Ray looked surprised. 'Oh, I see, I hadn't realised. Well, it's been a pleasure to have Beth Anne in my class. I wish you all the best, Beth Anne, and I hope you keep on acting,' she said, crouching down like Dad used to so she could see me eye to eye. Because this was the 1970s and long before such things were controversial, my teacher then opened her arms and gave me a big hug. I reciprocated.

It was still light when Mom and I walked out of the primary school I now knew I would not be returning to. 'Will Michael come with us when we move?' I asked Mom.

Mom paused before she answered with a question of her own. 'Would you like him to?'

'No,' I said.

Mom nodded, as if she had read my mind and my words were merely confirmation of what she already knew. 'That's what I thought. No, Beth Anne, Michael is not coming with us.'

'OK,' I said.

8

Stones

Grandma Lenore was an explorer. Not the sort of explorer I had read about in books – not like Magellan, Columbus or Peary. Grandma Lenore wasn't interested in planting flags in previously uncharted territory, but any territory already mapped was fair game. Grandma Lenore had – unusually for a woman of her era – worked for many years as a geologist; a room at the back of her Delaware home housed several enclosed glass display cases laden with rocks. At the base of each rock was a minute slip of white paper bearing a typewritten number. These numbers could then be cross-referenced in the binder wherein Grandma Lenore had recorded the name, location of origin, and date of collection of each individual specimen: 36, Rose Quartz, Mexico, 1958; 102, Obsidian, Hawaii, 1969, and so on. The display cabinets were locked, but sometimes, when she had a moment, Grandma Lenore would come to the back of the house, produce the delicate key, unlock the cabinets, and ask me which rock I wanted to inspect more closely. Anything that sparkled held particular appeal for me, followed by any rock with a noticeable crystalline structure. When I was holding my selected rock, Grandma Lenore would lean in closely, peer down through her thick glasses, and recount, in her grandmotherly voice, both her knowledge of that sort of rock's properties and the story of how that exact specimen came to be in her ownership. Out of the hundreds of rocks on display, I had one clear favourite: mica, a rock that both glittered and flaked.

'Fool's gold,' Grandma Lenore said, nodding, when I first pointed to number 61. 'It's called that because it looks enough like gold that people are fooled into thinking it *is* gold. It's not, but you can do a nifty trick with it.'

Grandma Lenore pulled at the top flake of the mica; it came off easily. 'Look, Beth Anne, it's nearly transparent,' she said, holding the flake up between her bespectacled and my not-yet-bespectacled eyes to demonstrate. 'Take this specimen, Beth Anne,' Grandma Lenore offered. 'Mica is easy to find. I'll have it replaced in no time.'

Grandma Lenore's mother – my great-grandmother – lived with Lenore and my dad's much younger half-brother and half-sister. Gran, with her hunchback and her pastel-flowered polyester shift dresses – the outfit of choice among great-grandmothers as far as I could tell – wasn't as much of a traveller as her daughter, but Gran was an explorer of another realm: language. Gran was a self-published poet; she had given all three of us copies of her most recent poetry collection for Christmas the previous year.

Grandma Lenore wasted no time in exposing us to adventure. Alice was probably still in nappies when Grandma Lenore took my siblings and I from Vermont to New York State to visit Ausable Chasm and Howe Caverns. Access to Ausable Chasm – a nearly two-mile long gorge cut around 10,000 years ago by the Ausable River through thick Cambrian-period sandstone – is gained by boat: specifically, by raft.

Grandma Lenore had no qualms about taking her three very young grandchildren out rafting. I don't remember her giving us safety guidelines beyond those of the tour guide; she assumed we had the intelligence, even at our tender ages, not to fall into the river. What

Grandma Lenore did lecture us on, however, was geology, with a level of enthusiasm that was contagious. When the raft pulled close to the stone walls of the chasm and the guide pointed out fossils of ancient jellyfish, Grandma Lenore saw to it that all three of us were able to lean in and take a closer look.

The silent solidity of the gorge was both regal and intimidating. At one point, when the raft was poised to pass through a particularly narrow passage, my fear got the upper hand. I was scared not just for myself, but also for my brother and sister, for whom I already considered myself responsible.

'The stone walls are closing in,' I said to Grandma Lenore, panicked. 'The boat isn't going to fit, and Alice and Andy can't swim.'

'These stone walls aren't going anywhere anytime soon, Beth Anne,' Grandma Lenore said, smiling her slow smile. 'And Alice and Andy – and you, I hasten to add – are all wearing life jackets. The captain of this raft has made this trip countless times before; we're in safe hands. Do you know how long it took the river to carve this gorge into the sandstone?'

I shook my head. The raft floated closer to the pinch point.

'Hundreds and even thousands of years. Water wears stone away slowly but very effectively, and often very beautifully, as we can see here. After this, we're going to the caves, and there you'll see another way that water can shape stone over time.' Grandma Lenore kept smiling as she hummed a little ditty.

The raft passed through the eye of the stone needle without incident, just as Grandma Lenore had predicted. The gorge walls stayed where they were, all-seeing yet impassive. Stone, it seemed, was more reliable than humans; I added this information to my mental inventory of the world. Grandma Lenore had proven herself a knowledgeable and reliable guide, and I relished the rest of the boat ride as an apprentice explorer rather than enduring it as an anxious big sister.

Gorges were nice, but it was caves that Grandma Lenore loved the most. To go from the bright summer sunshine of the river to the cool damp dark of Howe Caverns was shocking, and my ambivalence about the outing as a whole briefly returned, but Grandma Lenore wasn't having any of it.

'This is one of the most amazing cave systems in the Northeast,' Grandma Lenore said, by way of introduction. 'Do you see the stalactites and stalagmites? The stalactites come down from the ceiling. They're formed by the slow dripping of water carrying limestone deposits. Can you hear it?'

Andy and I listened. Alice may have been listening too; it was hard to tell if she understood much of what Grandma Lenore was saying. Andy and I both nodded seriously at Grandma Lenore.

'That dripping is the sound of new stalactites being formed. The stalagmites come up from the ground, usually right under stalactites. Sometimes they even come together – you'll see that when we get to the Pipe Organ formation.'

The Pipe Organ formation did not disappoint. 'Wow!' I said in appreciation.

Grandma Lenore's glasses moved up ever-so-slightly as her eyes crinkled. 'Isn't that beautiful?' Grandma Lenore asked, and when she did, I had the sense that Grandma Lenore was not asking me rhetorically, as an adult would, but asking me joyfully, as a child my own age might.

We were each allowed to buy a souvenir from the gift shop. I selected a small pouch of polished stones. After we had made the purchase, Grandma Lenore told me to cup my hands together; she poured out the pouch's contents, lifted the stones up one at a time, and named them for me: malachite, agate, smoky quartz. I loved hearing the names as she reeled them off.

That trip to New York State was the first of many adventures

Grandma Lenore had in store for me and my little brother and sister. She took us some years later to more caverns, this time to the Luray Caverns in Virginia; then, combining underground and overground exploration as she had in New York, Grandma Lenore drove us along a substantial portion of the Skyline Drive, a scenic route that overlooks the Blue Ridge Mountains in Virginia.

'There's a popular song by John Denver called "(Take Me Home) Country Roads" – have you heard it?' Grandma Lenore asked us as we sped along.

'Yes!' I answered, and began to sing. 'Wait a minute, Blue Ridge Mountains, that's where we are now! It's like we're in the song!'

'We *are* in the Blue Ridge Mountains, that's right, Beth Anne,' Grandma Lenore said. My name sounded special when spoken in my grandmother's quavery voice. 'But John Denver hasn't done right by these mountains. He sings about them being in *West* Virginia, but they're almost entirely in Virginia, just like the Shenandoah River that he also mentions. His song has probably increased tourism to the mountains, so I can't fault him for that, but he might have wanted to get his facts straight before he released it.'

I observed Grandma Lenore from the passenger seat while she drove blithely along despite the steep drop on my side of the road. Not only was Grandma Lenore unimpressed by stardom, as in the case of John Denver, she was also seemingly oblivious to danger. Had it been Mom at the wheel, there would have been no impromptu geography lessons, and there most assuredly wouldn't have been any lifting of the left hand to wave towards the subject of the lesson, the mountains themselves. Mom would have been gripping the wheel with both hands, looking straight ahead, and ordering the three of us, in no uncertain terms, to stay still and be quiet so she could concentrate on the daunting task of getting from point A to point B without succumbing to terror brought on by her severe acrophobia. Because I myself didn't suffer from fear of heights – quite the contrary – I found Mom's challenges with exposed roads endearing and bemusing, but I had to admit that Grandma Lenore's dismissal of caution was both refreshing and empowering. It was not that Grandma Lenore was foolhardy; she just believed that risk should be assessed, mitigated and then forgotten in favour of engagement.

Grandma Lenore ensured that we didn't forget her during the long spells between visits; she sent us cards for birthdays and holidays and presents for Christmas, yes, but even better, she signed us up as members of the National Wildlife Federation which entitled us to receive their glossy kids' magazine jam-packed with high-quality pictures of adorable wildlife, *Ranger Rick*. I ate *Ranger Rick* up like candy when it arrived, often taping the pull-out poster – sparring fox cubs, soaring eagles, stalking lionesses – to my wall. Sometimes when we moved house there would be a gap in delivery, but sooner or later *Ranger Rick* would reappear, and only then would I accept our new lodgings as home.

Grandma Lenore, curiously, never seemed to be present when we visited Dad's family on the farm in Pennsylvania, where Great-Grandma and Great-Grandpa Evans lived. I had stayed at the farm as a baby for many months while Dad was in Vietnam, and enough impressions had accumulated during that time for me to create a file for the Evans' farm under 'Home'. When I returned to the farm later – first with both parents, after Dad had been sent home from Vietnam but before he had left Mom, then with Dad only – I knew I was on primordial ground.

The Evans' farm was all about textures. The floors downstairs were almost all covered with thick Oriental rugs in a regal palette of deep reds, strong blues, and delicate creams. Each rug was woven into intricate geometric patterns, and perhaps best of all, some of the rugs had fringes at the top and the bottom. I was intimately acquainted with each rug, having crawled on each extensively, and I knew where the fringes were when I wished to weave my fingers into them or pull on them string by string. The furniture on top of the rugs was uniformly solid and antique: the dining room table, for example, stretched for what seemed like miles in either direction, and each leg was decoratively chiselled.

The collies at the Evans' farm were not entitled to the rugs as I was, but they had free run of the long wooden porch outside the farmhouse. Although I tested their good manners to the core, the collies – well trained as they were – never so much as growled at me. Instead they let me treat them like living rugs, diving into them where they lay resting, plunging my hands into their long coarse coats, cuddling up beside them or even on top of them and burrowing my nose into them to breathe in their earthy animal scent.

Every once in a great while, an adult would walk me past the sheep field to Spider's stable. Spider was an elderly gentleman of a horse, and just like the collies, he knew he was expected to tolerate me when I stuck my hands into his mane and patted every inch of him I could reach. Usually whichever adult had brought me to the stable gave me a treat to pass on to Spider – a bit of apple or carrot. Despite Spider's gigantic teeth, he took the snacks gently, albeit with an element of drool.

I even knew what the sheep on the farm felt like. The sheep were markedly less prepared to have small hands thrust towards them than the collies and the horse, but if restrained they had no say in the matter. I was fascinated by the kinkiness and warmth of the sheep's fleece, but I didn't trust them; their frequent unpredictable *baas* reminded me of Alice crying, a sound I dreaded and sought, whenever possible, to avoid.

I had the advantage of being the Evans' first great-grandchild, and when I lived on the farm, I was doted on not only by my great-grandparents, but also by my grand-aunt and uncle, and especially by their children, who were much younger than Dad but much older than me. The farm was not like other places – the door always seemed open to visitors. There was a constant stream of people, and all of those people loved me and, later, my brother and sister. That didn't mean we could do whatever we wanted – the folks on the farm, experienced in animal husbandry as they were, had certain expectations even of children, but – again, from their knowledge of animals – they also knew that happy children, like happy animals, thrive best when clear boundaries are coupled with clear affection.

It was not my choice to stop going to the Evans' farm. That choice was made for me too soon, when I was far too young to register a complaint, for reasons I could not fathom but the adults understood.

9

Piano

The white wooden house in Waterbury had a witch window on the second floor. 'It's tilted, so witches can't fly through on their broomsticks,' Mom told us. The bedroom Alice and I shared had a spacious walk-in closet – more like a small room, really – that could also be accessed from Andy's room. That closet was our kids' clubhouse. Alice, at three, was at last able to communicate with words instead of screams (although she reserved screaming as a valid form of communication), and that was all that was required for her membership in our club. I printed my first newspaper in that closet: a single sheet of paper, with the news stories in columns, just as they were in the real newspaper. The feature story was about my pet spider, who had claimed the closet prior to our arrival and whom I saw no reason to evict. Andy agreed to illustrate the spider feature and two other articles: one about the kittens we had recently adopted and another about Christmas, although Christmas was still several months away. Alice played no part in the creation of the newspaper, but she was the all-important subscriber. Never mind that she couldn't read; I read all of the front-page, which was equivalent to reading the entire newspaper, aloud to her, embellishing the stories with dramatic details not included in print, such as the mewling of kittens and Santa impersonations. Judging by Alice's response to our first issue, Andy and I could count on her as a faithful patron.

Our house was at one vertex of a triangular park. The white clapboard village grange, with its evenly spaced, institutional windows, was within view across the intersection at our corner. Mom said people played Bingo at the Grange, which added to the building's already substantial cachet. The Grange resembled a church, but instead of a full steeple, it had a sort of half-steeple enclosing an enormous siren. The Grange even had a label, formed of tall black wooden letters and numbers: Grange 237. I wondered where the other 236 granges were, and if they looked identical to 237. I would have liked to try my luck at Bingo at the Grange; maybe I could have won, or maybe I could have at least beaten Andy. I couldn't be sure any more that I would triumph over Andy at checkers – he was already beginning to outwit me – but Bingo had nothing to do with skill and everything to do with luck, so my odds were better.

Bingo, however, was for other people. Instead of attending events at the Grange, I appropriated the wooden gazebo in the middle of the triangular park. Alice, although she could now be part of our club at home, still wasn't old enough to venture into the park with me, and Andy preferred to hunt for insects in our own yard, but lacking an audience didn't stop me from using the hexagonal gazebo as a stage, quite the contrary; I felt most free to perform when no one else was about, and usually nobody was. I leapt about under the wooden roof belting out numbers from *Fiddler on the Roof*. We were still visiting Dad and Annie at least once a month, and Annie had landed the part of Yente the Matchmaker in a local production of the musical. Annie's preparation included, but was not limited to, playing the original Broadway recording of *Fiddler* on repeat on the farm stereo in Shelburne; I learned all the words to all the songs. Yente had no solo singing parts, but each time the record reached one of the chorus songs including Yente, Annie underwent a lightning-fast transformation: from twenty-something divorcée with a new love interest who happened to be my dad, to seventy-something crone, picking boyfriends for the village girls. To inhabit Yente, Annie puckered her petite face to produce as many wrinkles as her youthful skin could manage, quickly developed a slight hunchback, and added a generous helping of extra vibrato to her already tremulous singing voice. Annie's favourite number was 'The Dream', wherein Tevye is visited by the ghosts of both his Grandmother Tzeitel and Fruma Sarah, the deceased first wife of the butcher that Tevye's daughter is meant to marry, but whom she does not love. 'The Dream' is a dramatic encapsulation of every well-known human emotion, running through happiness, surprise, anger and fear, all in less than seven minutes, and Annie did them all justice, but she was at her most convincing when playing Fruma Sarah, who enters with a blood-curdling scream and leaves only after acting out the corporeal punishment she aims to inflict on Tzeitel should she go ahead and marry Sarah's widower, Lazar Wolf the butcher.

By the time Annie was rehearsing for *Fiddler on the Roof,* I was well acquainted with what anger and fear looked like off-stage, so the first few times Annie became Fruma Sarah, I was on my guard. Was Annie going too far? Would the feelings become real to her – would she lash out in real anger at me or my brother or sister? Was Annie in control of the character, or was the character going to claim control of her? Only after I had watched Annie go in and out of character several times did I trust her enough to sit back and enjoy her enthusiastic one-woman staging of 'The Dream'.

Back home in Waterbury Center, Mom was planning to purchase an upright piano. She must have asked for money from her parents; she was still working as a waitress at the Holiday Inn and would not have been able to afford the piano without help. Mom took us along when she went to pick out the piano. I have no idea how she knew where she needed to go – did she ask the pianist who played some weekend nights in the bar at the Holiday Inn? Did she happen to strike up a conversation with a pianist guest at the restaurant? Did she call around, using the Yellow Pages?

However she settled on the dealers, Mom struck gold. We walked into the showroom and were greeted by several grands with their lids open and their smiles of ivory teeth glinting under the lights. The wood of the handful of varnished, unpainted pianos ranged from fair to dark; a couple of the painted pianos were painted white, but most were painted black. All were partnered with benches, or more often stools, placed strategically at the exact distance necessary from the open keyboards to invite prospective owners to play. I was transfixed.

'We're not looking here,' Mom said breezily while Andy, Alice and I stood rooted to our spots. 'We're going down to where the second-hand pianos are. The staircase is that way. They've made sure the stairs are far away so you have to walk past the Steinways, just in case they can tempt you,' Mom added, her purposeful steps across the showroom floor demonstrating that she was impervious to their ploy.

The pianos downstairs were less shiny but no less mesmerising. If anything, the sheer quantity of instruments and the more jumbled display made the used piano showroom even more appealing. A salesperson materialised; he and Mom began to discuss how best to match her needs to her price range.

'There's a piano over here that you can play while I speak to your mother,' the salesman said to us, gesturing towards an upright workhorse. 'Just no banging,' he cautioned. I looked at Mom, who nodded her permission. With Andy's and Alice's eyes on me, I approached the piano the salesman had pointed out. I arranged myself on the stool and attempted to play. What I played could in no way be considered musical, but the mere act of making sounds on this gigantic instrument enthralled me. I abdicated my place sooner than I would have liked to offer Andy and Alice their turns. Alice was still playing, if one could call it that, when Mom came over and hushed her.

'Tim here thinks this piano in the corner may be the one for us,' Mom said, 'so I need to test it. That means you need to stop playing for a little while, Alice, although what you were playing sounded lovely.'

This was not factually accurate but I let that slide. I had already sussed out that Mom's strategy to encourage us to become musicians was to praise any effort towards music-making, however unmelodious.

I wanted to show Mom I was on her team, so I echoed her words as she walked back to the piano next to Tim. 'That was great playing, Alice, but now you have to be quiet.'

Alice nodded solemnly and my sibs and I waited while Mom adjusted the stool of the piano several feet away. We held our collective breath when she raised her hands above the keys. When her hands came alive and Mom began to play, six eyes opened wide in admiration. What we had played on the workhorse piano was noise, but what Mom was playing was music. We cast furtive glances at each other to agree wordlessly among ourselves that our mother was no ordinary human but rather a conjuror.

Mom was in high spirits on the drive home. 'We have to wait a few days before they deliver the piano,' she told us. 'I'll have to dig out my sheet music. It's still in a box somewhere.'

The piano arrived in due course and we were given stern instructions on how to treat it with respect. Now that the piano was in our front room, I thought that Mom would play it all the time. How could she resist the lure of the glistening white keys offset by the jet black of the accidentals? And yes, if I asked when she was in the right mood,

Mom would humour me by playing a couple of songs, but only when we had all been tucked in did she play the piano her way. Only then did she open the Cat Stevens' *Catch Bull at Four* songbook, turn to 'Sitting', and play like she meant it. Mom never sang when she played for herself, but she didn't need to; she was skilled enough as a pianist to make the instrument sing for her. And sing it did, so much so that shivers ran up and down the length of me and the delicate hairs on the outside of my forearm stood to attention. I didn't need Mom to sing; I knew all the words from the record anyway, and the lyrics ran through me as I lay in my bed in the dark.

Another night-time favourite of Mom's was the first movement of Beethoven's Piano Sonata #14 in C# minor, the 'Moonlight Sonata'. The opening chords against the repeating triplets, all blended together by the sostenuto, and then the lament of the melody – the piece was like an expression of truths Mom could only articulate through music. I yearned to hear Mom play because I was in awe of her ability to create music of such beauty, but the pain, completely visible just under the notes, chilled and haunted me. I fought against sleep when Mom played the piano in the naive hope that perhaps, if I could only stay awake and concentrate very, very hard, something about the music would give me the key I was missing, and I would be able to unlock my mother once and for all, for her sake, and for all of ours.

* * *

I couldn't understand why Annie was so nervous about actually performing *Fiddler on the Roof* in front of an audience. She knew not only her part, but the parts of all the other characters too, and while I recognised that Annie's singing voice was not rich and accurate like Dad's, it struck me as perfectly adequate for the songs required of Yente the Matchmaker. I don't know if it was her stage fright that prevented Annie from inviting us to the show itself. Maybe she felt she could manage, at a push, to have her own children in the audience, but not her new partner's children. Perhaps the show just fell on a weekend when we were not scheduled to visit. Dad went though, and he took photos afterwards of Annie in stage make-up and costume, triumphant and laughing, as she stood cradling her post-show bouquet, flanked by Melinda and Brian. Dad showed us the pictures, already proudly affixed into the photo album, when we next came to visit. Those pictures were fun to look at, but it was the pictures immediately following that really grabbed my eye.

'It's too bad, actually, that you couldn't have come to the show,' Dad said, still reminiscing. 'Annie was fantastic, and the rest of the cast was also very good. Chava's dancing would have been inspirational for you . . . It certainly was for Melinda; she's been dancing up a storm ever since.'

I ignored our exclusion and remained focussed on the right-hand side of the photo album. The pictures there reminded me of something I had seen before; looking at them I could again feel the heat and hear the whoosh and the crackling.

Dad would have preferred to keep talking about Annie, but he noticed my attention was elsewhere.

'That's when the barn burned down,' Dad said. 'It happened on Halloween night. We had all been out trick or treating. That's what we saw when we came home. Ironically, Brian had dressed up as a fireman for the night, but neither he nor the real firemen could save the barn.'

I let that sink in. While Mindy and Brian had been merrily knocking on doors and asking for candy, Mindy dressed up as a hobo and Brian as a fireman, the barn we had all played in so many times, with its vast doors, its hay lofts, and its nesting birds, had been engulfed by flames that reduced it to nothing more than a pile of burned wood and ashes.

'We were very lucky,' Dad mused. 'If we had been home, sleeping soundly in our beds, the fire could have spread, and God knows the farmhouse isn't fireproof either. It's not full of straw like the barn was, but a fire like that could have torn through this house in no time.'

'Who started it?' I asked.

Dad furrowed his substantial brows. 'They're not sure. It was probably just some kids, out for some alternative Halloween fun. The police haven't charged anyone.'

I stared at the black outline of the then still-standing barn set against the orange inferno in the photographs.

'I miss the barn,' I said. 'I miss your store too.'

Dad laughed ruefully. 'Me too, Beth Anne,' he said. Then Dad seemed to remember that he was meant to be a role model. 'But no one was hurt in either fire, which is a blessing. And now Fred and I have our new store, which is even better than the old one. So it all works out in the end.'

Except it didn't. The barn wasn't rebuilt, and sometime after it burned down, Dad and Annie, with Mindy and Brian in tow, moved away from the farmhouse in Shelburne.

* * *

Before Dad and Annie left the farm, however, we moved too, away from the white house in Waterbury Center. Mom had gotten a new job, as a paraprofessional in the Montpelier school system, and we moved to be closer to her new workplace. I didn't want to leave the house with the witch window. Mom had not been uniformly happy during our time there – there had still been bottles and tears – but there had been no loud arguments, no breakage of porcelain, and no cars leaving skid marks as they drove away too fast. I thought, given the chance, that maybe if we stayed put, happiness might begin to tip the balance, but it was not up to me.

Mom couldn't move the new-to-us piano on her own. It was hauled up into the back of a friend's pickup truck, where it was tied down with ropes and surrounded by boxes with covers over them to keep them from damaging the piano when they bumped against it, as boxes inevitably would, given the Vermont roads. The piano, as I watched it recede into the distance, reminded me of the recently killed deer I had seen in pickup trucks during the hunting season, laid limp and heavy on the flatbeds with the life extinguished from their huge black eyes.

10

Pointing

The outside of the apartment building we moved to in Montpelier – on Elm Street, a few streets behind the state capitol – was painted green, which felt both appropriate and nostalgic. Mom, ever the botanist, had often mentioned that the trees that once spread wide canopies of green leaves over the streets of her childhood in Bethlehem, Pennsylvania, were elms – the same elms that had later succumbed to Dutch elm disease. Mom was still in mourning for the elm trees of Bethlehem. Maybe living on Elm Street would bring her some peace, like my toy horse, Spider, offered me some comfort for my enforced absence from Spider, the real horse, at the Evans' farm in Pennsylvania.

I can't remember anything about where I slept in that apartment on Elm Street. I don't know if I shared a bedroom with Andy, or Alice or even both of them. I do remember the front room facing the street that housed both the piano and the TV; half-curtains covered the lower panes of the two large windows in the outside wall next to the TV, but only valances adorned the upper panes, permitting any available light entry and providing a clear view of the limestone and phyllite cliff opposite. That my mother, with her fear of heights, had rented an apartment directly across the road from a forty-foot exposed grey rock face can only be attributed to some degree of desperation, and perhaps to the happenstance of the road above the rock face – Hill Street – bearing her maiden name. To be fair, Mom didn't spend much time looking out of the windows, but I did. The cliff was so close that I could see the narrow horizontal edges where I might be able to gain a fingerhold were I to undertake an ascent. Only the intermittent and noisy passage of cars and the infrequent and quieter traverse of pedestrians interrupted my route-planning.

The foot-square black and white TV, complete with bunny ears designed to improve reception, rarely pulled my attention away from the diptych of the rock face outside and the piano inside, but for a couple of days not long before my birthday, the diminutive TV assumed oracle status. Mom, cigarette in hand, sat mesmerised by the news of President Nixon's resignation. Just before Gerald Ford took the podium to assume the presidency, Mom called us all in to the front room. Never had Mom insisted that all three of us watch TV with her, so I knew whatever was about to take place must be of utmost importance.

'Sit down and be quiet, kids,' Mom told us. 'This is history in the making.'

I had only the vaguest notion of politics when I listened to Gerald Ford's speech. I had gathered, from Mom's comments directed at the TV as the Watergate scandal broke in the run-up to his resignation, that Richard Nixon was not only a bad president, but also a very bad person. Richard Nixon was the polar opposite, it seemed, of George Washington and Abraham Lincoln, who had been both excellent presidents and very good people (I had learned of Washington and Lincoln at school; Mom seemed indifferent towards Washington, but approved wholeheartedly of Lincoln). I knew Gerald Ford was the vice president, which was like being second in line, and I grasped that

Ford was only moving to first in line because Nixon had been pushed out. I also knew Mom was relieved to see the back of Nixon, but I couldn't gauge her satisfaction with his replacement.

As for me, I was thrilled. Everything Ford said made perfect sense to me, and I pledged, in my young heart, to do as now-President Ford said: to go forward with my fellow Americans, to seek peace with all nations, to respect a higher power as the absolute authority, and to forgive even those who, like former President Nixon, had acted despicably. I caught the quiver in Ford's voice and the tears welling in his eyes when he mentioned President Nixon and they were not unfamiliar. Ford, it seemed to me, believed that Nixon had once been, and could still again become, a good person, just like Ford believed that the United States, before Watergate, had been a good nation and, now that 'the long national nightmare' was over, would become a good nation again. I was very fuzzy on what 'the long national nightmare' Ford referred to had entailed – Watergate, as I understood it, had something to do with tapes, newspaper reporters and theft – but I had been woken by fear in the night often enough to know that the end of any bad dream was a significant victory.

As a schoolgirl in the 1970s, I had recited the Pledge of Allegiance countless times to the best of my ability (I would not learn the words properly until fifth grade), but it wasn't until that day, August 9th, 1974, that it clocked that the teachers made me recite that oddly worded vow to hammer home that my loyalty – heretofore reserved for my family, pets and peers – should extend to my nation. Only on that day in August did I begin to understand that I was not just a girl, but an American girl.

* * *

Tovah told me decades later that the first time she saw me at school, my long blonde hair was loose and I was wearing bedroom slippers.

'You weren't like anybody I had ever met before,' Tovah said. 'I mean, who wears bedroom slippers to school?'

Nobody wears bedroom slippers to school if their lives are within the usual 'normal' parameters of the bell curve, but I didn't want to make Tovah feel sorry for me retroactively, so at the time I just smiled.

Tovah Klein, for her part, was unlike anyone I had met before either, because Tovah, in addition to being whip-smart and fabulously creative, was also willing to be my friend. I had my siblings, both full and nearly step-, and I had been happy to play with Kevin's Big Wheel, but Tovah was my first bestie. I may not be able to remember my room on Elm Street, but I remember not only Tovah's room, but the layout of Tovah's entire house, including her brother's room, one of only two rooms in her house that we were not permitted to enter: 'Gene's Room,' read the colourful wooden letters affixed to the bright green wooden crocodile on the door. I found the cheerfulness of the crocodile anomalous: the groans and shouts that sometimes emanated from Gene's room were at odds with the door decoration's mood of whimsy and optimism. I was afraid of Gene, but I wasn't afraid of Tovah's big sister, Talia, whose bedroom was also off limits. I admired Talia hugely and wished, more than once, that I could have had a big sister just like her. Talia played the violin with enormous skill; the music that flew from the strings via her bow entranced me, as did Talia's dark corkscrew locks and the flicker of wildness in her eyes. I reasoned that with Talia as my big sister, I would be safe, just as I thought Tovah was.

Tovah wasn't, though, and that was why we became inseparable: because we knew without saying that two were safer than one, that two were stronger than one, that two already broken – as we were – could, together, still become a whole.

It was Tovah who introduced me to *Bulfinch's Mythology*. Both of us had been able to read since long before we met, and *Bulfinch's* was chock-full of stories so fantastically exciting that neither of us could get enough of them. Reading *Bulfinch's* alone did not suffice; we learned the stories by heart and rewrote them – producing our very own (vastly thinner) edition of *Bulfinch's*, complete with illustrations of all the important gods, goddesses and creatures. Best of all, we acted the stories out; Tovah's mother showed us which sheets in the airing cupboard we could appropriate when we required togas, and we were allowed to bring sticks found in nearby Hubbard Park into Tovah's house and fit them with strings to serve as bows (the arrows, however, were kept imaginary). We played favourites: both of us preferred Greek to Roman mythology, both of us wanted nothing to do with Hera (Zeus's wife) or Zeus himself for that matter, and both of us hero-worshipped Artemis and Athena. It was those goddesses we most often chose to embody while leaping around in Tovah's room armed with sticks and clad in sheet togas. I loved particular Muses – Calliope, muse of epic poetry, and Terpsichore, muse of dance – even more than the goddesses themselves, and I took responsibility for several of the Muse entries in our Montpelier *Bulfinch's*. I was over the moon when I received my very own copy of the official *Bulfinch's Mythology* for Christmas that year.

Tovah's December presents arrived earlier than mine, because Tovah and her family celebrated Hanukkah rather than Christmas. Tovah explained to me that her mother's family had been made to leave their homeland because of the Nazis, and I accepted her explanation without question. Tovah's mother was wistful whenever she spoke of the home of her youth, so although I wasn't certain exactly who the Nazis were or exactly what they had done, I was angry at them on behalf of my best friend's mother. The Nazis had left her with a hole in her heart that would never be mended, and for that I, in turn, would never forgive them. Tovah's mother was an intelligent, soft-spoken, caring woman, but the grievous nature of her broken heart meant that part of her was always absent, and the blame for that lay squarely on the Nazis' shoulders.

Tovah's father – a particularly short man with glasses who favoured trousers with braces and read voraciously – had not been forced out of New York City by the Nazis or by anyone else. He had made the conscious choice to leave the Big Apple and forge a new life for himself and his family in Vermont's bucolic state capital. The Kleins were just another whitecap on the same wave that had brought my own father and mother to the state, a wave of educated young adults disenchanted with the establishment who hoped that in Vermont they would be able to lead the more principled lives they had envisioned for themselves and their families. Tovah's father was entirely unlike Tovah's mother – where she was remote, he was very much in the moment. He was prone to long explanatory monologues that Tovah often disregarded but that I soaked up like a sponge.

I was not Jewish. On n of our piano lay a hymnal bound in faded burgundy bearing the   the *Moravian Youth Hymnal* over an image of the conquering   ; around the Christmas and Easter holidays, Mom traded James Taylor and Beethoven for carols and hymns. Mom let us know that in so doing, she was following in the footsteps of her ancestors; her very own great-grandfather had served as a Moravian minister. Not only did Moravians do music, they also did baking. One of Mom's few consistent Christmas traditions was to bake Moravian sugar cake, a potato-based coffee cake sprinkled liberally with butter and brown sugar. What was not to like?

It didn't bother me at all that Tovah belonged to another faith. Mom never said it was a problem, and Tovah and I were so well schooled in the variation of beliefs held by the ancient Greeks and Romans that it seemed perfectly natural to us that our own religions were not identical.

Jew or Christian, Greek or Roman, sometimes a girl or a goddess just needed a refuge, and the same enclosed shelves that held the toga sheets provided us with the be-all and end-all of lairs; we were both small and nimble enough to climb up to the top shelf of that cupboard and wedge ourselves in. When one of us pulled the door nearly closed, the cupboard became so dark that even the two of us, both skilled at reading in dim light, were unable to see well enough to read. Which was just as well, because there wasn't room in the teeny closet for us to open *Bulfinch's* or our own version of same once we were inside.

It may be that the door became stuck one afternoon, closing us in completely and leading to one of our two near-death events as childhood friends. I can't be sure if the walls began to encroach and the air became warmer and less nourishing simply because my desire to pretzel myself into a tiny space had diminished, or if the panic I felt came when I realised my escape from the cupboard no longer lay within my control. Either way, the airing closet lost its appeal for me, as did all small enclosed spaces and the doors that demarcate them. We abandoned the airing cabinet. Instead Tovah and I ventured outside, where we were free not only from doors, but also from parents.

Not content to limit ourselves to others' ancient or less-ancient creation stories, Tovah and I spun our own. In the nearby park we collected tiny twigs and seed pods from trees. The twigs needed to be no more than two inches long, and in a modified Y-shape, to simulate arms and to allow for the papery pear-shaped seed pods to be stuck on as heads. As soon as a figure gained a head, it became a Datian. The Datians lived in groups within patches of lush thick moss. Some of them were able to fly, via wings of maple seed pods that had spiralled down from the benevolent trees above to be affixed with Elmer's glue to their backs. Tovah was the keeper of the Datians. Her mother granted us a special box with many compartments – likely once a sewing box – where we kept both the finished Datians and extra Datian components. It must have also been Tovah's mother who gifted us with scraps of cloth – fabrics woven with substantial threads in rich colours, quite unlike the thin calico printed with bright flowers I was accustomed to – so we could dress our delicate wooden creatures. We wrote the Datian scrolls on birch bark rather than paper, so the Datians' history was significantly condensed, as birch bark did not lend itself to inscription.

I loved playing mythology and Datians with Tovah, but there was something more I wanted to do with my new best friend. The cliff across from my apartment had called to me for months. I asked Tovah if she would come with me when I felt ready to scale it; Tovah hesitated. Perhaps it took a week – perhaps a month – but eventually I persuaded Tovah that climbing up the cliff opposite my home to reach the guard rails of Hill Street would be a fabulous experience, a once-in-a-lifetime accomplishment, an opportunity that we would be unwise to miss.

When the day came and we stood at the base of the expanse of grey rock, Tovah pointed to a nearby tree. 'That's sumac,' Tovah said. 'Mama made sumac iced tea last week, remember?'

'I remember,' I answered, grateful for the diversion. I could feel the velvety fuzz of the sumac fruits Tovah's mother had used for the tea in my tactile memory, the tight drupes the same colour as the cover of my mother's *Moravian Youth Hymnal*. I recalled the distinctive flavour of the sumac tea, so far from the Lipton's iced tea with mint my own mother sometimes brewed.

I approached the rock and attempted to begin climbing. Now that my hands were clutching the thin edges I had thought would make good handholds, I understood that the inclination of the rock was much steeper than I had anticipated from across the street. I didn't gain more than a couple of feet of elevation before my hands popped off and I landed, surprised, back on horizontal ground.

'Huh. It's harder than I thought,' I remarked to Tovah, who had looked on in consternation. She, who had not been convinced about the merits of the climb from the start, made no comment.

'I'll try again,' I volunteered, and clawed my way back on to the rock, only to be ejected a second time. 'Maybe it's a better idea to not go straight up.'

'Maybe,' Tovah agreed.

We moved several yards to our left, to the line between the vegetation and the rock, and scrambled up several metres. At this lesser slope, it wasn't truly necessary to bend towards the ground – in fact my balance might have been better had I stayed more upright – but I wanted to climb, not walk, and touching the rock with my hands shifted what I was doing from the wrong category to the right one. This time Tovah followed me, bending over the rock just I was, several feet below me. Even this far more sensible and achievable route was thrilling – by the time we were halfway up, if we veered to the right, we would be in vertical space, with nothing but several metres of air between us and the sumac trees beneath. If we were to trip on an errant root and lose our footing, the resulting fall would be dangerous – perhaps even fatal, at least in my seven-year-old mind. The proximity of possible death led me to feel I was a heroine in a myth of our own invention, whose fate hung in the balance between tragic and valiant.

'We're almost there,' I said to Tovah when the Hill Street guard rails came into view. 'But this is going to be the hardest part.'

Tovah's face was so white that her freckles, normally nearly the same colour as her skin, stood out like the spots on a cheetah. 'What if we can't actually get to the top?' Tovah asked urgently.

'We have to get to the top,' I answered, setting my jaw with determination. 'We can't go back down the same way. That would be even worse.'

As we crouched there, preparing for the final terrifying yards, a flush of tears came over me.

'Whatever happens,' I said to Tovah, 'you're my best friend.'

With that I lunged towards the dull silver of the guard rails at the edge of Hill Street. My left knee scraped against the jutting pebbles of the aggregate concrete separating the elevation of the road above from the cliff below; bright red blood trickled down my leg but I ignored it and grabbed hold of the metal rail so warmed by the sun that it was hot to the touch. Triumph.

Elated, I extended my free hand towards Tovah. 'Come on, you're nearly there!'

Tovah took two giant steps then grabbed hold of my outstretched fingers, which tightened quickly into a firm grasp as I began to pull her towards me.

'You're bleeding,' Tovah noted, as she reflexively dusted herself off then uncurled her body into an upright position.

'But we did it,' I crowed, giddy with adrenaline.

'Look at all the steeples,' Tovah said, gesturing towards the churches below with her hand, newly liberated from its role as pickaxe.

'They're so pointy,' I noted.

Tovah laughed. 'They're pointing to your God. Had you seen the sign by the sumac trees at the base that said 'Danger Area – No Trespassing' before today?'

'Yes,' I said, 'but I knew the rock would be safe for us.'

Tovah held my eyes for a moment, questioning.

'Let's go home,' Tovah said finally. 'My mom made lemonade.'

11

Fish in the Water

Tovah's father had a friend called Marvin Kessler. To be fair, Marvin was friends with both of Tovah's parents, but he had more in common with Tovah's dad: both hailed originally from New York City; both were literate, cultured Jewish men who had transplanted themselves to a town without a skyscraper in sight, a town where a significant portion of the population didn't even own a passport (and those who did used them mostly to cross the border for day trips into Canada), a town where the only public transportation was the van for the elderly.

Marvin was a third-grade teacher at the school where Tovah and I attended second grade. I had no business in Marvin's classroom during the course of a normal school day, but Mom took me, Andy and Alice to visit Marvin's classroom once; it must have been after school hours or, more likely, a weekend day. By then Marvin and Mom had somehow met and somehow fallen in love. I knew they were in love because of the way Mom seemed to be floating rather than walking as she explored Marvin's classroom, because of the way Mom kept her face from falling into any unattended expression in Marvin's company, and because of the additional lilt in her already musical speech when she spoke to Marvin, and even when she spoke to us in Marvin's presence. Marvin's classroom – wonder of wonders – had a built-in loft that served as a mini-library. From where I stood next to Marvin's desk, I could see beanbags on the floor of the loft and low bookshelves lining the walls. The desire to climb up and immerse myself in the tantalising books washed over me, but I had no idea how this man with his halo of loose black curls extending four inches from his head in every direction would react were I to storm his temple.

I tapped my mother on the arm to steal her attention away from her new beau. 'Could I go into the reading loft?' I asked.

'Not this time, Beth Anne,' Mom said. 'We're not staying for long. Marvin just needed to collect some papers.'

'I'll tell you what we *can* do though, Beth Anne,' Marvin said, his gold-rimmed glasses glittering as he turned towards me. 'We can go outside. You can meet my friend George. He's a sculptor and an art teacher. He's teaching a paid art lesson outdoors today – let's go pay him a visit.'

My disappointment at not being allowed into the loft was visible for only a fraction of a second; Mom was oblivious, but Marvin was not.

'I promise you can come back another time and explore the loft,' Marvin consoled me. 'If you end up in my third-grade class in September, you'll be able to spend hours up there every day.'

My mind reeled as I contemplated the enormity of free and unlimited access to books during the school day. Marvin strode out of his classroom and into the hallway, with Andy and Alice mutely in tow.

Mom turned in the doorway when she noticed I was hanging back, still plotting how to finagle my way into that book loft. 'Come on, Beth Anne,' Mom said. 'You can't stay here on your own. Marvin said you could visit another day.'

I couldn't quite convince my feet to move. I stayed rooted to the spot.

'Come *on*,' Mom said, in her next-level tone, the tone that was one step short of shouting. 'Andrew and Alice are waiting.'

Mom knew, already, what would work – it was unspoken but understood that she and I shared the burden of responsibility for my brother and sister; while the balance scales of that weight tipped significantly to Mom's side, she had many and lighter masses in her pan, while I had far fewer but far heavier. I followed Mom out into the hallway, and from there into the playground, where George and his handful of students were all sitting in folding metal student chairs with attached plywood desks. The chair–desks were dotted higgledy-piggledy around the asphalted playground rather than arranged in orderly rows as they would have been indoors. While the students looked comfortable, George should have arranged alternative seating for himself, as his frame – not heavy, but solid, like one of his own marble sculptures – did not at all fit the dimensions the student desks had been designed for.

When George spotted Marvin leading us towards him, he laid his pencil down on top of his open sketchbook and spread his arms out wide in welcome, with a smile that was slow to begin, but which, once started, spread like fire from his mouth to his entire face, and from there to the rest of his body. It was as if, because he was accustomed to sculpting emotion into every single inch of the stone he was working on, no matter how enormous that stone might be, George couldn't help but turn the whole of his physical body over to every feeling that came over him.

'Marvin,' George said simply, in welcome.

'George,' Marvin said, much more airily. 'George, I'd like you to meet my friend Elizabeth.'

George's sea-green eyes moved in Mom's direction. I watched as

George evaluated my mother the way an artist would assess a model; his tiny nod gave her his seal of approval.

'Nice to meet you, Elizabeth,' George said, extending his substantial hand towards Mom. 'These must be yours?'

'These are mine – Beth Anne, Andrew and Alice. Say hello, kids.'

'Hello,' we all said obediently.

'Beth Anne looks like an angel with that hair,' George said, as his gaze settled on me. His own hair was jet black and pin straight, but cut in long layers, like a rock star. By seven I had already heard countless adults remark on my hair and I normally ignored them, but something about the way George commented was different, and I felt my cheeks burning.

'Thank you,' I mumbled.

'No, thank *you* for coming to visit me, so I could see that hair for myself,' George said. His arm swept out in an arc as he pointed towards the other desks. 'These are my students – they love art so much that they're here at school when they don't have to be – can you believe that? They're sketching whatever they see. Trees, mostly. Do you all draw?'

Andy and I nodded immediately; Alice joined in as soon as she saw the two of us nodding.

George clapped his hands together, causing his pencil to roll off his sketchbook and onto the ground; I dashed forward, picked it up and handed it to him.

'Thanks, Beth Anne,' George said. I was impressed that he already remembered my full name. 'Maybe you'd like to take a spare sketchbook and find something to draw yourself? Your brother and sister are welcome to draw as well.'

The three of us turned towards Mom, but it was Marvin who answered.

'Another time, George – we only came to pick up some papers from my room. I just wanted you to meet Liza and her kids,' he said, and I noted the undercurrent of male appreciation that passed between Marvin and George, as if Mom's undeniably beautiful shell was even more important than the being it contained.

I was crestfallen that we couldn't stay longer. Not only had I not been allowed to climb up to the book loft, but now I was being denied the rare opportunity to seize a real artist's pencil in my eager left hand and transfer my vision of the world around me to a pristine sheet of thick paper in a real artist's sketchbook. I had to bite my lip to keep from crying. Alice, who was like a horse in her sensitivity and who, because she was younger, had not yet learned to bottle her disappointment, burst into tears.

'It's OK, Alice,' I said, to myself as much as to my sister. 'We'll colour at home.'

'I want to colour here,' Alice whimpered.

'We can't colour here,' I said with finality. 'We have to go.'

'Alice, the next time I see you, I'll bring my spin art set,' Marvin said, with the confidence of a seasoned teacher who, like a magician, was able to transform children's tears into smiles with a deft hand. 'Have you ever done spin art? It's fabulous. You take this special card and put it in the middle of a device that looks like the bottom of a bucket with most of the top cut off. When you turn the machine on, the card starts spinning around and around, like this,' Marvin demonstrated, whizzing his hand in circles. 'Then you take these tubes of paint – they look like miniature ketchup bottles – and you squirt just a splodge of paint onto the card, and it splatters out in every direction, creating your very own pattern. No two designs are alike. All my kids love it.'

Alice had stopped crying and was staring transfixed at Marvin.

'So what do you say, Alice – would you like to try spin art next time I see you?' Marvin asked my now-quiet baby sister, as if to seal the deal.

Alice nodded.

'Wonderful,' Marvin sang out. 'Now, George, it's been great to see you but we really must be off. See you at school on Monday.'

'Lovely to meet you all,' George said. 'Get back to your sketches, kids,' he added, observing that several of his students had been as engaged by Marvin's description of spin painting as Alice. The students in question dutifully resumed their sketching. 'Maybe you'll be in my art class next year,' George said to me.

'Maybe you'll be in my third-grade class,' Marvin added, for the second time that day.

I let myself imagine again what it would be like to have daily admittance to Marvin's book loft. When I added weekly drawing sessions outdoors with George to the tableau, school was transformed from somewhere I knew I had to go to somewhere I longed to go. I wanted that future very, very much.

It was not to be. We left the apartment on Elm Street and moved to a modern post-and-beam chalet, awash with light from its many windows, not far from the Mad River Valley Glen ski area in Waitsfield. This chalet would have been the best house ever if moving there hadn't meant that I could no longer walk to Tovah's house; in fact, moving to Waitsfield meant that I saw Tovah far less often than I had before. Thankfully for Tovah and me though, by the time of that particular relocation, Mom and Marvin had become more than just friends, and because Marvin counted Tovah's parents among his inner circle, it happened that Tovah and I were still brought together to continue our adventures, both exterior and interior.

I missed seeing Tovah every day, but I didn't miss her as much as I might have, because Marvin – a frequent visitor to our new home – excelled at fun. As soon as it was hot enough, Marvin proposed an outing to the Lareau swimming hole, described by Marvin as 'the best swimming hole in the Mad River, where you can be boring and swim in your swimsuit, or you can go just round the bend and swim in your birthday suit.'

I was scandalised at the idea of swimming without my suit on, but more than keen to cool myself off in a quick-moving river current. 'Yes! Oh please, Mom, let's go swimming! With our suits on,' I specified.

'As an ex-lifeguard,' Mom said, 'I can tell you for a fact that suits make it easier to help swimmers who get themselves into trouble – it's a lot easier to grab hold of a suit than skin – so don't worry, Beth Anne, you'll all be swimming with your suits on. Go collect beach towels for the three of you, then change into your swimsuit, put your clothes back on over top, and tell Andrew and Alice to do the same.'

My suit felt stretchy and slippery under my clothes when I came back to the kitchen with Andy, Alice and the towels.

'Everybody ready?' Mom asked.

'They look as ready as they'll ever be,' Marvin said. 'To the bus!'

Marvin's car was as unusual as his hairstyle. It wasn't a car at all – it was a dark green VW bus with substantial amounts of white trim. The exposed headlights on the front were like eyes, one on each side of the sizeable silver VW logo nose, and the bumper acted as a sort of mouth, all lending the bus far more personality than the green Saab 95 V4 wagon we had graduated to after our Datsun. Getting into the bus itself was a novelty – the back door slid to the side instead of either opening out like a standard car door, or not even existing, like on our Saab, where Mom had to lower the driver's seat every time she wanted to let us clamber in or out – but that was nothing compared to the unconventionality of the seating, which was something between a bench and a sofa. The seating surrounded a fake wooden foldaway table, and just beside that, most incongruous of all, was a sink. A sink in a car – wonder of wonders. All of this was benevolently overseen by the figure carved in red resin sitting cross-legged in the middle of the dashboard, hands clasped loosely together, eyes lightly closed: Buddha, meditating in a permanent effort to achieve enlightenment. Marvin was Jewish by birth and upbringing, but just as he had opted for elective surgery to remove his belly button to erase his visible connection to his mother, so too had he taken steps to scrub out his association with the religion of his ancestors and his childhood. Neither the absence of the navel on his body nor the presence of the Enlightened One in his VW bus, however, could wipe out Marvin's corporeal or spiritual history, just as my mother signing the divorce papers and taking off her wedding ring could not annul the fact that she had been married to my father and borne him three children, of whom I was one.

'Can I have a Triscuit?' I asked Mom in the front seat as we bumped along towards the river.

'Not yet,' Mom said. 'When we get to the river – when we've put down our blanket – then you can.'

When we arrived though, the water was too enticing for me to waste time on even my favourite cracker snack. I pulled my clothes off to reveal my baggy swimsuit – purchased, as all of our clothes were, at least one size too big to make it last longer – then tossed my clothes haphazardly towards Mom as she shook and re-shook the picnic blanket to make it lay as smoothly as possible. I splashed my way into the quickly flowing water. The current was noticeable. I had to curl my toes around the pebbles beneath my feet – most of them rounded by years of wear, some newer and more jagged, all slick with a thin layer of plant growth – to stand my ground. When I released my feet and began to swim, the current worked against me, but it was like a gentle tug rather than a strong pull, and even my child's doggy-paddle stroke was more than enough to keep the river from whisking me away.

Andy – one of those boys who looks like a linebacker even in primary school – was already holding his breath and submerging himself in the deepest pool of the swimming hole for as long as he could manage. He came up panting each time, with treasures from the riverbed that would have warmed Grandma Lenore's heart. Each new find joined its predecessors. Andy knew that, before leaving, Mom would ask him to select a few of his best rocks and leave the others behind, but that didn't in any way curb his enthusiasm – if anything, it may have spurred him on. I wasn't like Andy. If I knew I wouldn't be permitted to bring each and every one of my hand-picked rocks home, I would parse as I went along, ensuring that when the five-minute warning sounded, my handful of rocks was ready even before I was. Even with river rocks, I wanted to be the one to decide when it was time to say goodbye.

The current, as far as Andy and I were concerned, was exciting, not hostile. Alice – a four-year-old will-o'-the-wisp – felt otherwise; she had ventured in so far that the river, judging from the sheer panic in her eyes and the rigidity of her body, threatened to capture her. Alice screamed.

'What's up, Alice?' Marvin said from the blanket, where he sat with one hand around the neck of a beer bottle and the other on Mom's upper thigh.

'I can't stand up,' Alice yammered.

Marvin handed his beer bottle to Mom, who placed it in the cooler for safekeeping.

'You think the river's bad – now you're really in trouble,' Marvin joked, as he splashed through the current towards where my baby sister stood motionless.

Alice's eyes, already nearly all pupil and no iris, blackened further still and her mouth opened in a silent 'O'. Marvin was still new; Alice couldn't be empirically sure whether he was coming to rescue or betray her.

'Give me your hands,' Marvin commanded, holding his own hands out for Alice to grasp.

Alice did as she was told.

'Now keep your head up and float on your belly,' Marvin told Alice.

Alice started to cry again.

'Come here, Beth Anne,' Marvin said. 'This is a two-person job. You hold Alice's hands, and I'm going to hold her belly, so she learns how much fun she can have at the swimming hole if she just relaxes.'

'It really *is* fun,' I told Alice, swimming over to join them. 'You'll see.'

I took hold of Alice's hands, even smaller than my own. 'Just keep looking at me,' I instructed my sister.

Marvin scooped Alice off the ground, and I yanked her upper body away from the running water. We held her there, suspended, until her face bloomed with delight.

'Now kick, Alice!' Mom shouted from the shore.

Alice kicked.

'I'm going to take my hands away, Alice,' Marvin said, 'but you keep holding Beth's hands, and keep kicking your feet.'

It worked. I instinctively placed myself upstream from Alice, so the current would work for her rather than against her, buoying her from underneath. Alice kept her head above water, and all was well: Alice was swimming, with only my hands as help.

Until the fish started nibbling at my legs. I didn't know, at first, that the curious tickle, the pinprick not quite negligible, was caused by piscine mouths. Only when the sensation continued did I glance into the river.

'Fish!' I shouted, loudly enough for not just my family, but for every visitor to the swimming hole to hear. I reflexively dropped Alice's hands and began to swat my legs as best I could under the water while also jumping in place. Alice, unceremoniously released, dipped under the surface of the river and came up spluttering.

'Fish are biting me!' I yelled.

Alice had righted herself, but the water was up to her neck. When she caught sight of my scaly assailants, any grudging trust she had given to the river vanished. Alice let out a piercing shriek and sped out of the water towards Mom, who by this time had worked out what would happen next and was casually holding a dry beach towel outstretched to envelop whichever child reached it first. Within seconds Mom had wrapped my sister up and encircled Alice's shivering body with her arms to warm her.

I was both horrified and fascinated by the earth-coloured fish – none more than three inches long – darting about like the dots in an optician's field test.

'Andy!' I called out accusingly. 'There are fish in the river! They bite!'

'I know there are fish,' Andy responded without alarm. 'They only bite if you stand still for too long.'

I took this as an affront. 'I was only standing still because I was helping Alice! What if they start eating you?'

'They won't eat you,' Marvin called from the beach. 'They're just suckers. They'll only sample you. They won't do you any actual harm. Now if we were upriver at the nudist beach, then you might have more to worry about with the fish, because who knows where they might end up if you didn't have your suit on.'

'Marvin,' Mom admonished, but her eyes crinkled with laughter, 'the kids will never go in the water again if you talk like that.'

Suddenly my swimsuit seemed like the best coat of armour I could possibly wish for, protecting my most vulnerable body parts from a fate too ghastly to contemplate. Between my swimsuit and my speed, I calculated that I could foil the fish. I kept swimming, as did Andy. We came out only now and then to eat Triscuits and report to Alice that the fish really weren't that bad, entreating her to get back in the water.

Alice was having none of it; she didn't budge from the shore for the remainder of the afternoon. Just before we packed up though, when Alice was hot from the sun but content from the Triscuits, Mom suggested that Alice might like to cool off. Alice agreed, and Mom and Alice walked hand in hand first towards the river's edge, and then, step by tentative step, into the river itself. I couldn't make out her words, but I could hear Mom's voice, soothing and assuring Alice with every inch.

I dove down to fetch a particularly white pebble. When I surfaced, Mom was holding Alice in the deeper part of the river, where the water formed a still pool, the same way Marvin had held Alice in the current, the same way Mom had long ago held me in the swimming pool in Burlington where I had later tried to find her. Alice was swimming to the best of her ability, just as she had when I had clasped her hands. While Marvin and I had eventually tired of helping her, Mom did not: at least not there, and not then. The next time Marvin proposed an outing to the Lareau swimming hole, Alice said nothing, but she was the first of the three of us to put her suit on.

12

Mr Peabody

The house in Waterbury had a witch window, but this new house in Waitsfield had skylights, slanted roofs and an open second storey, allowing the ceiling of the living room to rise unbelievably high, as if the room had cathedral aspirations. There were bedrooms on the second storey, but not as many as there would have been had the living room not claimed much of the space above it for its own. From the landing on the second floor, you could peer down onto the living room through the balustrades. I was the only child allowed an upstairs bedroom, deemed sensible enough not to squeeze through the posts and careen headlong to the floor far below. Andy and Alice were assigned a shared bedroom in the basement. Alice had a crib against one wall; Andy had the bunk bed along the wall opposite and had chosen the top bunk. Although I recognised it was a privilege to have my very own bedroom and my very own double bed, I envied Andy the top bunk, and sometimes – particularly at night – I longed for the presence of my siblings. To hear them breathing – to sense the additional humidity caused by the exhalation of their young lungs – helped ward off the fears that came to me as I waited for sleep. To compensate, I sometimes crept through the dark house down to their room and snuck under the covers of the bottom bunk.

During the day, we sometimes played in my siblings' room. We'd made up the best game ever, in which Andy and I took turns in jumping from his top bunk all the way across the room to land in Alice's crib. Alice was too small still to clear even the short stretch of empty floor between the two beds. Her important job was to sit on the bottom bunk of the bunkbed, watch Andy and I jump, and give us each a score out of ten for style. Thankfully neither Andy nor I ever required a score for accuracy, as neither of us ever landed on the floor.

We got worms in Waitsfield, maybe from the swimming hole. The itch was like nothing I had previously experienced – worse even than chicken pox – but it was mesmerising to see the squirmy white creatures appear in the loo and to think that I had pets in my own body. I longed for cuddly, warm-blooded pets. We hadn't been allowed cats in our apartment in Montpelier, and I missed the cats we had owned in Waterbury. I thought about them sometimes as I lay awake at night. When we left Waterbury, Mom told me the cats had been given away to people who would look after them. I wondered who those people were, where they lived, and if they might let me come and visit the cats. I was willing to be reasonable – I wouldn't aim to reclaim the cats, only to say hello. I worked up the courage to approach Mom about the prospect one day.

'No, Pumpkin, we can't go see the cats,' Mom said, and her voice sounded pinched. 'But we aren't going to live here forever, and when we move, we'll get a new kitten or two. How would that be?'

A future kitten or two would be good, but a present visit with the cats we had given away would have been even better. I didn't say that out loud, and I was intelligent enough not to ask again.

Mom and Marvin were still in love. It was Marvin's idea to take us to the Easter Egg Hunt in Hubbard Park back in Montpelier. Easter, in Vermont, is not often warm, and that year was no exception.

Speaking to the excited children and their chilly parents before the countdown to the hunt began in earnest, the announcer informed us over the PA system that there was only one giant golden egg – whoever was lucky enough to find that particular treasure would be able to exchange it for an Easter basket of epic proportions. One golden egg, and I aimed to find it. I collected the brightly-coloured foil-wrapped eggs I spotted, but rather than staying with the gaggle of kids, I veered off on a trajectory of my own that I hoped would lead me to that coveted prize. The smaller chocolates became fewer and further between, the screeches of triumphant children became less audible, and I became aware that Mom and Marvin had assigned themselves one of my siblings each, but had left me to my own devices. There were still people about; I was by no means abandoned in the park, but when I looked for the Hubbard Park Tower – a similar lookout point to the one in Burlington that we had climbed often in more temperate weather – and found its whereabouts obscured by the cloud cover, I was disoriented. Where had I started from? Where were the others? What if they had left without me? Panic crept in, squeezing my ribcage with its cold, powerful fingers, and I broke into a run, hoping to retrace my steps.

'May I have your attention, egg hunters,' requested a tinny megaphone voice through the fog. I froze mid-run and listened intently, localising the source of the sound. 'I'd like to announce the winner of the Golden Egg Easter Basket. Brenda Cook, of Barre, found the egg all by herself. A big round of applause for Brenda, please!'

The speaker had given me ample time to pinpoint her coordinates, and now the throng of children and adults encircling the lucky winner came into view. There was Marvin's hair, and there was Alice's burgundy snowsuit. As I came still closer, I saw that Alice's face was smudged dark with chocolate, but her eyes were bright; she didn't seem the least bit bothered that Brenda Cook rather than Alice Evans was accepting the basket laden with chocolate and wrapped in cellophane secured with an enormous bow of yellow ribbon. My own insides were squishy with jealousy, although even my considerably more modest basket held enough chocolate for a week, but relief at being reunited with my sister and ad hoc father outweighed my envy of Brenda Cook, and I was soon happy again to be Beth Anne Evans.

Marvin came back to Waitsfield with us after the Easter Egg Hunt that Saturday. He would stay the night, Mom said, and share Easter dinner with us the following day. Marvin was thrilled by the quantity of snow in our ample, rolling yard.

'Let's make snowmen!' Marvin exclaimed. 'That'll keep us all busy while your gorgeous mother fixes dinner!'

Andy and I were game. Alice wanted to go inside and warm up, but Marvin took her under his wing, promising that their snowman would be far better than any stick-armed tower of snowballs Andy and I could scrape together, and that was enough to convince her. Andy and I divvied up the tasks: Andy took on the base, while I went to beg Mom for raisin eyes and a carrot nose. When I returned, triumphantly holding the facial features I hadn't already eaten en route, I let Andy have his share of the snacks while I cobbled together another snowball and plonked it on the base. Andy shoved the carrot in the middle as a nose, and together we dotted raisins into position as eyes and a mouth. Satisfied, we ran around to the other side of the house, where Marvin and Alice were busily building their own snow structure. Rather than a snowman, however, Marvin and Alice had created a shape that looked oddly familiar: a six-foot high cylinder topped by a bulge with two portions. Two particularly large snowballs flanked the sheath at its base.

'Ta-da!' Marvin warbled. 'Beth Anne and Andy, meet Mr Peabody!'

My brother and I, mystified, looked at the snowman. 'Ours is better,'

I said. 'Yours doesn't even have a nose.'

'Ours doesn't need a nose,' Marvin explained, 'because while yours is an entire snowman, ours is the distillation of a snowman. It's a snow penis! I forgive you for not recognising the male organ, Beth Anne, but Andy, I'm a bit surprised you don't know a dick when you see one. Your sister named him – Mr Peabody. Get it? Pee-body? Penis? So young, but already so witty! Ha!'

Sculpting a penis out of snow would have given any teacher I ever had reason to march me to the principal's office for a stern talking-to at least, but although Marvin was a teacher himself, we weren't at school. If he thought making a snow penis was funny and calling it Mr Peabody was even funnier, then who was I to argue? After all, the subversion of the snowman brief had Andy doubled-over with laughter and Alice grinning from ear to ear. I let go of my misgivings and joined in the mirth, adding several handfuls of snow to the balls at the base.

Both Mom and Marvin were flying high, maybe thanks to the fresh air, maybe thanks to the chocolate they had lifted from our baskets. Even the depletion of the emerald bottle during dinner didn't dampen Mom's spirits as it so often did when Marvin was not present. Instead of sobbing, Mom was smiling, and her euphoria began to rub off. I let myself imagine that maybe – just maybe – now she had Marvin, Mom would never sob again.

I went to bed elated, as soothed by the sound of the adults talking as by the burble of a brook in spring, but then the chatter began to subside, and another noise took its place – a sort of whimpering, like a puppy crying for its mother. My ears strained to ascertain the source of this nerve-jangling disruption. Was it Alice, her tummy distended from too many chocolate eggs, mewling in the basement? Was it indeed the puppy I had longed for, brought in under cover of darkness to surprise me on Easter morning? Was it my mother, moaning in pain? Had I been wrong to entrust her to Marvin?

The sound intensified, and was joined by another, a deep grunting. There was no question now that the noise was both human and emanating from my mother and her boyfriend. What I couldn't determine though, was whether or not Mom needed my help. I sensed the urgency, like the siren of an ambulance rushing to its destination, but would my intervention prevent injury, or would it do just the opposite, impeding the arrival of the emergency vehicle?

Falsely convinced of my power to alter the outcome, I emerged from my room and tiptoed towards the landing overlooking the TV room. I peeked down from between the wooden balustrades and spied my mom and Marvin intertwined on the sofa. Both were naked. I understood instantly that what I was witnessing was completely inappropriate for my young eyes and retreated immediately to the safety of my bedroom, closing the door as quietly as possible behind me.

13

Fish Out of Water

om and Marvin were in love, yes, but Mom was also broke. I'm sure we moved to Marvin's house in East Montpelier mostly for the first reason, but the second reason likely figured in the equation. However we came to be there, I was not complaining – at least not very much – because moving in with Marvin meant becoming housemates with not only Shiva the white shepherd, but also Rima the cat. I had a double bed again, this time with a brass headboard. Just outside my room, along the wall, was a bookcase filled with a mishmash of books, some aimed at adults, some perfect for precocious soon-to-be third-graders, thanks to Marvin's profession. My favourite of Marvin's books was *The Reluctant Dragon*, written by Kenneth Grahame and illustrated by E. H. Shepard. In this tale, set in the English Downs, a poet boy befriends a poet dragon and must then convince both the townspeople and St George the dragon-slayer that his friend – drawn as a sort of cuddly sauropod but with feathery long ears and a vaguely equine head – is nothing to fear. I pulled *The Reluctant Dragon* from the shelf again and again, with the sort of veneration normally reserved for holy texts. Rather than take the book somewhere more comfortable, I insisted on sitting cross-legged on the floor just beside my bedroom door to read it, so that when I was finished, I could place it carefully back in the exact same location from whence I had taken it.

'Ah, Beth Anne, if you like that book so much, you're going to absolutely love the song I'm about to play for you,' Marvin said animatedly, when he happened upon me poring over *The Reluctant Dragon* for the umpteenth time. 'Come with me.'

I hastily reshelved the precious book and trotted after Marvin as he headed for the room with the record player. We either hadn't owned a record player or hadn't unpacked our record player since leaving Burlington. I was over the moon that Marvin made frequent use of his, and I couldn't wait to hear the song he had selected for me.

When Marvin set the needle on the record, Peter, Paul and Mary began to sing about another dragon, Puff, who, just like Grahame's dragon, made friends with a boy. So far, so good, but then came the fifth verse. When I understood that Little Jackie Paper had abandoned his dragon friend, leaving Puff to crawl back into his cave all alone, I couldn't believe it.

'I don't like it,' I told Marvin, who was not only listening contentedly but also singing along in his nasal tenor voice.

Marvin's eyebrows rose up above the top of his gold-rimmed glasses.

'What? How can you not like "Puff the Magic Dragon"?' Marvin asked, alarmed.

'I liked the start, but I don't like the ending. Jackie shouldn't just leave Puff – Puff is his best friend. Puff is sad without him. Jackie isn't being very nice,' I declared.

'Jackie isn't really being mean, he's just growing up. He stopped believing in dragons. You'll see – when you're a teenager, you may stop believing in dragons too,' Marvin prophesied.

'Even if I did, I'd still go back to visit Puff,' I said staunchly.

'Have you read *The Giving Tree*?' Marvin asked. 'The boy in that

89

story goes back to visit his friend, but only as an old man.'

'No.'

'I'll bring it home from school for you to borrow.'

Marvin kept his word, and I paged through my first Shel Silverstein, captivated both by the story and the simple yet effective drawings. Instead of a dragon, the boy in this story visited a tree, which happily gave of itself as the boy grew into a man. Once grown up, the man deserts the tree, until – as Marvin had already revealed – the man returns many years later, hunched and stocking-footed. By that time, only a stump is left of his childhood friend, but even that is offered up by the tree and taken by the former boy, now indeed an old man.

I didn't like the boy in this story either, but I begrudgingly accorded him good behaviour points for at least not running off entirely like Little Jackie Paper. I was conflicted about the tree: I admired her self-sacrifice, but at the same time I was angry with her for giving the boy so much that she became a mere shadow of her previous expansive, fruit-bearing self.

'Why doesn't the tree ever tell the boy no?' I asked Marvin.

'Because she *wants* to give the boy everything,' Marvin explained dreamily. 'It makes her happy.'

Privately, I dismissed Marvin's explanation. If I were the tree, I would have drawn the line at giving my apples. Despite my issues with the plot, I still liked *The Giving Tree*, although it was a mere shadow of *The Reluctant Dragon*.

Marvin, spurred on by my love of yarns, began to spin his own for me. Sometimes Alice and Andy would pile on top of my double bed too, making sure they didn't squish Rima the cat, who loved to sleep on or under my quilt. Marvin told us stories about good princesses and bad kings, about kind dragons and evil dragons, about forests, knights and castles. There seemed to be no limits to Marvin's imagination. He rarely paused to consider the plotline, just rattled on, taking any children within earshot along with him. The longer we stayed in East Montpelier, the better the stories became, until Marvin settled on his ideal heroine – Lulela – and her perfect steed, Pegasus (Marvin must have felt there was no need to rewrite certain elements of his tale). Lulela was young, but she was also plucky, resourceful and indomitable. In short, Lulela was everything I wanted to be, and Marvin – without a doubt – not only knew that, but had shaped his heroine's character accordingly.

As the weeks passed, Rima the cat grew plumper and her feline body became more unwieldy. When I asked Mom why Rima was getting fat, Mom laughed.

'She's not fat, Beth Anne – she's pregnant,' Mom said. 'Rima's going to have kittens.'

I couldn't believe my ears. To gain not only a dog and a cat through Marvin, but our very own kittens as well – that was a stroke of unimaginably good luck.

'How many kittens will she have?' I asked Mom. 'When will they come? What colour will they be? Will we keep them?'

'Woah, woah, slow down,' Mom said, holding her hand up in a 'stop' gesture. 'I can only answer one question at a time. I'd guess, based on her belly, that Rima will have five or six kittens, but it could be as few as one or as many as ten.'

Ten kittens! Unfathomable. 'When will the kittens come? Will they stay with us?' I asked again.

'We can't be exactly sure when Rima will give birth, but when she's nearly ready she'll start making a nest as best she can. She might even make her nest in your bed – doesn't she often sleep with you? We won't be able to keep all of the kittens, Beth Anne, but we might keep one, to keep Rima company,' Mom told me.

That settled it. The one that stayed would be my kitten, although I would of course share her with Andy and Alice.

I had learned how to sleep without rolling onto Rima. Her warmth reassured me when I woke from the recurring nightmares that I didn't tell the grown-ups about. Rima's purr was like a tiny engine, staccato and insistent, but I dreamt about baby pigs rather than trains the night Rima bore her litter in my bed. I slept all the way through the birth and Rima's removal of the sacs and only woke when the teeny, blind kittens began to mewl for milk in the early morning. Rima's corner of my bed was covered in sticky liquid and blood, but I couldn't have cared less: there on my bed were six lumps of wet fur with their exhausted mama, and they were miraculous.

I rolled delicately off the bed opposite Rima and made my way to the room that had been Marvin's and was now Marvin's and Mom's. I tapped my mother on her bare shoulder.

'Mom,' I whispered, tapping in sets of three.

'Hmm . . .' Mom mumbled.

'Mom, Rima had her kittens! Come see! She had six, and they're so, so cute,' I said, in a voice one step up from a whisper, but still barely audible.

'What's the cat doing?' Mom managed.

'Rima? She's feeding them. They're so sweet. They're all drinking from her.'

'They're nursing,' Mom rephrased. 'OK, well, it sounds like she's being a good mom, so there's not much else we can do. We can't move them yet – that would traumatise both Rima and the kittens.'

I stood immobile, remembering the mess in my bed.

'What?' Mom said, now awake enough to be annoyed.

'It's just that my bed isn't clean now.'

At this, Mom woke fully. Before my eyes she transformed from drowsy off-duty mother to alert on-duty nurse. 'Of course it's not. That'd be the placentas.'

I looked at Mom blankly.

'The placentas are what kept the kittens alive while they were in Rima's belly, but the kittens don't need them any more, and in fact, if they didn't come out, that wouldn't be safe for Rima, so it's actually a good thing that your bed is messy,' Mom explained. 'Why don't you go keep an eye on Rima and the kittens, but don't handle them yet – leave that to their mom. I'll be there in a minute.'

Satisfied, I returned to my bed, perched on the clean side, and soaked in the glorious sight of the new additions to my ever-expanding family.

I learned more about birth in East Montpelier, thanks to Rima, and I also learned more about death, thanks to fishing. The red resin Buddha smiled his secret smile and Shiva hung her head, tongue lolling, out of the passenger seat window as Marvin drove us in his VW bus to the nearby pond to introduce us to a sport that did not adhere to the practice of ahimsa but did put fresh fish on our table that evening.

The pond was down the dirt driveway, along the main dirt road, and up another dirt road. The last stretch was riddled with potholes. Andy, Alice and I took turns in speaking at the deepest pitch we could manage so the combined vibrations of the engine and the road surface would imbue our voices with gravelly vibrato. We found this pastime uproariously funny and engaged in it often. Mom, when she was with us, sometimes got fed up and shushed us, but Marvin always drove on jovially.

I wasn't sure the last road we drove on to reach the pond was really a road at all, and we never saw anyone else fishing at the pond. Although Vermont is dotted with ponds, plenty of which are rewarding for the recreational fisherman, Marvin guarded his pond closely, like a desert-dweller who had discovered a hidden freshwater spring.

The process of preparing to fish was exciting and repulsive in equal measure. Andy had volunteered to help Marvin collect earthworms prior to our outing. Marvin set the worm jar next to the tackle box at the end of the wooden dock and turned to address us.

'I don't have four poles, but while we were gathering worms, Andy and I also managed to locate some sticks that will work as poles for two of us while the other two use the real poles. Andy gets to start with a real fishing pole because he dug up lots of these worms,' Marvin said, pointing to the pink, slimy bodies writhing behind the glass.

That seemed fair enough, although it didn't escape me that the end result would be that the boys would fish with poles and the girls would fish with sticks. Still, so long as I had a chance with a pole after Andy, I would be a generous big sister and cede to my little brother.

'First we have to put worms on the hooks,' Marvin said. 'Andy, why don't you pick the best worm out of the jar, and I'll show you how it's done?'

Andy held the glass jar at eye level, settled on a worm, reached his hand into the squirming annelids, pinched his favourite between his thumb and index finger and lifted it out gleefully. Every part of the worm not immobilised by Andy's grasp flapped helplessly in the air.

'That's a nice plump worm, Andy,' Marvin said, taking the bait from my brother. 'Now you've got to fasten the worm on the hook. The hook is very, very sharp, so be careful. You take the body of the worm and put the hook right through the middle, like this.'

Marvin matter-of-factly impaled the earthworm; I shivered in disgust despite myself. 'But that's not enough to keep the worm firmly on the hook, especially if a big trout bites, so you need to make an extra hole at the head of the worm, like this . . .' Marvin demonstrated by piercing the still-thrashing earthworm a second time. The velocity of the S-shapes the worm had been carving in the air with its body slowed and finally stopped. The hook was ready for its next – and for us, tastier – victim.

Andy was hanging on Marvin's every word, enthralled. Alice solemnly sucked on the first two fingers of her right hand and the rose satin binding of the security blanket she brought with her everywhere. It struck me that the satin, although now greyed by frequent washing, had originally been the same colour as Andy's earthworm. It was, as usual, impossible to discern if Alice was listening. She was prone to glue ear, and until her Eustachian tubes developed enough to provide adequate drainage, my little sister wouldn't hear the world like I did. Maybe this was why whenever Alice screamed – a not uncommon occurrence – the decibel level felt as though it might pierce my own eardrum. Marvin sometimes called her a banshee.

Andy and I both felt fish tugging on our lines, but only Marvin caught a fish that first afternoon. After an hour spent in pleasant idleness under the Vermont sun, the initial shock of the worm execution had worn off, so I was taken by surprise when Marvin unhooked the glistening brown trout, whacked it forcefully against the wooden deck, then slit its throat with his fishing knife.

Mom was well pleased with Marvin's trout. 'Just wait, kids,' Mom said, as she sharpened the knife on a whetstone. 'You are in for such a treat!'

Mom, it turned out, was adept at cleaning fish, thanks to her childhood summers spent at the cabin at Lake Wallenpaupack. Despite her skill, however, at dinner that evening I nearly gagged when my mouthful of flaky fish, fried to perfection, included tiny bones. I spat my fish out reflexively while Mom and Marvin looked on in horror.

'Beth Anne Evans, what do you think you're doing?' Mom said sternly. Andy and Alice stopped eating and stared at me.

'There are bones in the fish,' I said.

'There are not. I filleted that fish myself; there are no bones left. Look, Andrew has eaten nearly his whole portion,' Mom said. Andy, who had not been paying attention to exactly how much of his meal he had eaten, looked down at his plate, then puffed up with pride.

I ignored Andy. 'Andy will eat anything,' I said disdainfully. 'There *are* bones. I'll show you.' I gingerly took a tiny bite of the trout and, locating the bone in my mouthful, managed to isolate it so I could spit it out as proof.

'Oh, for heaven's sake, Beth Anne,' Mom said, when I produced the offending piece of skeleton. 'That's only a pin bone. There's no way to remove those, and they're completely edible; they just add a little crunch. Alice and Andy haven't been complaining.'

'Alice has barely eaten any of her fish.'

Now it was Alice's turn to glance at her plate. Unlike Andy, Alice knew exactly how much she had eaten, and she averted her eyes from Mom's gaze.

'Alice, I expect you to eat your fish,' Mom scolded her. 'And you too, Beth Anne. The pin bones are good for you – extra protein. Just use your teeth a little more. Pretend you're Shiva.'

I did as I was told. At least it wasn't liver. Liver was so hateful that even the threat of being made to sit alone at the table after everyone else had finished could not make me eat it. The trout, if I took bites small enough and chewed very thoroughly, did taste good; the bones still disturbed me, but I did my best not to let on.

By the time Marvin proposed a return to the fishing pond a couple of weeks later, my tribulations with the pin bones had all but been forgotten, while the feeling of sitting peacefully on the deck waiting for a tug on my hook remained vivid.

I reminded Marvin, after another bumpy ride up the unmarked road to the pond, that I had dibs on the proper pole this time. Andy's face clouded over, but Marvin was a man of his word.

'Of course you get the pole first, Beth Anne. You didn't think I'd forget, did you?' Marvin seemed genuinely affronted.

'You might have,' I said. What I didn't say was, 'Maybe you'd remember but break your promise, or maybe you were lying to begin with about letting me have the pole first this time.'

'Nah, I wouldn't forget. Does this mean you want to hook your own worm too? We've got an entirely new jar full. . .' Marvin held up the Mason jar like a game show presenter displaying a prize.

I crinkled my nose. 'Andy can hook my worm.'

Marvin laughed. 'No guts, no glory,' he tossed out.

I wasn't completely sure what Marvin meant, but I took up the gauntlet.

'Actually, Andy, never mind, I'll hook my own worm,' I said stoutly. With that, I wrinkled my nose still further, plunged my hand into the Mason jar, and snatched out a worm. I was about to grab the shiny metal hook when Marvin intervened.

'That's a fine-looking worm, Beth, and I'm sure the trout will love it, but the hook is sharper than you think, so take it easy, or you might hook your finger as well as the worm.'

I heeded Marvin's advice and took hold of the hook well above the sharp point, where the metal was still straight rather than curved. Under Marvin's attentive observation, I poked first one, then another hole in my sacrificial worm. I held the bait up for inspection.

'Good. Now you need to learn how to cast. The first step is to hold the pole correctly. Oh, you're a leftie, aren't you?' Marvin said, placing his hands on my shoulders and repositioning himself on my left side.

'I use both hands to throw,' I told Marvin, who was fumbling with the awkwardness of managing the pole wrong-handed.

'Do you?' Marvin said, relieved. 'Then let me show you right-handed. Because we're all on this deck - very close together - we're not going to cast so much as pitch, because of the risk of the hook catching one of us instead of a fish like it's meant to. You still have to let the line spin out from the reel though, like this.'

The rod – controlled by Marvin's hands, but taking my hands along for the ride – snapped to the side and out. I heard the click-click-click of the reel as the line fed out. Ripples emanated in concentric circles from where the worm had broken the water's surface.

'What happens now?' I asked.

'Now you wait,' Marvin answered, and proceeded to help Alice and Andy with their stick poles.

I liked waiting for the fish to bite. Because I had a real rod, I was meant to remain standing. Andy and Alice, with their stick rods, were permitted to sit down, and Shiva had offered herself to Alice as a back rest. None of us felt compelled to speak, because in truth we were all occupied, calmly preparing ourselves for the battles we hoped to wage soon against our cold-blooded opponents. If we had wished to talk, that would have been fine too. Marvin, unlike Mom and Dad, was uncritical, and it was freeing to sense that no matter what any of us siblings said or did, he would take us where he met us and roll with it, rather than sending us back to square one.

The waiting, that second time fishing, didn't last long.

'Something's pulling,' I told Marvin, who quickly reeled his own line in, laid his pole down and again added his hands to my rod.

'You've got something there, Beth Anne, and it's not a minnow,' Marvin said. 'You need to reel in until the line is taut. You do it.'

I rotated the handle. The pull on the line weakened.

'That's the wrong way, Beth Anne. You're feeding line out. Reverse direction.'

I reddened with shame, sure that Marvin would scold me for letting dinner slip away, and worked to undo my error.

'Good!' Marvin said. 'Now keep a tight grasp. This is when the fish swims around for a while. We let him tire himself out, then we reel him in.'

The top two feet of my rod bent towards the pond. The fish was doing his best to yank me into the water.

'Is the tip of the pole going to break?'

'No, Beth. Fishing poles nowadays are made from fibreglass – a very strong, but also very flexible material. Keep holding tight and let me know if you get tired.'

The fish and I carried on, him swimming as far from me as the line would let him, me refusing to give ground. I imagined him on the other end of the nearly invisible line, his golden eyes the size of dimes – eyes that would stay open even in death – trying desperately to rid himself of the hook. My fish was a fighter and I admired him for it, but soon the tautness of the line began to subside.

'He's getting away,' I said, disappointed.

'He's not, he's just losing strength, but the hook could fall out of his mouth if the line gets too loose, so now we have to land him,' Marvin said. 'Pull hard and I'll bring him up.'

Seconds later my fish was out of the water, his entire body in motion save for where the hook trapped him; the spots on his body reminded me of a cheetah, the fastest land animal on Earth. I wondered briefly if I had just caught the fastest fish in the pond – if I had, why hadn't he been fast enough to swim away like he should have to avoid what would happen to him next? I looked away involuntarily as Marvin completed the kill.

'I'd say that fish is at least a foot long, Beth Anne, and not just that – see that pink stripe on his side? This isn't an ordinary trout. It's a rainbow trout. Wait until your mother fries *this* fish up for dinner – you won't be complaining about pin bones tonight.'

Mom's face lit up when we tumbled into the kitchen.

'Beth Anne has something for you, Liza,' Marvin announced. 'Show her, Beth Anne,' he added, putting the cooler full of ice down on the kitchen island.

I clambered up on the bar stool nearest the cooler and raised the lid, revealing my rainbow trout on its bed of half-melted ice.

'Wow!' Mom exclaimed, and it was a real 'wow,' not the pretend 'wow' she sometimes trotted out when required. 'Did you catch that yourself? It must be twelve inches long! It's longer than your arm!'

I ate up the praise like candy, smiling bashfully.

'Go play for half an hour or so, then we'll have dinner,' Mom told us.

Maybe it was because I had caught the fish myself, or maybe it was because Mom had taken special care to remove as many bones as she possibly could, but no pin bones marred my savouring of the more meaty and less fishy rainbow trout that night. Mom and Marvin were chatting merrily, Andy was chomping away as usual, Alice was on her way to finishing her plate, and I was resting my feet on Shiva when an uncommon sensation of well-being flooded through me.

'This is the best dinner I've ever had,' I burst out, as the happiness spilled over.

Mom and Marvin both stopped talking and turned towards me.

'That's how it feels when you catch your own food,' Marvin said. 'You're fulfilling your primordial hunter instincts.'

Mom chuckled. 'You know all about primordial instincts,' she said to Marvin.

Marvin winked at Mom. 'You're pretty familiar with them yourself,' he retorted.

14

Potholes

My happiness faded as the evening wore on and the level of liquid in the glass bottle sank. There were various types of bottle, and there was a direct correlation between their size and the amount I disliked them, with the biggest bottles – the green gallon jugs with the Carlo Rossi or Gallo labels – being the most hated by me, but seemingly the most treasured by Mom. By the time Andy took himself to bed and I took Alice to bed, that evening's bottle, which had first been opened at dinner, was less than a third full, and the comportment of the adults had changed accordingly. Mom was still laughing, but it was anyone's guess when that laughter would turn itself inside-out and become sobs or shouts. I couldn't say for sure whether Mom's grief or her fury was more terrifying.

I said good night to Alice, then crept back to my room, closing the door firmly behind me. Sleep, I knew, would come when my body gave out, long before my mind wished to follow suit. If I had not been trapped in a child's body – a body that still demanded energy to grow – I doubt I ever would have fallen asleep before the rest of the house was completely silent. I had no empirical evidence to believe that my vigilance mattered – I had proven myself neither able to hinder the depletion of the bottles nor able to ensure that evenings ended peacefully – but I clung resolutely to the idea nonetheless.

Mom knew, by that time, that I wasn't going to sleep easily at night. On good nights – nights when the bottles opened were smaller or nights when they didn't appear at all – Mom sometimes said a prayer when she came to tuck me in or, once in a great while, sang me a lullaby. Mom's only prayer went like this:

'Now I lay me down to sleep,
I pray the Lord my soul to keep.
If I should die before I wake,
I pray the Lord my soul to take.'

'You don't have to say the second part,' Mom told me. 'It might be a bit fatalistic for a child. But the first two lines are reassuring, aren't they? You don't need to lie awake worrying, Beth Anne, because God is looking out for you.'

'I don't want to die before I wake,' I said.

'You won't. You're going to live a long and healthy life. This prayer is from a long time ago, when life was harder and people died much earlier. Before they invented antibiotics.'

'What are antibiotics?'

'Like the penicillin you have to take when you get strep throat.'

I squished my face in disgust. I couldn't swallow pills, so every time I needed penicillin, Mom had to grind the pills into a fine powder in her mortar and pestle and mix them into apple sauce, either home-canned or store-bought. Home-canned was better; store-bought had a peculiar consistency and didn't really taste like apples at all. Both were sweet, but even the sugar couldn't mask the horrid bitterness of the medicine.

I preferred the lullaby, which, like the prayer, was always the same. The lullaby went like this:

'Sleep, my child, and peace attend thee

All through the night.
Guardian angels God will send thee
All through the night.
Soft the drowsy hours are creeping,
Hill and vale in slumber steeping
I my loving vigil keeping
All through the night.'

Years of regular smoking had already taken a toll on Mom's vocal cords, giving her a quieter, breathier voice than she may have had as a child, but years of playing the piano to a high standard meant Mom had near-perfect pitch; she sang melodiously and with feeling.

'What's a vigil?'

'It's when somebody stays awake. 'I my loving vigil keeping' means I'll be looking after you all night long.'

'But you won't really, because you'll be going to sleep.'

'I'll go to sleep eventually, that's true, but sometimes when you need me in the night – like if you have strep throat and your fever gets really high – you come in to get me and I wake up.'

I nodded, satisfied with Mom's explanation.

'And also, like the song says, even when I'm asleep, God is watching over you.'

Mom had a curious relationship with God; she seemed to both believe and not believe at the same time. When she assured me at night that I was in God's hands, it was less like Mom was relaying a certain fact and more like she was herself making a request, asking a God she wasn't sure existed to please send his or her angels to bring me through to morning. I wished that Mom could leave me with prayer or a song every bedtime, but the nights when she did were as rare and as precious as finding real gold among the fool's gold when panning.

I wasn't sure if Mom ever said a prayer or sang a lullaby for Andy and

Alice when she tucked them in. When, for whatever reason, bedtime duty fell to me, I left Andy – who, at fifteen months younger, was much more of a peer and much less of a little brother – to sort himself out, but I often tried to copy Mom's best good nights to me when I said good night to Alice. I censored the prayer to avoid any mention of death, cutting it down to just the first two lines. I edited the lullaby too, not out of consideration for Alice's age, but because I myself hadn't learned the words properly. I generally started with confidence, hummed my way through the middle, then finished strong, singing the lines about the vigil resolutely. I wanted so much to keep that promise for my baby sister, although I had broken it by falling asleep every previous night.

Tousle-haired and pillow-creased, I emerged from my bedroom the morning after the rainbow-trout dinner and assessed the state of the rooms below like a forensic scientist. Unwashed dishes – some not even rinsed off – festered next to the sink, the gallon-sized Carlo Rossi jug sat empty and a second bottle had been opened and partaken of, a throw cushion from the sofa lay on the floor, and a trail of peanut M&M's led from one corner of the coffee table to the bright yellow packaging that must have been set down carelessly enough for the candy to spill out. Based on the evidence, I anticipated that Mom, when she eventually appeared, would be tired and irritable, while Marvin would be unshowered but in good spirits.

Andy was already ensconced so deeply on the sofa that I almost didn't see him, but the movement of his jaw as he munched on stray M&Ms gave him away, as did the TV, tuned to Sunday morning cartoons.

'These are re-runs,' I said to Andy.

'Mmm,' Andy replied, as his teeth ground up and down and from side to side.

'At least it's *The Jetsons*,' I noted, grabbing a handful of M&Ms myself and crawling onto the sofa next to Andy.

Alice came in, rubbing her eye with her left hand; as usual, the first two fingers of her right hand were jammed in her mouth, along with as much of the pink satin lining of her security blanket as she could manage. Alice snuggled in next to me, leaning her delicate head with its oddly grey silky hair against my shoulder. We sat there like that silently, the three of us, through the rest of *The Jetsons* and the cartoon following. Even with the peanut M&Ms, my tummy was starting to rumble. I hadn't yet been entrusted to prepare even something as simple as cereal for myself or my siblings, and the contents of the kitchen were off limits without permission. Mom and Marvin wandered in halfway through the third cartoon of the morning – surprisingly, and counter to my deductions, both seemingly pleased to be awake.

'Hi, kids!' Marvin called out.

'Hi,' I answered, on behalf of the three of us.

'I'll get out the cereal and make some toast,' Mom said. 'Come get your bowls.'

When I came close enough I noticed that both adults still had wine on their breath.

There were only four chairs around the kitchen table. 'I can take my cereal to the sofa,' I volunteered.

'No, no, you stay there, Beth Anne,' Marvin protested. 'Your mama can come sit on my lap, can't you, Liza?'

To my amazement, Mom took Marvin up on his offer and perched on his right leg.

'All the milk the kids are having is making me thirsty,' Marvin said. 'I'm going to have some milk too.'

With that, Marvin lifted up my mother's top and put his mouth on her nipple. He began to suckle like the kittens had suckled Rima. My face got hot and I bowed my head.

'Let's move to the sofa,' I ordered Andy and Alice, picking up my bowl and turning my back on my parents. I tapped Alice on the shoulder to make her break her wide-eyed stare.

'Marvin,' Mom scolded half-heartedly, 'I don't think the kids like that.'

'They might not like it, but I do,' Marvin said.

I avoided Marvin for the rest of that day, and maintained my scepticism for the rest of the week, but the following weekend Marvin brought home something new: a rock tumbler. The fire-engine-red plastic base of the rock tumbler was about the size of a child's picture book; the barrel where the action took place was lemon yellow and covered in something that looked like a long flesh-coloured bandage, but was actually a rubber sleeve designed to increase the barrel's traction on the drive shaft.

'I've wanted to try one of these for ages,' Marvin said, as Andy and I peered at the device. Mom was half-watching TV over her knitting. Alice was folded into the sofa where it came nearest to Mom's easy chair. Mom laid her knitting down every so often to lift the heavy glass on the side table to her lips.

'It came with these samples,' Marvin said, holding up a small handful of nondescript rocks. 'Once they've been through the tumbler, you'll see they're actually semi-precious stones – they'll be so beautiful that you'll want to make jewellery out of them. Assuming the tumbler works.'

I respected Marvin's intellect - if Marvin said gems were hidden within the drab rocks he was encouraging Andy and me to place in the tumbler barrel, then although the idea was hard to believe, it was worth entertaining.

'The way it works is, we add a bit of grit that the company has helpfully supplied, then I take the tumbler to the garage, plug it in, and it spins and spins for about a week. At the end of the week, I unplug the machine, we open the barrel, *et voilà*, semi-precious agate!'

Andy looked distraught. 'A week? Why does it take so long?'

'Do you have any idea how long it takes for rocks to be polished in the natural world?' Marvin asked, using his teacher voice.

'More than a week?' I suggested.

'Ha!' Marvin laughed. 'I'd say it's more than week. Have you ever heard of Niagara Falls?'

'Yes,' Andy answered, for us both.

'Do you know what it looks like?'

Andy said simply, 'A big waterfall.'

'I'm sure there's a picture of it in *Encyclopedia Britannica*,' Mom contributed from her easy chair as the smoke from her newly lit cigarette curled into the air above her.

'Have you taken the kids there yet, Liza?' Marvin asked.

'Not yet. I won't take them until they're old enough to stand far, far away from the guard rail. I used to be a lifeguard, remember, so I have a healthy respect for water. I'm also terrified of heights, so Niagara Falls with these three would be my idea of hell.'

'Niagara Falls is a life-changing experience,' Marvin said reverentially. 'And, most importantly for the purposes of this discussion, Niagara Falls – which, Andy, is indeed an enormous, spectacular waterfall – was formed by the movement of water over rock for much longer than a week. We'll take you there someday, kids.'

'What will these rocks look like when they're semi-precious?' I asked, directing Marvin's attention back to the here and now.

'They're already semi-precious,' Marvin said. 'Their beauty is just hidden. Not like your mother's beauty, which is there for all to see,' he added.

I nodded. Marvin was right – Mom was beautiful, and I was pleased that he wasn't afraid to say so. Mom's face was open and symmetrical; her almond eyes matched her chestnut hair. Her years of synchronised swimming and lifeguarding had left Mom strong, but not visibly muscular; she was like a lioness, supple and quick when necessary, but more than content to loll in the sun whenever possible.

'Will they be smaller?' Andrew asked, staying on topic.

'They won't be that much smaller,' Marvin replied. 'They'll look much like the polished rocks Beth Anne has in that little pouch from her grandmother on your father's side.'

'From Ausable Chasm?'

'Exactly. Do you two want to follow me out to the garage and see what the rock tumbler looks like when it's working?'

'Yes, please,' I said for us both, without hesitation.

Marvin led the way to the mudroom, pulled on his boots and saw to it that we followed suit, then traipsed across the driveway to the side door of the garage, cradling the device in the crook of his right arm. Once inside the garage, Marvin turned towards the substantial vice at the right-hand edge of the long workbench along the wall nearest the house.

'We'll put the tumbler right behind this,' Marvin said, indicating the vice. I was intimately acquainted with the vice – although I had been warned to never, ever touch anything in the garage without an adult present, I had not been able to resist inserting my left index finger into the space between the two metal bars and spinning the crank, over and over, until I began to feel pressure on the sides of my finger. As soon as the sensation went from peculiar to uncomfortable, I reversed direction, releasing my finger unscathed. I had been fortunate: had I made the mistake of further tightening the vice, I might have done myself irreversible damage. When Marvin ordered us to leave the rock tumbler strictly alone and to not, under any circumstances, touch it while it was in motion, I thought back to the finger incident and I vowed not only to follow his directive myself, but also to prevent Andy or Alice from going anywhere near the machine.

Marvin plugged the tumbler in and turned it on; the belt whirred and the rocks inside thunked from side to side.

'Now we leave it, for a week at the very least,' Marvin said.

I didn't have to actively prevent my siblings from fiddling with the tumbler over the course of the week because they were young enough for out of sight to still mean out of mind, but I hadn't myself forgotten about the work the rock tumbler was doing. I poked my head in periodically during the following days to check that the machine was still clunking away; I needed only to hear the dampened thuds to be satisfied.

The following weekend, while the grit and water continued to work away at the surface of the rocks we had placed in the barrel, Marvin suggested another fishing trip. I leapt at the chance. I very much wanted to catch another fish – for the thrill of the hunt, yes, but more importantly, for the flush of pride that had come from providing for our family and for the opportunity to bring about another night of celebration. Even if the exuberance of that evening had spilled over into a morning of disinhibition, I craved my mother's laughter so much that I was more than willing to accept mornings after nights before.

Marvin loaded the fishing gear and the three of us kids into the VW and we set off down the road. It had rained heavily during the week. The potholes in the dirt road, normally jarring enough to make our voices rumble, now made us squeal as we fought gravity to keep from being tossed around the interior of the campervan.

Marvin was a teacher, and he had trained himself over many years to avoid swearing in front of children. Mom had no such qualms, however – her speech was liberally peppered with profanity whenever she felt the circumstances warranted it, which was any time her world tilted off-kilter. It was startling when Mom swore, but it wasn't shocking. When Marvin shouted 'Oh, fuck!' as he lost control of the

109

steering wheel and the VW nosedived into a ditch, my first thought was not, 'Oh my God, we're turning upside down!' but rather, 'Oh my God, Marvin swore!'

Then I shrieked, because the VW had done a complete flip, and because my sister was crying.

'Shit,' Marvin said. We were now all upright, except for Alice – who was lying on what had been the roof of the bus, moaning – and the red resin Buddha glued to the dashboard, who still sat cross-legged, benevolent and impassive, despite being unceremoniously suspended upside down.

'Alice!' I shouted. 'Alice!'

'My head hurts,' Andy mumbled, pressing his hand against his forehead. 'My elbow hurts too.'

Marvin did a quick triage. 'None of you are bleeding,' he reported, 'but Alice may have a concussion. I think we're going to have to take her to the hospital.'

'How are you going to do that? The car is upside down!' I yelled. I was leaning over Alice whose olive skin had taken on an ashen hue.

'Alice!' I shouted at her. 'Alice! Are you OK? Alice! Talk to me!'

'Beth Anne, not so loud. If Alice bumped her head, all that noise will further rattle her brain. What needs to – oh fantastic, someone's coming,' Marvin interrupted himself, listening intently. 'Let's hope I can still get out of the bus.'

Exactly which door Marvin opened has blurred in my memory, but one way or the other, within seconds Marvin was standing in the dead centre of the dirt road, waving his hands like a madman. A Ford pickup truck came bouncing along the road and came to an abrupt halt a few feet in front of Marvin.

The driver's windows were already down to provide natural air conditioning in the Vermont summer heat, so it was through his open window that the driver said laconically, 'Went over, huh?'

'I did, yeah. The rain last week made the potholes worse, my wheel went down and I flipped. I was maybe going kinda fast given the conditions – we were in a hurry to get out fishing,' Marvin said, appealing to what he guessed were the driver's sensibilities.

The driver, noting Marvin's out-of-state accent, nodded knowingly. Of course Marvin had flipped his van – flatlanders were no match for Vermont potholes.

'Need help?' the driver asked gruffly.

'Yeah, I could really use a hand. I've got three kids with me – the little one needs to see a doctor. Could you maybe drive us back to the house so her mom can take her to the hospital?'

'I've only got room for two in the cab, and the back is full of firewood. Can you leave the other kids here?'

'Sure. The other kids are older and not badly hurt - they'll be fine. It's not far, so they won't be here on their own for long.'

The pickup truck driver nicked his consent. Marvin came back to the van where Alice was holding her head and looking dazed.

'I'm going to lift you up, Alice, honey,' Marvin said with uncommon tenderness. 'Andy and Beth Anne, you just need to wait here while this nice man drives me home to get your mom.'

'Can we walk home?' I asked.

'No,' Marvin said, 'just stay here for me. I'll be back in fifteen minutes or so.'

Marvin scooped Alice up and cradled her like a baby. Her head rested in the same bend of Marvin's right arm that had held the bright red rock tumbler only a week ago. When he saw Marvin's burden, the pickup truck driver jumped out of the driver's side and held the passenger side door open for Marvin and Alice. Marvin climbed in gingerly; the driver closed the door after him, did a U-turn and drove the truck back up towards our driveway.

Andy and I watched the truck disappear. 'Do you think Alice is gonna be OK?' I asked Andy.

'Dunno,' Andy said.

'I hope so,' I said, more to myself than to Andy. I hummed to myself to keep my panic under some semblance of control.

After a wait that seemed interminable, Mom's green Saab exploded over the crest of the hill, travelling at a speed that indicated she had no intention of stopping.

'Mom! Mom!' I shouted, waving.

Mom waved perfunctorily but kept on driving. I couldn't see Alice.

'That was Mom, but Alice wasn't with her,' I said to Andrew. 'Why not? What if Alice died, Andy? What if we don't have a little sister any more? Oh my God . . .'

Andy's face reddened and his cheeks puffed out. Just before Andy broke into tears, the Ford pickup truck trundled back into view. Marvin waved out of the window.

'Marvin!' I shouted.

Andy's cheeks became less like those of a squirrel.

'Alice isn't with him either though,' I remarked.

Marvin shook the Ford pickup truck driver's hand, then sprang out of the truck. 'Hey kids,' he said. 'Thanks for waiting. We'll see if we can right the bus ourselves, and if we can't, we'll just leave the Buddha to watch over it and walk home.'

He seemed perfectly at ease, whereas I was anything but. 'Where's Alice?' I demanded. 'Is she dead?'

'Dead?' Marvin asked, surprised. 'Do you really think I'd be this calm if your little sister were dead, Beth Anne?'

I was silent. I worked out that Marvin's return question meant that Alice was not dead, but I wasn't sure if Marvin genuinely wanted me to confess that I had no idea if he would be calm if Alice died.

'Of course Alice isn't dead,' Marvin said more kindly. 'I'm not sure why you think she is. Didn't you see your mother drive by?'

'Yes, but I didn't see Alice,' I said, and finally my own tears began to flow, cascading down my cheeks like twin waterfalls. 'I don't want my sister to die,' I sobbed, as the shock of the accident caught up with me.

A look of understanding came over Marvin. 'I know why you didn't see her. She was lying down in the back seat. That was the most comfortable position for her.'

Marvin put his arm around my shoulder. 'Your sister's going to be just fine, Beth Anne,' Marvin said, 'although I'm not sure I can say the same about my VW bus.'

Marvin's friendly gesture only increased the intensity of my tears.

'I'll tell you what, Beth Anne,' Marvin bargained, 'you trust me, and believe that Alice is going to live through this, and when we get back to the house, we'll see if the gems are ready.'

I perked up.

'In the rock tumbler?' Andrew said, suddenly interested.

'Yes, in the rock tumbler,' Marvin affirmed.

I brushed my cheeks with the back of my hands then pulled up my T-shirt to wipe my nose.

Marvin arched his eyebrows. 'Do you do that often?' he asked with distaste.

'What?' I said innocently.

'Wipe your nose on your shirt.'

'Only after I cry.'

'Well then, I guess we better try to keep you happy,' Marvin laughed.

15

Chocolate World

Alice had the whole back seat to herself on the way to the hospital that afternoon, but none of us were that lucky when we went on trips to Pennsylvania to visit Nanny and Poppy. The two kids who had pulled the back seat straws had to clamber in past the inclined driver's side seat while the fortunate child who had been assigned the front seat stood idly by, smugly twiddling their thumbs. Mom had to lean way in to fasten the seat belt on the kid on the passenger's side of the back seat. Why she didn't usually opt to open the passenger side door as well, to make it easier for herself and the child on that side, I don't know; my guess is that Mom was so accustomed to being over-extended that the trade-off of complexity for perceived time saved seemed worthwhile, but Mom also lived with the constant worry that one child would close a car door on the fingers of another child, and if she only opened the door on her side, she could more easily control when that door was closed. I had to curb my desire to giggle whenever I was the kid standing outside while this operation took place. Mom, a trained synchronised swimmer, was normally graceful, but performing the seat belt manoeuvre required her to stick her bottom out as counterweight so she wouldn't tip into the car; even when taking that measure, she looked awkward and off balance, and from years of jostling my younger siblings I sensed that it would take only a moderate push to topple her. If she had trouble fastening the seat belt, which she often did, Mom would sometimes mutter profanities, but because she was in such close proximity to us and was doing her best to be gentle, her tone was apologetic, and the words that would upset me in any other situation only made it harder for me to keep a straight face. The best place in the car for me, though, was not the front seat. No, the best place for me was the driver's side back seat, because Mom would lean over me not once, but twice: once to help the sibling to my right, and once to help me.

Mom was not a natural hugger. I'm sure that at some point I must have sat in Mom's lap, but I have no corporeal recollection of how that felt. I didn't go to Mom for cuddles or kisses – that pattern had not been established in our family, and because of my family's hermetic ways, I was mostly unaware that other families were in the habit of giving each other daily physical expressions of love. The closest we came, outside of goodnight kisses, was snuggling on the sofa, and even then, that was usually just some combination of us kids, because Mom almost always smoked or picked up her knitting in the evenings, and for both of these she sat in her separate armchair. I'd learned to respect Mom's need for personal space, but still yearned to be closer to her, which was why I loved to sit on the left-hand side of the back seat. While Mom struggled to fix the seat belt of whoever was next to me, I'd take in big whiffs of her Charlie perfume, sometimes freshly applied, sometimes residual from frequent use; I'd feel the warmth of Mom's nearby body and notice the delicacy of her ears, far more dainty than my own. I'd suck in my gut to keep myself as small as possible, but sometimes even then, Mom nudged me in passing. When that happened, I'd marvel at how her arms were both solid and malleable at the same time, and apologise for being in the way.

'Sorry,' I said when bumped at the start of the journey to Pennsylvania.

'This goddamn seat belt – you'd think they'd make these easy to operate if they really want people to wear them.'

I was well familiar with Mom's loathing of the tension-loaded belts – she often removed her own shoulder belt after fiddling with it repeatedly in futile attempts to make it more tolerable – but my previous offers to go without the belt had been waived, and besides, I was secretly grateful for this whole process so I kept quiet. I observed Mom's gnarled hands, which were already showing the effects of her lifestyle through their proclivity towards redness; the bluish-purplish veins showing under Mom's skin were fascinating and repulsive in equal measure. I was squeamish, and the idea of Mom's blood travelling along that venous highway – which is what Mom had told me veins were, a transport path for blood – was so overwhelming that I had to look the other way, out the window, to where Alice was making faces at me while waiting for Mom to finish. I stuck my tongue out at Alice in return.

The click of Andy's seat belt led to a noticeable relaxation of Mom's body. 'There we go,' Mom said. 'Finally. Now let's double-check yours, Beth Anne.'

I pulled my body back even further, making myself as flat to the seat as I was able so Mom would have an unobstructed view of my seat belt, but I couldn't remember what Mom would want me to do with my hands, so they flitted between straight down against my sides and then crossed high on my chest.

'Just keep your hands still,' Mom ordered.

'Where?'

'Where what?'

'Where should I keep my hands still?'

'In your lap? I just need to see your belt.'

I moved my hands from my chest to my lap and clasped them firmly together while Mom tended to me. Mom's attention, when turned directly towards me, was a bit like that of an unpredictable house cat, the kind that purrs and plays one moment, but hisses and arches its back the next. I could never be quite sure if interacting with her would leave me soothed or metaphorically scratched. When focussed on my health and safety – or that of my siblings – however, Mom's attention was only ever that of a lioness looking after her cubs. Mom checked my seat belt with the same care evident in her management of my long, thick, honey-coloured hair. Each click of the belt, each stroke of the brush, was Mom telling me something she couldn't often tell me any other way, and I hung on her every unspoken word.

Something about the mix of the open road, the hours stretched out before her, and the allure – if not the actuality – of going home led Mom to start each trip to Pennsylvania as though it were a party.

'Would you look at that sky, kids? We couldn't possibly have asked for better weather for driving,' Mom said, easing seamlessly into fourth gear. The car whizzed along under Mom's expert direction. 'We're going to Hershey's Chocolate World this time – you'll love that.'

Chocolate World sounded tasty, but I was a traditionalist. 'Why can't we go to Dorney Park, like we did last summer?'

Dorney Park was an amusement park that was only one step up from a travelling fairground: the rides were packed tight and the crowds were raucous, but the cotton candy was light as a feather and oh-so-sweet. I recalled pulling the strands out from the candy hive and how the sugary pink fuzz had almost sizzled when it touched my tongue.

'I love Dorney Park,' I said plaintively.

'You'll love Chocolate World more. In the gift shop you can get bags of only Special Dark Miniatures.'

My eyes opened wide. Both Mom and I loved Special Dark the

most. Andy liked Mr Goodbar, with the bright yellow wrapper and the peanuts. Alice seemed to favour plain milk chocolate or Krackel, in the red wrapper with the crisped rice, but no one was entirely sure which miniature was really Alice's favourite because Alice was fickle in her affections.

'But are there rides at Chocolate World?'

'There are some, and if there aren't enough, Hersheypark is right next door. It'll be fun.'

'I'm hungry,' Andy complained.

'We're not stopping yet. We'll stop for dinner later. It's nowhere near dinnertime now,' Mom said airily.

We had tried all three ways to drive to Pennsylvania: via Fair Haven, Bennington or Brattleboro, but the Fair Haven route, cutting past the lower reaches of the New York Adirondacks, was Mom's clear favourite. She was a very competent driver, but not fond of multi-lane traffic: she found busy highways tiring and preferred to travel *through* the landscape, on smaller roads, rather than *past* the landscape, on interstates. In winter, Mom would choose the Brattleboro route with its monotonous stretches of highway, as it was the most reliably snow-free. One might have expected her to pick the Bennington road, which afforded fewer twists and turns than driving via Fair Haven, and yet most often Mom snubbed Vermont by crossing into New York State as soon as she possibly could.

Maybe Mom drove just south of the Adirondacks out of habit, or even nostalgia. During our years in Burlington, we would have entered New York State either by driving north to South Hero island and hopping on the ferry for the quarter-hour transport to Plattsburgh, or by heading south and passing the border at Fair Haven, just as we could now from East Montpelier. Dad loved boats – he'd have chosen to take the ferry every time if Mom had let him – but Mom had a fear of water, and would have pushed for the ferry-less, bridge-less Fair Haven route.

It takes many hours to drive from either Burlington or East Montpelier to Bethlehem, Pennsylvania, and the trip, because of its familiarity, often fell into a certain rhythm. The initial frisson – 'We have suitcases! We're going on a trip! We get to eat out!' – lasted only thirty miles or so. After that, we began to amuse ourselves in ways that typically started as benign child shenanigans only to progress – slowly if Mom was lucky, quickly if she was not – to the more irritating sort of mayhem that three children under the age of eight excel at creating, even in cars.

Mom followed a particular pattern of escalation. To begin with, Mom would keep her eyes on the road ahead but adopt a stern voice: 'Kids, stop making so much noise! It's hard to concentrate with you yelling like that.'

This first warning would pacify us for perhaps five minutes. Then we'd start up again, getting more and more rowdy until we'd pushed Mom to the next disciplinary step, which was to swivel her head almost completely towards the back seat, look the noisiest child straight in the eye, and say, 'Beth Anne, I cannot drive when you're making such a racket. You're the oldest – you should be setting a good example for Andrew and Alice. Now I want you to quiet down and sit on your side. Pretend there's an imaginary line between you and Andrew – and don't cross it!'

This more serious rebuke bought Mom more time than her previous intervention. If all went well – if the two of us in the back seat turned our attention to the landscape whooshing past at an incomprehensible speed or to the books Mom ensured we had with us for the journey – Mom's efforts would end right there. If nothing caught our eye through the window, however, or the books were deemed boring, Mom could be forced to wield her ultimate weapon: pulling over.

By the time Mom resorted to pulling over, she would be well and truly furious. At home, Mom's anger was something to be avoided if at all possible – she wouldn't hesitate to combine shouting with swearing, particularly if the levels in the ubiquitous wine jugs were depleted. But there were no bottles in the car, and as much as she might have liked to throw her hands in the air, at least one of Mom's hands had to remain on the steering wheel. Mom even swore less in the car. At home, she might hurl profanities and hope they would just miss us, like high-speed but badly aimed baseball pitches. In the car, there was no room for deflection and nowhere to run – any expletives flung would hit us, and Mom didn't want that, not really.

'Mom! Andy keeps trying to tickle me! He won't leave me alone!' I complained on this particular occasion.

'I'm not tickling her,' Andy protested, his hand on my side. 'This isn't tickling.'

'You can't tickle me,' Alice said with superiority from the front seat.

'That's what you think,' I retorted, wrapping my arms around the back of her seat and jamming my fingers into my little sister's armpits as she shrieked.

'That's the last straw!' Mom shouted. 'I've had enough! I'm pulling over on the side of the road until you three are ready to settle down.'

Mom followed through on her threat, veering jauntily across the white line onto the bumpy verge and coming rather suddenly to a standstill.

The very first thing Mom did upon stopping was take off her seat belt entirely. Mom not only hated but also resented her seat belt; she hated the sense of constriction and how the shoulder strap dug into her neck, and she resented that she had to wear a seat belt at all, because she felt it should be her choice – not the government's – whether she lived or died in a crash. Mom breathed out as she released herself from the seat belt's unwanted embrace.

'The longer we stay here, the longer it'll take to get to Pennsylvania,'

Mom announced.

'He started it,' I said, pointing at Andy. 'He won't stay on his side, and he keeps tickling me.'

Alice accused me from the front. 'Beth Anne is tickling me!'

'I'm only tickling her because Andy is tickling me. So it's all Andy's fault.'

Mom had dug a cigarette out of her leather handbag while listening to our litany of complaints. 'It doesn't matter whose fault it is, and I really don't care who started it,' she said, taking a deep drag on her Marlboro. 'What matters is that now it has to stop. We've barely even left home – we've still got hours on the road – and at this rate, we're going to have to give up and turn right around.'

'No!' I shouted. 'I want to go to Chocolate World!'

'Well, if you want to go to Chocolate World, and if you want to see Nanny and Poppy, you're going to have to behave a little better.'

I had mixed feelings at best about seeing Nanny and Poppy, but no way was I going to miss out on Chocolate World, not now that Mom had told me about the bags of Special Dark miniatures.

'We'll be good now,' I said petulantly.

Mom knew she had won the battle, but she drew out the pit stop, whether to finish her cigarette, to make her point clear, or both. 'Are you really ready to be good?'

'Yes,' I said, in my most responsible voice. 'We're ready, aren't we, Andy and Alice? Because we want to go to Chocolate World.'

'OK,' Mom said, pulling open the car ashtray and grinding out the embers of her cigarette.

Not long after I promised to behave, we crossed the state line into New York.

'There's a billboard!' I called out, leaning over Andy to jab my finger against the window.

'Beth!' Andy yelled.

'Sorry, Andy, I just wanted to make sure you saw the billboard.'

'What does it say?' Alice said from the front.

'It's an ad for Coke,' Mom answered.

'Can I have a Coke?' Alice asked.

'We don't have any Coke in the car.'

'There's another one,' Andy said, pre-empting me by poking his own finger against his window. The smears of our greasy fingers stayed visible, clouding the view of the billboards slightly. 'It's for Chevrolet.'

'Aren't you glad we're not subjected to billboards in Vermont?' Mom reflected.

Her phrasing meant I should answer in the affirmative, but I found the billboards provided welcome diversion from the monotony of being a passenger. 'I like them,' I confessed. 'Don't you?'

'I don't want to be bombarded by advertising,' Mom countered.

I held my peace and carried on spotting the giant messages urging us to consume various goods and services.

By the time we reached the multi-lane interstates, all three of us children knew that the time for silliness had passed. Mom's grip on the steering wheel tightened, she checked her mirrors with much greater frequency and she took to complaining aloud about other drivers.

'Fine, just pull right in front of me, you bastard. Whatever happened to the three-second rule?'

I didn't comprehend what the other drivers were doing wrong, but I wished they would stop so Mom could become a carefree traveller again. It wasn't just the traffic that changed Mom's demeanour though, it was also her proximity to home, because while her feelings of homesickness for her hometown and her grandparents were straightforward, the same could not be said of her feelings for her parents.

As so often happened on our trips to Pennsylvania, dusk was falling by the time we approached my grandparents' house on Hickory Street. Andy and Alice had both dozed off miles ago, after our stop at the rest area for a fast-food dinner, another highlight of the journey. Only I kept vigil with Mom.

'Where will we sleep this time in Bethlehem?' I asked; our room assignments varied at the house on Hickory Street. 'Can I sleep with you?'

'You're too big to sleep with me now, Beth Anne. I can't have both you and Alice in a double bed with me – I wouldn't have any room.'

'Can I sleep in the basement with Andy?'

'We'll have to wait and see what Nanny and Poppy have planned.'

'I don't want to sleep by myself.'

There was something sinister about the house on Hickory Street. Nanny favoured cut-glass bowls and porcelain figurines of chubby children in white and blue, who appeared happy enough but whose faces were entirely devoid of colour. All of Nanny's precious collectables, of course, could shatter into tiny pieces in a child's hands, or for that matter in the hands of a clumsy or angry adult; one moment of inattention and the cut-glass sugar bowl might end up splintered on the floor. Mom could never relax at her parents' house –– and so neither could I.

Our car meandered through the leafy residential neighbourhood in the twilight.

'Should I wake Andy and Alice up now? So they're ready to get out of the car?'

'You can try. They seem pretty fast asleep.'

I nudged Andy with a flat palm. 'Andy! We're almost at Nanny and Poppy's house! Wake up,' I commanded.

'Hnnnhhh . . .' my brother mumbled, shifting only slightly.

'Alice! Alice, we're nearly there!' I snaked my arm around to the front seat and patted my little sister on the head; she didn't stir at all.

'They're really asleep,' I said to Mom, apologetically.

Mom nodded, then said with uncharacteristic tenderness, 'Let them be, Beth Anne. They'll wake up soon enough when we get there. Or they won't, and I'll just have to carry them in.'

My siblings were light enough and Mom was strong enough to do just that if required, but I was proud that I could stay awake when Andy and Alice couldn't. Mom had told me herself that she appreciated my company, especially as night drew in, so sleeping was simply not an option. Still, part of me yearned to be cradled in Mom's arms like the others sometimes were, to be borne, groggy and half-conscious, from the discomfort of the car to the cool sheets of a freshly made bed.

Mom's parents must have been keeping watch, peeking through the curtains whenever they heard the quiet rumble of a car travelling slowly past, because when our car finally pulled into the driveway, Poppy was on hand to greet us, even though the driveway was outside the basement rather than next to the house proper. The house at Hickory Street was a split-level ranch house, but most of the basement was unfinished, with concrete floors, save one large finished bedroom with two single beds.

I caught sight of the twinkling as Mom rolled the window all the way down to confer with Poppy about where exactly he would like her to park the car.

'Fireflies!' I burst out.

Poppy came over to the driver's side of the car, and laid his crossed arms on top of the hole in the door frame where Mom's window had just disappeared; Mom wouldn't be able to roll her window back up again without displacing the weight of her father's upper body. Poppy leaned his face into the car and spied my unblinking eyes, wholly focussed on the flashes of light visible in the murky darkness of the yard. Nanny had asked for a garden that felt private although it was not fully enclosed, and Poppy had happily obliged, planting dense, high box hedges around the perimeter, interspersed with trees that had grown from saplings when the house was built many years ago into lofty providers of shade in the daytime and darkness at night.

'Well, hello, little lady!' Poppy said. The pitch of Poppy's voice, much higher than I would have expected from a man of his age and size, took me by surprise as it did every time; his voice had an ever-present strained quality, as if it were continually hovering just shy of shouting. I stared at the lump above my grandfather's right eye, which had been present for as long as I had known him, and wondered what it felt like when his glasses – gold-rimmed like Marvin's, but aviator-style rather than round – rubbed against the protrusion.

'Hi,' I said.

'How come you're awake when your brother and sister are asleep?' Poppy asked. 'Have you been causing trouble?'

I didn't know how to answer my grandfather's questions. I was awake because it was my job as the eldest; I had been helping Mom, by keeping her company, rather than causing trouble. Neither of these would be the right answer to give. It shouldn't be my job to stay awake, and I knew it; I should have been asleep this late at night, and we all knew it.

'I'm looking at the fireflies,' I said.

Andy started to stir more convincingly. 'Fireflies? Are we there?'

I was thankful for my brother. 'There's tons of them, Andy! Can you see them? Mom, can you let us out so we can catch some?'

'Oh, sorry,' Poppy said gruffly, 'here I am, blocking your exit. Shall I get a Mason jar and the two of you can fill it with fireflies?'

'Yeah!' Andy and I shouted in unison. Alice shifted her weight but slept on.

'Thanks, Dad, but not tonight," Mom answered her father. 'I want the kids to get a good night's sleep. How about you hunt for fireflies tomorrow night, kids? I'm sure there will still be plenty to catch.'

'Aww, why not tonight?' Andy complained.

'It's time for bed now. We're getting up bright and early to go to Chocolate World – I don't want you whining because you're tired while we're there.'

That did the trick. 'Just let us look at them for a few minutes,' I begged.

'Alright,' Mom agreed.

Mom stepped out of the car and stood still, entranced despite herself. 'You could practically read a book by that light, there are so many of them.'

I could still squirm through the tiny space between the edge of the driver's side door and the upright driver's seat if I absolutely had to, but it was not my preferred mode of exit. I interrupted Mom's reverie.

'Can you please let me out, Mom?' I asked.

Mom snapped back to the present, wherein she was both a child – yes – but also a parent. 'Sorry, Beth Anne. I was so caught up with watching the fireflies myself that I forgot you were still in there.'

'That's OK,' I said. There was a loud thwack as Mom pushed the lever and the seat inclined forward. I crawled out, followed by Andy. Alice slept on peacefully in the front passenger seat, oblivious.

It was as though all the stars had fallen from the sky and were now exploding in my grandparents' garden like countless miniature supernovas, only instead of burning out, each firefly just carried on flashing, over and over.

'I've never seen so many,' I said, awestruck.

'We've had a wet winter – that's good for the little critters,' Poppy said cheerily. I bristled slightly at the thought that his loud voice might wake my sister. 'Did you know, kids, that the chemical that makes fireflies light up is called *luciferin*? Have you heard of Lucifer? It's another name for the Devil.'

'Mm-hmm,' I confirmed.

'They don't much look like the Devil's beetles though, do they? Although they do set the night on fire,' Poppy remarked.

I felt that Poppy had marred the beauty of the fireflies' display through the mere mention of God's sworn enemy, but I kept that to myself. I couldn't let Poppy have the final say though – I needed to reclaim the wondrous light show from him. I needed it sanctified.

'They look like stars,' I said.

'They do, Beth Anne,' my mom agreed. 'Like shooting stars. Maybe you should make a wish. Maybe you should make a hundred.'

'It doesn't count if it's not a real star,' Andy stated.

'Oh, Andrew,' Mom said playfully, 'it counts if you want it to.'

16

Understudy

B ack in East Montpelier, another sort of star shone that summer. Marvin's flair for the dramatic extended beyond the classroom and into the theatre, and both Marvin and his friend Art, Tovah's father, had won roles in the local amateur theatre's production of the Gilbert and Sullivan operetta *Iolanthe*. Not just any roles: Marvin had bagged the part of Strephon, and Art took on the character of the Lord Chancellor. I was deemed old enough to accompany Marvin to rehearsals occasionally, much to my delight. Art always brought Tovah along, and the two of us were overjoyed to be seeing each other regularly again. Tovah had an actual role – with a name and spoken lines – in the fairy chorus; I was assigned the part of Tovah's understudy. There had been no understudy for my previous star turn as a mouse in my primary school's first-grade production, so I was unfamiliar with the concept, but the director – whose idea it had no doubt been to assign roles to the two of us on the assumption that occupied children were manageable children – explained that to be a successful understudy, I needed to memorise all the same lines and songs as Tovah herself, but that I would only be called upon to perform on stage in the unlikely event that Tovah found herself ill on the big day. This was amenable to us both, and Tovah and I set about learning the fairies' songs with gusto. Not only did we master all of the fairies' chorus numbers, we also committed all of our fathers' featured songs to heart. My favourite of Strephon's songs was 'If We're Weak Enough to Tarry', a duet sung with Phyllis that affirms the pair's desire to wed, and soon. I hoped that Marvin the man was professional enough to keep his own wishes and his character's wishes separate, however, as I wanted to keep Marvin in our family, not watch him run off with the woman playing Phyllis. This appeared to me a grave danger, as 'Phyllis' was almost as beautiful as my mother – how could Marvin act so convincingly in love with Phyllis during rehearsal only to shed an emotion so seemingly genuine as soon as Strephon went offstage?

I asked Marvin about this as we bumped home in the VW bus one warm evening after rehearsal.

'Are you going to marry Phyllis in real life?'

Marvin burst out laughing, then patted me on the leg. The red resin Buddha, still affixed to the dashboard, retained his state of meditation.

'Debbie – sorry, 'Phyllis' – is married to 'Lord Mountararat' – whose real name is Jerry – and they have two kids, Beth Anne. Debbie would have no interest in marrying me even if I fancied marrying her. Ours is a purely professional relationship. Anyhow, I'm in love with your mother, and if I'm going to marry anyone 'in real life,' it would be her. Does that put your mind at ease?'

'Are you going to?'

'Am I going to what?'

'Are you going to marry my mother?'

Vermont roads are not like Pennsylvania roads. They demand the drivers' attention, especially the dirt roads, and particularly at night; possible hazards include deep potholes, fallen branches and unexpected deer crossing. So Marvin could afford only the quickest glance in my direction, but from that he gauged correctly that I was not being flippant. I was not yet in third grade, but I was the eldest of three, as Marvin would see it, or of five, as I saw it by including Melinda and Brian. I felt I had the right to know.

'Maybe,' Marvin answered cagily. 'Do you think I should?'

This was a no-brainer. Even at my tender age, I was worldly-wise enough to consider things Marvin and my mom had done best done by married couples, but more importantly, I liked Marvin: I liked his energy, his creativity, his sense of fun and his refusal to ever talk down to the three of us.

'Yes,' I replied without hesitation. 'Yes, I think you should.'

At the next rehearsal I was permitted to attend, we practised a simple dance to accompany the fairies' first song, 'Tripping Hither, Tripping Thither.' We wove in and out across the floorboards, singing all the while, as the director admonished us to turn our heads whenever possible in the direction of the future audience. This combination of dancing and singing begged for a level of concentration that merely singing did not. To succeed, I needed to cast aside preoccupied, precocious Beth Anne Evans and embody my fairy character fully, flitting around the imaginary stage as though at any moment my similarly imaginary wings might lift me straight off the ground. I was hooked. I was no stranger to impersonation – Tovah and I considered ourselves expert Greek goddesses – but freewheeling Athenas are child's play, while members of the fairy chorus in an actual production of *Iolanthe* are legitimate drama.

During our ride home that evening, I had more questions for Marvin.

'Why can't I be in the real fairy chorus? Why do I have to be Tovah's understudy?'

Marvin smiled broadly. His teeth still caught me off guard when he smiled like that; they looked sharp and powerful, more like those of a dog than a man, because of his particularly large and pointy canines.

'Bitten by the acting bug, are you?'

A frisson passed through me. 'Yes,' I admitted.

'I don't blame you,' Marvin said, still grinning. 'I was bitten a long time ago. There's a very practical reason you can't be in the fairy chorus, Beth Anne. It has nothing to do with your talent – I think you're a marvellous fairy – and everything to do with the fact that your father is planning to take you on vacation over Labor Day. You won't even be in Vermont the weekend of the performance.'

This was the first I'd heard about a possible trip out-of-state. 'I won't be in Vermont? Where will I be?'

'Massachusetts. Your dad and his girlfriend are taking her kids and you three to Cape Cod. You'll love it – you'll get to swim in the ocean. Bad timing though, for a budding Thespian,' Marvin ribbed.

Swimming in the ocean sounded appealing, but I wasn't sure it offset missing my chance at *Iolanthe*.

I demonstrated my developing skill for forward-thinking. 'Will there be another play next year?'

I noted Marvin's approval of my burgeoning autonomy. 'Yes,' Marvin said.

'Can I be in that play?'

'You can certainly audition,' Marvin answered. 'I can't promise you there will be a role for a – what – eight-year-old? You'll be eight in August, won't you?'

I puffed up with pride. Eight seemed ever so grown-up. 'August sixteenth,' I confirmed.

'That's not too far away,' Marvin said. 'What do you want for your birthday?'

'I don't know,' I said, hedging. I had already worked out that 'what do you want for your birthday?' was a trick question: if I asked for something I could be disappointed, so it was better to ask for nothing.

'I'm sure we'll figure something out,' Marvin said.

We hadn't seen Dad as much since we moved in with Marvin. Before that, we had carried on visiting Shelburne every two or three weeks. Our weekends with Dad often included an outing to Dad's newly remodelled home-decorating store; I had spent enough time in the new shop to be intimately acquainted with the decor. There was a substantial gated play area in the shop, with toys Dad had helped select, where children could amuse themselves while their parents consulted with the salespeople about which wallpaper would best match which carpet, or which paint would best withstand their young charges' exploring hands. The carpet in the play area itself was thick, dense and multicoloured: a geometric pattern of rich reds and deep blues. It was an entirely anomalous floor covering for a children's play area, which is what made it so perfectly suited to its purpose. Alice was consistently limited to the play area, while Andy and I were free to come and go from the store proper to the gated enclosure as we wished. The prerequisite for unrestricted movement was the ability to open the child gate; Andy should not technically have been old enough to operate the safety latch independently, but being abnormally skilled with mechanics, he had mastered it easily.

One Sunday after we had moved in with Marvin, Dad came on his own, without Annie and her kids, to take the three of us hiking. It was a fine Vermont morning in early summer. The strength of the sun warmed our skin, but there was a light cooling breeze and the humidity hadn't yet shifted into high gear, so each intake of air refreshed us, rather than overheating us as it would in high summer. I was wearing one of my most prized dresses, which doubled as a pinafore with a long-sleeved top underneath in colder weather. The dress was sewn of black and white calico, but with tiny squares instead of the more typical flowers, a U-neck, gathers at the waistline and white zigzag ribbon trim. It was summer enough to wear the dress with nothing underneath and I had paired my dress with clunky sneakers and tube socks. Mom asked, before we left, if I might want to add another pair of socks as my trainers were still slightly too big – they had been acquired with 'room to grow' – but I declined, impatient as I was to be off.

Dad, cognizant of the limitations of Alice's little legs, had done his research. He had managed to find a trail that, although long enough to tire me, was achievable by my sister, afforded fantastic views along the way and offered the satisfaction of bagging a summit.

Dad forgot to be mournful that summer day. His unnamed loss was still there under the surface, but there was no mistaking his joy at being out on the path in the beautiful green mountains.

'Did you hear that? That was a swallow!' Dad said with excitement.

'I heard it but I didn't see it,' I said from ahead.

'That happens with a lot of birds,' Dad informed me.

'My legs hurt,' Alice moaned.

'This hike is making your legs stronger with every step!' Dad encouraged Alice. 'You're doing great!'

Alice smiled her winsome smile. She was already darker than the rest of us; the sunshine turned her skin from olive to chocolate by her birthday in June every year. She extended her slender brown hand upwards for Dad to take, and he obliged. Dad was gentler with Alice, who craved closeness, than with Andy and me, who didn't. Alice, at four, still sought out arms to lift her and laps to rest in whenever and from whomever she could.

Andy, who was furthest in front, was poking a stick into a fallen log.

'What have you got there?' Dad called out to him.

'Ants,' Andy said. He carried on with his investigations until first I, then Dad and Alice, caught up to him.

'Wow, there sure are a lot of them,' Dad said, examining the colony Andy was disrupting. 'Ants are actually pretty smart, did you know that? Each ant has a particular job to do in a colony the size of this one. They stay very busy.'

Andy acknowledged this with a simple 'Huh'.

'I had an ant farm for a while when I was a kid,' Dad told us. 'It was fascinating, watching them dig their tunnels and carry their food from place to place.'

'What happened to it?' Andy asked. 'Did it break?'

'No,' Dad answered. 'After a while the ants started to die. Eventually the time came to try to release the surviving ants back into the wild, so to speak.'

'I wouldn't want an ant farm in my room,' I said. 'What if they broke free? I'd rather have kittens than ants in my bed.'

'It wasn't like they were running around loose. They were in their formicarium.'

'Their what?' Andy asked.

'Their formicarium. Like an aquarium, but with sand. It was an Uncle Milton's – they revolutionised the ant farm scene. All the cool kids wanted an Uncle Milton's ant farm,' Dad said, and I heard the sarcasm but I couldn't interpret it. Did Dad mean that he wasn't cool, that ant farms weren't cool, or both? Or neither? It reminded me of the time Dad had called on the phone and pretended to be someone he was not.

'Hello?' I said, just as I was meant to, when I picked up the phone.

'Hello,' Dad said gruffly. I suspected it was Dad, but the uncharacteristically scratchy voice threw me, and I couldn't be sure. 'I'm a representative for Campbell's Soup. I'm looking for Beth Anne Evans. Is this, by any chance, Beth Anne Evans herself?'

If I had been more world-weary, I may have seen through Dad's ruse immediately, but I was a naive child stunned that someone from Campbell's Soup not only knew my name but wished to speak to me.

'I'm Beth – Beth Anne Evans,' I stuttered.

'Fantastic! I've got excellent news for you! You've won a year's supply of Campbell's Tomato Soup!'

'I – I have? Really?' I adored Campbell's Tomato Soup. It was my most favourite canned soup of all time, far outstripping chicken noodle. Dreams of eating tomato soup not just for lunch but dinner as well flooded my imagination. I couldn't wait to tell Mom – I pictured in my mind's eye how pleased she would be.

I shifted to practicalities. 'When will it get here?' I asked.

'I'll bring some when I come pick you up next time. Beth, did you really think it was Campbell's Soup calling? It's me – it's your father,' Dad clarified, adopting his normal tone of voice.

I was crestfallen. 'So I won't be getting any Campbell's Soup?'

'I can bring you a couple of cans when I come – would you like that?'

'Yes,' I said, as cheerfully as I could manage.

Dad paused. 'Did I really trick you? Couldn't you tell it was me?'

The gears in my mind whirred as I attempted to formulate the correct answer. Would it be better to say I had thought it was Dad all along because he hoped I would be so well acquainted with his voice that I would never mistake it for another, or would it be more flattering to him to have fooled me into believing in his assumed identity?

I settled on combining the two. 'I thought it was you at first,' I confessed, 'but then you sounded so serious – and plus, I love Campbell's Tomato Soup – so then I started to think it wasn't really you.'

'But it was!'

I took Dad's chuckle as a sign that my answer had sufficed. Dad changed the subject. 'How's school?'

'OK,' I said. 'When are you coming?'

'That's what I called for, to talk to your mom about that,' Dad said.

'Is she there?'

'No,' I said, 'she went out shopping.'

'I'll try back a little later then,' Dad said. 'Can you let her know I called?'

'I'll tell her,' I promised.

'Beth Anne?' Dad said now, next to the clear and present ant colony on the mountainside. 'Did you hear me?'

Caught out, I flushed, but the rosiness my cheeks had already incurred from exertion disguised my embarrassment. 'No . . . Sorry, Dad. What did you say?'

'You were miles away, weren't you?' Dad said, amused. 'I said there's a pine tree over here that would be a perfect backdrop for a picture. Can you all come over and pose?'

We did as Dad asked. I leaned one hand against the tree trunk and placed the other hand on my hip, all seven-year-old swagger. Andy stood slightly in front of me, but because he was still much shorter, he blocked neither my view of Dad, nor the camera's view of me. Alice knelt down in front of us both.

'Say "cheese",' Dad called out.

Only Andy obliged. 'Cheese,' Andy said for us all, while I smiled broadly without showing my teeth. Alice just looked at Dad with a quizzical expression.

'And again.'

'Cheese,' Andy said alone, again.

Dad was satisfied. 'That's going to be a great shot. It's such a beautiful day – and now we'll have something to remember it by.'

That was when his lip twitched. Something about the idea of the photograph made Dad melancholy. Was it that Alice and I hadn't said 'cheese' properly?

'Do you want to take another one?' I asked. 'I promise to say "cheese" this time.'

Dad laughed and the shadow in his eyes vanished. 'You don't really have to say "cheese", Beth Anne. That's just something photographers say to get people to smile.'

* * *

Marvin didn't ask us to pose for photographs; he had other ideas.

'This feels like the first day of summer,' Marvin announced one hot July morning.

'The first day of summer is in June, after the summer solstice,' Mom said languorously.

'No, it's not,' Marvin said. 'The summer solstice marks midsummer. The vernal equinox is the official start of summer. All my third-graders know that.'

'Shame I wasn't in your third-grade class. I would have had the biggest crush on you and I would have known all about the seasons.'

'You vixen.'

'You fox. Anyhow, you were making some grand announcement about the first day of summer, which it's not, but it sure is hot enough,' Mom said, wiping tiny beads of sweat from her brow with the back of her hand.

'I most certainly was. It's my tradition, here in my hilltop castle in East Montpelier, to celebrate the coming of summer by streaking around the house. Children, as serfs of my manor, I invite you to join me in this excellent celebration of the encroaching harvest. Take off your clothes,' Marvin directed us.

Alice, Andy and I all gaped as Marvin cast off first his shirt, then his shorts, and then finally – to my horror – his underwear.

'Come on,' Marvin taunted, standing stark naked by the screen door. 'Last one round the house is a rotten egg!'

I glanced at Mom. 'Go ahead,' Mom said. 'Streak round the house if you want to. I'm not running anywhere in this weather.'

I tore off my T-shirt and my own shorts, then hesitated, leaving my once-white but now grey-from-repeated-washing undies on.

'Just take them off,' Marvin said encouragingly as he held the screen door open. 'It's very freeing. It'll make you faster too – no clothes to get in your way.'

I delayed another second, then gave in, pulling my undies off and kicking them onto the sofa. Alice and Andy were in various stages of undress, and I seized my chance to win the streaking race, dashing under Marvin's extended arm carefully so as to avoid any accidental contact with his body, and out of the front door.

The summer heat hit all of me, even the bits never normally exposed to the elements, as I began to run once, twice and three times around the house, laughing riotously as I easily lapped Andy, Alice and even Marvin, who must have been running more slowly than usual to allow Alice to beat him. The feel of the air on all parts of my body was both delicious and salacious. I knew that streaking around the house with Marvin, and at Marvin's request, was wrong, just as Eve must have known that eating the forbidden fruit at the serpent's suggestion was off limits, but I did it anyway, just as my ancestral forbear had taken that bite. We both paid for our misplaced trust later.

I ran into trouble in the bathroom of the house in East Montpelier. The previous winter, when my throat, as was its wont, became a hotbed of infection, I was introduced to Aspergum when Mom, eager to avoid the mortar and pestle, forked out the extra cash for the branded pain-relief gum. The orange flavour was mesmerising – it started zesty, then the tang faded as the chalky taste of the aspirin came to the fore. Aspergum was the best part of having a sore throat, although I was never a suave gum chewer, prone instead to determined chomping.

The Aspergum was kept on a high shelf in the bathroom cabinet.

Because the house was actually Marvin's and he had furnished it as a single, childless man, there was a wicker laundry hamper in the bathroom, the sort a parent would have relocated to prevent accidents in the room every parent recognises as the most dangerous room in the house. The hamper was a three-foot-tall woven cube, with bits of wicker sticking out here and there, and closed with a strap in dark brown leather with a brass buckle. The hamper was just waiting for me to scramble on top of it in a bid to access the package of Aspergum. Once the hamper was dragged into place in front of the cabinet, I didn't even need to stand on my tiptoes; I could easily stretch out my hand and claim the Aspergum for myself. Back on the floor, I moved the hamper to in front of the door – an unnecessary precaution, considering I had already put the silver hook through the eye of the simple bathroom lock – and sat with my back against the wicker weave, aware of the odd piece of bamboo poking into my skin. I opened the package of Aspergum and took two pieces to start with. I chewed until the orange flavour disappeared. Two pieces wasn't enough to satisfy me so I popped two additional pieces out of their protective foil. The clump of gum grew larger, but after a few minutes, the new gum was indistinguishable from the old. I added two more, then two again, until I had a wad of gum nearly the size of a golf ball in my mouth and it became unwieldy to chew. When my jaw began to ache, the fun was over. What I hadn't considered, however, was how to dispose of the gum without drawing attention to myself. I would have to hide the evidence somehow. I had chewed gum often enough to realise that I couldn't just put the clump in my pocket to dispose of at my convenience without covering it first, so I tore off a generous amount of toilet paper, spat the gum out of my mouth, wrapped it carefully, and only then plunged it deep into my pocket.

Guilt among children is often short-lived. It took only a moment for me to get sidetracked after leaving the bathroom, and later, having completely forgotten about the wad of gum, I neglected to empty my pockets before tossing my shorts into the same hamper that had provided me with the means of committing my misdemeanour.

Two days later, I was summoned by my full name.

'Beth Anne Evans,' Mom shouted, in the voice that meant business.

I put my book down immediately and hastened to where Mom stood, fuming, beside the washing machine, holding a hard, white, circular object.

'What is this?' Mom said, in her most reprimanding tone.

I wracked my brain.

'Let me refresh your memory,' Mom said angrily. 'It was in your shorts pocket.'

The light dawned. I hung my head. 'Gum,' I said softly.

'Gum,' Mom echoed, like a lawyer cross-examining her witness. 'And what *kind* of gum exactly?'

My mother was no fool. I could tell her it was Wrigley's, but it seemed to me that hers had been a rhetorical question and she knew as well as I did what kind of gum it was.

'Aspergum,' I nearly whispered.

'What? I didn't quite hear you.'

I looked straight into my mother's brown eyes, now flashing yellow with fury.

'Aspergum,' I owned up.

'Aspergum,' Mom repeated. 'Aspergum. Beth Anne, what were you thinking? Aspergum is not candy, it's medicine, and you can make yourself sick if you take too much medicine. You can even die, if you take too much medicine and nobody notices. Did you know that? You've been very lucky. I'm surprised you didn't develop a tummy ache at the very least from that much aspirin. Why do you think we keep the Aspergum on the top shelf of the medicine cabinet? So that you kids will leave it alone unless you really need it. You are not to take Aspergum ever again without my permission.'

Mom paused to let that order sink in. I had let my eyes fall again to the floor, and I could feel the tears coming when Mom stepped towards me, put two fingers under my chin, and gently lifted my head until my eyes again met hers. Her anger had evaporated, but my shame remained.

'Don't ever take medicine without asking me first, Beth Anne,' Mom said. 'And gum belongs in the trash, not in your pocket,' she added, with a faint air of amusement.

17

Somersaults

I was not the only one to land myself in trouble with the wicker hamper. I don't know why Alice had decided that she too wanted to access the medicine cabinet – maybe she was also drawn by the lure of the Aspergum – but the repercussions of her efforts were far more dramatic than those of mine. Alice managed to drag the hamper into position, climb on top and stand, but when she went to open the cabinet, she was unprepared for the alteration to her centre of gravity; Alice fell, hitting her chin on the edge of the white porcelain sink at a moment when her tongue, unfortunately, was between her teeth. A scream, even more blood-curdling than Alice's typical screams of discontent, emanated from the bathroom. Mom charged in. Alice, thankfully, had forgotten to fasten the hook and eye lock, but even if she had remembered, it wouldn't have prevented Mom from gaining entry. Mom opened the door with enough force to have torn the screw for the eye sheer out of the door.

'Oh shit!' Mom exclaimed, as Alice continued to shriek. 'Beth Anne, get Marvin up here immediately. You're OK, Alice. I'm just going to hold this towel here – just stay calm. Marvin! Where the fuck is he?'

I dashed through the house shouting for Marvin at the top of my lungs. Marvin swooped in through the front screen door, leaving it to close abruptly in Shiva's face. Shiva, surprised at her unexpected exile, looked at me with her big eyes. I allocated her the ten seconds it took to let her in, then sprang after Marvin, who had already reached Mom and Alice.

'Liza – what's going on?'

'Alice has nearly bitten straight through her tongue. She's in shock and needs stitches. We've got to get her to the emergency room as soon as we possibly can. You're going to have to drive, so I can hold her on my lap.'

I saw now that Alice's chin and neck were marred by bright red blood. 'Oh my God – is Alice going to be OK?'

No one answered me. 'Should we take your car?' Marvin asked.

'We can't – I'm running on empty.'

'Fine, I'll go get the VW ready. Good thing they've repaired some of the potholes – should be fine for ambulance speed.'

Panic struck me. Marvin was going to drive quickly in the same VW bus that had flipped on the way home from fishing.

'No!' I yelled, as Marvin exited the premises and Mom, with Alice in her arms, rushed after him. 'No! No!'

'Beth, shut up!' Mom ordered. 'Alice is going to be fine, we just have to get her to the hospital.'

With that Mom clambered through the side door of the bus. Marvin closed it swiftly after her and jumped into the driver's seat.

'No!' I yelled again. 'Don't take her in the VW! Don't take her in the bus! She needs an ambulance!'

Marvin, who had the objectivity of a non-biological parent, rolled down the window and said in a level but firm voice, 'Beth Anne, be quiet and get out of the way. Your sister needs to get to the hospital, and you're not helping her or your mother. Go back inside and look after Andy until we get back.'

Unbidden and unwelcome tears streamed down my cheeks as the motor revved and Marvin tore away. I shouted again and began to race after Marvin, who outpaced me within seconds. 'Not in the bus! No, no – Alice!'

I kept running. I ran down the dirt driveway and out onto the main road. I ran until the bus disappeared from view. Then and only then did my legs buckle from the exertion, leading me to fall to my knees on the road, banging my hands in frustration on the dirt, which was the colour of strong tea with milk. I grabbed fistfuls of the pebbles that lay on top and flung them into the ditch at the side, as if both punishing the ditch for previous crimes and warning it against future infractions.

When the tears abated and my legs felt capable of supporting me, I remembered that Andy was now alone with only Shiva to look after him. Slowly I got to my feet and turned towards home.

Alice reappeared safely much later that evening. The stitches in her tongue, when I saw them the following day, looked like very poor embroidery with strong, thin black thread.

'Why are they so jagged?' I asked Mom. 'You can sew better than that.'

Mom laughed. 'Sewing tongues isn't like sewing fabric, Beth Anne, and anyway, I wasn't the one holding the needle. What's important is that they line the tongue up properly, not that they win prizes for even stitches.'

I was relieved when the VW bus was not the vehicle selected for our next trip to Pennsylvania. We had only recently been to see Nanny and Poppy, but Mom said it was important for us to visit again.

'The time has come for Marvin to meet my parents,' Mom said, with her jaw ever-so-slightly clenched.

'Do you think Nanny and Poppy will like Marvin?' I asked. I thought about the artificially happy children in pale porcelain at

Nanny and Poppy's, and then the jolly wine-red resin Buddha on Marvin's dashboard – would the owners of such fundamentally different figurines be able to find common ground?

'Probably not, but that's not the point,' Mom said.

When I met new people, I wanted to know as soon as I could whether or not the new person might be my friend; the point always was to see if I liked them and if they liked me. Adults, though, sometimes didn't make sense.

'Is the point to go to Chocolate World?' I asked.

Mom laughed. 'No, Beth Anne. We won't be going to Chocolate World this time.'

'Are we going back to Dorney Park instead?'

'No, not there either. I want to take Marvin to some of the places I love best in Pennsylvania.'

'Are we finally going to Lake Wallenpaupack?'

Lake Wallenpaupack was a lake of mythical proportions, an enormous freshwater lake brought into existence in 1926 by the Pennsylvania Power and Light company to provide both hydroelectric energy and flood control. Mom had learned to swim in the lake's clear, cool water, which she could access at will from the small wooden cabin her grandparents owned on the shoreline where both Mom and her sister Joanne had spent most of their childhood summers. Mom spoke of the lake the way Tovah's mom spoke of Switzerland – a place so beautiful it beggared belief, so idyllic that strife was unheard of, so distant and unattainable that it might as well be heaven.

The mere mention of the fabled lake sent Mom into such a reverie that she neglected to answer my question, so I tried a new tack, pushing my advantage. 'Maybe because Marvin is coming we should actually go to Lake Wallenpaupack?' I suggested. 'As a special treat?'

In previous conversations about Lake Wallenpaupack, Mom had sometimes marked the end of the line of inquiry by saying wistfully,

'Someday I should take you three there. We couldn't go to the same cabin – my parents didn't want to take it over when Grandma and Grandpa Weller grew too old to manage the upkeep, and I was in no position to buy it, so it's not in the family any more – but I'm sure we could find somewhere cheap and cheerful to stay, and you'd love the lake. It's perfect for swimming even if you're just learning because the slope into the deep water is so gradual, and there's nothing to be afraid of – no current like in the river, no crabs like in the ocean.'

I wanted very much to go to Lake Wallenpaupack. I had learned, through trial and error, that rather than mentioning that desire, I was meant to keep silent, but the occasion of Marvin's Pennsylvania premiere had made it seem reasonable to again propose the lake as a destination.

'No, Beth Anne, not this time. Someday I'll take you there,' Mom said, her eyes hooded and far away.

I considered what other special place Mom could possibly be thinking of to share with Marvin. Maybe it was the Moravian bookshop, the well-lit but oddly laid-out purveyor of not only books by the thousands, but also food and decor particular to the Pennsylvania Dutch traditions: jarred sauerkraut and pickled beets, cake tins emblazoned with the distelfink, and candles of the exact size necessary to power the spinning Christmas angel chimes.

The grown-ups had an arrangement whereby Marvin drove the VW bus and Mom drove the Saab, but this trip was lengthy enough to warrant Marvin asking Mom if she wanted him to drive the first leg.

'I should be fine – I've driven this route plenty of times on my own. It'll just be nice to have adult company,' Mom answered.

The Saab was noticeably heavier with the addition of a second parent. Each pothole in the dirt road felt like a crater; an awful scraping sound accompanied one particularly jolting dip.

'What was that?' I demanded from the back seat.

'That was the car bottoming out,' Marvin said. 'Your mom may have to drive a little more slowly,' he added laconically.

'There's a lot of extra weight in the car,' Mom shot back.

'Is the car broken?' I asked.

'The car is fine, Beth Anne,' Mom said. 'There's nothing to worry about.'

Now it was Marvin's turn to riposte, which he did wordlessly by arching his eyebrows, first at the noise the car had acquired following the trench-like pothole, and then at Mom.

I reimmersed myself in the Shire. Marvin had correctly assumed – no doubt based on his large sample size as a third-grade teacher – that a child who loved dragons would also love Middle Earth. By now, I was on my second reading of Tolkien's classic *The Hobbit*. We had left the dirt road and I had reached Rivendell when the car's coughing became unignorable and a noise like fingers on a chalkboard ensued.

'Damn,' Mom muttered. 'I think the muffler came off.'

'I think you're right,' Marvin concurred. 'Pull over.'

'What do you think I'm doing?'

'Do you have any wire in the car?'

'I've got some spare wire clothes hangers, but they're buried under the suitcases at the moment.'

'Great. I should be able to rig the muffler with them so it'll get us to Bethlehem.'

'Kids, why don't you get out of the car for a minute and stretch your legs,' Mom said after pulling up the emergency brake. 'We're going to be here for a while.'

We were still in Vermont, so rather than concrete, there was luscious green grass on the gentle slope at the side of the road, perfect for me to practise my somersaults. Alice was annoyed.

'It's my turn! I want to do one!'

'OK, do one,' I said, with the cruelty of a big sister fully aware of the less-developed skills of a little sister.

Alice tucked her head down as she had seen me do many a time, crouched and gave it her best go, but still her body refused to cooperate and she tilted to the right, legs flopping out diagonally, rather than completing the full turn.

If ours had been the sort of carefree, light-hearted family of television commercials, both Alice and I would have erupted in fits of giggles. Instead, tears sprang out of Alice's eyes and her mouth twisted into a frown. 'I still can't do it! Why can't I?'

In truth, somersaults may have been more challenging for Alice because of her perpetual ear problems – anything that requires balance is harder when ears aren't working properly. That awareness, however, would take decades to acquire, and in the meantime I pegged Alice as uncommonly clumsy and added that to the list of my little sister's vulnerabilities. As with all the chinks in my siblings' armour, sometimes I did what I could to protect the weak spot, and sometimes I aimed with cool precision on the same fissure. On that particular day, the excitement about our journey had not yet worn off, and I knelt down next to Alice.

'Do it again,' I told Alice. 'I'll try and help you.'

Alice wiped her tears across her face with the back of her delicate hand. 'OK,' she agreed. My little sister resumed her ready position.

'You've got to keep your head tucked way down,' I said. 'Try to roll the base of your neck on the ground.'

'OK,' Alice said again, gravely.

'Go!' I ordered.

As Alice flipped, I grabbed her legs and tried to pull them out straight, in my best approximation of how Mom had taught me to do the forward roll years ago.

'Ow!' Alice yelled, and her grimace of frustration was overlaid by a mask of pain. 'Mom! Beth Anne hurt me!'

'I was only trying to help her do a somersault!' I protested.

'Kids, cut it out. Marvin can't concentrate when you're making such a racket.'

This prompted both Alice and I to turn our attention to Marvin, whose body, back flat on the ground, could be seen jutting out at a jaunty angle from the rear bumper, but whose head had disappeared under the Saab. Marvin looked so silly that I forgot I had been tattled on and started to laugh. Alice, similarly, forgot she was both humiliated and wronged. She trotted over to Marvin and plopped down beside him, stretching herself out at a complementary angle. I hesitated, waiting to see if Marvin would tolerate her presence. When he carried on working, unperturbed, I took my sister's lead and lay down on Marvin's other side, peering towards the car's undercarriage where Marvin's hands were busily doing what they could to make the Saab fit for travel. Marvin still said nothing, but the addition of an extra child interfering with Marvin's work pushed Mom's needle into the red.

'Beth Anne and Alice, get up right now and leave Marvin alone. Can't you see he's trying to work?'

I sprang up like a jack-in-the-box but Alice, who took longer to register, remained prone.

'Alice!' Mom shouted. 'Get out of Marvin's way!'

Marvin's muffled voice wafted out from beneath the car as he freed a hand to pat Alice reassuringly. 'It's fine, Liza. I'm nearly finished anyway. Give me two more minutes and we'll be back on the road.'

I wanted to lie back down next to Marvin and carry on playing mechanic, but my wish to please my mother – or at least to not displease her – held me at bay. Instead I resumed my roadside somersaults. Andy, oblivious to both the gymnastics and the car repair, carried on searching for insects in the high grass further from the road.

Marvin was true to his word, and less than five minutes later the Saab was back on the highway, still noisy, but without the horrible scraping of the exhaust pipe dragging along the road's surface.

The rest of the trip passed uneventfully. We stopped at the rest area in Plattekill for dinner at a restaurant of questionable quality but indisputable convenience. Mom favoured Plattekill because of its proximity to Newburgh, where we had lived briefly with Dad when Andy was born. Each time we passed Newburgh on our way to Pennsylvania Mom mentioned Andy's provenance. Each time, the three of us were nonplussed. Only many years later, when Mom drove me to upstate New York to look at colleges, did Mom make a detour into Newburgh itself to show me the house Andy had come home to. It was a small white clapboard three-bedroom starter home with black shutters, set back only the length of a two-car driveway from the main road, although it seemed more secluded than the distance prescribed because it was built on a steep hill. Passersby would not have easily been able to peer in, but those in the house could easily observe passersby. Would it have mattered if there had been no slope? Would the cracks forming in my parents' marriage have mended themselves under even fleeting scrutiny? If the house itself had been capable of influence, had it missed an opportunity? The house seemed so innocent, resting there among the green grass with a stranger's car in the drive, but I could not absolve it of possible complicity.

When the blood sugar from the dinner stop wore off, Andy and Alice grew drowsy and Alice fell asleep leaning into my shoulder. While I would have tolerated this in the winter, in the present summer heat, the stickiness of the layer of sweat on my arm was unwelcome. I pushed my sleeping sister over towards Andy, who was leaning against the door on his side.

'Alice, get off,' Andrew groaned, pushing Alice's body back towards me harshly enough to wake her.

'I want to lie down,' Alice complained.

Andy acquiesced. He descended into the wheel well and stretched out; he was small enough, and fond enough of close spaces, to consider this arrangement comfortable. The floor in the back, unusually for cars of that time, was perfectly flat from one side of the car to the other. Alice spread out across the newly freed space Andy had vacated. Both my siblings dozed off, but I, as usual, did not.

An hour or so later, after again wending our way through the wide suburban streets of my grandparents' city, we pulled into the driveway at Hickory Street. As always, Poppy appeared within seconds to greet us. This time, however, he was swiftly followed by Nanny, whose curiosity about Mom's new companion was immediately apparent.

'You must be Marvin,' Nanny said, offering him her smooth, limp hand, which, unlike that of my mother, never washed dishes without gloves and never pulled carrots from the earth either with or without gloves.

'I am indeed,' Marvin said, holding Nanny's hand up to his mouth to kiss it. Nanny was so taken aback by the gesture that she laughed her little girl laugh. My mother cringed.

'Well, we're so pleased to meet you, Marvin,' Nanny said, recovering her usual ladylike aloofness.

'The pleasure is indeed mine,' Marvin said gallantly, with a slight bow.

'What fine manners,' Nanny said approvingly, and I could almost see the smoke coming out of my mother's ears.

'Marvin, we need to get the kids to bed,' Mom said now.

'Nice to meet you, Soldier,' Poppy said now, extending his right hand to Marvin. When Marvin took it, Poppy flung his left arm across Marvin's back and clapped Marvin's shoulder repeatedly. 'Hope you had an easy journey? Liza told me she's looking forward to showing you some of the local beauty spots. But of course, you've already found Bethlehem's most beautiful,' Poppy said, looking appraisingly at Mom.

Now it was Nanny's turn for disapproval, expressed by a narrowing of her eyes. 'Jim,' Nanny chided.

'After Dolly, of course,' Poppy hastened to add.

'Like mother, like daughter,' Marvin said, and he and Poppy exchanged the sort of glance I would swap with someone in my class who had also got full marks on her spelling words when no one else besides us had.

Mom returned from carrying Alice in to the waiting bed. 'Andrew, wake up,' Mom said, leaning awkwardly into the back of the car to shake my brother. When Andy didn't respond, a note of urgency crept into my mother's voice.

'Andrew,' Mom said. Then my mother did something I had never seen her do before and never saw her do again. She slapped my brother, where he lay scrunched into the footwell, square across the cheek. 'Andrew!'

My brother's glazed eyes opened slowly. 'Mmm . . .' Andy grumbled.

'Andrew, it's time to go inside. Can you get up?' Mom said, in the nursing-school voice she used with me when my fever was too high.

I didn't understand why Mom was suddenly panicked, and I was dumbstruck that she had woken my brother so violently. I was busily running through my brother's possible crimes when Mom took me by surprise again; she reached all the way in to the floor of the back seat – a position that no adult could adopt without considerable discomfort – scooped my brother up off the floor, pulled him out of the car, and leaned him up against the hood of the Saab. Then she knelt down in front of him, put one hand in each of his armpits and shook him gently.

'Andrew,' Mom said. 'Andrew, I want you to take some deep breaths, and then I want you to stand up on your own.'

By this time all the adults knew that something was amiss.

'Liza, I'm sure he's just tired after the long trip,' Nanny said dismissively. 'Just carry him in – he'll be fine.'

'Mother, we just got here, and you don't know what's happened on this trip,' Mom said icily. 'The muffler has holes in it and it's jury-rigged. Why don't you take Beth Anne inside?'

'No,' I said bluntly.

Nanny didn't insist. Instead she shrugged and said to Marvin, 'Why don't you come in with me, Marvin dear? I'll fix you a drink. You must be thirsty after the long drive.'

Marvin sought – and Mom granted – permission wordlessly. 'A drink would be most welcome, Dolly,' Marvin said, stepping towards the open door to the garage.

Relief at her mother's exit did not wash away Mom's evident alarm. 'Andrew, I want you to try and walk into the house,' Mom said seriously.

Andy cooperated to the best of his ability and took a few wobbly steps as Mom walked slowly backwards steadying him, but when Mom, satisfied, released him, Andy crumpled onto the driveway. Mom's reflexes were fast enough to break, but not prevent, his fall.

'Fuck,' Mom said to her father. 'It's carbon monoxide poisoning. Do we have to take him to the ER?'

'Liza, he'll be fine,' Poppy said. 'He may have hit his head on the way down just now, but that'll be the worst of it. I've seen this sort of thing before – as long as he wakes back up now . . .'

My brother's eyes flickered as if on cue and he looked up at Mom and Poppy in confusion. 'Why am I on the ground?' Andy said.

'You fell down, Andy,' I announced.

'You fainted, honey,' Mom said, more specifically. 'You're a little ill from sleeping on the floor of the car. Poppy is going to carry you to bed – you're too heavy for me to carry, and I don't think you can manage walking yet – and when you wake up in the morning, you'll be as good as gold.'

'OK,' Andy said, extending his arms upwards towards Poppy, then clasping his hands behind Poppy's thick neck, lined with veins protruding from the effort of carrying my solidly built brother.

Mom went ahead of Poppy and held open the garage door. I waited for them all to go through, then walked into the yard on my own and waited. After several minutes, Mom's shape was silhouetted by the bare electric light hanging in the garage. She opened the door, but blinded as she was by the sudden darkness, she couldn't see me.

'Beth,' she called out. 'Beth Anne, what are you doing?'

'I'm waiting for fireflies,' I said, from where I stood in the middle of the night-damp, dark green lawn.

'There are no fireflies tonight,' Mom said. 'Now come indoors.'

18

Red

At breakfast the next morning Nanny served defrosted white Wonder Bread. There was a particular taste to the bread in Bethlehem, a chemical grace note that was noticeably absent from our own often homebaked and never frozen bread.

I turned up my nose. 'I think the bread is mouldy,' I said, although I had already inspected the bread and found none of the green or blue circles that sometimes decorated the bread at home.

Nanny looked offended. 'I froze this bread the day I bought it and defrosted it last night. It certainly is not mouldy.'

'Just eat your cereal, Beth Anne,' Mom said under her breath. 'Leave the bread if you don't like it.'

'You're a growing girl, Beth Anne. You should eat everything placed before you. Some children aren't lucky enough to have toast with jam in the morning,' Nanny said sanctimoniously.

I finished the toast, but once safely out of Nanny's earshot, in the car on our way to Longwood Gardens, I asked Mom for an explanation.

'Why is Nanny's bread so yucky?'

Marvin laughed heartily. 'You have one up on her there, Liza. You may be the black sheep but you've got the best bread. I'd much rather

have your buns for breakfast than Dolly's stale, old, yucky white bread.
'

Mom giggled, then reached across and patted Marvin playfully on the thigh. She seemed to have forgotten my question entirely.

I persisted. 'Why is Nanny's bread so bad? Mould tastes like penicillin, so it's not mould, but Nanny's bread is worse, because you can't even cut off the mouldy bits. There's something wrong with the whole slice.'

'It's because she freezes food for too long, Beth Anne,' Mom said. 'She's always done it. She thinks she's being so virtuous, but the bread just sits there for months and months, soaking up the tastes of all the other food around it, and then when she finally defrosts it, it's barely edible. This is why I almost never freeze food. How my grandmother, who can cook like Julia Child, raised a woman who can't chop onions because,' and here my mother screwed her face into a simper, "They make me cry," is beyond me. It's because she was Lily's only child – my grandparents spoiled her rotten. Thank goodness I had three – none of you will ever suffer the same fate. You may go hungry, but you won't be spoiled, and it may not be fun to go hungry, but at least hunger only lasts until the next paycheck. Being a selfish bitch who can't lift a finger lasts a lifetime.'

'Liza,' Marvin remonstrated, 'just because you hate her doesn't mean your kids have to. Don't you want to teach them respect for their elders?'

Mom bristled. 'Only if the elders deserve respect. My mother doesn't fall into that category.'

'Serving defrosted Wonder Bread doesn't warrant this level of scorn.'

'It's not about the bread,' Mom said.

'The kids don't know that.'

'They will someday.'

'They don't now.'

'I just don't want them to be anything like her.'

'It's good for kids to have grandparents,' Marvin said. 'I adored my Bubbie. My Bubbie froze all sorts of things – she thought the freezer was such a revolutionary invention, she was determined to use it as much as she possibly could. That generation didn't grow up with freezers, remember. Your mother worked her whole life – without convenience food and a freezer she wouldn't have been able to do that.'

'I wish she hadn't been able to,' Mom countered. 'She loved everybody else's children – she told us about them all the time – but she never loved us.'

'I'm sure she loves you, Liza.'

'If she ever did love me, she didn't show it when I most needed her to,' Mom said ruefully. 'It's too bad for her if she loves me now – which I doubt she does – because the feeling is not mutual.'

I'd been following the conversation to the best of my ability, but the logical conclusion seemed far-fetched, even to me, so I sought confirmation. 'Do you hate Nanny because she always gave you yucky bread?'

Both adults laughed. 'No, Beth Anne,' Mom said. 'I don't hate Nanny because of the bread, and neither should you. If you really can't stomach the defrosted Wonder Bread, just tell Nanny you only want cereal for breakfast.'

'But they only have Special K.'

'That's because my mother is constantly on a diet. She is under the misguided impression that if she eats Special K for breakfast every day, it will somehow make up for all the cookies she treats herself to when she feels she deserves a little something because life is so unfair.'

'Liza,' Marvin said again.

'Sorry,' Mom said, although it was crystal clear that she wasn't. 'Anyway, what's the matter with Special K?'

Andy volunteered an answer from the back seat. He had been strictly forbidden to sit on the floor ever again, which, for this outing, was not a problem as we had the enormous privilege of travelling in the far newer and yards more luxurious Volvo sedan that Poppy, with unprecedented largesse, had lent us. Poppy had even volunteered to take the Saab to the garage he trusted. He could have done the repairs himself and saved her some money, he told Mom, but he understood that given the time constraints of a visit from out-of-state, that wasn't possible.

'Special K,' Andy began, then followed with the most damning insult known to six-year-olds, 'is *boring*.'

'Beggars can't be choosers,' Mom retorted. 'But we'll have lunch at Longwood Gardens, so you all get at least one meal that's not your grandmother's cooking,' she added, sneering involuntarily.

'There's probably something Freudian about your mother not feeding you the way my Bubbie fed us,' Marvin said.

'There's plenty that's Freudian about my mother,' Mom said. 'But nothing that we're going to mention in front of the kids. Look, kids – we're here! This is Longwood Gardens. Do you remember it now?'

Mom had asked us that morning if we recalled our previous trip to the world-famous botanical gardens. Although I had vague memories of a place crowded with flowers, I couldn't be sure if the place I had called to mind was real or imaginary. Only when confronted with the splendour did I accept that the cascades of flowers of all colours, shapes and sizes were not something I had conjured out of thin air, but rather something I had indeed experienced.

Mom was like a kid in a candy store in the gardens. 'Would you look at those lotus flowers? They're as big as your heads! And the leaves are so gigantic – doesn't it make you want to walk across them? I bet they're strong enough that they'd almost hold you, Alice,' Mom said, stroking Alice's hair. Alice leaned in towards Mom the way cats do when they want their human's attention. Mom, from twice Alice's height, wouldn't have seen Alice's faint smile when Mom, rather than stepping away, left her hand on Alice's shoulder after it reached the end of her hair and, with it, gently pulled her youngest in. I was only a head taller than Alice, and, also just like a cat, had learned to keep one eye on my human, so Mom's gesture of tenderness towards Alice gave me permission to take my cat's-eye off Mom and revel fully in the glorious riot of flowers and plants all around me.

Mom might have been snuggling my sister rather than me, but in the greenhouse, the air itself held us close; so close, in fact, that even our ability to breathe was affected. My impulse when faced with the shockingly hot and humid air of the East Conservatory – a building, my mother said, that had 'risen like a phoenix from the ashes of the azalea house' – was to recoil in fear. Mom, however, took an enormous lungful of the moist air and announced, 'I love this so much – it's like a sauna, only better, because saunas are nowhere near as beautiful.' That was my cue to reinterpret the environment of the glasshouse: it wasn't threatening, it was a throwback to being held very tightly against your mother's bosom – so close you could hardly breathe, but you didn't mind, because you knew she was squeezing you because she loved you – only in this case your mother was green.

It was the next day's outing – embarked upon in our newly repaired Saab – that introduced me to an even more wonderful sort of hug – one carved in stone. We ventured all the way to Philadelphia, somewhere Mom had rarely - if ever - taken us before, to visit the Rodin Museum. Marvin's good friend George, the art teacher in Montpelier whom I had once hoped in vain would teach me, was a sculptor on the side. We had all seen a few of his sculptures – rounded forms carved forth from substantial slabs of Vermont marble – in George's studio when Marvin had taken us to visit George and his wife Marianne. Now Mom wanted us all, Marvin included, to stand in the presence of *The Kiss* and witness what George was striving towards.

'I used to come here, every once in a while, when I was at nursing school in Philly,' Mom told us, as my brother, sister and I gaped, mouths wide open, at the naked stone bodies, some alone and some entwined, in rapture and despair, all around us.

'Usually I didn't even come in because I didn't want to pay, but I'd walk through the gardens because that was free. Other times I just couldn't resist – I'm sure you can understand why. Wasn't he a genius? Have you ever seen two people more in love than this man and this woman?' Mom asked rhetorically, waving her arm theatrically towards an undressed couple, infatuated beyond measure, embracing ecstatically for all eternity.

As I gazed awestruck at Rodin's masterpiece, I underwent a seismic shift of opinion on the subject of sexuality, a subject with which I was more familiar than was possibly healthy for a girl of my age, thanks to the disinhibition of both my mom and her lover. I had thought, up until that point, that the physical expression of love between two adults was uncomfortable at best and terrifying at worst, but if mutual desire could be as magnificent as it was for these figures in white marble, then maybe I had been wrong all along. Maybe passion was not something to hide, but something to celebrate. Maybe Mom and Marvin, by displaying their passion so unashamedly, were just being artistic?

Marvin, however, derailed my train of thought with a pithy question. 'They're most definitely in love, but have you noticed that this sculpture was originally intended as part of *The Gates of Hell*? And not only that – the word on the street is that *The Kiss* was for Camille Claudel, Rodin's mistress, rather than Rose, his wife. So love may be beautiful, but it's not straightforward.'

Mom refused to be completely deflated, but she did turn away from

Marvin to address us instead. 'Rodin fell in love with Camille Claudel, the woman in this sculpture, when she came to him as a student. She was a fine sculptress in her own right, even before she met him. Actually, if Camille Claudel hadn't had her heart broken by Rodin, she might not have ended up having a nervous breakdown and spending the last thirty years of her life in an insane asylum.'

'Touché,' Marvin said admiringly, fond as he was of repartee. 'On the other hand, here we are talking about Camille Claudel. Chances are we wouldn't be doing that if Claudel hadn't become Rodin's student, lover and muse. She did benefit from her association with him, even if he perhaps benefitted even more from his association with her.'

'I don't think there's any 'perhaps' about who gained the most from that relationship,' Mom said, with a touch of hostility. 'In a truly egalitarian society – a society in which women were equal to men – Camille Claudel wouldn't have needed Rodin in the first place. Who knows – she might even have become more famous than him. If she had received the recognition she so richly deserved, she might not have lost her mind, and we might be surrounded by her work here as well as, or even instead of, his.'

'I'm not sure her work would be strong or plentiful enough to warrant a museum like this,' Marvin said, spinning slowly in place with his arms extended like the car salesmen on TV.

'You haven't read up on this, which actually further proves my point,' Mom fumed. 'Claudel destroyed a lot of her pieces before she was institutionalised.'

'What is it about women and smashing things?' Marvin said meaningfully.

I had been following the verbal ping-pong with some trepidation as the hostility level mounted. Now I entered the fray, hoping the distraction would at least wipe the scowl off Mom's face, or perhaps – better still – re-establish the original amorous tone of the exchange between my two guardians.

'Look at that humongous hand over there,' I said. 'Why did he make just a hand without a body?'

'I think that may have been a study piece for a larger sculpture,' Mom said.

'Who has hands that big?' Andy asked, wandering away from *The Kiss* and towards the enormous clenched hand.

'Someone who would be really good at tickling,' Marvin proposed, in the particular tone adults reserve to indicate to children that they want to engage in play. I didn't have to glance back to know that Marvin's own hands would be held out in front of him, waiting to tickle the nearest child, and when Alice squealed delightedly, I sensed that Marvin had hit his target. Her high-pitched laughter was still such a novelty – before Marvin's entrance on our family stage, I couldn't recall Alice ever having laughed – that Mom's indignation vanished and a wide, easy smile spread across her face.

Andy and I wasted no time on pleasantries upon our return to Hickory Street. We left Alice, who didn't mind Dolly's fussing and wouldn't object to sitting on Jim's lap, to supply the charming child presence while we took our own less-charming selves down to the basement, where we were sleeping this time around, to play records.

Mom and her sister Joanne jointly owned a portable Magnavox Micromatic record player – whether it had been given to them as a present, or whether they had pooled their pocket money to buy it, I wasn't sure. However Mom and her sister had come by the Magnavox, neither of them had felt enough sole ownership or perhaps enough fervour to take it from the family home. They had even left the white leatherette box containing their cache of 45rpm vinyl. The box was emblazoned with the image of a girl wearing a sleeveless belted dress with a full circle skirt, hair coiffed in a perfect nape-length flip – just like my mom's in the intriguing picture from her high school yearbook – lightly holding the hand of a boy in a button-down shirt and Oxford shoes; the couple's dance floor was a red and white 45rpm single, suspended among the stars like a new-found musical Milky Way. The box fastened with a metal clasp that made a satisfying click when opened or closed, but that click paled in comparison to the clack of the first of the stack of five or six lovingly chosen singles falling onto the turntable, and both of those sounds were outshone by the scratch of the diamond stylus as the needle entered the groove and the Shirelles sang out in unison. The 45s ranged from the silly ('Thumbelina' by Jimmy Boyd) to the sublime ('Runaway' by Buddy Holly) and I played them over and over, until I knew all the words to 'Thumbelina' and could sing the entire sax solo of 'Runaway' note for note.

As much as I would have liked to ignore my rumbling stomach to carry on with my musical education, my mother wouldn't entertain my suggestion that I skip dinner in favour of Patsy Cline. I was torn away from the Magnavox and made to endure a bland dinner of overcooked meat and boiled vegetables, and then told in no uncertain terms that I needed not only to bathe but also wash my hair, to rid my mane of the impurities Mom assured me it had collected on our outing to the big city of Philadelphia.

'I'll pop Andrew in the tub first – he's quick and easy – then I'll tackle you and Alice,' Mom said. 'I'll go run the water now.'

'Do the kids want bubble bath?' Dolly asked.

'Oooh! I do!' Alice squealed.

'I'll put some in,' Mom said, leaving the table for the bathroom.

'Of course the *girls* want bubble bath!' Jim bellowed, in his too-loud voice. 'What about Andy though? Andy might be already too much of a man for such things,' Jim added, winking obviously at my brother and clapping him on the back as if to welcome him to the lads' club.

Marvin wasn't having it. 'I'm as red-blooded as the next man, but I find nothing as relaxing as a good soak in foam. Bubble baths don't make you a sissy, Andrew, they just make you a hedonist, and there's nothing wrong with that.'

'I beg to disagree,' Dolly said drily.

'With what part?' Marvin asked. 'The sissy part or the hedonist part?'

Dolly looked disgusted, but Jim guffawed approvingly. 'Nothing wrong with hedonism,' Jim repeated. 'I guess you'll be telling me next I should stay in the tub for hours on end if that's what I want to do.'

Dolly's jaw had clenched shut as if she were personally affronted by all this crazy talk. 'No one should stay in a bath for hours on end. It would dry your skin out, for one.'

'If Jim feels like having a good long soak in the rose-scented lather, what is there to stop him?' Marvin asked Dolly. 'Jim's a man of leisure now – he's worked hard all his life, supporting you and your daughters. I think he deserves an hour in bubbles, don't you? You could even keep him company. Beth Anne and Alice think it's more fun to bathe together, don't you, girls?'

Colour flooded Dolly's cheeks and she rose abruptly from the table. 'I must go start the dishwasher,' she said coldly.

'She has a woman's sense of humour,' Jim said apologetically.

'Maybe my suggestion will plant a seed,' Marvin replied, just at the moment that Mom returned to the dining table.

'What kind of seeds are you planting now?' Mom asked, glancing from Marvin to Jim and back again.

'Bath seeds,' Marvin said innocently. 'And there's somebody sitting right over there' —Marvin pointed at Andy, with both index fingers for added emphasis— 'who needs watering.'

'Yes, there is,' Mom agreed. 'Let's go, Andrew. Beth Anne, why don't you play upstairs here with Alice for a few minutes while I scrub your brother? Maybe you could even give Nanny a hand. Where is Mother, anyway?'

'She retreated to the kitchen,' Marvin said. Poppy cleared his throat. Mom eyed them both up and down, then shrugged her shoulders.

'I leave you two alone for five minutes and you're already thick as thieves,' Mom said.

'I'm just making a good impression on my future father-in-law.'

'Marvin . . .' Mom half-spoke, half-whispered.

'Your what, now? Your "father-in-law"?' Jim exclaimed. 'Liza, is there something you'd like to mention?'

Marvin was unruffled. 'I thought you would have told them by now, Liza,' he said lightly, in response to the silent daggers Mom was casting at him with her eyes.

'I planned to tell my parents tomorrow evening,' Mom said, speaking past her father to Marvin.

'Dolly, did you hear that? Liza and Marvin are getting married!' Jim bellowed towards the kitchen from the table.

'Jim, honestly, you don't need to shout so loudly that all the neighbours can hear you,' Nanny said, as she came towards the table, hands still encased in bright yellow gloves with cuffs that continued some way up her forearm.

Mom, by this time, had left her annoyance behind and was standing by her new man. 'It's true,' Mom asserted. 'I'm going to be Mrs Elizabeth Kessler.'

'Yay!' I shouted. 'That means Marvin will be our dad forever! Did you hear that, Alice? Mom and Marvin are getting married!'

'Do you really think that's a good idea, Elizabeth?' Nanny wondered. 'I mean, you haven't known each other for more than a few months . . .'

'Nearly a year, Mother,' Mom corrected Dolly, dropping Marvin's hand unceremoniously in her sudden haste to resume bath-time duties. 'Now I'm going to go and make sure Andrew isn't drowning, while you come to grips with having a Jewish son-in-law.'

'This has nothing to do with Marvin being Jewish,' Dolly said, affronted. 'I've been friends with the Singers for years, and I certainly wouldn't have objected to you marrying their son David.'

Mom rolled her eyes. 'Yes, Mother, you've mentioned that several times over the years. So what's the problem then, if it's not your Protestant sensibilities?'

'Liza, don't talk to your mother that way,' Jim said sternly.

'I'm a grown woman with three children – I'll talk to her any way I want,' Mom retorted.

'I just think it's a bit rash,' Nanny said. 'Why do you have to hurry into another marriage when the last one went the way it did?'

'I don't know why I brought you here,' Mom said to Marvin. She pivoted as if to leave, then spun back to deliver her parting shot. 'I do, actually. I wanted you to meet my grandmother. That's whose approval matters – not yours,' Mom hissed at her mother. She marched out of the room, slamming the bathroom door behind her.

Nanny winced behind her thick plastic glasses. 'Don't get me wrong,' she said, turning to Marvin. 'I have nothing against Jews, and you seem to be up to the challenge of being Liza's husband, but I don't see why you need to be in such a hurry. Unless there's something else Liza hasn't told us.'

Marvin chuckled. 'There's nothing else Liza hasn't told you. Three children is plenty. I appreciate your point of view, Dolly, but Liza and I are very much in love and that's why we plan to marry.'

'Is Mommy going to wear a white dress?' Alice asked.

Poppy nearly choked on his mouthful of beer. 'I should hope not,' he said. 'That train left the station a long time ago.'

'I believe she's leaning towards red,' Marvin answered Alice, and the laddish undertone was not lost on Jim, who nodded knowingly. 'Didn't you mention something about bourbon earlier, Jim? Feels like time for a nightcap.'

'I did. I'd be happy to pour you one,' Poppy said. He rose from the dining table and crossed the room – in half the number of steps it would have taken me – to a smaller round table, dressed similarly to the dining table with a nearly floor-length starched white tablecloth. Jim delicately removed the stopper from a hefty cut-glass decanter, poured two fingers' worth of amber liquid into each of two substantial cut-glass tumblers, and set the decanter back on the shiny brass tray.

Marvin accepted the tumbler Jim offered him with the merest hint of a bow, then raised his glass to his lips, but instead of drinking took a prolonged sniff.

'Here's to our future son-in-law,' Poppy proposed.

'Here's to my future wife,' Marvin toasted.

Both men raised their glasses and drank.

19

Eight

There were not just two, but three doors that opened to the master bathroom at Nanny and Poppy's house: one from the master bedroom, one from the small foyer at the back entrance to the upper level of the house, and one – opposite the upstairs guest bedroom – from the corridor that led from the living room to the master bedroom. Of these, the door I paid least attention to when in the bathtub was the door from the foyer. I was more aware of the door from the hall, but the only door that, if opened, caused me to freeze as if I was playing magic statues and the music had come to an abrupt stop was the door from the master bedroom. Only one person employed that door to enter the bathroom when I was immersed in the bath, and that was my unaccompanied grandfather. It did happen sometimes that Poppy would make an appearance via another door, but if so, it was nearly guaranteed he would then be just in front of or just behind my mother, or – in very rare cases – my grandmother. As soon as I ascertained that Poppy was not alone, the involuntary deer-in-the-headlights response faded, sometimes so rapidly that even a finely tuned ECG would not have been able to pick up my passage through that state, but if I sensed that the door to the bathroom from the master bedroom had slowly and tentatively opened wide enough for Poppy to pass through, I became as paralysed as any whitetail blinded by bright lights on an otherwise deserted Vermont highway.

As I had grown older, Mom had increasingly insisted that I bathe with Alice rather than on my own when we visited Nanny and Poppy. It was true that Alice's presence made me feel slightly less vulnerable during Poppy's unannounced visits to the bathroom, but my body was still naked in the water and his eyes were still hungry – perhaps even hungrier – when there were two little girls in the tub instead of just one.

The evening of the engagement announcement, after Andy had been roughly towelled off and pyjamaed, Alice and I were playing with the bubbles in the tub when my insect-like hygroreceptors picked up a subtle lessening of the humidity in the air. My mom, when coming to check on us, was never shy about swinging the bathroom door wide, so the barely measurable reduction in atmospheric moisture could mean only one thing.

'Hello. girls,' Poppy said, sliding into view.

I became aware that although the bubbles were still high, they were neither covering me as much as they could nor as much as I suddenly wanted them to. I scooped in as many armfuls as possible and held the bubbles to my chest like a glistening ephemeral bath towel. 'Hello,' I said to my grandfather, as coldly as I could.

'I came to see if what Marvin said earlier is true – is it really more fun to have company in the tub?' Poppy's light-hearted manner was forced, and his voice was tight, like a rubber band that had been stretched nearly to breaking point.

Alice and I said nothing.

'So, who's washing who? Is it the big girl washing the little girl, or vice versa?'

Holes were forming in my foam shield, but if I moved my arms now to repair it, my upper half would be exposed. I hugged the remaining bubbles even closer and kept my arms in a protective X, like a Catholic girl at Communion before confirmation, crossing her arms to indicate to the Father that she receives neither the blood nor the body.

'We're each washing ourselves,' I said.

'Have you done a good job and washed your whole bodies? Even what's under the bubbles?'

'Even our toes,' Alice said cheerfully. I scowled at her and she looked back at me in confusion.

The lump on Poppy's forehead seemed to jut out that little bit further. 'Maybe I should—'

'Maybe you should what?' Mom said, throwing the door from the hallway open and barging in. 'Maybe you should leave bathing the girls to me?'

I loosened, but did not release, my crossed arms, now the only barrier between my torso and Poppy's gaze. Mom's arrival had discombobulated my grandfather enough to tear his eyes away from the two nude little girls in his bathtub, but he was still in the room.

'I've got this under control, Dad,' Mom bristled. 'Why don't you go keep Marvin company? You two seem to be getting along like a house on fire.'

Jim grinned. 'You picked an interesting specimen there, Liza. Very witty, and well educated of course, as you'd expect.'

'As you'd expect of whom? A third-grade teacher? Or a Jew? Is that what you really meant to say?' Mom knelt down beside the tub and addressed us. 'Are you both squeaky clean now?'

'Yes,' Alice and I said in unison.

'Good. When your grandfather goes, we'll get you out of the tub and into your pyjamas. Nanny has some chocolate Jell-O in the fridge.'

I thought of the tough, nearly black skin, like thick ice on a frozen lake, that always covered the soft, creamy pudding. I imagined piercing it with my spoon and savouring my chocolatey reward. I felt Poppy staring at me and realised with a start that I had let my guard down; my hands were at my sides and the bubbles were gone.

'Go!' Mom said to her father, and it was no longer a request, it was a command.

Poppy ceded. 'I'll see if your intended wants another drink.'

'I'm sure he won't refuse,' Mom said.

The next morning, after Mom had wrestled us all reluctantly into our clothes, we walked down the hill and across the street to where my great-grandparents on my mother's side now lived. My great-grandparents' home on Broad Street, in downtown Bethlehem, had felt like the set of a period drama, chock-full of antiques and authentic to the bone. I still recalled the once lush burgundy shade of the overstuffed, crushed velvet armchairs I had claimed whenever I could in the Broad Street sitting room. There wasn't space, in the new flat in the elder housing five minutes' walk from Jim and Dolly's, for most of Lily May and Harry's belongings. Mom and Aunt Joanne had each taken some pieces of the Wellers' furniture, but Nanny had declared that she would offer no part of her mother's home sanctuary in her own: 'What do I want with all those old things? I'm a modern woman with a modern house. Someone else will appreciate all that oak far more than I would.' My great-grandparents had chosen with great care what to take with them to imbue their final address with at least a hint of the character of the home they had built for themselves over the many decades of their adult life, but it was not the same and it was not enough. Sitting in the living room area of their open-plan residence, they resembled the lead couple from the cast of that same period drama who find themselves inexplicably aged and unceremoniously plonked onto the set of a Seventies sitcom. Both of them seemed ill at ease and even physically smaller in their new surroundings. My great-grandfather's pipe-smoking, positively Holmesian at Broad Street, now seemed like the dated pastime of a pensioner when performed in a room with a shag carpet, while my great-grandmother's exuberant floral shifts, which had blended so seamlessly with the Broad Street interior, clashed markedly with the avocado counters in the kitchen of the new apartment.

Diminished though they were, my great-grandparents retained their ability to instantly transform my mother. Mom needed only to cross the threshold to step into her own personal verse of Revelation, wherein all her tears were wiped away and she was again the open and trusting child she had once been, long ago. I wasn't sure what secret power these silver-haired, slow-moving relatives possessed, but I admired it deeply and would have given my right arm to acquire it so that I too could make my mom that happy through my mere presence.

Marvin was subdued and respectful at my great-grandparents' flat. There was no hiding his several inches of tight dark curls standing straight up in every direction and no getting around his Brooklyn dialect, but Harry and Lily May, unlike Jim and Dolly, made no comments about the difference between Marvin's religious background and their own. Instead, Lily May asked Marvin about his third-graders. Did he enjoy teaching them? Were they well behaved, or did he struggle to keep them on task? And Marvin asked Harry about his pipe. Had he gone over to cigarettes when they first appeared, only to find he preferred his tobacco loose and tasted rather than tightly rolled and inhaled? What about the pipe itself – was there a story behind it? (Of course there was.) When, at the end of the visit, Mom shared the good news of the approaching wedding with her grandparents, both listened attentively and then offered Mom and Marvin their warmest congratulations.

Mom was in seventh heaven by the end of our hour with her grandparents. As the door closed behind Andy – last out because he had been engrossed in some sort of Andy-like activity prior to leaving and thus missed the cues given for imminent departure – I declared aloud, 'I love Great-Grandma and Great-Grandpa Weller.'

Mom took my hand and swung it merrily back and forth. 'I love them too,' Mom said.

When we returned home to East Montpelier, Mom began to sew furiously. Her sewing table was stacked with yard upon yard of red and yellow calico – the red sprinkled with thousands of brown-eyed Susans mixed with white forget-me-nots, the yellow graced with black floral wreaths each encircling between one and three diminutive bright red geranium flowers. Mom had the red bolt spread out; she delicately placed a collection of three or four shiny silver pins – head in, sharp side out – between her lips, then plucked them out one at a time to deftly affix the flimsy brown tracing paper with its mysterious instructions onto the fabric.

'What will your dress look like?' I asked Mom.

Mom showed me the front of the Butterick pattern, where three slim figures – drawn mannequins, recognisable as women, but without proper faces – posed to illustrate the front, side and rear views of the finished dress with its full sleeves, below-knee to floor-length hem and decorative yoke in a complementary fabric.

'Oooh . . .' I gushed. 'Will ours look the same as yours?'

Mom removed the extra pins carefully from her mouth to answer. 'Mine will skim my ankles, but yours will come to just below your knees. And mine is red with a yellow yoke, but yours will be all sunshine yellow, because that's who you are – you're my little Sunshine.'

'What about Alice's dress? And what will Andy wear?'

'Alice's dress will be the same red fabric as mine, but the same style as yours: short sleeves, no yoke, just the one fabric.'

'And Andy?'

'I found some very hippy corduroy – red hearts, orange stripes, that kind of thing – and I'm going to make Andrew some elasticated-waist trousers out of that. I bought him a mustard-yellow turtleneck two sizes too big last winter – I'm guessing he'll still fit into that in October.'

'October?' I repeated in alarm. 'Why October? Why not now?'

Mom laughed. 'Somebody's excited about being a flower girl, huh? October, mostly because it's going to take me about that long to sew three dresses, a pair of trousers, and a satin-backed waistcoat.'

'What's a waistcoat?'

'A vest. Waistcoat is the fancy British English term.'

'Is Andy wearing a fancy British waistcoat?'

Mom laughed again. Her laugh had come more easily since the wedding announcement. 'No, not Andrew. Marvin's wearing the waistcoat. Andrew is still growing too fast to spend time and effort sewing him something like that.'

I was relieved to hear that Andy wouldn't have the preferential treatment of two new items of clothing to my one, but I was still not satisfied with Mom's explanation for the – in my view – unnecessary delay of the wedding date. What if Mom or Marvin got cold feet? My first dad had been a good dad, but when I thought about Michael, my second dad, and the day he'd taken Andy to the woodshed, ire rose up instantly like the intense white flame of a chemical reaction. I wanted Marvin to be my third dad, nobody else, and October seemed a long way off.

'October is forever away,' I complained.

'October will be here before you know it,' Mom assured me. 'And lots of exciting things will happen between now and then to make the time go faster. You have your birthday next week, then you go to Cape Cod with your father, and then you start at a new school.'

'I don't want to start at a new school. I want to stay with Tovah at my old school.'

'We can't drive you all the way to that school from where we're going, and you'll make new friends at your new school. Now go find something else to do, because I need to get this finished,' Mom ordered, pulling four pins from her plump pincushion, shaped like a cheery tomato, and sticking them in her mouth.

My birthday was in the middle of August, which meant school was never in session on the big day. For the family celebration, I could bank on a cake with candles, I could expect a rousing (if not perfectly in tune) rendition of 'Happy Birthday' led by Mom and accompanied by my siblings, and I could hope for a couple of presents, covered neatly by Mom, whose training in hospital corners during nursing school had generalised to wrapping paper. I had come to expect that every birthday would be the same, so I was unprepared when my eighth birthday broke the mould, although I shouldn't really have been surprised, because life with Marvin was not like life before Marvin.

On Mom's birthday, just ten days before my own, Marvin woke Andy, Alice and me up earlier than usual for an August morning. He gathered us in the kitchen, then laid out his battle plan.

'It's your mom's birthday today, kids,' Marvin reminded us, although we already knew, 'and we're going to make her the best breakfast in bed she's had in ages.'

The three of us went from wiping the sleep from our collective eyes to buzzing with purpose. Marvin divvied up the tasks according to perceived ability: I was responsible for spreading butter and jam on the toast, Andy was sent outdoors to pick at least one flower, and Alice was instructed to draw a picture of the birthday girl on a piece of scrap paper, to be folded into a makeshift card. Marvin saw to it that the breakfast tray included a strong cup of coffee, a pack of cigarettes, and an ashtray.

Mom's eyes were open but still groggy with sleep when we appeared in the bedroom doorway.

'Happy birthday to you,' Marvin began singing, and we all joined in, clapping enthusiastically as the song ended.

'Oh . . . thanks,' Mom said, in that embarrassed way she reserved for presents she didn't like. 'I haven't had breakfast in bed in a long time. Maybe because I don't really like to eat in bed,' she added.

'Andy could only find dandelions,' I confessed, as if perhaps a better choice of flower would have made breakfast in bed a welcome, rather than a bothersome, intrusion. 'But Alice drew you a picture, and I let the butter sink in before I put the jam on.'

Only now did Mom glance at the flimsy folded paper with the uneven edges on which Alice had sketched an image that, with its jumble of curved and straight lines, accurately depicted Alice's enthusiasm for the assignment but resembled Mom only tangentially.

Mom softened. 'That's so special, Alice. Those must be my eyes there – and that's my mouth. Is that some writing too?'

'It's "I love you Mommy",' Alice explained.

No emotion passed through Mom without causing at least a ripple. Mom had worked for years in high school as a lifeguard, scanning the pool for any telltale signs that a swimmer's laughter had turned to distress in the blink of an eye and a lifeguard's assistance was required. The tables had turned and I was Mom's lifeguard now, watching her every movement, always poised to dive in and help, but wondering with every intervention if my skills would be up to the task this time.

Mom caught herself before tears spilled over. Her initial annoyance returned as she inspected the ashtray and cigarettes. 'I don't normally eat in bed and I certainly don't smoke in bed. I'm not Marilyn Monroe.'

'Who's Marilyn Monroe?' I asked, thinking she might be an adult I had met but whose name I hadn't learned.

'She's an actress,' Mom said.

'She's a bombshell,' Marvin elaborated.

Mom gave Marvin a dirty look. 'It's *my* birthday,' Mom reminded him, 'not Marilyn's.'

'She's a nobody,' Marvin corrected himself.

Mom nodded with satisfaction. She sipped at the coffee. 'Nice coffee,' she said. 'Maybe breakfast in bed isn't so bad. But it does remind me a bit of the hospital. The patients usually ate in bed – they had metal trays back then. Sometimes they'd spill and then we'd have to change the sheets. It made more work for us.'

'But today we've done all the work,' I pointed out, 'so you don't have to, because it's your birthday.'

'Will you change the sheets too, if I get toast crumbs on them?'

'Yes,' I said without hesitation.

'Beth Anne, you don't even know how to strip a bed,' Mom pointed out.

'I could learn.'

'Why don't you kids go watch TV for a while now?' Marvin suggested. 'I have a birthday present I'd like to give your mother in private.'

Alice's face lit up with curiosity. 'What is it?' Alice asked.

'If I told you, it wouldn't be private,' Marvin said.

'Tell me what it is!' Alice insisted, tugging on Marvin's shirt tail.

Mom patted the top of Alice's head. 'He's kidding about the present, Alice. Now kids, as a special treat – because it's my birthday – you can watch anything you want on TV.'

'I want to watch *The Price Is Right*,' Andy said. The summer sun had sprinkled still more freckles liberally across Andy's cheeks and nose. I had searched my own reflection for freckles countless times, but just as for the evil stepmother in the story, the mirror refused to show me what I wanted.

When my own birthday rolled around, I recalled the breakfast in bed we'd made for Mom – she might not want crumbs between the sheets, but I had no such qualms. I thought it would be heavenly to be waited upon like that, to lie in bed like a queen and nod regally at the efforts of my subjects to please me. I would never have dreamt of asking for breakfast in bed before Marvin. While I'd been vaguely culturally aware of the concept, the term only took on a concrete meaning after Mom's birthday. With Marvin installed as our new dad, however, the odds seemed considerably better that my unspoken wish might be granted.

And it was. The morning of August sixteenth I woke up bright and early, but rather than jumping out of bed, I retrieved my copy of *Prince Caspian* from the bedside table, fluffed up my pillow, arranged it vertically against the knobbly spindles at the head of my bed, and began to read. Rima the cat, when she worked out that I had no plans to make my bed, burrowed herself into the warm cavern between my duvet and the sheet. I stroked her for a moment, then opened my book and completely forgot about Rima, because I was no longer Beth Anne Evans in bed on her birthday morning, I was Lucy Pevensie, just woken in the night by Aslan. Narnia was not just a story to me – as with all my favourite books, the world the author created became my world, and what happened to my favourite characters happened equally to me. I had just been made a lioness by Aslan for my willingness to wake my siblings and insist that they follow the lion with me, when my real-life siblings – who, to my occasional disappointment, were not called Peter and Susan – flung open the door of my real-life bedroom and surprised me out of Narnia. Mom was right behind them, holding the tray I recognised from when my siblings and I had prepared breakfast in bed for Mom ten days prior. Marvin was next to Mom, holding a wrapped present.

'Happy birthday!' Mom proclaimed.

The others echoed her. 'Happy birthday, Beth Anne!'

I inspected the breakfast tray. Andy had managed to find a fresh dandelion; I touched its yellow head, bright as a tiny sun, and felt the hard centre where the stalk ended and the flowers erupted. I picked the flower out of the glass, fingered its hairy light-green stalk, then turned it upside-down and let the milky-white liquid from the end of the stalk ooze onto the back of my hand.

'You don't need to do that any more now your wart's gone,' Mom said.

'It might stop me from getting another one,' I said.

'Maybe. Alice was in charge of the toast, so she hasn't made you a card yet.'

I glanced at Alice, who had snatched the rectangular package from Marvin's hands and now thrust it towards me. 'Open it,' she ordered.

I hesitated. 'Is this my only present?' I asked. If the answer was yes, I thought it might be better to save the present until later and derive as much satisfaction as I could from the breakfast for the moment.

Marvin laughed. 'Of course this isn't your only present! This is just your morning present! You'll get your big present after dinner, when the cake is ready. Your mom says the singing needs to wait until then too, because you can't have the song without the candles, and you can't have the candles without the cake.'

My cheeks reddened. 'Shall I open this now then?'

'Absolutely. That's what we're all standing around for, to watch you open your morning present. So get a move on, because I've got a cake to bake,' Mom joked.

'Should I try to save the paper?' I asked Mom.

It wasn't Mom who replied. 'Liza, she doesn't need to do that. There's plenty of wrapping paper to be had,' Marvin said.

'There is, but there's also no reason not to keep it. It's perfectly good wrapping paper, and I can recycle it when Andrew's birthday rolls around. Go ahead and save it, Beth Anne. I'll put it in the wrapping paper drawer.'

I did as I was told, identifying the locations of the clear tape and using my fingernail to slice the bond between the tape and the paper.

It was a large book with a sturdy vinyl cover made to look like wood grain. There was no title on the front cover – in fact, the front cover looked exactly like the back cover.

'Oh!' I exclaimed, impressed by the book's size and durability, but perplexed as to what sort of a book this could be. I cracked the spine; there was no print. Each page was thick, optical white and completely blank. 'Is it for colouring?'

'It could be for that,' Marvin said, 'but you could also use it as a journal or for stories. You're always reading other peoples' books – this is for writing your own. There's an inscription on the first page.'

The flush on my cheeks intensified as I took on board that Marvin thought that much of me. I turned to the first page and read aloud. 'To Beth Anne, the writer and artist, on her eighth birthday, with love, Marvin and Mom.'

I closed the book and hugged it tightly. 'It's beautiful,' I said. 'I love it.'

'Just wait until you see your other present,' Mom said. She was smiling already in anticipation.

'Can I have it now?' I said, trying it on.

'No,' Mom said. 'After dinner.'

'That's OK,' I said, acquiescing. 'After all, I've got a whole book to fill. I'd better get started.'

20

Sagamore Bridge

Mom was right about the bigger present; it was even more amazing than the journal. After spending the sweltering August afternoon splashing in the river at our old swimming hole, we returned home for a dinner of my choosing – burgers – in my case, a burger absolutely loaded with every possible condiment except mayonnaise: blood-red ketchup, sunflower-yellow mustard and pickle-green relish. A burger was most tasty when the sauces dripped out over my fingers, and because it was my birthday, Mom didn't even look askance when I took care of the excess sauce by licking my fingers. Mom prepared my favourite potato salad as an accompaniment, a Pennsylvania Dutch recipe served warm, with a dressing tangy with vinegar rather than cloying with mayonnaise. I was not allergic – none of us were allergic in the 1970s – but I disliked mayonnaise, a food selectivity that my mother had registered, but one which she believed was best treated with desensitisation rather than avoidance. Except, apparently, on my birthday.

After dinner I was expecting to keep sitting at the table where I would be presented with my presents, as I had done on every other birthday I could remember, but Mom and Marvin had other plans.

'Sorry,' Mom said, 'but your present was too big to wrap.'

I felt a tinge of disappointment. It would have been marvelous to tear off vast expanses of wrapping paper with abandon, without even asking whether or not the paper should be saved. Then a second, still more discomfiting thought struck me – what if my present was so gigantic that some unfortunate fate had befallen it? What if it had broken, or what if – worse still – my parents had conferred among themselves and come to the conclusion that the present was unsuitable on account of its size?

Alice was reading my face and caught the telltale twitch of my lips. 'The bike is in the garage, Beth Anne! It's red!'

Mom looked over our heads at Marvin. 'Four year-olds don't really do secrets,' she said to him, and by extension, to the rest of us.

Marvin chuckled, and Alice, who by now had both remembered that she was not meant to reveal the nature of the present, clapped her hand over her mouth.

'A red bike,' I repeated, thunderstruck. 'Can I see it?'

'Of course you can,' Mom said. 'Let's all follow Beth Anne out. We'll come back to the table for the cake.'

The fire-engine-red Schwinn stood gleaming next to the workbench where the equally red, but suddenly far less interesting rock tumbler stood. I fell instantly in love with every inch of the bicycle: its red and white leather seat, decorated with an 'S' for Schwinn, the elegant curves of the frame, and most of all, the tassels, sparkling even in the comparative gloom of the garage. It was as if the Schwinn had been made for me and me alone. Kevin's Big Wheel, held up as the pinnacle of personal transportation in my esteem for so long, now seemed a mere toy compared to this beautiful machine that beckoned towards untold adventure.

'When do I get a bike?' Andy asked jealously, and my pride in my new Schwinn swelled.

'Well,' Mom said, 'You do have a birthday coming up in November . . .'

'How long until November?'

'Let's see if we can work it out,' Mom suggested patiently. 'What month comes after August?'

I jumped in. 'September. Can I ride it?'

'Beth Anne,' Mom chided, 'I didn't ask you – I asked Andrew. I'm trying to make sure Andrew knows the months of the year.'

'Sorry. Can I ride it? The Schwinn? *My* Schwinn?'

'Of course you can ride it,' Marvin said. 'What are bikes for? Especially birthday bikes. Birthday bikes demand to be ridden.'

Mom hesitated. 'I don't know if it's such a good idea to take it out right this minute, Beth Anne. Riding a bike may be harder than you think. You have to learn how to use the training wheels on these dirt roads. Maybe you should wait till tomorrow.'

I was crestfallen but put on a brave face. 'OK,' I agreed.

'Liza – she's eight years old and she just got a new bike. Let her have some fun,' Marvin insisted. 'Come on, Beth – let's take your new wheels for a test drive.'

'September, October, November,' Andy said, still counting off. He left the counted fingers extended; the other fingers remained curled tightly shut. 'Three. It's three months until my birthday.'

Mom looked pleased. 'That's right, Andrew! Great job working that out.'

I batted Alice's curious fingers away from the bike's tassels. 'My tassels,' I hissed.

Alice's face contorted. 'She hit me! Mom!'

I denied the charges, although I had swatted my sister in plain sight. 'I didn't hit Alice – I just need her to move so I can take the bike out.'

'When do I get a bike?' Alice demanded, through tears. 'My birthday already was!'

'Maybe Santa Claus will bring you a tricycle,' Mom consoled Alice.
'What's a tricycle?'

Andy jumped in with the answer. 'It's a bicycle with three wheels.
Tri-cycle, get it? Tri- for three, cycle- for, um, wheels.'

I rolled my Schwinn towards the garage door. The training wheels
were some distance behind my field of vision, and the wheel on the
right knocked into Alice's foot.

'Ow!' Alice shouted, looking genuinely aghast. She had been
prepared for grievous bodily harm by hand, but not by vehicle. 'You
ran over me!'

'You were in the way!'

Marvin was holding the garage door open for me to facilitate my
exit. 'I don't think she meant to hurt you, Alice,' Marvin said, his voice
tender as it always was when he addressed my little sister. 'She's just
in a hurry to feel the wind rushing through her hair as she zooms
along. Right, Beth?'

'Right,' I confirmed, and the bike was finally out. Marvin sur-
reptitiously stabilised the bike while I clambered on. I gripped the
handlebars so tightly that my suntanned hands went one shade lighter,
then arranged my feet on the pedals and pushed down as hard as I
could, hoping to fly. No such luck. The resistance from the gravel
driveway meant that although I was putting every ounce of power
available into my feet, the bike barely moved.

'It's not working,' I said. 'Maybe there's something wrong with it.'

Mom dismissed this idea. 'There's nothing wrong with the bike,
Beth Anne. It's brand new and in perfect condition. It's the gravel.
Bikes like this are really meant for paved roads. I remember when I
learned to ride, back in Bethlehem . . .'

That faraway look came into Mom's eyes. She was no longer with
us; she was in Bethlehem – she was home. I tried to go there with
her. I called up my grandparents' house, picturing Hickory Street as

the brighter Pennsylvania sun struck the leafier Pennsylvania trees, dappling the asphalt in light and shadow.

'The hill by Nanny and Poppy's must have been hard at first,' I said, imagining myself careening down the slope from my grandparents' house towards my great-grandparents' apartment.

'I didn't live on Hickory Street, Beth Anne,' Mom reminded me. 'We lived on Broad Street, close to where the Wellers lived before they moved to the housing for the elderly. The streets where I learned to ride were flat and drivers were used to kids playing in the street so they gave us a wide berth. As soon as the Memorial Pool opened up, Joanne and I started biking over on summer mornings, spending all day there and biking home in time for dinner. That's how I became a lifeguard – the pool staff knew me from all those summer days at the pool and they asked me if I wanted a job.'

I wanted Mom back in Vermont, not in Pennsylvania, and I wanted to speed away on the best birthday present I had ever received. I let the talk of the pool fall by the wayside and zeroed in on the salient point for me at that moment: although I had never witnessed it, Mom knew how to ride a bike.

'Can you show me what to do?' I asked Mom from where I perched on the leather saddle, still pushing to the best of my ability on the pedals, still moving at a snail's rather than a cheetah's pace.

Mom laughed. 'I haven't ridden for years, Beth Anne, and I wouldn't fit on that bike at all – in fact, I'd probably break it. Anyway, you don't need me to show you what to do – you pedal, and it looks like you're pedalling just fine already. You just need to try an easier surface. Walk down to the main road if you're so desperate to have a go. Just watch out for potholes. We'll have birthday cake when you're done.'

'We'll eat all the cake before you're back,' Marvin threatened, doing his best impersonation of the Big Bad Wolf about to eat Little Red Riding Hood. 'And then we'll eat you . . .'

Andy was impatient. If he couldn't have a bike, he at least wanted some cake. 'Beth Anne, come on, you can ride your bike tomorrow.'

I was stubborn. 'No,' I said to Andy, 'I want to ride now.'

Balancing was much more complicated getting off than it had been getting on, and I nearly toppled when my right leg came across to the left side. Steadied, I walked my bike down the driveway, admiring the glint of the chrome, the brilliance of the red and the shimmer of the tassels, with Alice trailing behind me.

'Why are you following me?' I said gruffly. 'You should go back home. Maybe Mom needs help sticking eight candles in the cake.'

'I want to watch you ride your bike,' Alice answered.

Sometimes Alice's company wasn't so bad. There was no chance she would outshine me at cycling, and if my bike were too small for Mom, it was conversely far too big for Alice, so I had an ironclad excuse to refuse should she beg me to let her have a go. Maybe somehow Alice could even help me go faster, by pulling or pushing or something. I wasn't sure if she'd be any help, but I capitulated and let Alice tag along anyway. After several minutes of noisy walking as the training wheels bumped over every anomaly in the driveway's surface, the main road stretched out ahead of me. Alice reached again for the streamers as I arranged myself on the saddle. This time I didn't object.

'They're so pretty,' Alice said with longing.

'When I get too big for this bike, it'll be yours,' I promised Alice, confident – with the overwhelming optimism of the very young – that my growth would be both rapid and substantial. What I didn't foresee – because of the further naive belief of the young that beauty lasts – was that within six months, a third of the tassels would be lost to attrition and those that remained, although still precious, would have sacrificed much of their sheen to the Vermont elements.

Alice, well-acquainted with second-hand goods, likely knew better than I did that mine was an empty promise, but whether because of her own youthful optimism or her inclination to believe her big sister, even this empty promise sufficed. I resumed pedalling hard, as I had done on the gravel outside the garage, and found that Mom was – unsurprisingly – correct; my speed was markedly better, although still not equal to the remembered rush of Kevin's Big Wheel careening downhill. I would get faster though, I felt sure, and when I did, no one – not Alice, currently sprinting after me, not Andy, back at home snitching frosting, not even Mom or Marvin – would be able to catch up with me.

I battled on for a few more days, always walking my Schwinn to the main dirt road at the bottom of our driveway rather than braving the slant of the driveway itself. When Dad came to collect the three of us for our first-ever trip to Cape Cod via the Shelburne farmhouse to which we would return to collect Annie, Mindy and Brian, I insisted on showing off my cycling prowess.

'I want to show you my best birthday present ever,' I told Dad, grabbing his hand and leading him towards the garage, 'Mom and Marvin gave it to me. It's a Schwinn.'

Dad winced. I thought I was squeezing his hand too hard and loosened my grip, but his pained expression did not disappear.

'What good luck that they picked something so wonderful,' Dad said, his voice oddly flat. 'I wonder what made them think of it.'

'It still has training wheels on, so I can't go at top speed yet,' I warned Dad.

'You won't need the training wheels for very long,' Dad said. 'In fact, it would be much better if you could learn to ride without them.'

'Mom says it took her a few months to learn with training wheels, and I only just got my bike.'

'Riding with training wheels and riding without them are not at all the same. My granddad took my training wheels off as soon as I got my first bike. I was whizzing around in no time.'

'Yeah, but I'm pretty fast even with the training wheels on. Wait until you see,' I bragged.

Dad acquiesced; he was wise enough to let my excitement trump his hurt. I determined to bike more impressively than ever before, because maybe when Dad witnessed me tearing off, leaving a cloud of fine dirt-road dust in my wake, he would admit that training wheels seemed to be working just fine for me, and the hood that had descended over his flecked green eyes would be pushed back.

Even my most concerted effort, however, couldn't take my Schwinn to the velocity I had hoped for, and Dad, while intrigued by my performance, maintained his previous position.

'That's a great start, Beth, but if you don't have those training wheels off by Thanksgiving I'll take them off for you.'

The pattern of spending Thanksgiving with Dad and Christmas with Mom had already been established, so I had no quibbles with Dad's basic premise, but I did spot a hitch in Dad's plan. 'So would I bring my bike with me when we come to visit?' I queried, wondering how me, my brother, my sister, and the Schwinn would all fit in Dad's car.

'No,' Dad said. 'We don't have a bike rack on the car. I'd do it here, before I whisked you all off to Shelburne. It takes almost no time to remove training wheels, Beth Anne,' Dad added, with the subtlest hint of mansplaining. 'Now let's go back to the house and round up your siblings. We've got to get back to Shelburne – Annie has dinner waiting.'

'What's for dinner?'

'Lasagna.'

'Mmm . . . I love lasagna. Let's see if I can bike up the driveway,' I said, suddenly in a hurry to deposit my bike safely in the garage and claim the front passenger seat of Dad's car as my own, a privilege only afforded me when Annie wasn't along for the ride.

* * *

The car was much more crowded on the way to Cape Cod, and Annie had the front seat the whole way, which – although disappointing – was to be expected. After what seemed like countless hours on the road, Dad started prepping us for our journey over the bridge.

'There are only two bridges onto Cape Cod,' Dad informed us, 'so the traffic may be substantial.'

'I expect it will be,' Annie said sardonically. 'It's a sunny August Saturday, and probably all the new renters will be on their way, just like we are. Not to mention if there's an accident, or even a bomb scare, like there was a while ago.'

'Well, that's the price you pay for vacationing on Cape Cod,' Dad said.

'I know,' Annie said, 'But I'm not looking forward to sitting in a traffic jam in this heat.'

'Maybe we'll hit the bridge at the sweet spot and sail right over,' Dad said optimistically.

Annie snorted. 'Maybe,' she said, but I could tell she didn't believe that for one minute.

Traffic did slow down as we approached the steel behemoth that was the through-arch Sagamore Bridge.

'Is there a bomb this time?' I asked from the boot of the sensible second-hand Volvo 145 Dad and Annie had purchased to replace Dad's green Datsun when it had dawned on them that there was absolutely no way two adults, five children, and seven suitcases would fit in the Datsun. The Volvo's only nod to sportiness was the red paint job, but even that couldn't offset the solid practicality of the wagon, built as it was to withstand impact with a moose from without or a horde of youngsters from within.

'A bomb?' Mindy, who hadn't been paying attention during the earlier parental discussion, repeated shrilly. The only bombs any of us children had directly experienced were the bombs that routinely exploded during the Saturday morning cartoons, particularly when Wile E Coyote was involved. No matter how stupendous the explosion, and regardless of the extent of the coyote's injuries, he always bounced back unharmed. Mindy may have thought that, should we indeed encounter a detonating device, we'd be treated to some glorious pyrotechnics, and we might briefly appear charred, but would be dusting ourselves off within moments, just like Wile E Coyote always did.

Alice, who had a more powerful instinct for self-preservation, could not appreciate the allure of explosives. She was also, as the youngest, the least well equipped to tolerate the exhaustion of the long car journey to an unknown destination.

'Alice,' Annie said in her most maternal tone, catching sight of Alice's tear-stained cheeks in the rear-view mirror, 'don't worry. I was just telling your dad that some time ago, the police had to close both of the bridges to Cape Cod when someone told them there was a bomb, but the police looked, and there was actually no bomb at all. You're as safe as safe can be, and in just a couple of hours you'll be able to dip your toes in the ocean! Won't that be wonderful?'

Alice wiped the tears from her face. 'Aren't there sharks in the ocean?'

'Yes,' Andy said, confirming Alice's fears. 'And sharks' skeletons are made of cartilage.'

'What's cartilage?' Brian asked, turning his face away from the view of the traffic to look directly at Andy.

'Cartilage is what your nose is made out of,' Andy answered.

'Maybe that's why my nose is so ugly,' Brian quipped.

'Your nose isn't ugly,' Annie retorted predictably. Brian was Annie's favourite: he knew it – we all knew it – but Annie would never in a million years have admitted as much. Annie's party line was that she loved us all equally; again, we five recognised that within that supposed equality, Brian was the most equal, Mindy the next, and Andy, Alice and I considerably less, but I approved of her good intentions even if they didn't fluently translate to emotional attachment.

'Your nose is aquiline,' Annie told Brian. 'Like the nose of a Greco–Roman sculpture.'

'Aqua-what? Aquatic? Is that why I'm such a good swimmer?'

'I'm a better swimmer than you are,' Mindy corrected Brian, jabbing him gently with her elbow from the middle of the back seat.

'That's because you have an even bigger shark nose than me,' Brian ribbed.

'I'm gonna break your shark nose for that,' Mindy declared.

'Kids, settle down,' Dad said from the driver's seat. 'We're almost on the bridge. Get ready to look at the view.'

The Volvo's engine hummed as the car ascended towards the bridge's midpoint. 'Boston is behind us,' Dad said, pointing vaguely towards the back seat. 'And the Atlantic,' Dad continued, with a dramatic sweeping gesture out his open window, 'is that way.'

I felt my stomach drop as the car drove over the crest of the bridge, but kept my face turned towards the expanse of blue shimmering at the eastern horizon. Never before had I seen the demarcation between earth and heaven as utterly level as it can only be over water, and there was something magical about the combined sharpness and emptiness of that dividing line that enthralled me.

My brothers and sisters had registered the view as instructed and then rapidly lost interest, but I twisted my body backwards to keep the ocean in my field of vision for as long as possible.

'Wow,' I said appreciatively, 'is that the Atlantic Ocean we're going to?'

'It's not exactly the ocean,' Dad explained. 'It's Cape Cod Bay. You can think of Cape Cod as an arm held out in front of you, like this.'

Dad took his right hand briefly off the steering wheel and crooked it like the arm of Popeye the Sailor.

'Ooh, look at those muscles,' Annie teased from the passenger seat.

Dad flexed his heretofore relaxed bicep and it did indeed rise, but only by a fraction. 'Maybe not,' Dad admitted, 'but my own brute strength is not the point of this illustration. This is a geography lesson.'

'Oh, sorry,' Annie said archly, 'let me just give Cape Cod a squeeze . . .'

Annie laid her long slender fingers, with their carefully home-manicured French-tip nails, on top of my father's arm and applied light pressure. She delivered her verdict of approval. 'That Cape Cod could withstand a tornado.'

'I grew up in Georgia, remember,' Dad said, more seriously. 'Even these muscles – although impressive, I admit – are no match for a tornado. Be that as it may – if this is Cape Cod, Beth Anne, then this part to the north is Cape Cod Bay. It's not the open ocean; it's protected by this arm of land.' Dad wiggled his forearm. 'There's a bay on the south side as well, and that part of the Atlantic is called Nantucket Sound, because the islands of Nantucket and Martha's Vineyard are off the southern coast. If you want to see the open Atlantic, you need to go to the eastern edge of Cape Cod, like here,' Dad said, tapping the outside of his forearm. 'We're going to Dennis, which is close to the elbow on the Cape Cod Bay side, because bays are more sheltered and better for kids to swim in.'

Dad, pleased to have imparted this information, put both hands back on the wheel, falsely believing that he had answered my question.

'But the ocean we saw from the bridge – is that the ocean we'll be by in Dennis? Is it the same bit?'

Dad looked confused, but Annie, whom I would later learn shared my abysmal sense of direction, understood what I was asking.

'She wants to know if Dennis was visible from the bridge, honey,' Annie clarified. 'Beth Anne wonders if she has now seen where we're headed. I'm not sure your geography lesson – excellent though it was – explained that to her.'

'Yes,' I said, grateful for Annie's assistance, 'that's what I wanted to know.'

I observed closely as a panoply of emotions cascaded across my father's face: bewilderment, disbelief, awareness, and finally – last but not least – tenderness.

'No,' Dad said, in the lower voice he employed when circumstances conspired to remind him that even I, the eldest at eight, was still very much a child. 'No, Beth Anne, you didn't see Dennis from the Sagamore Bridge. So I suppose it won't be quite the same ocean. But I think you're going to be very satisfied with the bit of ocean next to the house in Dennis.'

I relaxed into my seat, my back sticky from the heat. 'I think you're right,' I said to my father.

21

Waiting

The itsy-bitsy cottage in Dennis was so close to the Sea Street beach that Dad and Annie had no qualms about sending one or more of us from the beach back to the house to restock if we ran out of potato chips or soda. Beer and cigarettes were outside the kids' remit, but those supplies somehow never seemed to run low. There was an ancient sign at the top of the path leading down to the ocean enumerating the beach rules the Town of Dennis considered most important. Only three of the five of us could read the sign, and those who could – myself included – found its list of prohibited activities vastly entertaining, which could not have been the desired effect. The rules sign was like the lamp post of Narnia, the last bastion of the humdrum before the everyday black and white was replaced by the technicolour of the seaside holiday.

Cape Cod was not at all like Vermont. It didn't look like Vermont – the houses, thanks to stricter zoning regulations, were remarkable for the uniformity of their grey-shingled wooden exteriors whose only nod to individuality was the colour of their clapboard window shutters; the trees were not the straight, leafy maples of the mountains, but the crooked, needled pitch pines of the coast; the land was covered not in farmers' fields, but in sand dunes. Cape Cod didn't smell like Vermont – the briny sea air infiltrated my nostrils even inside the cottage – and it didn't sound like Vermont – from my narrow top bunk, the insistent rhythm of the waves, accompanied by Alice and Melinda's restful breathing, lulled me to sleep each night. Above all else, Cape Cod didn't feel like Vermont, not only physically – the burn of the hot sand on the undersides of my feet, the shocking cold of the ocean on my neck when I worked up the courage to immerse myself – but mentally, because whether on the beach or in the palm-sized cottage, I was not afraid. I had left fear back on the mainland. Crossing the Cape Cod Canal meant that we were indisputably in the sole care of Dad and Annie: Dad and Annie kissed, but only like actors did on TV; they bickered, but they didn't shout; they drank, but it didn't make them cry.

The routine in Dennis was comforting in its predictability. It was as if the adults were following a template – the beach holiday – so well known to them that it soon became familiar to all of us. The children woke first, then – at a more reasonable hour – the adults. After a hearty breakfast, Dad and Annie prepared the cooler and the beach bags while we all donned our swimsuits, and then our parents herded us down to the beach, where we all assisted in the selection of our patch, within the parameters prescribed by the adults. Hours of sunbathing, building sandcastles, playing wiffle ball, and swimming ensued, punctuated by chatting and snacking. In the late afternoon, when we returned to the cottage, we kids would play go fish while Annie fixed dinner and Dad either kept Annie company in the kitchen or joined us at cards.

On Tuesday night, after three days of go fish, Dad joined us again at the card table. 'It's time to widen your horizons, kids,' he announced. 'Go fish will only get you so far in life. It's time you learned a real game. I'm going to teach you gin rummy.'

'I like go fish,' Alice protested. 'I don't want to learn a new game!'

'Actually, Alice, as a special treat, you can be on my team for gin rummy to begin with. Of course you may get so good at gin rummy that you don't want me on your team after a few hands,' Dad joked. Dad was the best out of all of us at card games – he only lost when he wanted to lose. There was some ratio of wins to losses, transparent to him but nearly opaque to us, that Dad adhered to when it came to competition with children, but Dad was such an unconvincing loser that even when one of us claimed the win we sensed our victory was hollow.

'I do want you on my team,' Alice said to Dad, sensibly.

'In fact, should we all team up?' Dad suggested. 'Beth Anne, you can play with Mindy, and Brian, you pair up with Andy.'

I had nothing against Mindy, but I didn't want to share the glory should gin rummy prove to be my lucky game. 'I'd rather play for myself,' I said.

Dad, whose competitive nature I had inherited, approved of my drive to win in theory, but not in practice this time. 'We'll be playing with open hands, Beth Anne, just to learn the game, so we'll keep score, but the scores won't count. Once you've gotten the game under your belt, you can play a hand of your own.'

I acquiesced. Dad picked the cards up off the dark green vinyl of the folding card table with the deft hands of a card shark, and I looked on in awe as he riffle shuffled, ending with a bridge. Already by eight I had tried and failed countless times to replicate the card bridge, taking half of the split deck in each hand and applying pressure with each thumb only to sigh, unsurprised, when the cards shot out in every direction. Dad dealt three hands of ten, we laid our cards out on the table and play began.

It took only two rounds for me to learn the rules, and I was eager to play in my own right, but the same could not be said for Brian, who had lost interest and gone out to play swingball, nor for Alice, who lobbied Dad to pick from the discard pile every time she saw a face card – whether she could use the card or not – simply because she admired the royal regalia.

'If you want to play a hand of your own, Beth Anne, that's fine. Mindy, you can team up with Andrew if you want, but I'll stick with Alice, because she's on fire at the moment,' Dad said. Mindy, Andy and I raised our collective eyebrows, but Alice smiled her gap-toothed smile proudly, completely willing to believe that her face card 'strategy' was advantageous.

Mindy, who was more canny than me, turned to Andy and said sotto voce, 'If we play together, I think we might beat Beth Anne. We probably can't beat your dad, but who knows, maybe if we get lucky . . .'

Andy nodded. 'Can I hold the cards?' he asked.

'Sure,' Mindy answered.

Only when I went to pick up my cards did I realise that a hand of ten was not at all as easy to manage as a hand of five. Several of my cards fell onto the table, some face down, some – to my horror – face up.

'We have to start over,' I said, flustered. 'Everyone saw my cards.'

Dad remained calm. 'No, we don't,' he said. 'I didn't see them, and I don't think the others did either. Let me give you a tip about how to hold your cards. May I? I won't look, I promise.'

Dad held his hand out to receive my cards.

'How are you not going to look?' I asked, not wanting to be taken for a fool.

'OK, I will look,' Dad granted, 'but I promise to forget what I've seen straight away.'

I gave him my cards in a pile; he spread them instantly into a perfect fan. 'Here,' Dad said, leaning towards me. 'Hold them like this.'

Dad placed the fan of cards between my thumb and forefinger and pressed my thumb gently into a suitable position. 'Then when you need to sort them, don't let go with your thumb, just pull the card you're moving out with your other hand. So keep a firm grip on your hand the whole time.'

I looked over at Andy and Mindy – Andy was holding their shared cards as if he'd been playing all his life.

I scowled. 'How come Andy can do it without any trouble?'

Dad deflected. 'He can hold them, but can he play? Why don't you go first, Beth Anne, and we'll go clockwise from there.'

I still couldn't tell my left from my right, so clockwise versus counterclockwise was beyond my ken, but I trusted Dad to moderate the proceedings.

The game settled into a rhythm: the draw, the assessment, the discard. I'd played enough cards to have suits (hearts and spades) and even cards (aces, eights, and queens) that I preferred, but all of the cards were like talismen, exerting their hold on me to keep within the orderly microcosm of the game, where luck dealt me a hand, skill helped me play it and both determined the outcome. What didn't affect the result was cheating, which was firmly not allowed (except for Dad's occasional pre-ordained losses) – this was important, because it kept the game both fair and within boundaries.

I could have played for hours, but after a few hands, when the smell of the clam chowder had become so tantalising that all of us were pausing once a minute to inhale, like dogs sniffing for scents, Annie called out from the kitchen that it was time for us to leave our game and set the dining table.

Not everything at the Cape was as predictable as cards. Take the ocean. Glimpsing the sleeping blue giant in the distance from the heights of the Sagamore Bridge did not prepare me for meeting that same giant wide awake and playing with my feet on the beach in

Dennis. I was surprised at how noisy the ocean was at high tide – how the waves, even in a bay when the sea was calm, progressed from susurration through rumble to roar with every whitecap – and beyond that, I was astounded at its enormity. My parade of primary schools had each wasted no time before commencing indoctrination in American history and by second grade I was already familiar with my country's war of independence from British rule. The British, I knew, were the enemy – the stuffy men in the dapper red coats and white wigs kicking anybody who didn't like their church out of Great Britain and charging far too much money for tea – but they were also family. The battles that resulted in the signing of the Declaration of Independence by the Founding Fathers had been fought between those Founding Fathers (I believed at the time) and the fathers from the mother country – the British. It seemed more like a family feud than a war to me, or perhaps I chose to colour it that way, because not only did the British strike me as grandfatherly, but Mom had also informed us that we had an actual great-grandfather who was indeed straight from Birmingham, England, who had died before I was born (although not in the American Revolution), and who linked me directly to the Old Country. I was further tied to England by my love for the grandfatherly storytellers of the Narnia and Middle Earth tales, CS Lewis and JRR Tolkien. When I stood for the first time on that Cape Cod beach and cast my eye to the distant horizon, it was England I believed I would arrive at should I set sail in a straight line. I must have kept this belief to myself, otherwise Dad would have quickly disabused me of that notion by informing me that Portugal, not Great Britain, lay directly across the immense body of water that was the Atlantic Ocean. Or perhaps my desire to see England was so strong that even if Dad did once correct me, I let the inconvenient truth roll off like water off a duck's back and carried on privately waving across the pond to Great Britain as I saw fit.

Nothing about the ocean stayed the same from moment to moment; even the ocean's location was changeable. The rivers I swam in at home in Vermont were always in motion internally, but their path, as far as I could tell, never changed. The Atlantic, however – subject as it was to the powerful pull of the moon – was constantly moving, in a way that I could make neither rhyme nor reason of: sometimes the beach stretched out for what seemed like miles before the water's edge, leaving tide pools scattered around like polka dots; sometimes the ocean seemed on its way to devouring the dimpled white sand laden with stripy beach towels and squat metal-framed folding chairs. If the ocean had been cooperative enough to follow the same pattern every day, I might have accepted its vicissitudes, but the ocean didn't care what worked for me.

I railed about this lack of consistency to my father. 'We get to the beach at about the same time every day, but the ocean isn't in the same place two days in a row. Why not?'

'The ocean is where it always is, Beth Anne. It's the tide that changes, not the ocean itself. The tide is linked to the gravitational pull of the moon, and low tide and high tide are later each day because the moon rises later each day, by about an hour.'

'I wish it was never low tide,' I complained. 'I don't like having to walk so far to get to the water.'

'I prefer high tide too,' Dad agreed, 'because I'm a sailor at heart. If we had a sailboat – maybe a little Sunfish – we'd only be able to take it out easily at high tide. At low tide it would be a long slog with the boat on wheels – I wouldn't be up for that, and I don't think any of you would be.'

I liked the idea of a sailboat very much, and the idea of pulling a boat along on wheels sounded like an adventure rather than a chore. 'I would pull the Sunfish down at low tide,' I assured Dad, who appeared dubious, but I chalked that up to his underestimation of my strength. I held both arms out at right angles and flexed my eight-year-old biceps to demonstrate my capability. Dad nodded in appreciation.

'So when are you going to get one?' I asked.

Dad sighed. 'It's not a question of just going to the store and buying a boat, Beth Anne. Sailboats – even little ones like a Sunfish – cost a lot of money, not just to buy but to maintain.'

'Maybe you could ask for a sailboat for Christmas?' I suggested. After all, I had just been given a fabulous bicycle for my birthday – maybe Santa Claus, like Mom and Marvin, had a penchant for transportation.

Dad pulled thoughtfully at his moustache. 'Maybe I could,' he conceded.

Most incalculable of all was the ocean's behaviour. I had learned to read the current of the Vermont rivers; I knew that the faster the water swirled on the surface, the stronger the pull would be of the water beneath, and the harder I would have to fight to maintain my position. If I wanted an easy swim, I looked for the pools and eddies; if I wanted more excitement, I started at the riffle and let the run carry me downstream. In contrast, the waves of the ocean, just like its tides, seemed arbitrary. If I stood waist-deep in the water, sooner or later a wave would come along with enough power to knock me off my feet, but I couldn't say whether it would be the fourth wave or the fourteenth; although I learned quickly that the higher the wave, the greater its punch, there were often waves that tricked me – waves that looked benign during their entire approach, only to then pick me up like so much flotsam and jettison me where they saw fit. I walked a tightrope between playing with the ocean and letting the ocean play with me, but it was a balancing act I couldn't resist, even when the ocean won, as it did one day when I had my hair down.

My hair, at eight, was still essentially uncut – trimmed, yes, but cut, no. If loose, it cascaded down my back in honey waves; if tied, it was as thick as an actual pony's tail. The tug on my scalp, when my locks were neatly pulled back, was constant and tiring, so I favoured allowing them free reign, as on that Wednesday when the rogue wave caught me and tossed me onto the ocean floor. My hair wrapped itself across my nose and mouth as I twisted my way back to the water's surface, only to be thrown down again by the rogue wave's successor. I opened my eyes – something I hadn't yet done in the sea – but it was futile; I was blinded by both the salt and the same locks that were suffocating me. Disoriented, I fought against the water, raising both my hands to clear my face so the sun, beating down through the green water, could lead me back to the surface.

I was in awe of the ocean. When Annie suggested on Thursday evening after dinner that we should all take an evening walk along the beach in our pyjamas to watch the sun set, there was groaning from some of us kids, but not from me. I was wearing my favourite nightgown: the white flowers now indistinct against the pink, faded from repeated washing, the elastic at the neck and at the end of the short sleeves stretched past functionality, the above-knee length considerably shorter than when I had first started wearing it at least one year previously, if not two. I was barefoot and the sand, where it lay now in shadow, was cool as it sifted between my bare toes. I was still the eldest, even on Cape Cod, but under no obligation there to keep track of my younger siblings, so I didn't. Instead I walked out far ahead of everyone else towards the tangerine sun which hung over the mighty water, suspended by threads of deeper orange and a lilac the colour of clove Necco wafers. When my head start was such that I could no longer hear the rest of my family chattering, I picked a dune on the right overlooking the beach, scrambled up and settled down like Christina in the field in the Andrew Wyeth painting that had followed us from house to house, to watch in rapture as the sun sank, inch by inch, below the horizon. Dad had been trailing me, leaving Annie to herd the other four, and Dad had his camera with him.

'Don't move,' Dad said when he was within earshot. 'Just stay as you are. Just keep looking at the sunset – I'm going to take your picture.'

I had been photographed, with and without my siblings, plenty of times before, and sometimes the photos had been staged – 'Lean against this tree', 'Get closer to your brother', that sort of thing – but this was the first time I was photographed as art. The picture Dad wanted wasn't of me looking at him, it was of me looking at the sunset – away from him – and the expression he had wanted to capture with me unawares had not been one of conventional childhood happiness, but one of yearning. I wasn't only myself, kneeling in sand before the glorious sun, I was a metaphor for something for my father, but while I was a tangible vehicle, the tenor of the metaphor – however much I wished to grasp it – remained beyond my reach.

22

Real Soon

Mom had warned us before we left for Cape Cod that we wouldn't be coming back to the same house. I didn't understand what was wrong with the house in East Montpelier, but then I hadn't understood what had been wrong with any of the houses we had left to that point, so it was unempirical of me to expect comprehension. I only hoped my bike wouldn't be forgotten. In previous moves, treasures had gone missing. My orange Hot Wheels dune buggy was a case in point; when I had enquired as to my toy's whereabouts after we left Burlington for Duxbury, Mom had looked at me blankly.

'Your what?'

'My Hot Wheels dune buggy. It had an orange top.'

'I don't remember that particular toy, Beth Anne. You must have other Hot Wheels? Why don't you play with them instead?'

'I don't. They're all Andy's.'

'I'm sure Andrew would share with you.'

'I left my dune buggy in the sandbox.'

Mom began to lose patience. 'Beth Anne – that wasn't an easy time. Maybe the dune buggy didn't quite make it out of the sandbox. Tell

Andrew he has to give you one of his Hot Wheels.'

This was not a viable solution. 'I'll know it's really his.'

'It won't be his any more, it'll be yours.'

Dad didn't drive us to our new home after the Cape Cod trip. Instead, Mom met us at a rest area close to our new, more southernly exit at what must have been a pre-ordained meeting time. I spotted Mom as soon as we pulled in; she was sitting in her car, several parking spaces away from the nearest vehicle, with all the windows rolled down; she was resting her arm on the car windowsill, tapping the ashes from her cigarette absent-mindedly onto the ground.

Dad chose to park next along in the line of cars, rather than further from the building but next to Mom. Maybe he wanted us kids to have the shortest walk possible to the public toilets, or maybe his mind had been so trained by the study of engineering that to leave a gap where one was not meant to be was unthinkable. Or, most likely, Dad had some inkling of how much Mom and Annie disliked each other and thought it best to put a reasonable amount of distance between them.

Mom stepped out of the car casually, leaving the door wide open. Instead of lessening the distance between herself and us by approaching, she turned towards us from where she stood, so the body of her car acted as a massive metal shield.

'Hi, Mom!' I called out.

'Hi, kids,' Mom said. 'If you need to use the toilet, go do it now – it's not a long ride to the new house, but it's a bumpy one. Hello, Mark.'

Dad and Annie had both extricated themselves from the car now, legs stiff after the long drive from Dennis, Massachusetts.

'And hello, Annie,' Mom added, and her tone was so cold that any notion I had entertained of giving Mom a hello hug or Annie a goodbye hug withered like a plant caught by an early frost.

'Hello, Liza,' Annie said icily.

'I need to pee,' Andy said, shifting uncomfortably in the middle of the back seat, where he had suffered through the last long leg of the journey.

'Me too,' Alice added, wincing.

We were nearly home, so I reassumed the mantle of responsible big sister as was expected of me. 'I'll take you,' I said to Alice.

When Alice and I exited the building, after our hasty flick through some of the more colourful tourist brochures carefully organised in a purpose-built wooden display unit in the visitors' centre foyer, Mom had returned to the driver's seat of her car and was either still nursing the same cigarette or had lit a new one. Annie was back in the front passenger seat of Dad's car, but her arm was draped over the back of the driver's seat, enabling Annie to more easily twist her body towards the back seat while she engaged Brian in conversation. Only Dad was exactly where he had been when I had turned my back on the adults to visit the restroom, and even his permanence was an illusion, because in reality he had spent our absence transferring our luggage, such as it was, from his car to Mom's. Dad opened his arms wide in my direction the moment I dithered, unsure which way I should point my feet.

'Come here, Beth Anne,' Dad said. 'And you too, Alice. You're not getting away without a hug.'

We both complied. Dad knelt down and wrapped us in a tight embrace, loosened only to beckon to Andy to come join the scrum when my brother moseyed out of the rest area building seconds later.

'I love you kids,' Dad said, his voice muffled by my hair. 'I'm so glad Annie and I had the chance to take you all with us to Cape Cod.'

Alice began to cry. Dad stood up, perhaps realising that he was making matters worse not better, and tousled her hair ever so gently. 'Don't be sad, Alice. Just think about all the fun we had, and remember that I'll see you again real soon.'

I knew that my 'real soon' and Dad's 'real soon' were not at all the same. For me, 'real soon' meant later that same day, or at a stretch, tomorrow; for Dad, 'real soon' meant in a couple of weeks, or worse, in a month or two, or even three. Maybe I would have told Alice that truth if we'd been solely under the aegis of Dad and Annie, because it wouldn't have then fallen to me to pick up Alice's broken pieces, but as it was – caught in limbo between the two cars and my two roles – I kept that insight to myself.

'Come on, kids,' Mom called out. 'Marvin's fixing dinner back at the new house.'

Andy had already wriggled out of Dad's arms and was meandering over towards Mom's car.

'Let's go, Alice,' I said. 'Let's go see your new room.'

'I don't want a new room,' Alice sobbed. 'I want my same room.'

'Alice,' I said, now using my best and most convincing big sister voice. 'Come on.'

Annie piped up from the passenger seat. 'Mark, it's been a long day, and I want to get Melinda and Brian home before nightfall.'

That was enough for Dad to set us on our way, repeating his earlier assurance. 'Run along now, girls. I'll see you again real soon.'

I escorted Alice, still tearful, over to Mom's car, and helped her into the back seat, displacing Andy, who then bagged the coveted front. We waved limply as Dad's car passed us on the way back to the interstate.

'The new house is great, but what's really special is the view from just off the exit,' Mom informed us when we were all settled in her car. Alice had wiped her face just before reaching Mom's car; she had not let any further tears fall, but only through Herculean effort.

I asked the question I'd been led towards. 'Why is the view from the exit so special?'

Mom, who had arranged the set piece, now took the goal shot. 'Randolph is in the most beautiful valley. The exit is up at the crest of the hill, and when you drive off the ramp, it's all there laid out before you – the Green Mountains, the pointy white church steeples – there's even a ski area, in case your father ever wants to take you skiing.'

I was easily persuaded. Maybe, if Mom loved the view so much, this home would be our last home. Maybe Mom would stay enthusiastic about this new location for years, maybe even for enough years for me to grow up.

Mom interrupted my reverie. 'But the house isn't actually in Randolph. It's in Braintree.'

'Brain Tree?' Andy spluttered, suddenly paying attention. 'Brain Tree?'

'That's disgusting,' I said, and the daydream of a forever home vanished like another mirage. 'Why is it called Brain Tree?'

Andy had a macabre theory. 'Somebody probably carved out a dead man's brain and stuck it on a tree there. Like in a war. So brain . . . tree.'

'Ugh!' Alice exclaimed, and her distress began to swell again.

I attempted to quell the tide. 'Andy, that's gross and there is no war. Stop scaring Alice.'

'I'm not scaring Alice,' Andy retorted. 'I'm just telling you why I think it's called Brain Tree.'

'Kids,' Mom implored from the front seat. 'First of all, keep your eyes open, because we're about to take Exit 4, and second of all, Braintree is the name of a town in England. Lots of place names in New England were taken from place names in England – that's why it's called "New England". Get it?'

'Maybe the town in England was called "Braintree" because some-body stuck a brain in a tree there,' Andy suggested, not to be deterred.

'Oh, Andy, stop it, you're going to make me throw up,' I said.

Mom, who had found it necessary to pull over on account of Andy or Alice's travel sickness in the past – I was somehow immune to that particular childhood ailment – reprimanded me. 'Don't talk about throwing up in the car, Beth Anne. The last thing I want to be doing right now is driving around with the smell of vomit in the car for the next month. Now would you look at that, kids?'

For the second time in as many weeks I was on a promontory overlooking a landscape of inconceivable natural beauty, but here, unlike from the crest of the Sagamore Bridge, the horizon was anything but a straight line. Instead, with its bluish-green peaks and troughs, the line between earth and sky reminded me of the scutes along the back of the eponymous character from *The Reluctant Dragon*.

'Do you see where the forest is cut away in straight lines, on that mountain over there?'

I followed Mom's pointed finger. 'Yes,' I confirmed.

'That's the ski area - Pinnacle.'

'Do you think it's good for sledding too?' I asked. We had sleds, but we didn't have skis – yes, maybe Dad would take us skiing, but I expected that would happen 'real soon', and I was already planning how to take to the snow in the meantime.

'They don't usually allow sleds on ski slopes, Beth Anne,' Mom informed me. 'That would be too dangerous for both the skiers and the sledders. But I'm sure there are plenty of fantastic sledding hills here. I mean, just look at those mountains – how could there not be?'

Mom had a valid point. We descended Route 66 deep into the valley; the houses, sparse along the hill, became more numerous as we reached the valley floor. We crossed a short bridge over a wide, shallow brook, and entered the village proper. The lawns became flatter, more rectangular and better manicured, the number of cars increased and then we came to a stop light. There had been no stop lights in East Montpelier, so the novelty was thrilling, although not for Mom, who – because the light was red – was required to perform a hill stop behind a pickup truck on an extremely steep slope. When the light changed, Mom – determined not to roll backwards into the car of what could be our new neighbours – revved the engine until our car sounded like a lion waking up hungry. Our car shot forward only to then come to another stop as Mom blinked to turn right.

'That hill stop will take some getting used to,' Mom said, 'but this next hill in the winter is going to be absolutely treacherous. It's pretty terrifying even now. Hold on to your hats, kids – get ready for Elm Street.'

This Elm Street, as it happened, wasn't at all like the Elm Street we'd lived on in Montpelier, which had been essentially flat although next to a steep cliff. I hadn't ever been tall enough to ride the roller coaster at Dorney Park, back in Pennsylvania, but if I had, I was sure the ascent would have felt like the initial slope of this Elm Street. After nearly a minute of holding my breath – as a precaution in case the car began to slip backwards – the road levelled out, and we passed several reasonably sized and a couple of enormous houses.

'Does our new house look like one of those?' I asked Mom optimistically, pointing at a building with space for at least six, if not ten, bedrooms.

'You'd like that, wouldn't you?' Mom said. 'No – it's certainly spacious enough for us, but it's not going to sleep your entire class, Beth Anne. Our house is on a dirt road, just like in East Montpelier. You tell me why a city girl like me keeps ending up living like a country bumpkin . . .'

'If we live on dirt roads, does that make us country bumpkins?' I asked.

'It certainly doesn't make you city slickers,' Mom said.

'But we used to live in Burlington? Alice was born in Burlington. She must be a city slicker,' I reasoned.

Alice tried her new sobriquet on for size. 'City swicker,' she said, her eyes alight with the gleam of exclusive ownership.

210

'Slicker,' I corrected Alice.

'Swicker,' Alice echoed as best she could.

'I'm not sure being born in Burlington really qualifies you as a city slicker,' Mom said. Alice looked confused, as though she'd been offered an ice cream only to then have the offer withdrawn.

Mom, who'd developed the skill of rear-view mirror checks to a fine art, noticed and backtracked. 'Then again, Burlington is the biggest city in all of Vermont, so maybe you are a city slicker after all, Alice.'

The initial flurry of homes after Elm Street flattened out slowed to a few scattered one-storey ranch houses, then these too petered out and the forest took over. Soon the road opened up on the right-hand side and the hill opposite us became visible, but because we had gained so much altitude ourselves, it was as if someone had taken a scythe and whacked off all but the peak. A brook wound through the fields spread out between us and the opposite summit like a dark jagged scar. My legs ached to run across that expanse of land, to scurry down the sandy bank of the brook on one side then up the other side, legs wet and ice cold on the outside but warmed by the exertion inside. If I could reach the most distant point, I was sure I would be rewarded, although I wasn't entirely sure with what.

The asphalt ended a couple of minutes later, when we came to a three-pronged fork in what was now Flint Road: we could take a sharp left towards Hollyhock Hill, a slight left up Flint Road, or a slight right down Labounty Road. Mom set our course for Flint Road and within seconds the sunlight all but disappeared as the forest engulfed us on both sides. The trees were thicker, taller and closer than they had been even in remote East Montpelier. And then, just when I was growing accustomed to the forest, Mom pulled in to a driveway on the left, next to a sprawling white wooden farmhouse.

'Welcome home, kids,' Mom said.

'I'm hungry,' Andy said.

'Maybe you can catch yourself a fish for dinner in the pond at the end of the driveway,' Mom joked.

'OK,' Andy said.

Mom, twigging that Andy was indeed keen to take her up on her offer, corrected herself. 'Actually, all of you need to stay well away from that pond unless there's an adult with you. And Beth Anne does not count as an adult.'

There were frogs by the pond, there was a climbing tree outside the kitchen window, and there were enough bedrooms for each of us kids to have our own, but I still missed East Montpelier. Marvin had lived in the house in East Montpelier for so many years that every square inch of floor space had been known to him and in being known, had been loved. This new house had maybe been loved by its previous occupants, but never by any of us, and that mattered.

I resented the inside of the new house like a daughter resents a father's mistress – what had my parents seen in this building that they didn't see in our home back in East Montpelier? Yes, this farmhouse was novel, but did that necessarily make it better? I didn't think so. Why couldn't they have stayed in the old house? What would happen if my parents became bored of this new location? When would I be finished with the upheaval that was part and parcel of every move to a new house, a new town or even a new state?

I had no such qualms, however, about accepting the land outside the farmhouse walls. I adopted the narrow path around the field across the driveway as my own personal track for walking, running or, best of all, biking. Mom and Marvin thankfully hadn't forgotten my Schwinn, and the perimeter path around the field on the hill proved the perfect velodrome. After several days of cycling around the acre, avoiding the occasional patties left by the cows that came over from the working dairy farm up the road to graze every so often, I felt ready to have my training wheels removed. Mom obliged, whipping a Phillips-head screwdriver out of her toolbox and setting my two wheels free, but she had never been a runner and she drew the line at giving me a running start for my maiden ride on two wheels, turning that job over to Marvin, who accepted. With Shiva loping along in front of us, Marvin pushed my Schwinn up to the top of the field so I could start on a flat rather than an uphill stretch.

'You ready for this?' he asked me rhetorically.

'I am.'

'Remember, Beth Anne – just keep pedalling, especially through the turns. And lean *in* to the turns, not away from them. It's counter-intuitive, but it works. If you feel like you're going too fast, pedal backwards to brake, just like you did with the training wheels on. Ready?'

'Ready,' I said, and I adjusted my position from straddling the bright red frame to seated on the red-and-white leather saddle while Marvin steadied me, his left hand on my left ribcage, his right hand gripping the bicycle seat.

'Here's how it will work,' Marvin explained. 'You start pedalling, fast as you can, and I'll run with you, counting down from four. When I get to "blast off", I'll let go and then you're on your own. Got it?'

'Got it,' I said, admiring my tassels as I leaned forwards, my hands clenched round the sticky white grips of the handlebars.

I tramped down and the bike began to move, unsteadily at first, then more surely. Marvin kept one hand on me and one hand on the bike seat as he trotted along, calling out numbers: 'Four . . . three . . . two . . . one . . . blast off! Keep pedalling, Beth Anne!'

The decreased friction of two wheels as opposed to four was immediately noticeable; now nothing – not even the pebbles of the dirt track – prevented me from reaching a speed I had previously only dreamt of. My streamers were living up to their name, the wind was rushing against my squinted eyes and I was invincible. I thought of Tovah and our studies of mythology; I missed her then as I raced along, because I wanted so much to tell her that I was no longer only a girl, I was also a centaur, but with wheels instead of hooves.

23

Prey

Instead of Tovah, I met the kids on the bus. The bus was a sunshine-yellow behemoth with black stripes that called to mind the giant bumblebees that zig-zagged among the purple clover. The sound of the bus lumbering down Flint Road was more like the fearful noise of swarming locusts, however, than the cheerful buzz of a friendly bumblebee. At the front, the bus had a protruding nose with a massive slatted grille – like the gills of a shark, and – in case there was any residual doubt as to its identity – the words 'School Bus' in black capital letters several inches tall over the enormous front windshield. The driver, Mr Chase, controlled the glass double doors at the front.

The first day Andy and I took the bus, Mom stepped aboard with us.

'Hi,' Mom said to the bus driver. 'This is Beth Anne, this is Andrew, and this is their first time on a school bus.'

'Welcome aboard, young man and little lady,' Mr Chase said.

Mom glanced at the kids already sitting casually on the green vinyl benches. When some of them returned her glance, she smiled her widest smile and waved. Some of them waved back – because that

215

was the polite response when waved at by other kids' moms – but others ignored her and carried on chatting. I was proud of my mom for being braver than me; I myself kept my eyes glued to the floor.

'Will you drop them back in the same place?' Mom asked Mr Chase.

'Yes, ma'am, that's my job.'

Mom looked Mr Chase directly in the eye. I'd seen a few male strangers flinch when she did that – some looked down, as though Mom had laser eyes like Superman and was about to set them on fire – but Mr Chase held her gaze comfortably.

'Take good care of them,' Mom instructed the bus driver.

'I'll do what I can, ma'am, but I'll mostly be driving the bus,' Mr Chase replied frankly.

'That's very honest of you. I imagine driving this big bus on these narrow dirt roads takes a lot of skill. You must be a good driver.'

'I've been driving this bus for a lot of years now, ma'am, so I guess if I weren't a skilled bus driver to begin with, I am now, but I'll tell you what – even for a good bus driver, these roads ain't fun when they're icy. Now if you could say goodbye to your youngsters, ma'am, I've still got kids I gotta pick up.'

'Of course. And I'm glad that you don't have to worry about the roads being icy just yet,' Mom said.

'Me too,' Mr Chase agreed.

Mr Chase, who had already been very patient, waited while I turned around to wave to my mother, who stood guard in our driveway until the glass doors of the school bus closed behind me. He even waited while Andy and I made our way down the striped black rubber matting of the aisle, past the faces of all the unfamiliar children – some staring, some taking no heed – to the first free bench towards the back.

Andy and I stopped sitting together before the end of the first week. Andy joined a posse of boys his own age, while a clutch of older girls – fifth- and sixth-graders – took me under their collective wing.

'Hey,' one of the older girls said as I was about to pass by on my way to what had become my preferred bench one morning after Andy had already left my side in favour of his new friends. 'What's your name again? Beth Anne, right?'

I blushed. 'Yes,' I said. 'Beth Anne. Or just Beth.'

'You have beautiful hair, Beth Anne,' the girl said. She was blonde too, like me, but her hair just skimmed her shoulders, while mine reached the hollow of my back. 'Can I braid it?'

'Sure,' I said, keen to ingratiate myself with this girl and her friends, because to have these older girls braid my hair would be much better than to have the boys at the back of the bus pull it.

'Come sit with us,' the girl said.

The first girl oohed and aahed as she wove half of my hair into a braid.

'Let me do the other side, Jessie,' begged a brown-haired girl in a short-sleeved orange turtleneck.

Jessie capitulated without a fight. 'It looks soft, Sharon, but it's really thick,' she said to her friend. 'My arms are tired just from doing the one side.'

Sharon pulled quite hard and I flinched involuntarily.

'Sorry,' Sharon said. 'I wanna be sure to get everything in.'

I nodded mutely.

'Where did you live before Braintree?' Sharon asked me.

'East Montpelier.'

'Why'd you move?'

'I don't know.'

Sharon looked at me in surprise. 'You don't know why you moved? Did your dad get a job here?'

I considered whether or not to try to explain to Sharon and Jessie, who was now listening intently, that I didn't live with my dad but that my mom's current boyfriend, who would hopefully one day be my stepdad, had not gotten a new job, though from what I understood my mom had. It all seemed too convoluted to explain, so I answered simply, 'No.'

'You don't sound like a Vermonter,' Jessie said, half-accusingly. 'Where were you born?'

'I was born in Illinois and I have some of my mom's accent. She's Pennsylvania Dutch,' I explained, and although I had meant to be humble, I could hear for myself the tinge of boastfulness in my voice.

Sharon and Jessie put me in my place. 'I knew it,' Jessie said triumphantly, 'she's a flatlander.'

'What's this about being Dutch? Is your mom Dutch?' Sharon said, as she yanked again on an errant strand of my hair.

I winced. 'Not Dutch. *Pennsylvania* Dutch – like Moravian?'

Sharon sighed. 'This is getting worse and worse. Mor- what?'

'Moravian – like from Moravia. Moravia used to be a country but then it was taken over by Czechoslovakia.'

Jessie and Sharon gaped at me. 'Czecho- what?' Jessie said.

'Czechoslovakia. It's a country in Europe.'

'I'll ask Mr Rice about that when we get to school,' Sharon said to Jessie. 'Can you spell the name of that country, Beth Anne?'

'C-Z-E-C-H-O-S-L-O-V-A-K-I-A,' I intoned, in my best imitation of the voice Mom had used so many times with me, especially when I had been struggling to master the spelling of my own name the previous year. It had taken me months of practice to reliably leave a space between 'Beth' and 'Anne,' to capitalise the 'A' of 'Anne,' and to write 'Anne' with two 'n's and an 'e' on the end.

'I can't believe you can spell Czecho-vakia when you're only in third grade!' Sharon said, her mouth hanging open. Sharon shouted over the not insignificant noise of the bus to her friends two benches away. 'Florence! Patty! You've got to hear this! The new girl can spell Czecho-vakia!'

'What? What's Czecho-vakia?' Patty yelled back.

'Patty, haven't you ever heard of Czechoslovakia?' Florence said, jabbing Patty with her elbow. 'It's a country in Europe – one of those little tiny ones. It's on the world map from National Geographic.'

I made a mental note of Florence's better-than-average general knowledge and hoped that Florence also liked to braid hair, so I'd get the chance to sit close to her soon.

'OK, smart alec, can you spell it then?' Patty asked Florence, placing both hands on her hips like Wonder Woman and fixing Florence with a matching Wonder Woman stare.

'I didn't say I could spell it, I just said I've heard of it,' Florence said, bristling. 'The new girl can spell it – ask her.'

Suddenly all four girls were looking at me expectantly. Had they been waiting for me to answer a question about my personal life, I might have crumpled like a villain confronted by the Fantastic Friends, but they weren't; they just wanted me to spell, and that was something I could do, something far easier than actually conversing. 'C-Z-E-C-H-O-S-L-O-V-A-K-I-A,' I repeated.

'See?' Sharon squealed. 'I told you she could do it!'

'What else can she spell?' Jessie wondered. 'Can you spell 'Montpelier', Beth Anne?'

I obliged.

'That was too easy. You have to think of something harder,' Sharon half-whispered to Jessie.

And with that, thanks to my dual circus sideshow appeal, my bus journeys for the rest of the year were straightforward: yes, I had to tolerate offering my hair to anybody who wanted to touch it, and yes, I had to perform public spelling when required, but either of those were a small price to pay to avoid being ridiculed or ostracized.

Unfortunately, the girls who adopted me on the bus were all Lower Branch girls, in grades four through six. The girls on the bus who were actually my schoolmates – the Upper Branch girls in grades one through three – were not nearly as easily entertained. With them, my special skills, such as they were, were more likely to incite jealousy than amity.

The Upper Branch of the Braintree Elementary School was a confusing place, not least because of its name. It made no sense whatsoever to me that the Upper Branch was for the younger kids and the Lower Branch was for the older cohort. The names, Mom explained, had to do with the river rather than the ages of the children, but I saw nothing in the river either to distinguish one section from the other – it was all river to me – and the nonsensical names were two of my many complaints about my new school, complaints that I kept to myself as far as possible. When Mom asked outright about the work we were doing at school though, I had no choice but to tell her that my work – once Mrs Neill had pegged my abilities in reading, writing and arithmetic – consisted almost exclusively of worksheets: flimsy papers with sums printed in purple ink, sometimes so freshly mimeographed that they were still damp.

'Why, oh why, is your teacher having you do worksheets?' Mom burst out.

'Because I finish before the others,' I said.

'So she's penalising you by giving you exceedingly boring, repetitive busy work? What about giving you something challenging to do? Or even just letting you read? Reading would be far more beneficial to your education than mind-numbing worksheets.' Mom spat out the word 'worksheets' as though it were a swear word. 'I'm going to have to speak to this Mrs Neill,' Mom fumed.

I imagined my mother, in a maelstrom of righteous anger, sweeping into the classroom where Mrs Neill presided. Mrs Neill had short salt-and-pepper hair that she kept in a strict state of precisely spaced waves, tamed through liberal use of hairspray so that no single hair was ever out of place. She wore glasses that ended in triangular points, like the cat's-eye tail lights of a '59 Chevy, but her beliefs about children and education hearkened back to the era of the Model T. There would be little common ground for Mom and Mrs Neill to stand on.

'I don't mind the worksheets,' I said.

This had the desired effect of unpicking Mom's wires – the vein in her neck retreated, her breath slowed and I hoped that if Mom did charge into my classroom, she might sizzle, but she wouldn't explode.

'How can you like worksheets?' Mom said, incredulous.

'They're good practice. I would rather read my book,' I conceded, and Mom stiffened up again, though not to the same degree, 'but worksheets are OK.'

What I didn't tell Mom was that if she *were* going to storm my Upper Branch classroom, what she should be talking to Mrs Neill about was my nearly complete lack of friends, not the mimeographed worksheets.

I brought packed lunch to school like the other kids, but my packed lunch was often not enough to fill my tummy, given the wide variation in the regularity and amount of our family's breakfasts and dinners. When and how much we ate depended on an algorithm shrouded in mystery, including variables like what food was in the house, whether or not Mom had gone to work that day, and how much both Mom and Marvin had partaken of the ever-present jug of Ernest Gallo; that last variable, one might think, would only affect the evening meal, but in fact – given Mom's ever-increasing thirst – it had the power to impact breakfast as well. I couldn't help but stare at the wonders contained in the lunchboxes of the other children – rich chocolate Devil Dogs wrapped in crinkly plastic, Lay's potato chips, kid-sized packages of Sun-maid raisins in tiny red boxes with the Sun-maid lady – who looked like a happier, agriculturally minded Snow White – on the front. The other kids noticed my hungry eyes, and would sometimes offload parts of their lunch they didn't want in my direction – a half-eaten egg salad sandwich here, a bag of slimy peeled carrots there. Every once in a while, one of them would take extra pity on me and offer me a bite of their midday treasure, or even the entire item, if they happened to despise the treat their mothers had carelessly or perversely included for them that day. I never turned down a gift of food and I appreciated my classmates' generosity, but I was less grateful for the nickname they gave me in consequence: 'Garbage Can.' The particularly cruel children found the name hilarious and used it every lunchtime.

'Guess what, Garbage Can?' one of my benefactor/tormentors said one Thursday. 'Mom packed bologna with mustard today and I hate mustard! Here you go!'

'Thanks,' I said meekly.

The girl and her friends crowded round me.

'Are you gonna eat it?'

'Yeah, come on, Garbage Can, how hungry are you today?'

I humoured the ringleader by chomping slowly on the unwanted sandwich, my mouth burning from the spicy French's mustard, until it was all gone.

'Ugh! Did you see that? She ate it! She really is a garbage can!'

'Oh, shut up,' said Janine, the only girl in the class who seemed to consider me a human being rather than a human sideshow. 'Penny, just leave her alone. Come on Beth Anne, come play jump rope with me,' Janine commanded.

'I can't jump rope,' I confessed, at a volume I hoped would be audible only to Janine.

Penny, with the predator-worthy hearing of an eight-year-old, heard every word.

'She can't even jump rope! What a loser! How could you not know how to jump rope? Every girl in the class knows how, except you,'

Penny crowed.

I stayed rooted to my seat and peered intently at the floor, willing it to open up like the pit of Hades and swallow Penny and her awful friends whole. Instead, Janine linked her arm in mine and dragged me into a standing position.

'You don't have to know how to jump to play jump rope, Penny,' Janine said, and I noticed that Penny, who had seemed to me to be at the top of the food chain, deferred to Janine's authority. For prey like me, Janine was the best friend I could have wished for, so I trotted along with her towards the playing field.

When we were out of earshot of Penny and her pack, I asked Janine the question that was begging to be asked. 'What do you mean I don't need to know how to jump to play jump rope?'

'You can swing,' Janine said. ' We always need people to swing.'

Ah. Janine was my friend, but she was also an eight-year-old girl, and she could help me, but she couldn't save me. No matter. I *could* swing – Janine was right – and if swinging was what it took to keep me under her watchful eye and out of Penny's clutches, then swinging was what I'd do, not just that Thursday, but every day Janine jumped rope.

I had only one friend at school, but I had a barn full of friends up the hill from our house – they just happened to be bovine rather than human. Mom believed that neighbours should at the very least be civil, and ideally quite pleasant, towards each other, so less than a week passed between our arrival at the farmhouse and Mom's appearance, with me in tow, at the door of our closest neighbours bearing a plate full of chocolate chip cookies.

'Hello,' said the matronly woman who answered the door.

'Hello,' Mom said brightly. 'I'm Liza, your new neighbour down the road. I just wanted to introduce myself. This is my daughter, Beth Anne. Her younger brother and sister are back at home.'

I smiled on cue and the woman smiled back at me.

'Hello, Beth Anne, how nice to meet you,' the woman said; she reminded me of my great-grandmother, but with a Vermont accent. 'I'm Mrs Mason. I'd offer you both some lemonade, but I'd best be gettin' supper on the table for Joe – he'll be comin' in from milking soon.'

'Milking?' I asked.

'We're farmers, Beth Anne,' Mrs Mason said. 'You must have seen our cows in the field? We've got a whole herd of 'em. You're welcome to come visit them one day – Joe loves to take youngsters through the barn.'

I perked up. 'Can I?' I asked Mom.

'Of course you can, but not with me,' Mom said to me, then added confidentially to Mrs Mason, 'I'm afraid of cows. And horses. And dogs I'm unfamiliar with.'

'Oh dear,' said Mrs Mason. 'A dairy farm is no place for you then, love.'

'I like cows,' I said to Mrs Mason. 'And horses, and dogs, and cats – and fireflies.'

Mom and Mrs Mason looked over my head to exchange a smile steeped in motherhood.

'So why don't you come up without your mom sometime, Beth Anne, and my husband will show you how we milk.'

I pestered Mom for days after our visit to the Masons' farm – 'Could I go visit the cows today?' 'No.' 'Tomorrow?' 'Maybe.' – until either the appropriate modicum of time had passed or Mom's resistance wore down, as it usually did in the end. I had learned how to chip away at her, like water running over rock, slowly enough so as not to irritate her, but persistently enough to bend the course of the river in my direction.

I walked up the dirt road towards the Masons' farm on my own. I was sensible about road traffic and kept my ears pricked and scanned the road ahead; if I became aware of a vehicle hurtling past me from behind or towards me from ahead, I was quick to jump into the encroaching forest until the danger had passed. After making my way up the hill, I looked back and forth in both directions for several minutes until I deemed it safe to cross, then darted over, climbed the steps, and knocked timidly on the Masons' door.

Nothing happened. I stood on the doorstep, debating internally: should I knock again more loudly and run the risk of being rude; should I remain in place, hoping that Mrs Mason was perhaps on her way to answer but taking longer than I would have expected; or should I scamper back across the road, run down the hill as fast as my legs could carry me, and pretend I had lost all desire to venture into the dairy barn?

Mrs Mason opened the inside door before I could wrap up my closing arguments in the court of my mind, thus resolving the question for me.

'Hello there, Beth Anne! I suppose you've come to see the animals? How brave of you to come all the way up the hill without your mom or dad!'

'My dad lives in Shelburne,' I explained. I assumed I didn't need to tell Mrs Mason why my mother hadn't accompanied me, as I expected our previous conversation had not slipped her mind.

Mrs Mason seemed to be taken off guard. 'Does he now? Is that your stepfather at the house then?'

'No, that's my mom's boyfriend. They're getting married soon. They have to wait until Mom finishes the dresses.'

'Oh, I see. Your mom sews, does she? Did she make the dress you're wearing right now?'

I was wearing the calico dress in a dusty-pink print with green sprigs and white daisies; the puffed sleeves were like compressed fabric renditions of the Chinese lanterns we'd made during an art lesson at school, gathered at each end but wide in the middle. I patted down the front of my dress proudly; it was one of my favourites.

'Yes,' I answered Mrs Mason.

'She's a very talented seamstress. Is that what she does for a living?'

I laughed defensively, thinking of the many times Mom had sworn in exasperation while sewing. Only when everything went according to plan – when the fabric, pattern, thread, and machine all cooperated to make Mom pleased with both the appearance and the fit of the finished product – did Mom glow with satisfaction upon completion of a sewing project. Anything less than perfection and Mom would toss the garment casually in the direction of its intended owner, announcing offhandedly, 'Catch – it could have been better, but at least it's done.' Mom was her own harshest critic and in all my eight years of watching her sew, only a handful of garments had met with her full approval. I inspected the clothes that did not meet her expectations, wondering where the mistakes were, but I could never spot them; to me, all the clothes Mom sewed for us were like magic tricks, like rabbits pulled out of hats, because with every garment, Mom took a piece of two-dimensional fabric and transformed it, through a process as unfathomable to me as a magician's sleight of hand, into something completely new. Although I thought Mom was amazing, she thought she was a failure, and I didn't like to contemplate how miserable life would be if, instead of driving off to work, Mom had to stay home and sew every day.

'No,' I said finally to Mrs Mason, after a much longer pause than she had maybe been expecting, 'she works part-time as an aide at the Lower Branch school. I go to the Upper Branch school, so I have to take the bus with my brother.'

'I see,' Mrs Mason nodded. 'That's nice. Well, I'm sure your mother's wedding dress will be beautiful.'

I blushed. 'Me too. Can I see the cows?'

"Course you can, honey. I just saw Joe on his way in. Let me call him and tell him not to take his boots off.'

Mrs Mason walked through to the back of the farmhouse, pulled the inner screen door towards her, and flung the wooden outer door open wide. 'Joe!' she hollered, blocking the screen door from closing. 'Joe! We've got sweet little Beth Anne here, from down the road, and she wants to meet *all* of her new neighbours! Can you take her down to the barn?'

Joe waved towards his wife to indicate both comprehension and consent. Mrs Mason took a step back, widening the gap between herself and the door frame, and pointed at her husband. 'Go ahead out, Beth Anne,' she said, in case I was still in any doubt.

The walk from Mrs Mason to Mr Mason felt airy and exposed, as if I were traversing a wooden suspension bridge stretched taut over a river without any forehand knowledge of whether or not the opposite bank would prove hospitable. I could feel Mrs Mason's eyes following me until Mr Mason, when he deemed me close enough, raised his hand again towards his wife, relieving her of responsibility and claiming me as his charge.

'You wanna see the cows, do ya?' Mr Mason said, with some bemusement.

'Yes, please,' I said.

'It's gonna be noisy in the barn – smelly too. Might be a bit of a shock if you've never been in a barn before.'

'I like cows,' I said, throwing my shoulders back defiantly.

'Alrighty. Come with me then.'

I skipped along just a couple of paces behind Mr Mason for the short walk out to the barn. The cows were audible before they were visible. The enormous doors at either end of the barn were open to let the breeze pass through, and the rumble of the mooing of an entire herd resonated in my chest.

When Mr Mason and I stepped over the threshold and they spotted us, the cows had even more to say. Fifty or so ruminant Jersey heads turned towards us and I laughed at the spectacle. The nose of each cow was around the size of my hand, and on inspection, each was dimpled like the folds of a human brain. Whiskers protruded from all sides of the bovine noses, barring the very top, and the cows' mouths were in near-constant motion as they chewed and chewed again. The barn was markedly warmer and more humid than outdoors, and there was a distinctive odour, but it was not wholly unpleasant – yes, it included the heady aroma of cow manure, but there was also the sweet smell of hay and the strong scent of fresh milk. I felt no inclination to hold my nose but instead slurped in deep breaths of this air unlike any other.

'How many cows are there?' I asked Mr Mason, who'd been keeping one eye on me and one eye on his herd.

'Forty-seven heifers, two bulls and a calf,' Mr Mason replied. 'Go ahead and pet them if you want. They won't bite. They can't bite, actually, 'cause they only got bottom front teeth. Daisy here is one of my favourites – give me your hand and I'll show you what to do.'

I extended my hand to Mr Mason, who took hold of it from above, raised it high enough to reach the bridge of Daisy's long nose, set it down on the whorl of hair between her eyes, and guided it down towards her nostrils, each as big as Alice's wide-open mouth when she screamed.

'It's longer than our dog's nose,' I remarked.

Mr Mason laughed. 'Your dog is nowhere near as big as Daisy, even if she's a Great Dane.'

'We used to have a Great Dane called Tasha, actually. Tasha knocked my baby sister Alice down the stairs once, and my mom got really mad.' I wasn't sure why I was telling Mr Mason this as it cast my mom in a bad light, but if his cows trusted him, then it seemed reasonable that I could too.

Mr Mason glossed over my unnecessary revelation. 'What kind of dog you got now?'

'A white German Shepherd called Shiva.'

'Shiva, huh? Funny name for a dog. I sure hope Shiva is smart enough to stay away from our cows,' Mr Mason said, with an edge of warning.

I came to Shiva's defence. 'She doesn't eat our cats,' I assured Mr Mason.

'That's a good start. You wanna see the calf?'

'Yes, please,' I said.

The calf was at the far end of the barn in an enclosure all of its own. Its legs were still spindly and its head, already oversized, was so out of proportion to its body that it was a wonder the calf could hold it aloft. The baby was a lighter shade of brown than the adult Jerseys, but its eyes – almost level with mine – were nearly as deep brown as a bar of Hershey's Special Dark. I knew what the eyes of a predator looked like – I had been looking into dogs' and cats' eyes from birth – but I had never come this close to a prey animal, and a wave of recognition washed over me. This beautiful animal, with eyelashes as long as my little finger, was as scared as I was.

'What's her name?' I asked, stroking the calf's nose the way Mr Mason had demonstrated earlier.

'*He* doesn't have a name,' Mr Mason responded. 'We don't usually name the ones we won't keep.'

I glanced up at Mr Mason. 'Why won't you keep him?'

The farmer, with the skill of a seasoned politician, gave me a palatable but incomplete answer. 'We don't have room for every calf that's born here. Our barn is only so big.'

'Can I name him?'

'You can if you want, but you might not wanna get too attached,' Mr

Mason cautioned.

I considered this briefly, while lost in the calf 's liquid eyes. 'Fawn,' I announced, 'because he looks like a baby deer.'

'That's a funny name for a calf,' Mr Mason said, 'but it makes sense. Come visit Fawn and Daisy and the rest of 'em whenever you want, Beth Anne.'

I patted Fawn on the top of his head. 'Thanks,' I said, to both Mr Mason and the calf.

24

Gold

Mom finished sewing the outfits that Alice, Andy and I would wear to her wedding to Marvin a few weeks after school started, but she had yet to hem her own red calico wedding dress when Marvin announced we would be attending a wedding a week from Saturday.

'What?' I asked, wondering how Marvin could have missed that Mom's dress was not yet ready.

'Not our own wedding, Beth Anne,' Marvin said. 'Don't get all jumpy. Our wedding is set for the day after Halloween – the Day of the Dead. Because all other loves are dead to us, now that we've found each other,' Marvin said in his sappiest voice, batting his dark eyelashes in Mom's direction. Mom blew him a kiss. 'And because your mother is so spooky,' Marvin added, waving his arms about like a very amateur ghost and making an 'Oooo' noise.

'Marvin,' I chided, swatting his ghost arms with my own arms of youthful flesh and blood, 'whose wedding is it then?'

Marvin cut the ghost act short and reassumed his usual identity. 'George's friend. There'll be a big party after at the Griffin's house.'

'Who are the Griffins?'

'Mutual friends. Should be a nice wedding, and the reception will be like no other party you've been to. The Griffins live in a breathtaking house, way up on a hill in Brookfield – they designed it themselves. It's nothing like this farmhouse.'

'I like this farmhouse,' I retorted.

'You'll like the Griffins' house even more.'

On the day of the wedding, Mom got cold feet. 'Do you really think it's a good idea for the kids and I to come along today?' Mom asked Marvin, fishing for an out.

Marvin placed one hand on either side of Mom's waist and drew her in close, then planted his lips on hers and gave her a noisy smooch. 'Yes, Liza,' Marvin said, ending the kiss but keeping his face mere inches from Mom's, 'I think it's an excellent idea. There's nothing like a wedding to get me in the mood – all that talk of undying love. Plus we may want to pinch some of their vows – we haven't quite finished writing ours, have we?'

'No, but I could stay at home and work on them,' Mom suggested. 'I won't know anybody at this wedding except you, George and Marianne. And the kids won't know any of the other kids at all.'

'They're *kids*, Liza,' Marvin said, peering over at me and Alice where we sat half-watching TV. Andy was outside looking for frogs by the pond, in flagrant defiance of Mom's edict forbidding us to play over there without adult supervision, which only strengthened Marvin's hand. 'They don't have to know anyone to have fun. There'll be other kids there – I'm sure by the time the party's over, all the kids, including yours, will be best friends with all the other kids.'

'Fine. But let's take two cars, in case I want to leave early.'

'Does that mean you're not going to sample any of the brownies?' Marvin asked, adding special emphasis to 'brownies'.

Alice's ears pricked up. 'Chocolate brownies?'

Mom smiled despite herself. 'They might look like yummy chocolate brownies, Alice, but they might taste horrible.' Mom squished her face up in disgust for emphasis. 'So promise me you won't eat any brownies at this party without checking with me first?'

I could understand that we shouldn't play by the pond – Alice had never taken swimming lessons, and Andy, though he could doggy-paddle, was the sort of brother who might end up in water far too deep for him because he'd been so focussed on chasing a frog, fish or even pond skater that he hadn't noticed he was in over his head. Most of Mom's other rules – even those I heartily disliked, such as 'You must try one bite of everything on your plate' – made some sort of sense, but I couldn't let this new directive about not eating brownies go unchallenged.

'What's wrong with chocolate brownies?' I asked. 'You've always let us eat them before, so long as we have dinner first. Do we need to ask just to be polite? Because it's a wedding?'

Mom and Marvin looked at each other over my head. It was frustrating that I was still too short to intercept the subtle nonverbal communication taking place inches above my sightline.

'That's right, Beth Anne,' Marvin confirmed solemnly after a short pause. 'At weddings you can't just help yourself to any old food you see lying around, because it's a special occasion, so some of the desserts – some of the brownies, in particular – may be specifically for adults, while other desserts are fine for everyone. That's why you have to check first. Got it?'

I nodded; Marvin's explanation was perfectly reasonable. Alice, however, seemed now to believe that we would be denied not only brownies but all possible desserts – her jaw had locked shut and her brow was furrowed in the early warning signs of impending tears.

'Don't worry, Alice,' I said. 'I'm sure there'll be brownies we can eat too.'

Mom, who seemed now to be stifling a laugh, seconded me. 'Of course there will be brownies for the kids,' she said. 'And if it makes you feel any better, Alice, I won't be eating any of the grown-ups' brownies either.'

Marvin appeared disappointed. 'Why not, Liza? Because you're driving?'

'Because I've tried grown-up brownies once before, and they just weren't my thing,' Mom said.

'Maybe you got a bad batch.'

'Maybe you should leave me alone. If I don't want to eat the brownies, I don't have to eat the brownies. I'll drink all the wine I want, but I won't eat the brownies,' Mom said, ending the discussion definitively.

Or so I thought.

'You might not want to drink *all* the wine you want,' Marvin demurred. 'You're taking your own car, remember?'

Mom looked as though she had been slapped. 'Exactly what are you implying, Marvin?' Mom asked. 'That I can't handle my booze? You're the one about to get high on brownies but you're telling me to lay off the wine? I'm perfectly capable of having a glass or two – or even three, if it's over a long period of time and I have something to eat – and driving home. I'm an excellent driver.'

Marvin remained calm. 'I never said you weren't.'

'Oh, so you think I'll become so impaired it will affect my driving skills. Do you really think I would endanger the lives of my children and myself by getting into a car if I were sloshed? That might be something my father would do, but not me. I know my limits, thank you very much. Or maybe what you're saying is that you think I don't? Do you think I drink too much, Marvin? Maybe if you do, we should reconsider our own wedding plans?'

The arguing led Alice, who had only just recovered from the potential denial of dessert, once again to the brink of tears. My own heart was racing; usually Mom and Marvin restricted their arguments to night-time, when we were all sleeping, or meant to be sleeping. I had two immediate choices if my goal was to prevent Alice from breaking down: end the fight or take Alice offstage.

I swallowed hard. 'Stop it!' I shouted. 'You're making Alice sad! And don't we have a wedding to go to?'

Mom and Marvin both froze, as if we had all been playing freeze dance and the music had come to a sudden stop.

Mom was the first one to thaw. 'We do have a wedding to go to, and Alice is not wearing that tattered dress. Why don't you take your sister upstairs, Beth Anne, and help her pick out a nice dress? And find one for yourself while you're at it.'

Andy, Alice and I rode with Mom; Marvin drove alone with the red resin Buddha. Shiva had to stay behind and protested by running after the green VW until Marvin shouted, 'Go home, Shiva!' out of his rolled-down window loud enough for us to hear in the car behind. To reach the church in Snowsville, we had to drive first up to the top of Braintree Hill, then right onto Peth Road; we could then either stay on Peth Road or turn onto Brainstorm Road. The roads were still new to us, and the thrill of travelling along a road with a name so close to mine had not yet worn off.

'Let's stay on Peth Road!' I shouted, as we bumped along. 'It's almost my very own road!'

'Maybe someday we should get out some white paint and make that 'P' into a 'B', huh, Beth Anne?' Mom joked. 'So no one will have any doubts about whose road it is.'

'Wouldn't we get into trouble?' I asked.

Mom rolled her eyes like a teenager. 'You're so conventional, Beth Anne. Don't worry, honey – I'm not really going to vandalise a street sign in our new hometown.'

Andy spoke up. 'I like Brainstorm Road better. Maybe if we take that road we'll get smarter.'

Mom laughed so much that her head shook and the sunlight bounced off her gold hoop earrings. Even Mom's eyes were shining today; she had applied Vaseline – her substitute for the eyeshadow she never wore – to the top lids to add extra sparkle. 'None of you need to be any smarter, Andrew,' Mom said. 'You're plenty smart already. It doesn't matter which road you all prefer today anyway – we're tailing Marvin, so whatever road he chooses is the one we'll take. Tell you what – whoever loses, we'll take their road next time.'

Marvin turned right on Peth Road and didn't turn left on Brainstorm.

'Yay!' I cried. 'We're on my road!'

'Fine,' Andy said begrudgingly. 'But it's Brainstorm next time.'

'I want a road,' Alice said.

'It's not really Beth's road, Alice,' Mom said to console my little sister. 'It's 'Peth' road with a 'P' and without the 'Anne'. And don't worry, because Andrew and I don't have roads here either. We're all in the same boat, really – all roadless. Like nomads in the desert.'

I partially disagreed; 'Peth Road' might not have been 'Beth Road', but it was close enough for me to feel ownership. And yes, we had been nomads, but surely our proximity to Peth Road must be preordained and our wandering in the desert must now come to an end.

The Snowsville church sprang up on the right-hand side of the road. It was peculiarly close to the asphalt, and Mom was taken by surprise when Marvin swerved suddenly onto the grass to park, as several other cars had done.

'Damn,' Mom said, 'he could have signalled. It's not like I knew where I was going.'

'Does that mean we've missed the wedding?' I asked, as we continued to hurtle along the narrow Vermont road that ran roughly parallel to Ayers Brook.

'No, Beth Anne,' Mom said with annoyance. I wasn't sure if the annoyance was meant for me, the situation, or both. 'It just means I have to find a place to reverse direction so I can make the turn to park at something less than thirty miles per hour. I wonder if I'll ever get used to driving in Vermont. It's not at all like Pennsylvania. Here's a farm – that should have a nice big driveway – yes, it does. We're back on track.'

Marvin was standing outside the church, chatting with a couple of people I had never seen before. 'What happened to you?' he asked Mom when we materialised at his side.

'You didn't signal, so I missed the church, and then I couldn't find anywhere to turn around. Hello,' Mom added, extending her hand in turn to the man and woman next to Marvin. 'I'm Liza and these are my kids – Beth Anne, Andrew and Alice.' We all waved on cue.

'We'd better get inside before the bride shows up,' the man said; he had a booming voice, grey hair and a grey beard. The woman with him had grey hair as well; she was wearing leather sandals with a special strap for her big toe, like the sandals favoured by the gods and goddesses Tovah and I had adopted as our own.

'We wouldn't want to upstage our own daughter,' the woman said.

'No one could upstage your daughter, Sandra,' Marvin said. 'Except possibly you,' he added, gallantly raising the sandalled woman's hand and kissing the tips of her fingers.

'Liza here could give Marie a run for her money,' the man said, bowing towards Mom and taking her hand, just as Marvin had taken Sandra's. Mom curtseyed in return, then tugged gently on Marvin's arm.

We were the last to arrive before Marie. The groom, who was also wearing sandals with a special strap for his big toe, perhaps in honour of his soon-to-be mother-in-law, was waiting at the step of the altar. He and the presiding minister chuckled under their breath at whatever story the similarly relaxed best man had just recounted. When the pianist broke off mid-piece and played the fanfare opening of the bridal march, everyone standing at the front of the church snapped to attention, and the guests, previously sitting at ease, jumped to their feet. Every set of eyes turned to admire Marie as she floated in, looking for all the world like a clothed Venus on the half-shell. The minister led the happy pair through half of the ceremony, and then the time came for a musical interlude. An extremely tall man with bare feet, wearing faded denim jeans and an even more faded denim shirt with the sleeves casually rolled up, rose from a middle pew.

'Forgot to line up some roadies,' the man said, as he strode towards the back of the church to retrieve a three-legged wooden stool. Everyone in the church laughed. The man placed the stool smack-dab in the centre of the centre aisle. 'Where are those roadies when you need 'em? Now I've got the stool, but I still need the guitar.'

A woman nearly as tall as the bald man, with a uniform white-gold shade of perfectly coiffed hair, crouch-walked the ten feet required to deliver the man's battered black guitar case. 'Thanks, Carly,' the man said. 'She beats all the roadies hands down.'

The man laid his case flat, then snapped the silver hinges and swung open the top, revealing the burnished wood of a guitar to rival the lyre of Apollo. Nimbly, the bald man lifted his instrument, slung the strap over his head, and began to adjust the tuning.

When he was satisfied, he squinted out at the invited audience. 'This is a song some of you may have heard,' the man said as he began to play, with the effortless style of a musician whose instrument is no longer a separate entity, but rather an extension of their own body. And when the denim-clad man with the pointy beard began to sing, he did just what Sandra had warned us against – he commandeered everyone's attention utterly and completely, rendering the bride and groom temporarily no more significant than any other couple in the church. It was as if the singer had brought his own spotlight, and the Vermont sun seemed to comply, seeking him out where he sat on his oddly shortened wooden stool, the toes of one bare foot curling down from the most convenient stretcher and the toes of the other splayed out on the floor of the aisle for all to see. For three and a half minutes, I was as mesmerised as every other person in the congregation. When the last plucked string had ceased to resonate, the musician raised his head, acknowledging the assembly's applause – normally reserved for the bride – with an 'Aw, shucks' smile.

'Who was that?' I whispered to Marvin.

'That was Charles Griffin. He's hosting the party afterwards.'

'The party with the brownies?'

'The very one.'

When we reached the wedding reception, the Griffins' house was brimming with adults. The church hadn't seemed crowded, but when the same number of people occupied what had, until recently, been a family ski lodge, the bodies were packed so close that it was hard to snake my way through to the kitchen in search of the food. There were trays of bite-sized sandwiches, platters of cheese cubes on toothpicks, and bowls of olives dotted randomly throughout the other rooms – those rooms that weren't closed off for renovations – and I sampled their contents on my way, but I was hunting for something more substantial. Andy and Alice trailed behind me, copying my tasters' menu strategy; Alice pursed her lips as though she had just bitten into a lemon after popping a green olive in her tiny mouth, but Andy retraced his steps to swipe an entire handful before catching us back up. The woman with the white-gold hair stood beside the hefty kitchen table, holding a glass of wine at chest height, talking animatedly with a clutch of admirers. I grabbed Alice's hand, motioned to Andy to follow, and planted myself as close to Carly as possible.

' . . . some work done, because Charles is building a recording studio, but it's coming along,' Carly was saying.

'The view is stunning,' one of the listeners said. 'I'm sure the house will be gorgeous when you're done. I notice you've already started your art collection.'

It was the right thing to say. 'Here's to Vermonters with a good eye,' Carly said, raising her glass into the space between herself and the art enthusiast. The other listeners followed suit, all enthralled by this towering and elegant woman, who'd chosen a back road in Brookfield over a boardroom in Manhattan; five wine glasses clinked, five adults sipped their wine, and only when they had all lowered their hands did Carly acknowledge my presence. Some adults would immediately drop their conversation with another adult if a child appeared; some would make it evident – with varying degrees of irritation – to interrupting children that they would need to wait their turn; while the mere bearing of other adults like Carly, and maybe the Queen of England, instructed interloping children as to when they would be received without so much as a word.

'Josh said there were hot dogs here?'

'Oh, you must be Liza's kids. How lovely to meet the three of you. Yes – you've come to the right place – they're just on the stove. One for each of you?'

We nodded our heads. 'Yes, please,' I said, speaking for us all.

Carly handed each of us a white bun. 'Hold this open and I'll pop in your frankfurters,' she said. She took a pair of tongs and tucked the hot dogs into each of our rolls like a saint dispensing alms for the poor.

'If you need any condiments – ketchup, mustard, relish – they're all on that table. Just help yourselves. We'll call you all back in when it's time for the wedding cake.' With that Carly dismissed us, just as cleanly as she had welcomed us, and seamlessly rejoined the conversation we had interrupted.

We dressed our hot dogs as we each saw fit – mine liberally laden, of course, with all three condiments – then snaked our way back through the still tightly packed and increasingly merry adults. The compression lessened downstairs, but the concentration of smokers increased until nearly every adult downstairs was nursing a flame, but not all of them were smoking the sort of cigarettes Mom favoured. Some of the cigarettes looked decidedly homemade, and there were unfamiliar smells in the room: a Christmassy gingerbread aroma and a sweet heavy scent I couldn't place. As I scanned the room to see if Mom was among the smokers, I observed that some of the adults seemed to have entered a state of private yet communal reverie, a state to which Mom's Benson & Hedges, despite each box's promising golden exterior, did not transport her. Mom wasn't there, so we continued outside to where Josh and Fern were waiting to resume our game of tag. After tag, Josh took a stick and drew a hopscotch outline in the dirt road.

'Who wants to go first?' Josh asked, and we all lined up, except for Andy, who deserted us in search of local insects.

By the time we had tired of hopscotch, the sun had taken on the appearance of a powerful searchlight, like the bulb of a lighthouse, as it sometimes did in the hour before dusk. When it was this close to evening, it was possible to look straight at the sun without being blinded, and standing on the dirt road outside the Griffins' house, the sight of the almost setting sun bathing the lush green mountains combined with the pleasure of a day of celebration – and perhaps with the fumes of the specially made cigarettes – to produce a rare euphoria. No matter that Mom's first wedding, the one to my father, had gone awry, like the wish of King Midas: Mom's next wedding, to Marvin, could be like this wedding today and convert love into a gold even purer than the metal, a gold so magical it would light up the couple and all of their guests from within, a gold so far beyond the mythological that it would never be tarnished, lost or broken.

There was, however, no exchange of gold rings at Mom and Marvin's wedding two weeks later; they had both agreed that they didn't need rings to commemorate the burning love they shared with one another. They were modern lovers, bound together through shared commitment, not by outdated symbols of the patriarchy.

Mom and Marvin married in our farmhouse on Braintree Hill. Marvin had a friend who was a justice of the peace and he officiated at the ceremony, held in our crowded living room. Mom wore her wedding dress, completed at last – several yards of red calico dotted with yellow flowers, accented by a yoke of yellow calico with red flowers. Alice and I wore our matching calico dresses, mine in the yellow of the yoke, Alice's in the red of the dress itself. Together we formed a fabric bonfire, a fact that went unnoticed by those in attendance, busy carousing as they were. The guests jostled each other jovially, drinking red wine and smoking indoors, because after all, the bride had a cigarette resting in her favourite deep-red ashtray, its ashes drifting soundlessly onto the cerulean blue enamel of the bowl's interior.

I was ecstatic that Mom and Marvin had married, but for my own wedding, someday in the distant future, I would wear white – like Marie, like a goddess – and my groom and I would offer each other rings of twenty-four carat gold.

25

Veal

Mom did speak to my third-grade teacher Mrs Neill about the mimeographed worksheets, but not with me present. The meeting did not go well.

'Mildred Neill is about a hundred years old,' Mom reported to Marvin at dinner. 'I think she's going deaf, or maybe she just couldn't understand my out-of-town dialect. Maybe she was making a point – uppity flatlander, coming in here, telling me how to do my job. That sort of thing.'

'I'm sure the fact that you're not from here has nothing to do with it,' Marvin said soothingly. 'She's just one of those teachers who stopped loving her job years ago, but has to hang on for her retirement money. We've got a few of those in Montpelier. They want to carry on doing what they've always done – they don't want to have to work too hard – until they can go off to greener pastures, either above if they're lucky, or below if they're not.'

'Anyway, Mildred says she can't give Beth Anne special treatment. There are lots of kids in the class who can't even read consistently on their own, so she hasn't got time to be coming up with interesting extra work for the few children who can. Thus the interminable worksheets.

She expects Beth Anne to just sit there doing mind-numbing busy work and be quiet. It makes my blood boil.'

'Liza – it might be boring, but doing a lot of rote work isn't going to lower Beth Anne's IQ.'

'It could though! She could get so fed up that she loses all interest in learning!'

Marvin rolled his eyes. 'Don't tell me I know your own child better than you do, dear wife. The likelihood of Beth Anne 'losing interest in learning' is about nil.'

Mom fixed Marvin with her steeliest stare.

Marvin capitulated, sort of. 'OK, zero is a little strong . . . maybe more like one in a million.'

Mom threw her hands up. 'It's more that I'm frustrated. I could do a better job than Mildred Neill.'

'So homeschool her.'

'I'm working, and God knows I need the money.'

'So become a teacher, instead of just a speech therapy aide, and be ready to take over when Mildred Neill either retires or dies, neither of which can be too far away.'

'Maybe I will.'

'Maybe you should. You'd make more money than you're making now, and you'd be an excellent teacher.'

'I don't have time to go back to school at the moment. I'm just barely keeping my head above water as it is. But I'm going to tell Beth Anne that if she ever wants to spend the day learning at home, she can. She'd probably teach herself a lot more than she'd learn at school.'

I was listening from the next room, where Andy, Alice and I were all colouring. It had taken me until third grade to recognise that my younger siblings, in addition to being my best – and my only reliable – playmates, were also like sponges that I could fill with knowledge and ideas. I had started to structure play sessions like today, when our assignment, set by me (it would be a year or so before either sibling demanded greater democracy), was to draw first a cat, then a tree and finally a house. Having completed the cats, all of us were studiously shading the leaves of our trees with variants of green from our Crayola 64 box: Alice's leaves were just whorls, some green, some pink, some yellow; Andy's were straight lines, only in 'Pine Green' because he had drawn an evergreen with needles; my tree was bedecked with foliage in every shade of green Crayola offered, even the very un-leaflike 'Sea Green'.

'Did you hear that?' I said to Andy and Alice, who shook their heads and carried on colouring. 'Mom's going to let me stay home from school whenever I want from now on.'

'I don't want to stay home from school,' Andy said, adding still more needles to the branches of his tree. 'I like school.'

'That's because you have a nice teacher. I have the horrible Mrs Neill.'

'Also because I like kickball,' Andy said.

Alice replaced the 'Forest Green' among the blues and selected 'Sepia' for her tree trunk. I picked the green crayon out under the pretext of needing it, although I had in fact already used it, then filed it away correctly alongside its green counterparts.

'I don't like kickball, I can't jump rope, and I'm sick and tired of doing worksheets,' I said firmly. 'I think I'll stay home tomorrow.'

'I want to stay home too,' Alice said.

'You're not even in school,' I said dismissively.

Alice shook her fist at me, still clenching the 'Sepia' crayon. 'Am too – preschool.'

'You don't even go every day.'

'I don't want to go any day,' countered Alice, put out by my belittling.

I wasted no time in testing Mom's loosening of my educational boundaries. 'I'd rather stay home today,' I announced the following

245

morning upon shuffling into the kitchen. 'I'd like to read and write a story instead. I'm halfway through *The Magician's Nephew* and I want to finish it.'

Mom, bemused, asked, 'And what will your story be about?'

'A new adventure for Lulela.'

'Who's Lulela?'

'The princess with the flying horse.'

'I don't want to go to preschool either,' Alice chimed in.

Mom laughed. 'Well, at least one of you is in luck – you don't even have preschool today, Alice. It's one of my days off, so you're home with me. Or with me and Beth Anne, if your sister gets her way.'

'I just can't face more worksheets today,' I wheedled.

Mom was easily swayed. 'Fine. But at the end of the day I expect to see how much you've done – how many pages you've both read and written. Deal?'

I did a discreet victory dance. 'Deal,' I agreed, with a broad grin.

I was saving the journal Marvin had given me for my previous birthday for when I had either something very important to write or a very artistic picture to draw; instead I took my stenographer's notebook, purchased as Mom's nod to my left-handedness, squeezed a pen through the cold metal rings at the top, and climbed the tree outside the kitchen window to my preferred writing nest. I straddled the thick branch, at least a foot in diameter, and rested my back against the trunk of the tree. Once settled, I flipped to the half-filled page where I had last left Lulela – in heated negotiations with a troll for the serum necessary to mend her steed's damaged wing – and took up the story.

An hour or two passed before a shout pierced the bucolic silence. 'Beth Anne! Get inside right now! The cows are loose!'

I clambered down as hastily as I could without endangering life or limb and ran around to the front of the house. Sure enough, several of the cows from the Masons' farm, permitted to graze in our field on certain days of the week, had wandered out of the field and were now dotted around our front yard and driveway, chewing contentedly. Mom was standing on the raised back deck, waving her arms furiously and yelling, 'Shoo! Shoo! Get out of our yard!'

Alice, who had either not been outside to begin with or who had already been sequestered, was peering through the window, watching both the mellow cows and our much less mellow mother's theatrics. Alice was so abbreviated that only the upper third of her body rose above the windowsill, giving her an oddly legless appearance. The tableau of my artificially short sister, my near-hysterical mother, and the enormous but benign Jerseys struck me as hilarious, and although I knew I shouldn't, I started to giggle.

'Beth Anne, this is no laughing matter! Get inside this minute!' Mom screamed at me. 'I don't know how those cows got through that fence! One of you must be leaving it open!'

'They're not going to hurt us, Mom,' I said, searching for Fawn among the escaped cows. 'I've seen them up at the barn.'

'You don't know what they're going to do. I've seen them run before – they can move faster than you think, and if one of them trampled you, Beth Anne, that'd be the end of you. Now do as I say and get the hell inside.'

When Mom swore while sober it meant she was serious, so I scampered in through the front door and ran straight around to the back to join Mom on the deck. Far from pleasing her, this further incensed my mother, who – temporarily forgetting the bovine threat – wheeled around to yell at me at close range. 'Beth Anne! When I say 'get inside' I don't mean 'get inside and then come back outside'. I knew I shouldn't have let you stay home today. It was probably you that left the fence open when you rode your bike in the field yesterday.'

I denied the allegation. 'It was not. And anyway, I just want to see if

Fawn is here.'

'They're raising that calf for veal, Beth Anne,' Mom said. 'It will live in the barn until they kill it.'

I recoiled. 'What do you mean, "veal"? Why won't Fawn grow up like the other cows – like those cows?' I pointed at the rebel Jerseys who, still impervious to the human drama, wandered slowly in search of more grass.

'Because he's not a cow. He's a bull. He'll never produce milk, so he won't be any use to them. They'll sell him for meat – that's the only way they'll make any money from him. These cows aren't pets, Beth Anne, they're livestock. They're the Masons' livelihood.' Mom turned back to face the immediate danger. 'Shoo! Oh, I'm going to have to call Mrs Mason and get her to send someone down to round these animals up.'

I was frozen in place, thinking of Fawn's huge eyelashes and the reassuring heat of his body that warmed my hand when I clapped his shoulder.

Mom spun around to face me again. 'I've told you to go— Oh dear. You didn't know, did you? We're carnivores, honey – we eat meat. That's just how it is. I didn't mean to upset you . . . I'm just not thrilled at having cows running amok in my yard.'

'Will they let me say goodbye?'

'Do you really want to say goodbye?' Mom asked. 'Maybe it would be better if you didn't? It might be easier not to?'

I couldn't believe Mom would suggest that I should let my friend go without a proper farewell. 'I love Fawn,' I said. 'Of course I want to say goodbye.'

'I'll let the Masons know,' Mom said, the anger in her voice momentarily replaced by tenderness. 'But now, for the umpteenth time, please go inside.'

The next time I went up to visit the Masons' cows, Fawn was gone.

I said nothing to Mr and Mrs Mason, but told Mom, my bottom lip quivering, when I returned home.

'Why didn't the Masons let me say goodbye?' I asked. 'You promised me you'd tell them.'

'Maybe they forgot, or maybe they were too busy,' Mom said, brushing over my sadness.

Whether in mourning, in protest, or both, I didn't return to the Masons' farm after Fawn disappeared, and I stopped eating veal parmigiana, which bothered Mom, but not Marvin.

'You can't just eat the tomato sauce, Beth Anne,' Mom said the next time she served me the once-loved, now-hated dish. 'You need some protein. Don't you want to grow up to be big and strong?'

'Liza,' Marvin said, 'Beth Anne gets plenty of protein. I admire her for standing up for her principles. She's growing up to be a girl of character and conscience – isn't that more important?'

'She can do that and still eat her dinner,' Mom remonstrated. But she added an extra dollop of tomato sauce to my pasta and split the spare veal patty between Andy and Marvin, who were delighted to accept their increased portions.

'I hope this isn't the start of a trend,' Mom said to me, her face ominous, 'because you need to keep up your iron levels so you have the energy to go downhill skiing with your father over Thanksgiving.'

'Downhill skiing?' I repeated in disbelief.

Mom nodded. 'Yes. Your father's an avid skier, and that is no small part of how I ended up in this godforsaken state. Sorry, I mean this quaint state with breathtaking foliage and 'White Christmas' winters.'

The first description was truer to Mom's sentiments. I heard the sarcasm in the second, far more flattering, portrait, but felt no compulsion to defend Vermont. Mom had a love/hate relationship with her adopted home state, and in any love/hate relationship, the love is of a particularly fierce nature, honed as it is by constant battle.

249

'Will there be snow at Thanksgiving?' Andy asked, very sensibly.

'There should be,' Marvin said, 'But even if there hasn't been much natural snow, Killington has snow guns, and the baby slope will be covered. It's not like Mark's going to send you down any black diamonds.'

Alice's eyes opened wide. 'What's a black diamond?'

'It's the hardest trail at a ski area, Alice,' Marvin explained. 'Nothing to do with the jewel. There's a rating system – green circle, blue square, black diamond, in ascending order of difficulty. You'll be skiing green circles.'

'Do you ski?' I asked Marvin, impressed at his knowledge of the sport.

Marvin shook his head. 'Boys from Brooklyn go to Coney Island for thrills, not to ski slopes. I tried it once – a friend of the Kleins persuaded me that I couldn't call myself a Vermonter without having skied at Stowe – but it wasn't for me. I like cross-country though,' he added.

Now it was Mom's ears that pricked up. 'Do you? Why hadn't you told me that? I hated downhill skiing – I mean, come on, a chairlift is no place for someone with a fear of heights like mine – but I've always wanted to try cross-country skiing. If it has to snow – if it has to be twenty below, which it doesn't really, not for my sake anyway – then I'd like to at least have some way to enjoy it. Why haven't we gone cross-country skiing yet?'

'You tell me. Why don't we take the kids to the Trapp Family Lodge? Do they even know that Maria lives in Vermont? Maria, that great enemy of the Nazis? Why does the most famous anti-Nazi heroine in popular culture have to be Julie Andrews playing a failed nun?'

'Oh, Marvin, now you're exaggerating. What about Anne Frank? She did far more to educate people about the horrors of the Holocaust, she wasn't Catholic, and she was real.'

'Maria is real too, and living in Stowe. You might have read *The Diary of Anne Frank*, but you're the exception, Liza, not the rule. Plus I think it's required reading if you want to marry a Jew. Which you did, Mrs Kessler.'

'That's Ms to you, Mr Kessler. Do you think Alice could manage cross-country skis, or would she sink into the snow?'

'Let's wait and see how the kids do with Mark.'

We were meant to wear snowsuits for skiing, but only Alice still had one. Alice's one-piece snowsuit was mulberry and had appliqued patches of brown imitation leather; wearing it, Alice reminded me of the Inuits I had seen in books, as she peered out from the depths of the fake-fur lined hood with her deep brown eyes set in her dark olive skin. Andy and I were still near enough in size to Melinda and Brian that we had been lent their snowsuits for the occasion. Melinda's snowsuit, in which I found myself, was bright yellow – Mindy already aspired to stardom and had nothing against standing out in the crowd. I didn't like the restricted movement that came with the snowsuit but was thankful for its warmth, and beyond that I was grateful for the fact that because I had Mindy's snowsuit, she couldn't be present herself. It wasn't that I didn't like Melinda – I did, so much so that I felt honoured to be wearing her starry snowsuit – but I liked my dad more, and wanted to share him with as few people as possible, as though Dad were a finite substance. Mindy wasn't really out for my share of my dad – she wanted her own dad's time and energy – but had Mindy come skiing, Dad would have given her his time and energy anyway. Andy's outerwear, borrowed from Brian, was boys' standard-issue navy blue, and I doubted very much that Andy cared one way or the other about the colour.

Dad took us to the lower half of the bunny slope and began our skiing instruction by showing us first simply how to stand on our now outrageously long 'feet', then how to slow down and stop using the 'snow plough', and finally, how to move down the hill in a modified S-shape. Andy picked up the basics of skiing almost instantly, except for the curve element, which he felt was superfluous; his only aim was to get down the slope as quickly as possible, preferably – but not necessarily – without falling. Alice and I weren't as comfortable on our skis, but within an hour we were all proficient enough to warrant Dad introducing us to the bunny lift. After only a few trips up and down, Andy started using the lift and skiing down the short trail independently. I could get down the hill, but I still wanted company for the trip up; the process of catching the lift, maintaining my upright position, then getting off efficiently (and without falling) was too intimidating for me to face alone.

In truth, it might have been more fun to wear my own cobbled-together ski gear if it meant Mindy could have come along and worn her snowsuit. Mindy would have been good company for me, as Dad, although he had fought nominally against communism in Vietnam, was distributing the lion's share of his time and energy to Alice rather than to me because she was the one who needed him the most. Dad's unspoken but not unnoticed goal for the outing was to instil in us a similar love for the sport of skiing to that which he harboured. He had already succeeded with Andy, and could see that I was well on my way, but quite rightly sensed that for Alice it was touch and go. A few times in passing I had caught Alice's slow, unwilling grin as her legs and skis cooperated and she coasted carefully down the mountain, but I'd also seen Dad pulling her up from a few unexpected falls. It was lonelier for me to ski on my own, but I was relieved not to be the one responsible for comforting Alice when the tips of her skis crossed and she toppled over into the snow. By early afternoon, even Alice could occasionally manage a half-decent snow plough.

I don't know how Alice ended up in the snow-making pond. Maybe Dad had sent her to the lodge to use the toilet and she became confused about where exactly she was meant to go, maybe her snow plough was less secure than Dad had realised and she simply lost control, or maybe Dad just let his attention stray for that one critical minute it took for Alice to tumble in. I'm not even sure if Alice was on skis or on foot at the time. What I do know is that moments after I saw her from a distance, safe but unaccompanied, close to the lodge, Alice somehow managed to wholly immerse herself in the Snowshed Pond. Whether called by Dad or a random onlooker, the ski patrol swooped into action and pulled my baby sister out of the water – albeit pale, sputtering, and twice her usual weight, thanks to the complete saturation of her mulberry snowsuit.

It must have been the ski patrol that stripped Alice down and then clothed her in garments left behind by previous skiers. By the time I reached her and Dad in the lodge, Alice had calmed down enough to smile wanly at me, her hands clasped tight around a white styrofoam cup of instant hot chocolate.

'Where's Andy?' she asked.

'No idea,' I said. 'He just keeps going up and down. I think he likes skiing the most out of all of us.'

'I hate skiing,' Alice said, her bottom lip trembling.

'You don't hate skiing,' Dad countered. 'You hate going for un-expected swims. As I do. You can't hold an unfortunate accident against the sport itself. Plus, you got to put on these very stylish clothes'—here Dad tugged lightly at the oversized unclaimed layers Alice was wrapped in—'unlike your sister, who's stuck in Melinda's blindingly yellow snowsuit.'

I glanced down at my borrowed snowsuit in surprise. I'd been wearing it proudly until that point, but now I reddened, like Eve must have done when her eyes were opened in the Garden of Eden. My embarrassment, however, unlike that of Eve, quickly turned to anger. I was suddenly so insulted on my sister-by-association's behalf that I temporarily forgot that my blood sister was still blue with cold.

'Don't tell Andy that I fell in the pond,' Alice said to me.

'OK,' I said, returning my attention with a thump to the sister there before me, and grasping immediately why Alice would prefer to keep her misadventure to herself. 'My lips are sealed.'

Dad harrumphed. 'Alice, there's nothing to be ashamed of. Of course we'll tell Andy what happened. It's important for him to know that just because he's buzzing up and down the mountain like Ingemar Stenmark, accidents do happen and you have to be careful on the mountain and even off the mountain, especially if you don't want to go for an unplanned swim in the snow-making pond.'

Dad nudged me good-naturedly with his elbow and winked at Alice when he mentioned the pond, but both my sister and I remained stony-faced. Whether because we no longer found them funny, or because we willed ourselves not to, neither Alice nor I laughed much at Dad's jokes any more. Maybe we never had; I could no longer be sure.

26

Ponytail

Shiva was under house arrest when we returned to Braintree. 'Don't let the dog out!' Mom shouted when Dad rapped ceremoniously at the door the Sunday after Thanksgiving. He needn't have knocked; no one in Vermont locked their doors, us included, so we could have let ourselves in, but Dad had been raised to be polite at all times, even when reluctantly returning his children to his ex-wife and her new partner.

Faced with the Catch-22 of possibly allowing the big white shepherd to escape or waiting awkwardly on the doorstep in the freezing temperatures, Dad deemed it preferable not to risk Mom's ire. He set the suitcase he'd carried from the car down beside him and we all listened to Shiva's enthusiastic barking.

'I think we'd better wait until your mom gets hold of the dog,' Dad said to us under his breath.

Mom swung the front door open, bent to one side from grabbing Shiva's leather collar. 'Why didn't you come in? It's too cold to make the kids wait outside.'

From the minute readjustment of his facial muscles, I read that Dad was both angry and determined to hide it. 'Sorry,' Dad said, his voice sheepish but his lips pursed. 'I'm not sure I could control your dog, so I thought it was safer to just wait.'

'It's not my dog,' Mom said, 'and given the German Shepherds you came across in the service, I don't see how you might think you couldn't handle a civilian pet.'

Dad bristled and changed the subject. 'The kids tell me they enjoyed your recent wedding,' he said. 'I don't think I congratulated you earlier.'

Marvin appeared behind Mom. 'Let me take Shiva, Liza,' Marvin said, reaching down to relieve Mom of Shiva's collar, and adopting the same tilted position that Mom was now able to abandon. 'Hi, Mark, thanks for bringing the kids back. Hope the skiing went well?'

'It did, thanks,' Dad said with continued artificial friendliness. 'Are you a downhill skier yourself, Marvin?'

To be a downhill skier, I suddenly understood, was to be like a girl who could jump Double Dutch: it was a badge of honour. Any answer other than yes would show Marvin as of a lower rank in a sort of battle, comparable to who was the best at jump rope, but somehow more all-encompassing.

Marvin, though, seemed at first not to be bothered about hierarchy. 'I told Liza before – I tried downhill once, but it wasn't for me. Cross-country is more my style.'

'I see,' Dad said, nodding indulgently, secure that he had won this particular skirmish.

Marvin wasn't finished, however. 'We'll be taking the kids to the Trapp Family Lodge when Liza's sister comes to visit. We're hoping to bump into Maria.'

Dad produced a forced laugh. 'That would certainly make it memorable for the kids,' he agreed. 'Well, I don't expect I'll see you before then, as I don't have the kids until after Christmas now, so have fun.'

'Thanks,' Marvin said. 'I'm sure we will.'

Dad hugged us each in turn. His moustache tickled my cheek and I thought I might sneeze, which distracted me from any sorrow the goodbye might have induced.

On the school bus the next morning, everyone was already talking about Christmas. The older girls were asking for Barbies and Barbie accessories, with the Barbie camper van at the top of several lists for Santa. Not wanting to be left out, when Mom asked us to draw up our own lists, I put the Barbie camper van in at number one.

'You are not getting a Barbie,' Mom said to me when I handed her my list.

'All the girls on the bus are getting Barbies,' I informed Mom.

Mom looked at me as though I had taken leave of my senses. 'Beth Anne, first of all, do you really think I care what "all the girls on the bus" are doing? Second of all, just because "all the girls on the bus" are doing something does not make it right. No doll has done more to further girls' hatred of their bodies than Barbie. No girl looks like that in real life, you know. Barbie is completely exaggerated. If I had boobs like Barbie they'd be out to here.' Mom helpfully demonstrated where her Barbie-proportioned breasts would extend to by putting both hands several inches beyond where her bosom actually ended.

'That wouldn't be so bad, would it, Liza?' Marvin asked.

Mom rolled her eyes. 'You vowed to love me just as I am, remember,' Mom reminded Marvin. 'Flat chest and all.'

'And I do,' Marvin said.

Mom snorted. 'Barbie's face doesn't even vaguely resemble a real woman's face. How many women wear eye make-up twenty-four hours a day? Not to mention her sickeningly blonde hair and her sapphire blue eyes.'

'You're just jealous,' Marvin said.

'I am not jealous, and you are not being the least bit helpful. Is that the kind of image you want Beth Anne to aspire to? Like some sort of bimbo fashion model? I want her to be proud of both her body and her mind, and I don't see how a Barbie doll is going to help her get there,' Mom said.

'You don't need to attack me, Liza,' Marvin said in a serious tone. 'I agree with you. Barbie's boobs do nothing to further the evolution of a healthy female self-image, Beth Anne.'

'I don't care about her body. I just want to style her hair,' I protested.

'There must be some other doll with long hair,' Mom said. 'And I don't think Barbie's hair is really made for styling anyway.'

'The girls on the bus say it is.'

'What else is on your list?' Marvin asked me, ending the Barbie discussion for the time being.

Although she wasn't impressed by my Christmas wishes, Mom threw herself wholeheartedly into Christmas that year on Braintree Hill. She had started, serendipitously, with Advent Sunday, the very Sunday we had come back from the Thanksgiving weekend with Dad. Before we went to bed that evening, Mom gave us hot chocolate and let us each poke a squat candle into the base of the brass angel chimes, following her demonstration with the first one. Mom lit all four candles using a single cooks' match, although by the time she reached the fourth one, it had burned down enough to singe her fingers.

'Damn,' Mom said, shaking out her index finger and thumb as the angels – who weren't really angels as I thought of angels at all – spun merrily around, the sound of their trumpets transposed into the tinkling of the chimes.

'Why do the angels look like cupids?' I asked. 'I thought Christmas was about Jesus?'

Mom carefully considered the plump winged toddler boys whizzing around the central brass star. 'They do look more like cupids,' Mom conceded. 'I hadn't ever thought of it. I think they're meant to be cherubim rather than adult angels. Maybe because they're so cute and pudgy. They look a bit like Andrew did when he was a toddler. We used to call him "Thunder Thighs".'

Andy, busy slurping his hot chocolate, only looked up when he felt four pairs of eyes on him. 'What?' he asked, wiping his mouth with his sleeve.

'"Thunder Thighs", huh? I can see why, given his fondness for all things alimentary,' Marvin commented. 'How do you know the cherubim aren't seraphim though, Liza?'

Mom sighed. 'I suppose you can tell the difference? I thought angels were particularly Christian, what with Gabriel and the heavenly host? Are there any angels at all in the Old Testament?'

'It's not the "Old Testament", it's the Torah – get it straight, Ms Kessler. And for the record, we Jews, even ex-Jews like yours truly, not only have angels, we even have an angel hierarchy. These tykes here,' Marvin said, pointing at the eternally trumpeting brass angels, 'aren't seraphim, because seraphim have no bodies, only wings and faces.'

'Thanks for filling us in, Mr Kessler,' Mom said, like a child who has just had their answer bettered by the teacher. 'Now, kids, I also had the foresight to buy an advent calendar back when we visited the Moravian Bookshop, in case I couldn't find the right kind here.'

Mom took hold of the cut glass knob on the top left-hand drawer of the massive oak chest of drawers that had accompanied us, like the piano, from home to home for the last several years. Unlike the piano, the chest of drawers had been inherited rather than purchased: when her grandparents had left their home and relocated to the flat closer to her parents, Mom – despite her track record of residential upheaval – had adopted a few pieces of their furniture. She kept fabric napkins and placemats she had sewn in the top right-hand drawer of the antique chest of drawers, and it surprised me to realise that during the months since our last trip to Pennsylvania, despite often being tasked with setting the table, I hadn't ever opened the left-hand drawer and discovered the stashed advent calendar. Then again I had learned that the best way forward, when given instructions, was to do as I was told without deviating from the task. If asked to set the table, I'd go straight to the right-hand drawer where the table linen lived. It was ill-advised to poke around in other drawers if I wanted to avoid questions like 'Why haven't you set the table already'?

I wasn't sure how many of my eight Advents had been marked by the pressing open of perforated paper flaps bearing the numbers one to twenty-four. As with several other aspects of our Christmas celebration, an advent calendar had featured often enough to be familiar, but not consistently enough to be a reliable tradition. I clapped my hands in delight at the unveiling of this year's stiff paper nativity scene, wherein a few human boys and a few girl angels – human boys all dressed for the cold, girl angels incongruously barefooted and sporting demure wings on top of their colourful robes – were on their way, past artificially sparkly snow-laden pine trees, to pay tribute to the newborn Baby Jesus as he slept under the watchful eyes of Mary and Joseph.

'I want to open first!' Alice shouted.

'I want to open on Christmas Eve,' I announced.

Andy wrinkled his brow and was temporarily silent.

'What about you, Andrew?' Mom asked. 'Do you have a preference?'

'If Alice goes first and I go second, Beth Anne will open last,' Andy said.

Mom neither questioned nor commented on Andy's workings-out, instead accepting his math skills as a matter of course. 'And is that OK with you, if you're in the middle?'

'I'm in the middle anyway,' Andy replied, referring to his age, so the matter was settled.

It was a Christmas season peppered with every ritual Mom had introduced in years past and spiced with a couple of welcome new traditions, the first of which wasn't even Christian. The same night Alice opened the first door of the advent calendar, Andy was tapped to light the second candle on the menorah, a special candelabra with room for nine candles.

'Why two candles? It's only the first Sunday of Advent?' I asked.

'It's the second night of Hanukkah. Only your mother got a present though,' said Marvin, 'because she was the only one home on the first day of Hanukkah yesterday.'

'Not fair!' I burst out. 'What did she get?'

'I got a big book of Christmas carols for the piano,' Mom said, pleased. 'The arrangements are really lovely.'

'Christmas carols for Hanukkah – I'm such a good Jew,' Marvin chuckled.

'Is Hanukkah the Jewish version of Christmas?' Andy asked.

'You could say that, but not exactly. We believe Jesus was a great teacher, but we don't believe he was God incarnate. There I go being a bad Jew again, saying 'God' out loud, but I'm not sure you'd understand if I left it out,' Marvin said, half to himself. 'Anyway, Jews are still waiting for the Messiah – Jesus didn't fit the bill for us. So we don't celebrate Jesus's birthday, which wasn't in December anyway, for the record. Instead we celebrate Hanukkah, when we took back an important temple from our oppressors, and we burn the candles because the oil in the temple which was meant to last only one night lasted for eight. Miracle!'

I counted the candles in the menorah again, then said, 'But there are nine candles.'

'That's because Jews can't count,' Marvin said.

The three of us looked at each other in confusion, and Mom shot Marvin a glance. 'Marvin, they're still too young to know you're toying with them. Tell them the real reason, whatever the real reason is.'

'Of course Jews can count,' Marvin said. 'We're excellent counters, especially of money, if you listen to the goyim. But we prefer lighting candles with another candle rather than using matches, so we light the shamash, then use that candle to light all the others.'

'I don't think it's fair that only Mom got a present for Hanukkah,' I said, steering the conversation back to more salient matters.

Now it was Marvin's turn to rise and walk to the oak chest of drawers, where he knelt to open the lower right door, stuck his right arm way into the far corner, and pulled out three net bags of silver foil-covered chocolate coins.

'Happy Hanukkah,' Marvin said, handing a bag to each of us. 'Don't eat all your gelt at once.'

The following Saturday Mom drove us all out to a forested part of Braintree Hill where she reckoned we'd be able to poach a tree.

'I'm not sure whose land it is,' Mom said, as the three of us exited the back seat and Marvin stepped out of the passenger seat. 'But I'm sure they wouldn't mind donating one of their smaller pines to a loving home.'

'I feel like Robin Hood,' Marvin said, taking aim with an imaginary bow and firing at the nearest tree. 'Bulls-eye! Come, Maid Marion, let us away, let us take our band of Merry Men – or in this case, merry children – and set about the redistribution of wealth, one Christmas tree at a time!'

Marvin marched gleefully through the snow, goose-stepping so as to minimise the forward resistance of each step. No walking technique in the world, however, would eliminate the vertical drag of each boot being raised in turn out of the deep, dense snow.

We settled quickly on a scraggly pine a foot taller than Mom. It was Mom who wielded the hatchet, and it was Mom who felled the tree.

Mom swung that hatchet assertively and with precision but even so, the process was much more drawn-out than expected. I had thought that the tree would topple in seconds, but it clung tenaciously to life.

'Do you want me to take over for a few minutes, Liza?' Marvin asked. 'I'm also handy with a hatchet.'

Mom paused and stood upright to push the hair off her forehead. 'Just keep the kids back. And here, hold this,' Mom added, shaking off her coat and tossing it in Marvin's direction.

She did reluctantly accept Marvin's help when we got the tree home. First the tree had to be put in the stand, made of heavy metal and painted a deep green. Mom was not happy with anything less than a perfect right angle between the trunk of the tree and the floor, so each of the four thick screws needed to be tightened just the proper amount.

'Don't wiggle it!' Mom shouted at Marvin, the designated tree-holder, as she knelt down and fiddled with the screws. 'I had it just the way I wanted it!'

'Liza, I haven't moved it at all. It's exactly as upright as it was when you let go of it,' Marvin said calmly.

'We'll see about that,' Mom threatened, but Marvin was unruffled. He managed to assist with the stringing of the Christmas lights with similar aplomb, letting Mom's complaints roll off him as he sang along with Bing Crosby in his mock-operatic voice.

My fear of the dark had never truly abated, which perhaps partly explained my infatuation with the Christmas tree. If I had trouble getting to sleep, as often happened, I could sneak out of my room and over to the tree. The room was sufficiently well-lit by the reflection of the moonlight bouncing off the snow and in through the windows – and my night-time vision was strong enough – that I was able to locate both the prong end of the extension cord and the outlet on the wall. Grasping the copper prongs, I felt my way to the slits in the plastic outlet; the plug didn't even need to be fully inserted before the tree flashed to life, with lights in every colour of the rainbow and in several garishly artificial hues besides. Mom did not subscribe to uniformity when it came to Christmas decorations, so the bulbs were a cheery mishmash of blinking and static, clear and matt. I had two favourites, chosen for two different purposes: a soft red matt bulb, the colour of a Valentine's Day heart, that produced enough heat to warm my hands but not enough to burn them, and a neon-blue flashing bulb that hypnotised me with the rhythm of its incandescence. The neon-yellow bulb must have belonged to the same set as the neon-blue light, but the two, strangely, were not coordinated in their illumination – if one remained on for three seconds, the other stayed on for only two, although I never empirically measured the actual duration of their frequencies. All I knew for sure was that if I patiently observed for a sufficient length of time, the blue and the yellow would, at some unforeseen, magical moment, light concurrently. There was something enormously satisfying about that phenomenon; it exerted a pull on me nearly as strong as the pull of the tide. As I waited for that synchronicity, those nights when sleep eluded me, I could occupy myself by gazing at the other lesser but still-loved bulbs, or the ornaments, so many already imbued with history, like the glass snare drum with its red and silver triangular patterns outlined in gold sparkles, or the reindeer with bodies of dried thistle, glued-on stick legs, and pine cone heads that we had made in bulk at one of our long-ago visits to the Evans' farm in Pennsylvania.

I reached out my hand to touch one of the reindeer – my skin was sensitive enough that I thought I could distinguish between each individual prickle. I applied the tiniest amount of pressure, as one does when testing the blade of a dull knife to determine whether or not it requires sharpening, and a tingle ran through my finger.

Mom's voice, scratchy with emotion, arose from the gloom in the far corner. 'I don't know if you'll ever go back there now.'

I'd been so preoccupied with my search for beauty that I had, uncharacteristically, completely neglected to reconnoitre my surroundings. In my defence, the orange glow of her cigarette would normally have given Mom's presence away, but tonight she wasn't smoking and she must have been sitting very still.

'Hi,' I said. 'I didn't know you were there. Go back where?'

'The Evans' farm. Your father called earlier – Frank Evans died. Helicopter crash.'

I ran through the list of Evanses whose first names I knew; there was no exact match. 'Frank?'

'Yes, Frank Evans – your dad's father. Well, his adoptive father. You probably don't remember him. He was at the farm the year your father was in Vietnam.' Mom's voice was flat, but strangled. She lifted the glass next to her on the side table and I heard her swallow. I didn't need to move closer to know what the liquid would smell like. I could call up the scent of wine far more quickly than I could produce an entry for Frank Evans in my mental encyclopaedia.

It didn't make sense to me that, having deselected Dad, Mom would be so upset about the death of his father, a man I couldn't even picture. It made even less sense that Frank's death would somehow preclude us from ever again visiting the Evans' farm, especially given that he hadn't been at the farm during any visit in my living memory. Given that she had rarely – if ever – spoken of Frank before, I assumed that Mom was devastated, as I would be, at the prospect of a future without trips to the sprawling Evans homestead and all the joy and wonder that that entailed.

'Don't worry, I'm sure we can visit the farm even without Frank being there. He wasn't there when we made the thistle decorations,' I reminded Mom helpfully.

Mom's voice was still constricted. 'There are some things, Beth

Anne, that kids don't understand. You're right – Frank wasn't there last time, or the time before, or maybe any time you can remember, but his death will still have an impact on your relationship with the Evans clan. I'm sorry.'

I ran everything I had learned during my eight years through my internal computer and after some shaking and sputtering, it spat out the result: Mom couldn't be right. It was sad that my dad's dad had died, even if he wasn't my dad's *real* dad, but it made no sense at all that my dad's grandparents and cousins would hold his death against us and no longer welcome us to their home. They had shown us how to make thistle animal Christmas decorations: they loved us.

'I think I can get to sleep now,' I said, guessing Mom would be pleased to hear this news. 'I think I'll go back to bed.'

'Good idea,' Mom said, taking another sip of her wine. I wondered idly if I could possibly have been so entranced by the Christmas tree that I had managed to turn off both my visual and auditory scanning, or if Mom had actually been sitting next to her glass of wine without drinking earlier. Perhaps my unexpected appearance and behaviour had distracted her sufficiently to make her forget to either smoke or drink. Maybe, I mused, there were other ways I could entertain her so thoroughly that she would let go of those crutches more often – maybe, but this was not the time to investigate further.

'Good night,' I said.

'Good night, Beth Anne. I'm sorry,' Mom repeated.

As I left the room, I heard the scratch on a matchbook followed by the subtle but unmistakable whoosh of a match-head igniting. This reassured me, as it meant that Mom was still herself.

Mom spent the morning of Christmas Eve making Moravian sugar cake, a yeasted coffee cake that required repeated proofing.

'Lily May used to let me poke the holes and fill them in with sugar,' Mom told the three of us, presenting us each with a tin foil pie plate covered in the soft dough. 'Now it's your turn. I'll show you how to do it.'

Mom took her own shiny pie plate and began sticking her index finger into the dough at regularly spaced intervals. Her fingers were objects of some fascination for me – unlike the rest of her skin, which ranged from caramel in the winter to toasted marshmallow in the summer, Mom's fingers were shaded more like boysenberries, thanks to her inadequate circulation. Hands weren't meant to be purple, but then again, my own hands lacked Mom's perfectly maintained crescent-moon nails of just the right length – not too long to interfere with housework or gardening, but long enough to look like a lady. The only white on my own nails was at the cuticle; I kept the tips bitten short.

'Good!' Mom exclaimed in approval as we all poked our own fingers into the pillowy mixture. I experimented with the resistance, making some holes shallow and others deeper, then noticing how much the dough sprang back.

'You want to keep the holes as even as possible, Beth Anne,' Mom said. 'You want them all to be big enough for the sugar and butter to really fill them.'

We had a special meal early that evening, but because our family was not a traditional family, it was not the same meal as the previous Christmas Eve. After dinner, Marvin and Mom had a surprise for us.

'Kids,' Marvin announced, 'I, your Jewish stepfather, have determined that you all know far too little about your Christian Christmas story. You think Christmas is about baked goods, trees and presents, when actually it's about the birth of Baby Jesus. But instead of taking my word for it, your mom and I are going to take you back up to our East Montpelier stomping grounds, up to the Old Meeting House for the Christmas Eve service.'

Mom smiled. 'Ironic that it took a Jew to get me to do my Christian duty and take you heathens to church.'

'We went to church for that wedding,' I reminded Mom.

'That doesn't really count,' Mom said. 'Now go get ready, all of you.'

Darkness settled hours before we arrived, but lanterns along both sides of the church walkway cast pools of shimmering light onto the snow and candles flickered in all of the church's windows. I was awestruck and would have stood for hours on the path had Mom not hurried me along.

'Come on, Beth Anne,' Mom said. 'It's beautiful outside, but it's warm inside.'

She was only partially right. The church was heated by two blazing woodstoves, one on each side of the altar, and like all buildings warmed by wood, even when the fires were well stoked, the bite of cold was always apparent, nibbling at the edges of the heat, ready to reclaim the room as soon as the fires' embers died down.

The minister that night told us the story of Christmas straight from the Bible, and together we sang the carols we had sung often at home, but here, the melodies were transformed by the richness of the voices of the congregation. I could distinguish my own voice, Marvin's nasally tenor and Mom's raspy alto, but it was the mingled harmony of all of our voices reverberating through my whole body that made the downy hairs on my arms stand up against the sleeve of my sweater. I felt like the lead character in my favourite Christmas cartoon, *How the Grinch Stole Christmas*; my heart felt outsized with Christmas spirit, and I thought that if I, like the Grinch, could only keep my heart filled with that joy, I might never be unhappy again.

The glow from the service permeated the car on the way home, and was still in evidence in the morning as we tore open the small and mostly useful presents Santa had left in our stockings – toothbrushes, pencils, colourful bouncy balls. The glow lingered still while we smacked our lips at the sweetness of the Moravian sugar cake and scrunched up our mouths at the tartness of the baked grapefruit. As soon as we sat down to open the presents Mom, Marvin and Santa Claus had left us under the tree, however, the Christmas spirit dissipated, like a tyre that has sprung a slow but irreparable leak.

'Don't just tear them open,' Mom commanded, and I heard a familiar chord of irritation creeping in. 'Take one present at a time, and we'll take turns. It's not meant to be carnage.'

Andy flaunted Mom's instructions and grabbed hold of two presents; hoping to avert disaster, I sprang into action.

'Andy!' I shouted. 'Mom just said not to take more than one present! Put one back immediately!'

Andy looked sheepish but unsurprised. He shuffled back towards the tree and deposited his less desired present smack-dab on the head of the snowman appliqued onto the skirt of the Christmas tree.

Alice was already clawing at the wrapping paper on the book-shaped present in her hands, demanding my further intervention. 'Alice! Stop opening until everyone is ready! Mom said so!'

Alice froze; she looked first at me and then at Mom.

Mom, contrary to my intention, seemed more rather than less annoyed. 'I don't need you to be my policeman, Beth Anne. Now why don't you open your biggest present – that might keep you so occupied you forget to boss Andrew and Alice around.'

I obliged. Maybe, when I had carefully removed the wrapping paper familiar from at least one, possibly two, Christmasses past, I would discover the spun-gold tresses of a quasi-divine Barbie and her camper van chariot. Maybe Mom was just saying that Barbies were out of the question and didn't really mean it. Maybe.

When I opened the package though, instead of the coy eyes of a hypersexualised Barbie, the wide, innocent eyes of a life-size baby doll looked out at me. This doll had long eyelashes, chubby hands set in a permanent partial clench, and five toes on each half-curled foot.

All of that I could tolerate, but at the top of her head, right where her brain should be, the doll had a two-inch hole out of which erupted a demonic cascading ponytail of lava-coloured plastic hair. Similar hair covered the rest of her scalp. Had the creators left it at bright red hair, I might have warmed to the doll, but the cavern in the doll's head was unforgivable.

I feigned joy. 'She's amazing!' I said. 'But why does she have a hole in her head?'

Mom, pleased at the reception of the not-Barbie, seemed to regain some of her previous equilibrium. 'Her hair grows,' Mom explained. 'If you yank at it, it shrinks; yank again, and it gets long.'

'Wow,' I said. I tried it out. Sure enough, if I pulled hard, most of the doll's hair disappeared with a jerk back into her head. Another tug, and the ponytail-length tresses reappeared. 'I'll call her Ruth,' I announced.

'I want a doll like that,' Alice whined, and instantly the doll became far more attractive to me.

'Why don't you open your own special present, Alice?' Mom suggested. Alice did as she was told, and three sets of cheerful eyes, two blue and one brown, gazed back at her through a thin sheet of clear plastic.

'Ooh!' Alice squealed.

'It's the Sunshine Family,' Marvin said. 'Like Barbies, but better.'

I zoomed over to Alice with Ruth in tow. Her dolls, I constituted, were superior in many ways to mine: there were more of them, they were more poseable, and most importantly, none of them had holes in their heads.

'I'll trade you,' I said to Alice. 'You can have Ruth, and I'll have the Sunshine Family.'

Alice looked daggers at me and clutched the box containing the three dolls tightly to her chest. 'No!'

'Come on, Alice,' I wheedled, 'don't you want this big doll instead of three little dolls?'

'Beth Anne,' Mom remonstrated, 'leave your sister alone. I thought you loved your new doll? I thought you wanted a doll with hair you could play with?'

'I do, and I did,' I said, backtracking, but the jealousy was too intense, and I couldn't leave it at that. 'I do love Ruth, but I love Alice's dolls more,' I confessed.

Mom threw up her hands in a gesture of exasperation. 'This is why I hate Christmas,' she said. 'It's a holiday based on an unachievable fantasy. I remember wishing every year that this would be the one year my family would have a happy Christmas. It wasn't even about the presents, I just didn't want there to be any arguments. But every year, like clockwork, my father would get drunk and shout. Now I understand why. There's no way any parent can live up to a child's expectations of a storybook Christmas.'

And with that, Mom stormed out of the living room. Marvin, Andy, Alice and I were all left shell-shocked.

'I guess we should have stuck with Hanukkah,' Marvin joked. 'Why don't we take a little break from the presents, kids, and I'll go try to replace your mother's Christmas spirit? Perhaps a glass of wine would not be remiss. It seems to have been her father's go-to Christmas beverage.'

Marvin's strategy worked, at least to begin with. Mom returned to the living room, glass in hand, after ten minutes or so. We kids finished opening our presents – I made sure to express only gratitude – partook of the ham and potatoes, and set about playing with our new toys. One glass, however, turned into two, which turned into three, and soon Mom was sobbing quietly in her favourite chair, while Marvin knelt at her side.

'Come on, Liza,' Marvin said gently, 'pull it together. Let's not end the holiday like this.'

'I can't,' Mom said. 'Don't you get it? I can't pull it together. I'm falling apart, more and more, with every passing day.'

Marvin turned to me. 'Beth Anne,' he said. 'Take your brother and sister and go play in your own bedrooms. I'll come in a bit later to read you the Christmas story of your choice.'

'Can it be the one from the Bible?' I asked.

'I'm not sure we have the New Testament in the house, but thanks to our recent refresher course, I could probably retell that story to your satisfaction. Now scoot.'

I did as I was told, shepherding each sibling with their cache of gifts to their own room, while I retired to mine, but not without first stopping to retrieve something from the middle drawer of the oak bureau.

Safely ensconced in my bedroom, I took the sharp, orange-handled silver scissors Mom used for fabric-cutting and hacked off every inch of Ruth's ponytail.

27

Outside the Lines

'Jesus, Beth Anne, what happened to your doll?' Mom said when she emerged, tousled and still squinting in the morning light, from the master bedroom the morning after Christmas Day.
I reddened but my answer was defiant. 'I cut her hair.'

'Why the hell did you do that?'

'I didn't like the way it grew. It wasn't like normal hair. I think she looks better with short hair,' I said. This last statement was completely false. Ruth looked even worse with the jagged remnants of her once luxurious ponytail sticking straight up at the top of her head, but there was no way I would admit that.

'Of course it isn't like normal hair,' Mom said, frustrated. 'It's a *doll*, Beth Anne. That doll was not cheap, and there's no way we're buying you another one.'

'I don't want another one anyway,' I said, and that was absolutely true, because I hadn't wanted a baby doll in the first place. I had wanted a Barbie. 'I like Ruth.'

I maintained ownership of Ruth for another week or so, but she had become a physical reminder of my stupidity – and worse, my ingratitude – and I came to hate her.

'Do *you* like Ruth?' I asked Alice, when my desire to absolve myself of the sins I had committed against both the doll and my parents became overwhelming, like a leaded cloak holding me underwater that I was desperate to cast off, so I could swim back up to the surface and breathe freely again.

'I like Ruth, even though you cut her hair, but I like my Sunshine Family more,' Alice replied, wisely anticipating where the conversation was headed.

'I know you don't want to trade,' I said, 'but do you want Ruth? Do you want her to be your doll?'

'Would I still get to keep the Sunshine Family?' Alice asked, not quite believing that I was offering her something for nothing.

'I told you – I don't want the Sunshine Family,' I said, throwing my hands up. 'I just want you to have Ruth.'

'OK,' Alice said.

'Great,' I said, feeling lighter already. 'I'll go get her for you.'

'I don't need her right now,' Alice said. 'I'm colouring.'

'But she needs you,' I countered and went to get the doll, depositing her on the free chair next to Alice at the table.

My health deteriorated after Christmas. I had boots with mottled felt liners – while warm when dry, the boots were a half-size too big for me as Mom believed in ordering clothing and footwear for longevity, so snow was able to find its way in, and the boots seemed to hold the cold almost more effectively than they held the warmth. Whether because of my icy feet or because my immune system was simply not equipped for the onslaught of the Vermont winter that year, in January my throat closed up with tonsillitis, and stayed mostly closed for the next several weeks. Fever became my new normal, and I trained myself to let it roll over me as I shivered under several blankets, occasionally interrupted by Mom's administration of ground-up penicillin in apple sauce. The illness brought simplicity

– I couldn't worry about missing school, about Andy and Alice, about Marvin and Mom, or about anything at all other than riding through the fever and the burning pain in my swollen throat. Sometimes the fever made the ride easier for me by bringing me visions, colourful blocks of light that danced before my inner eye and distracted me from the horrible discomfort of each swallow; when that happened, although it was better for me, it was worse for Mom, because it meant my temperature had soared into realms dangerously close to seizure or even death, which she knew, but I didn't.

'I'll get you a cold washcloth,' Mom said one day – or was it night, I couldn't tell – when my fever had skyrocketed. 'I don't understand why the antibiotics aren't working,' she added.

I gathered my strength, and in a voice hijacked by sickness, said, 'Maybe it's the apple sauce?'

Mom's eyes crinkled as she smiled, but the gauze curtain of my illness couldn't obscure that even as she smiled, her eyes were concerned. The illness was a price I was more than willing to pay for those fleeting seconds when I was suddenly present to Mom, when her fear of losing me to a capricious adversary superseded all her other fears. The cold cloth was soothing, but what mattered far more was the care with which it was placed on my burning brow.

One Saturday towards the end of February, when I was finally deemed sufficiently healthy, Marvin made good on his promise to take us all cross-country skiing at the Trapp Family Lodge. Alice complained bitterly – her dunking in the snow-making pond had put her off skiing entirely – but Marvin informed her that there were no snow-making facilities for these tracks, and thus no snow-making ponds. As a primary-school teacher, Marvin knew better than to argue that even if there were ponds – or rivers or brooks for that matter – Alice would be able to avoid them. He understood that from Alice's point of view, it wasn't her fault that she'd fallen into the pond at Killington, but rather it was that of the pond for simply being in the wrong place. Marvin's reassurance sufficed, and soon we found ourselves in the strong late February sunlight wearing sheepskin-lined rental ski boots with ridiculous black plastic protuberances at the front.

'I feel like Donald Duck,' I said. 'Quack! Quack!'

'Donald Duck is above quacking, Beth Anne. But he's not above saying'—here Marvin adopted his best Donald Duck voice —'Oh boy, oh boy, oh boy.'

We all laughed at Marvin, who was not only talking but also waddling like the famous cartoon duck.

'Those are for clamping the skis to your feet,' Mom explained. She took the hilariously long skis I had been allocated and bent over me to attach first the left one, then the right, to my boots while I leaned on her stooped back for support.

Mom selected the easiest of the myriad trails for us to begin with. She was a natural cross-country skier, whether from winters spent ice-skating or from innate athleticism; she coasted ahead as though weightless. My ski tips, however, seemed as drawn to each other as the North and South poles of a powerful magnet – whenever they crossed, I had to fight to stay upright, a fight I lost repeatedly, ending up prostrate in the snow at the side of the track. Andy and Alice weren't faring much better, and for the first fifteen minutes or so we kids spent most of the time falling and getting back on our feet. Soon, however, our skills improved, and we were ready to take on a hill.

'Now you really have to act like Donald Duck,' Marvin told us as we stood contemplating the V-shaped ski tracks ahead. 'I'll go first, to demonstrate the technique, and your mom can give you each a hand if you need it.'

Marvin turned each of his skis outwards and started up the hill, black curls bobbing with every step. 'Oh boy, oh boy,' he squeaked from ahead.

There was something so incongruous about a Donald Duck-impersonating Brooklynite staggering up a snowy ski track in Vermont that I couldn't help but laugh. Before long we were all laughing, even Mom.

'This is why I love him,' Mom said to us. 'He is not afraid of making a fool of himself.'

'I heard that, Liza,' came the response from halfway up the hill.

In the evenings, however, when all of us had been tucked in, Mom seemed to forget her reasons for loving Marvin. Half-heard disagreements became more frequent. Some heated exchanges were punctuated by crockery, hurtling through the air and smashing on impact. This sound – which I had long ago learned to recognise – alarmed me, but what scared me even more were the arguments that ended in sudden near-silence, save for a sort of scuffling reminiscent of the noise of moving furniture. Somehow even the worst fights with Marvin were preferable, however, to the evenings where Mom's only opponent was herself, and her only weapon was a gallon jug of wine.

The boundaries shifted as the winter wore on, and slowly the drinking previously reserved for after our bedtime began to colour outside the lines, first infiltrating the early evenings, then making inroads into the afternoons when Mom wasn't at work. I decided, after much thought, to take matters into my own hands. I had worked out, by that time, that the problem was the wine. I reasoned that if the wine were to disappear, so too would all of Mom's anger and sadness.

Mom was in her favourite chair, half-sleeping, when I took action one Tuesday afternoon when I had been granted yet another day of 'home-schooling' and Alice was napping in her bedroom. Furtively, I tiptoed out of the TV room, crept into the kitchen, and opened the cupboard under the sink where Mom kept her active gallon, at that moment a little less than half full. With giddy excitement I yanked the mottled cork out – this proved easier than anticipated, as the cork had been only half-heartedly reinserted after Mom's last glass. I tipped the bottle into the sink; the pale yellow liquid with its sweet yet sour smell poured out like an alcoholic waterfall, and I revelled in the certainty that the dull silver drain would be both unable and unwilling to cough the wine back up, no matter how impassioned Mom's rage. When the volume in the bottle reached a particular level, the flow began to hiccup – glug, glug – coming out in spurts, rather than in a steady stream. The smell nauseated me, but I was determined to carry on until the last tiny drop had vanished. I kept one eye on the entrance to the TV room, both wishing and dreading that Mom's shape would materialise in the doorway so she could witness at first-hand my reckless destruction of her closely guarded treasure. My vigilance was unnecessary – although I held the bottle aloft until what remained within would not have intoxicated a fly, I was not caught red-handed.

Mom went to refill her glass only after Alice had woken from her nap and Andy had returned from school. Marvin was not yet home from work and Mom was preparing to cook stew for dinner; a glass of wine on the side was called for by every recipe, although that was never mentioned in the actual cookbook. My eyes bored into my mother's back as she lifted her glass from the side table and walked leisurely towards the kitchen. I steeled myself for a barrage of expletives heretofore unencountered.

Nothing. 'Beth Anne, can you change the chan—' Alice started, but I cut her off.

'Shh,' I hissed, giving Alice my most intimidating evil eye. 'Be quiet for a minute.'

I left my finger at my lips and held very, very still.

Andy, unmoved by my gesture, asked, 'What? Why do we have to be qui—'

'Andy! Shut up!' I commanded in a whisper. Andy rolled his eyes, then padded over to the TV and changed the channel himself, looking to Alice for confirmation that she wanted to watch 'Match Game' instead of 'One Life to Live,' which, of course, she did.

Still nothing from the kitchen. I couldn't believe my luck. As soon as I had relaxed, however – when I was well and truly involved in the drama of who would win the sought-after cash prize on 'Match Game' and had nearly forgotten the drama of the empty bottle – Mom sidled up to the sofa.

'Did you pour out my wine, Beth Anne?' Mom asked, in a measured voice somehow more terrifying than a scream.

I was taken off guard. My face, which I had hoped to compose in an attitude of innocence, gave the game away immediately, although my mouth temporarily refused to form words and my head seemed locked in position, unable to indicate either yea or nay.

'Beth Anne, I'm asking you a question. Did you go into the cupboard and pour out my wine? Tell me the truth.'

'Yes,' I said simply, looking my mother straight in the eye and willing her to ask me why.

Mom, her expression inscrutable, held my gaze. Finally she broke her silence. 'Don't ever do that again,' Mom said. She didn't wait for a response. She didn't need to – Mom was wholly confident that any direct orders she gave us would be fully obeyed.

I crumpled into myself. My only viable escape route from the spectre of Mom's overconsumption had been cut off at the pass. Even when my favourite panellist, Richard Dawson, said something so witty that not only the studio audience but all of the other panellists as well chortled with laughter, I remained sunken.

As winter slowly retreated and spring gained a foothold, Mom became sunnier, but it was a sunlight with continued scattered showers. On one particularly bright day, Mom announced that Aunt

Joanne and her friend Ted Noke would be coming to visit at Easter; Aunt Joanne was moving to Alaska and wanted to come to say goodbye before she added four thousand miles to the distance between us.

'Is Ted Noke Aunt Joanne's boyfriend?' I asked. I'd met Ted Noke at least once previously and remembered him fondly for his exceptional sketching skills, so I hoped for an affirmative answer, but Mom looked aghast.

'No,' Mom said, as if I had proposed something completely out-landish. I had no idea why Mom thought Ted Noke would be so unsuitable a match for her sister, and it clashed with my perception of him, so I inquired further.

'Why not? I like Ted Noke. He drew us all pictures last time he came to visit,' I said.

'Aunt Joanne might have wanted Ted Noke to be her boyfriend,' Mom said carefully, 'but Joanne isn't the kind of person Ted Noke is interested in romantically.'

This was even more mystifying. Aunt Joanne was just as pretty as Mom, albeit differently shaped: where Mom was rounded, Aunt Joanne was angular. Aunt Joanne was at least as smart as Mom, and she drawled when she spoke, like a cowboy, or like a country singer being interviewed on the radio. Also, as I must have known earlier, but had only recently learned again as an autonomous person, Aunt Joanne was my godmother – that alone, I thought, with a child's delusions of grandeur, should have made Ted Noke want to walk Aunt Joanne down the aisle. How often could you marry someone and gain a goddaughter as marvellous as me?

'What's the matter with Aunt Joanne? Why doesn't Ted Noke like her?'

Mom, I could tell, was walking around an elephant in the room as she answered, but the elephant, although very obvious to her, was completely invisible to me. She sighed. 'Nothing's the matter with

Aunt Joanne, Beth Anne,' she said patiently. 'And nothing's the matter with Ted Noke either. Just because a man and a woman are friends, it doesn't mean they have to be boyfriend and girlfriend. Don't you have any friends who are boys at school?'

'No,' I said. I neglected to mention that I had barely any friends who were girls either.

'What, are all of the boys just – boys?' Mom probed.

'Yes. They're all stupid.'

'Hmm, I don't think that's the case, but that's certainly age-appropriate,' Mom said, both to me and to herself. 'But you have your brother. Your brother isn't your boyfriend but he's your friend.'

'He's not my friend, he's my brother,' I countered.

'Aunt Joanne is my sister, but she's also my friend,' Mom said. 'That's why I wish she weren't moving to Alaska. I know we don't see her often, but now we'll see her even less. It would be hard for her to step up as a godparent, should she ever need to, when she's four thousand miles away.'

'What do you mean?'

'Well, officially, godparents are meant to look after the children if the parents can't for some reason. Like if the parents die in – I don't know – a car crash or some other sort of accident. That's when the godparents are meant to take over.'

Mom noticed that I was now looking not only perplexed, but also bereft. 'Don't worry, Beth Anne. In a way you're lucky that your dad and I aren't together because there's no chance at all that both of us will be killed in a car crash at the same time. The silver lining of divorce, I suppose.'

I tried to appear more cheerful, as if Mom's dire logic had succeeded in comforting me. I managed a wan smile.

'Speaking of men and women who are,' Mom raised her hands to surround the next phrase with unironic air quotes, '"just friends", one of Marvin's friends, Ellie Tillerman, has invited us all over to her house for a party while Joanne and Ted are here.'

I perked up. 'Really? When?'

'Good Friday. Rather odd to have a dinner party on Good Friday, when you're meant to be sitting around contemplating the Crucifixion; Ellie must not be much of a churchgoer. And for Marvin, of course, it's not a holiday at all – it's just another Friday.'

Mom was fond of playing a particular hymn from the *Moravian Youth Hymnal*, 'Go to Dark Gethsemane', in the run-up to Easter; it was in a mournful minor key, and I wondered if for Mom, playing that hymn counted as appropriately reverent, whereas hosting or guesting a dinner party did not.

'Should we stay home instead?' I suggested. 'We could all sing some Easter songs? Does Aunt Joanne know the *Moravian Youth Hymnal*?'

Mom laughed. 'Of course Joanne knows the *Moravian Youth Hymnal*. She grew up with it just like I did, but I'm quite sure Joanne would rather go out to a dinner party than stay at home singing hymns. You'll like Ellie's house – she has horses.'

Ellie had a tanned open face and a hint of a bow-legged walk, possibly from her hours spent in the saddle; she squinted in the manner of someone whose vision has gone uncorrected for too long. Ellie knew our names before we were formally introduced; she even had the order right, welcoming me as 'Beth Anne' and my sister as 'Alice', not the other way round as some adults did upon meeting us for the first time. It bothered me when grown-ups jumbled up me and my sister – it felt like being demoted from the older, most responsible sibling to the baby – so I appreciated Ellie's accuracy.

Ellie took those of us who wanted to go straight out to meet the horses. Andy was more interested in the platter of crudités and the sour cream and onion dip than in stroking an enormous animal of no immediate use to him, and Mom, given the choice, would rather stay a safe distance away from any animal bigger than a cat, so the two of them stayed indoors, Andy eating and Mom smoking, while the rest of us trundled out to the barn.

The horse barn was not like the cow barn up the road at the Masons' farm. There was none of the scent of day-old milk, the air was not close and heavy with moisture, and there was nothing of the din of a herd of cattle. Yes, the horses snorted and stamped when we entered, but unlike the indiscriminate lowing of cows, the noises of the horses seemed considered, almost conversational.

'No, Duchess, I'm not taking you out, so there's no need to get excited,' Ellie said soothingly to the horse craning her head the furthest out of her stall. Reflexively, Ellie patted Duchess on the neck, then reached up and scratched behind her ears. 'I have some people here who'd like to meet you though.'

Ellie beckoned for Alice and me to approach, which I did timidly and Alice did fearlessly. 'You can pat her,' Ellie said. 'I'm not sure you'll even reach though, Alice – let me lift you.'

With the additional height, Alice was able not only to pat Duchess's neck, but even scratch behind her ears, just as Ellie had.

'Do you want to try giving her a treat, Beth Anne?' Ellie asked, placing Alice delicately back on the floor.

I turned to Aunt Joanne, who, just like Ted Noke and Marvin, appeared to be reliving her own early encounters with horses through witnessing ours. She nodded her assent in Mom's absence.

'OK,' I said, accepting the carrot Ellie offered me. I thought of Spider, the horse on the Evans' farm, and I reminded myself to keep my hand flat despite the tickle of Duchess's lips so as to avoid the chomping of her huge teeth.

'You already know how to do it, I can tell,' Ellie said.

Duchess snapped up the carrot, her breath warm against my hand, and I stepped back, delighted.

'Do you three want to pat Duchess?' Ellie asked the adults, who formed an orderly queue and took it in turns to come forward and introduce themselves to the chestnut mare with the white blaze on her nose.

Meeting the horses – Duchess, Venus and Ruby – was the highlight of an otherwise monotonous evening. The adults all seemed to get along famously, but we were the only children present, and because Ellie had no children of her own, there were no toys, crayons or books suitable for young readers in the house. There wasn't even a television, but Ellie did offer us a deck of cards, which Andy and I gratefully accepted. Alice wasn't in the mood for cards and she soon nodded off in a corner of the couch, tucked into a ball, looking much like Shiva when she returned from her daily adventures. How many times had I cuddled up next to Shiva, digging my hands into her stiff, sandy fur, dry at the ends but oily next to her skin, and let her barrel chest, rising and falling rhythmically with her breathing, support the entire weight of my head.

The morning after the dinner at Ellie Tillerman's, the Masons called from the farm up the road.

'Was she?' I overheard Mom say. 'Oh dear – I'm so sorry. You're absolutely right. No, we would normally have left her inside while we went out, but I called and called for her, and Marvin called as well, but there was no trace of her. Yes – I understand. We'll keep her under control from now on, and if we can't, well . . . well, then maybe this isn't the right home for Shiva.'

There was a pause as Mom listened. Aunt Joanne wandered in; she yawned showily, took a seat at the table, and opened the second to last issue of the weekly local newspaper. 'Of course – we'd rather she stay with us as well,' Mom said into the phone, 'but I do realise that this is your livelihood. Please let us know if it happens again. Thanks, Helen.'

Mom replaced the heavy black receiver in the cradle.

'What's up?' asked Aunt Joanne, who had been alternately nodding in agreement and shaking her head in disbelief while reading the latest batch of Letters to the Editor.

'It's Shiva,' Mom said. 'This is the second time she's caused trouble. They nearly shot her last night because she was running the cows. One more strike and she's out.'

'Why do you let her up there?' asked Aunt Joanne, who was a cat person.

'We don't "let her up there",' Mom said with exasperation. 'She just goes. I can't control her – she's Marvin's dog – and even if I could, would I want her chained to our property the entire time? No. No, I wouldn't.'

'Surely being confined to your property is better than being shot or given away?' Aunt Joanne asked, eminently sensible.

'Not for me it isn't,' Mom retorted. 'Then I have to put up with her going insane from boredom – barking incessantly, digging huge holes in the garden, looking at me with those pathetic eyes. Maybe she would be better off somewhere else.'

'She would not,' I said. I puffed up like a bantam, then proclaimed, 'I'll walk Shiva. I'll make sure she never goes outside without me.'

I knew I would have to be very grown-up indeed to keep the white shepherd on the straight and narrow, but I was absolutely certain I was up to the task. I would take Shiva out for a walk now, just to prove it.

'Where is Shiva?' I asked.

'She came and slept with us,' Aunt Joanne said. 'I think she's snuggling with Ted at the moment.'

'Oh,' I said, my plans thwarted. 'So maybe I can't walk her right now but I can walk her every single other day.'

Mom shook her head as if failure was a foregone conclusion, but

Aunt Joanne gave me a vote of confidence.

'That's right, Beth Anne. Shiva's resting now – she's probably tuckered out from all her shenanigans last night – but you can walk her later, and tomorrow, and all the tomorrows after that. I'm sure you and your mother and everyone else in the house will do whatever it takes to keep Shiva from ever running the cows again.'

28

Tomato Seedling

Like every other child who has promised to look after a dog – to feed it, walk it, play with it every day – my vow to take responsibility for caring for Shiva was broken within days of being sworn. Hours, actually. I did try – once Shiva had rested for the morning, and, more critically, once I'd had lunch, I asked Mom to help me ready Shiva for her first walk with me.

'She doesn't like walking on a leash, Beth Anne,' Mom cautioned. 'She'll either pull so hard you won't be able to control her, or she'll go on strike and refuse to move. Or maybe a combination of both.'

Mom attached Shiva's hand-beaded leather collar as she spoke.

'She looks prettier with her collar on,' I said. 'It's like a necklace. And don't worry – maybe she doesn't walk for you, but she loves me and I'm sure she'll walk with me.'

Mom snorted. 'So now you think Shiva doesn't love me? She's Marvin's dog – do you think she knows something I don't?'

I revised my line of reasoning. 'Of course Shiva loves you, and so does Marvin, but what I mean is I might be more fun to walk with.'

I wasn't. Shiva did just as Mom had said she might – she first sat on her haunches, then eased herself into a supine position, front legs straight out in front of her. No amount of cajoling or pulling on the lead could sway her.

Mom was checking on me intermittently through the window. She left me to persuade Shiva for longer than most parents would have, but as two minutes became five, and five neared ten, Mom opened the door to the back deck.

'Just unclip the leash, Beth Anne,' Mom called out.

'But what about the cows? If Shiva runs the cows again, then . . .' I let the sentence hang there, uncompleted, as the prospect was too heartbreaking for me to contemplate.

'The cows aren't in the field right now and if you're keeping an eye on her, she'll stay with you. Remember, she got into trouble last night because we'd gone out without putting her inside.'

Aunt Joanne's head appeared behind Mom; Joanne was so tall she didn't even need to crane to see past her older sister. It was hard to imagine being dwarfed by my own little sister, Alice; I hoped, with the self-importance of an eldest child, that I would maintain my status as the tallest of, if not the three of us siblings, than at least the two of us girls.

'Your mom is right, Beth Anne,' Aunt Joanne said, in her low, gravelly voice. The overlay of the Pennsylvania Dutch accent endemic to the Cliff bloodline made her sound like a latter-day Marlene Dietrich. 'Go ahead and set Shiva free. She won't run away, not while you're out there. Actually, you haven't shown me your new bike yet – how fast can you circle that acre?'

Andy squirmed out from under Mom. 'Race ya!' he cried as he ran towards his own chariot.

'Cheater!' I shouted, as Andy mounted his bike and pedaled furiously towards the open gate at the foot of the field.

I dashed off to grab my own bike then sped after him, determined to beat my brother despite his significant head start.

When, after circling the acre at full tilt, I reached the arbitrary finish line of the open gate in triumph, I glanced over to the doorway: Aunt Joanne was still watching, bemused, but Mom had disappeared.

Aunt Joanne was not a natural hugger, but when she and Ted Noke had loaded their suitcases into her light blue Saab – the car that would shortly transport her all the way to Alaska, where her new job as a paralegal awaited – she wordlessly opened her arms and enveloped Mom, who was similarly not a natural hugger, but made an exception on this occasion to bid her giant little sister adieu.

'Look after yourself,' Aunt Joanne said to Mom.

'I'm not the one moving thousands of miles away to some snow-covered state full of polar bears,' Mom said. 'I should be telling you to look after yourself. Then again, I needn't bother – you've always managed to keep yourself safe.'

'I've had a different set of circumstances,' Aunt Joanne replied, her tone apologetic. Did she mean that she hadn't been made to move to the wild and hostile mountains of Vermont, as Mom had? Did she mean that she didn't live anywhere near farms, so didn't need to contend with oversized ungulates, as Mom did? Or did Joanne mean that she hadn't been born the eldest, so wasn't laden with the burdens of that position in the birth order, as both Mom and I were? Aunt Joanne, I was sure, feared neither heights nor cows, so I reasoned Aunt Joanne must be referring to the duties of an elder sister that she had gratefully been spared – this was notably empathetic of her, I thought, and that raised my aunt (and godmother) still further in my esteem.

Wine had flowed over the Easter holiday, but Mom had kept either her intake, her emotions or both under control while Aunt Joanne and Ted Noke were with us. As soon as our visitors left, however, the storm of evening arguments gathered apace, punctuated by the thunder of slammed doors and the lightning of smashed crockery. Marvin, previously so keen to devote his weekends to our entertainment and acculturation, started spending some weekend days, and even nights, elsewhere. While his absence guaranteed my parents wouldn't argue, it also increased the likelihood that Mom might end up shouting at one of us, or – worse – that I would find my mother slumped in her easy chair in tears when I came out of my bedroom in the middle of the night for a drink of water.

Just as the evenings were a lucky dip, there was also no way to predict what sort of mood Mom would be in when I came home from school or when she arrived home from work, whichever came first. This was another benefit to skipping school if it was one of Mom's days off – staying home allowed me to read the tea leaves as the day progressed, so that crying jags or fits of anger in the evening, while still unwelcome and unpleasant, were at least less of a surprise. I calibrated myself like the finest barometer, attuned to any shifts in the pressure of the weather system that was my mother, and deluded myself into believing that my own atmospheric physics might somehow affect hers.

All that school missed didn't go unnoticed by Mrs Neill. At dinner on an evening that had been comfortably normal, Mom raised the issue of the following school year.

'I had a call from Upper Branch today,' Mom said, wiping her mouth after her bite of baked potato.

'What did they want? Did Mrs Neill suggest Beth Anne would be a better teacher than she is?' Marvin asked, grinning at me like the biggest know-it-all.

I blushed. 'I wouldn't be. I couldn't tell the other kids what to do.'

Marvin disagreed. 'Sure you could. You tell your brother and sister what to do all . . . the . . . time.' He dragged out each of the last three words for emphasis.

I reddened further. 'I don't *always* tell them what to do. Just a lot of the time.'

Mom interrupted. 'Anyway, it wasn't Mrs Neill, it was the principal. We're going to have to go to a meeting, because basically Beth Anne has so many absences that they're considering holding her back a year.'

I was outraged. 'What? They're going to flunk me? Only Barry Sampson is flunking! How can they flunk me when I do all the work Mrs Neill gives me to do?'

'Calm down, Beth Anne. I haven't finished telling the story yet,' Mom said. I slathered more sour cream on my potato and took a huge bite to demonstrate my reluctant compliance.

'They can't hold her back, Liza,' Marvin said. 'It would be nearly criminal to keep someone as bright as Beth this bored for yet another year. That could turn her off learning indefinitely, just like you've been saying.'

'They know that too, so they also considered letting her skip a year,' Mom said.

I nearly choked on my mouthful of green beans. 'What? I'd be in fifth grade instead of fourth grade? But I don't want to do that either! Janine is my only friend in the whole school and I want to stay with her!'

'I'm sure Janine isn't your only friend, Beth Anne,' Mom said. 'But don't panic – what will probably happen is that the two will cancel each other out, and you'll stay in the same grade you're in now, with Janine.'

'Can I skip a grade?' asked Andy. 'I'm bored too, and I already have friends in the grade above me.'

'No,' Mom said. 'Honestly, don't they know anything about how to teach smart kids in these schools?'

'They've got their hands full, Liza,' Marvin said. 'They've got a class full of kids, little to no help, insufficient funding and resources, and they're in Vermont, which, while very progressive in some places, is still very backwater in others.'

'Mrs Neill being a stunning illustration of the less progressive elements,' Mom said.

'Right,' Marvin agreed. 'So I wouldn't worry about it. Beth Anne will go into fourth grade, just like Janine and the rest of her class, and hopefully her fourth-grade teacher will be more forward-thinking.'

As mud season gave way to spring, Mom started preparing her garden plot for planting. Tomato seedlings appeared in the kitchen windowsill, in ink-black soil in flimsy cardboard pots that were perfectly square at the top. The stalks were downy with fuzz, and too delicate at first to touch; when the seedlings were established though, I could run my finger from the base of the stalk to the first leaves and my finger would come away bearing the intoxicating scent of the tomato plant, rich with the promise of fruits to come.

Mom's state of mind was not the only unpredictable variable at play when I returned from school. She was also given to rejigging the layout of our home. I might come home and head for the TV only to discover the TV was against the wall opposite to where it had been previously, or in a different room altogether. Even the piano was not immune to such relocation: Mom possessed the sinewy, superhuman strength necessary to manage moving a piano on her own and used that strength whenever she deemed it necessary. Sometimes Mom got a bee in her bonnet that would lead her to repurpose entire rooms in our sprawling, haphazard farmhouse, so the dining room would become the living room, or the play room would become the sewing room. I found these changes discombobulating, but I had learned to live with the state of constant physical flux and could manage that far better than the equally constant emotional flux. Besides, wherever the things of the house found themselves, Shiva would navigate through them, or, if outside, past the pond or through the field, to greet me after school each day, her eyes bright and her straw-coloured tail wagging.

Except that one day Shiva didn't. She didn't run up to the bus to meet me, she didn't beat me to the front door by bounding down the driveway, and nor did she tackle me when I stepped through the front door. Mom wasn't inside either, although her car was home; perhaps she was working in her garden, and Shiva was too occupied digging worms alongside to notice my arrival.

I traipsed around the house and found Mom, as I had guessed, kneeling on the ground with her wooden-handled trowel, whose point, I knew from experience, was surprisingly sharp; Shiva wasn't with her.

'Where's Shiva?' I said.

'Oh hi, Beth Anne,' Mom said, straightening her back. She dusted off her hands, stood up, and composed her face in an expression that filled me with visceral dread.

'The Masons called – Shiva was running their cows again. The Masons can't afford to lose any cows, Pumpkin,' Mom said, as though this explanation would make whatever Mom was going to say next not only understandable, but inarguable.

I stiffened. 'Where's Shiva, Mom?'

'Marvin took Shiva to Ellie Tillerman's house,' Mom said.

The star inside me collapsed and was replaced by a black hole. 'But Ellie Tillerman has horses! Shiva might run the horses! Isn't that just as bad? Why couldn't we just keep Shiva inside?'

'Ellie used to have a dog of her own and the horses got used to it, so they won't be scared of Shiva and they won't move in a way that makes her chase them,' Mom said. 'It's for the best, really – Ellie was missing her dog, and she gets to borrow ours, the Masons' cows won't be in danger, and Shiva won't get shot, which is what the Masons said they'd be doing next.'

'When does Shiva get to come home?'

I could see the clouds forming as Mom answered. 'Beth Anne – I'm sorry you'll miss your friend, but you have to accept this. Now why don't you go inside and see what Alice and Andrew are up to?'

This was my cue, but I refused to take it. 'Will it be two weeks? A month? Two months?'

Mom snapped. 'It's not my fault the fucking dog chases cows, OK? It's not my fault she doesn't come when called – I didn't train her, Marvin did. She's not my dog, she's his. I wouldn't blame the Masons for shooting her when she's going after their cows. Maybe if they didn't shoot to kill, but shot her in the leg, she'd learn her lesson.'

The gravitational pull of the black hole in my centre increased exponentially; I froze, preparing to self-destruct. When a beat passed and I was still there, hot tears sprang to my eyes.

'Stop crying,' Mom ordered, 'it's not going to do any good. Nobody is going to shoot that damn dog, Beth Anne. Certainly not *Ellie*, not when it's Marvin's dog.'

Mom said 'Ellie' in a mocking sing-song, the way Janine said 'goody-two-shoes' about the girls at school she didn't like, and the hostility surprised me enough to staunch my tears, at least momentarily.

'Why didn't you let me say goodbye to Shiva?' I demanded to know.

'Oh for fuck's sake, Beth Anne,' Mom groaned, 'it's not like the dog died. Now go inside, and let me garden in peace.'

I stayed rooted to the spot, as if I were one of the tomato seedlings. Mom ignored me and turned her attention back to the actual seedlings. She stabbed the ground with her trowel, using more force than necessary, but then, when the moment came to transfer the nascent tomato plant from the safety of its cardboard planter, her demeanour underwent a dramatic shift. I studied her through a fog of tears, transfixed, as she delicately removed the seedling from its pot, then still more gently shook the excess black soil from the roots. Mom solicitously placed the plant in the hole she had prepared, then carefully replaced the soil and tamped it lightly with the back of her trowel. Mom repeated the process three times as I looked on, sobbing soundlessly.

Finally Mom sighed and raised her head. Her voice, when she spoke, was softer, but still unyielding. 'Look, Beth Anne, I know you love that dog, but it's just not practical to have her here right now, OK? It's better to have her alive somewhere else than dead here though, isn't it?'

The mere mention of Shiva's possible demise was enough to make my shoulders shake involuntarily as grief overtook me. I spun around and sprinted away from the conversation I wanted to undo, from the tomato plants I envied, and from the real gravitational pull at the centre of my universe.

29

Fireflies

The intermittent flashing of fireflies lit up our yard and acre of field towards the end of May. I took satisfaction in noting that we had at least as many, if not more, of the unassuming yet fantastical beetles per square metre on our property as my grandparents had at their house in Bethlehem. I had to concede, however, that it wasn't actually our field that was the most entrancing, but rather the one across the dirt main road, where the lightning bug density was the greatest. A substantial, intimidating split-rail wooden fence stood between the pull-off from the road and that field; we were strictly prohibited from setting foot on the other side of that fence. Mom claimed it was the bulls' field, and although I had not once seen any bulls in the field, she was absolutely not willing to gamble where potentially murderous beasts were concerned. While I respected the overriding injunction, I stretched what was permitted by climbing the fence – the heavy top rail was level with my nose – and perching aloft, holding on to the closest post. On evenings when the fireflies appeared, I headed straight for that split-rail fence, because the incongruity of their incandescence against the inky dark of the forbidden field made the spark from each bug all the more wondrous. The trick was to remain on the fence for long enough to soak up the beauty of the tiny living stars, but not so long that my whereabouts became known. I tried to introduce Andy and Alice to the appeal of the fence during firefly season, but Alice – likely because her recurrent ear infections had disturbed her sense of balance – did not enjoy climbing, and Andy preferred trapping the fireflies to admiring their beauty out in the field; he was content to stalk his marvellous quarry on our side of the road.

Left to my own devices on top of the fence across the road, I imagined that maybe the fireflies, similar in so many ways to the stars twinkling in the night sky above, could hear wishes, just as the celestial bodies could. Maybe, between the sparkling both above and below, my wishes would have better odds of reaching God, who – according to the hymns in the *Moravian Youth Hymnal* and the minister at the church service we had attended before Christmas – was the only one truly in a position to grant them.

'Please, God,' I began tentatively and under my breath, 'bring Shiva home to me.'

The heavens were not rent by my beloved pet falling from the sky to my feet, but the fireflies seemed to flash with greater intensity, which I took as encouragement to repeat my wish once, twice, then ten times, until gradually my wish became a prayer.

One Wednesday a postcard arrived from Aunt Joanne. On the front, enormous mountains covered in snow rose up like sentinels; on the back, Aunt Joanne had scrawled in her spidery handwriting, 'Greetings All. Arrived safely in Alaska. Astounding scenery. Not as cold as you'd expect. Joanne.'

'It probably suits Aunt Joanne, Alaska,' Mom mused, 'she has that frontier spirit. It's just a pity it's so far away.'

'Why didn't she write "Love, Aunt Joanne"? And why didn't she write anything about Ted Noke?' I asked.

Mom looked at me quizzically. 'You do remember that Ted Noke isn't her boyfriend, don't you, Beth Anne?'

'I remember, but I thought she might have written something about Ted Noke anyway.'

Mom's expression became one of mild consternation, as though she had only then become aware that my reality didn't match hers. Which it didn't, because I was eight, and she was thirty-nine. 'Ted Noke didn't go to Alaska with Aunt Joanne, remember?' Mom reminded me, as if she still couldn't quite believe that I thought he had. 'Aunt Joanne might not have even spoken to him since she moved up there – what do I know? She hasn't spoken to me and I'm her sister, but then maybe she talks to her friends more. She probably does, come to think of it.'

'When will we see Aunt Joanne again?' I asked. 'Will we go to Alaska?'

Mom coughed on the drag she was taking of her cigarette. 'Umm, no, Beth Anne. I told you this too – Alaska is literally thousands of miles away. And we're certainly not all hopping on a plane just to see my sister – that would cost hundreds of dollars. It's more economical for Aunt Joanne to come visit us sometimes.'

Mom's mention of money led me to consider the Tooth Fairy. Our family's Tooth Fairy was seriously inconsistent: sometimes she left quarters for our offerings of milk teeth, sometimes even half-dollars, but occasionally the Tooth Fairy would forget about our lost teeth entirely. When that happened, my siblings and I needed to ask Mom to remind the Tooth Fairy that we had tooth money outstanding. Now and then, when the Tooth Fairy had her act together and was feeling especially flush, I sometimes woke up the morning after losing a tooth to find a shiny silver dollar under my pillow; sometimes Andy and Alice did too. Still, even if we saved all our tooth money for a year or two and pooled it together, some quick mental maths indicated that we would barely manage twenty dollars, let alone hundreds. My face fell.

'I forget sometimes that you're not even nine yet, Pumpkin,' Mom said, noticing my disappointment. 'You seem so grown-up most of the time. I know I tell you things I shouldn't, and I probably treat you like you're older than you are.'

I wasn't sure what to say. On the one hand, I was honoured that Mom saw me as a peer, but on the other hand, I sensed that I had failed her, through the accident of my age – I was not the friend Mom yearned for.

'That's OK,' I said, hoping to prove that although I might not know how to get to Alaska, I could still be trusted with all manner of confidences, 'I can handle it. I like it when you tell me things.'

Mom's eyes welled up. 'I love you, Beth Anne,' she said. 'You've always been my little ray of sunshine. It's Aunt Joanne's loss that she won't get to watch you grow up.'

'We could call her on the phone, like Dad calls us sometimes,' I suggested.

Mom clenched her teeth and her eyes went from moist to steely.

'Your father seems to think that phone calls make up for all those weekends he hasn't seen you,' Mom said.

I should have known better than to mention Dad, but the wound left by the divorce was like a scar whose itch, while it healed, sometimes became so unbearable that I was compelled to scratch it, tearing the painstakingly regenerated top layer off and gazing on in satisfaction as the red blood trickled out, only then to regret my lack of impulse control as the hot sticky fluid ran down my leg. Still, in for a penny, in for a pound. 'Could we call him sometimes, instead of waiting for him to call us?' I asked. I had seen Mom dialling numbers on the rotary phone, and the three of us had often played with the receiver, but always with the ringer depressed. None of us had any idea how many numbers were actually required to make a phone call, nor what the key combination of numbers would be should we want to reach our father.

'It's better that he calls you, Beth Anne,' Mom said. 'Let him pay for it,' she added grimly.

Janine asked me at school the next day if I could come to her house for a sleepover during the impending school summer holidays. I told Janine that I would ask my mom, but I didn't actually ask, for two reasons: first, because I was afraid Mom would say no, and second, because I was afraid Mom would say yes. Janine wasn't like Tovah, whom I still missed – she had been like me, a child out of time, whereas Janine was firmly rooted in both time and place. I wasn't sure I would know how to act at Janine's house, and anyway, I didn't want to create more problems for Mom to solve. When Janine inquired a couple of days later about the outcome of my request, I lied and told her my mom had said no. Janine was disappointed, but consoled me by telling me there were other girls who weren't allowed on sleepovers – that was when I knew Janine had become not just my protector, but also my friend.

It was late afternoon on the penultimate Friday of the school year when the argument started. The wine bottle had been on the table since at least Mom's arrival home from work, if it had even been put away from the night before. As soon as Marvin crossed the threshold of the front door, Mom was at him.

'So, are you staying here tonight, or are you going off to visit your dog?' she asked, as if she were a trial lawyer nailing the opposing side's witness to the wall.

'As a matter of fact, I was planning to go pay Shiva a visit,' Marvin answered measuredly.

'Yeah, right,' Mom said, her voice shot through with hostility. 'I know, OK? I know it isn't Shiva you're going to see. Why the hell did you ask me to marry you if you couldn't even go one full year without fucking someone else?'

'I told you going into this, Elizabeth, that I'd rather have an open marriage arrangement,' Marvin said, his tone still level.

'And I told you that was bullshit,' Mom growled. 'Open marriage, my ass. That's just a way for men to fuck as many women as they want. Let the woman decide she wants to sleep with someone else and forget it, that "open marriage" slams shut faster than the blink of an eye. I've had it with men who can't keep their dicks in their pants. But more than that, I've had it with women who play along. I'm going over there, Marvin, and I'm going to give Ms Ellie Tillerman a piece of my mind, and maybe take a piece of hers in return.'

Mom lunged towards the kitchen counter and drew the butcher's knife out of the knife block.

Weaponry took the situation to an unprecedented threat level, and my drive to protect myself and my little brother and sister kicked in. I ran into Andy's bedroom where he was once again engaged in modifying his Lego house, as he had been interminably since Christmas. 'Get out!' I screamed at Andy. 'Get out of the house! Now!'

'Why, what is it?' Andy asked, irritated that I was brutally tearing him away from his colourful plastic bricks.

'Mom and Marvin are fighting, and Mom has a knife! We've got to get out of the house!' I shouted. 'Just get out! Now!'

Andy looked more put out than distressed, but did as he was told, dropped his Lego pieces and loped away, leaving me to fetch Alice. Unlike Andy, Alice had already been listening to the row; she had retreated to her bedroom of her own volition and was now balled up under the covers, holding a pillow over her head to drown out the noise. Her body under the bedspread was shaking.

'Alice,' I said, pushing her as gently as I could, given the urgency.

'Alice, come on, you've got to get out of here. We've got to go outside. Mom has a knife.'

'I don't want to go outside,' Alice cried, her words muffled by the pillow. 'I don't ever want to go outside again. I just want to stay here.'

'Alice, you can't stay here – I don't know what Mom's going to do,' I pleaded.

Why I thought outside would be somehow safer than inside I have no idea; it was an instinctive, rather than a logical thought process, carried out by my reptilian brain rather than my neocortex, but once made, the rest of my brain jumped on board, and there was no turning back.

'Alice,' I begged, on the verge of tears, 'Alice, you're not safe here. You've got to come outside. Come on!' With that I threw back the blankets, exposing my sister's quaking form. I rocked her back and forth by the shoulder. 'Alice, come on!'

Finally Alice complied and we ran outside. Andy was already headed for the pond, while Alice and I stayed in the driveway, close enough to the house to hear our parents' voices, but far enough away to obscure their words.

My strategy backfired. The house could not contain the fire of my mother's rage and without warning both parents tumbled out onto the back deck. Mom was still clutching the butcher's knife, its dark brown wooden handle splotchy from years of repeated immersion in steaming dishwater; as she neared the edge of the deck, Mom raised the knife overhead with both hands. Marvin was both nimbler and stronger than Mom and before I could work out if she aimed to stab Marvin or herself with her utilitarian but deadly weapon, he had seized my mother by both wrists and forced down her hands. Marvin was strong, but Mom, with red-zone levels of adrenaline pumping through her blood, was almost the more powerful. Try as he might, Marvin couldn't both keep Mom's wrists still and simultaneously pry her fingers from the weathered wood.

'Liza!' Marvin shouted. 'For fuck's sake, Liza, just let go of the knife, and then we'll talk.'

'Fuck you!' Mom wailed, her face contorted. I could see she was tensing every muscle, like a lioness preparing to spring at its prey, directing every fibre of her body to aid her in breaking Marvin's grip. Mom's fury bestowed her with outsize force, and Marvin's hands were beginning to waver, like Andy's arm when I was about to beat him at arm wrestling.

But Marvin was sober, or nearly sober, and that gave him the winning advantage. At the exact moment that Mom overpowered him, ripping her hands free, he grabbed my mother by the waist, lifted her like a life-sized doll, and threw her off the back deck.

Time dilated as I traced the arc of my mother's body – the body that had conceived and given birth to me, my brother and my sister – as it rose at a slight angle; each millimetre her body travelled seemed to last an eternity. I willed the laws of physics to lapse, to make the peak only one more point on the trajectory that would carry my mother upward and still upward until she'd had time to grow wings, until she could fly away from all of her pain and sorrow, until she could come back to us as the angel that fluttered within her, caged but yearning.

The laws of physics remained in place, however, and Mom's body landed on the ground with a dull thud. Only then did I realise I had been shrieking. I sprinted towards my mother, leaving Alice where she had collapsed from horror at the side of the driveway, as Mom's disfigured body arose from the grass she had recently mown.

'You fucking broke my bones, you bastard,' Mom groaned, writhing into a hunched but upright position, 'but I can still fucking drive." Mom stumbled towards her car, right hand still clasping the butcher's knife, left hand clutching her now-broken ribs. Marvin watched, silent and immobile, from the deck.

Mom was in the car, the engine running. Without knowing quite how I had gotten there, I found myself at the closed passenger side window, banging on it with both my fists, shouting at my mother to stop. The butcher's knife lay between her seat and the passenger seat, the steel glinting in the last rays of the June sunlight.

Mom rolled down her own window. 'Beth, get the fuck out of my way, and don't you dare try to stop me,' she threatened.

I took two steps back, obeying her out of sheer force of habit, but when Mom revved the engine and sped out of the driveway, my personal safety became inconsequential and I raced after her, first pounding on the rear windscreen, then losing contact and running, running, running until Mom's car had disappeared from view.

Only then did I remember Alice. I'd run like that after Alice once, but now I had run away from her, leaving her alone with the man who had just almost killed my mother. My legs were burning, but I forced them to serve me as I pelted flat-out back towards the house. I got to the driveway to find Marvin starting the ignition of his VW bus. Alice was still hunched over in the verge, and even Andy had emerged from the relative quiet of the pond; he stood wordlessly at the far end of the driveway.

'Where are you going?' I yelled at Marvin. 'Are you going to kill her?'

Now it was Marvin's turn to roll down his window. 'I'm not going to kill her, Beth Anne,' he said tiredly. 'I'm going to try to stop her from killing herself or anybody else.'

And with that, he tore out of the driveway, leaving the three of us – me, my brother and our baby sister – alone in the gathering dusk, without even any fireflies to light our way.

30

Rocks

Quiet as deep as the soundlessness of space enveloped us. We were like three flickering stars in a constellation, separate yet linked, divided by distance that was negligible under normal circumstances, but now seemed as insurmountable as a journey to the moon. For some time none of us stirred, as if we were waiting to see, given the unexpected eclipses of both our sun and our moon, whether or not we could still exist. When time passed and we remained, we haltingly made our way towards each other, forming our own centre of gravity. To be more accurate, Andy and I walked slowly towards Alice, who still hadn't risen from the ground.

'I didn't think they'd come outside,' I said to my brother and sister by way of apology. 'We can go in now.'

Neither Andy nor Alice mentioned that they would have been better off staying in their respective rooms – safely both out of sight and, critically, unable to see – rather than dragged outside by me and forced to witness events whose marks would prove indelible. My brother and sister were generous like that, partly, to be sure, because of their forgiving natures, but mostly because we all instinctively recognised that if our parents deserted us entirely, I was our next best bet, unprepared and insufficient though I was to fend for us. Andy and I pulled Alice to her feet, then I headed to the front door, giving the back deck a wide berth; my siblings tagged along after me, as they had done so many times before, and would do so many times again.

Once inside, my inadequacy as a leader was instantly revealed, because although I wanted to, I was unable to call anyone to help us. Dad might come, I thought, if I could tell him what had happened: that both parents had driven away, that we had no idea when or if they might be coming back, and that we hadn't had dinner. Dad was far away – I understood that – but he wasn't as far as Alaska. The distance to Alaska meant that Aunt Joanne, although she was my godmother and meant to look after me in emergencies, was out of the question, and I couldn't bear facing the Masons again, not after what had befallen Fawn. That left my friends Tovah and Janine: both of them, I assumed, would have done their best to help us, but I had phone numbers for neither. Even if I had known my friends' numbers, I wasn't sure I'd be able to call them successfully because I had never placed a phone call in my life.

Not only could I not be trusted to enlist outside assistance, I could neither cook nor reliably tell the time. We scavenged what we could find, bravely disregarding Mom's rule prohibiting taking food without asking, and then, an indeterminate amount of time after night had fallen, I sent my brother and sister to bed.

'When is Mom coming back?' Alice asked mournfully when I said goodnight.

'I don't know when she's coming back, Alice,' I answered, not mentioning the distinct possibility that Mom might not ever be coming back.

Alice tried another tack. 'When is Marvin coming back?'

'I don't know that either,' I said. 'We just have to do the best we can while they're gone.'

I was sitting on the sofa, half-reading and half-slumbering, when Marvin returned; he was not surprised to find me still up.

Marvin was no longer my friend. I had loved him like a father and he had betrayed me. I cut right to the chase. 'Is Mom dead?'

Marvin tossed his car keys onto the table with more force than necessary; the keys skittered across the wood until they collided with the salt and pepper shakers. 'She's not dead, Beth Anne. She's in jail, which is where you end up if you intentionally destroy someone's property.'

I was familiar with jail from the board game *Monopoly*. I tried to picture my mother with her hands wrapped around the bars, surrounded by the orange wall, desperate to escape.

'Why didn't you get her out? Couldn't you pay?'

Marvin looked at me with new-found respect. 'You mean bail? How do you know about bail? Have you been watching too many detective shows on TV?'

Marvin was trying to be funny, but I didn't think, at that moment, that I would ever laugh again.

'Not from TV, from *Monopoly*,' I said. I stared at him. 'Why didn't you bail?'

'You mean why didn't I bail her out? Well, Beth Anne, in case you hadn't noticed, your mother is an alcoholic. I have a good understanding of how alcoholics work, and if you cover for them – if you bail them out of jail, for example – then you're enabling them, and they never really have a reason to get sober. You want your mom to stop drinking, don't you?'

I hated Marvin then, because he had put me in a corner. I would have to agree with him, even if by extension I was then consenting to leaving my mother with her hands clenched around metal bars and her teeth gritted in agony. I dropped my head to escape Marvin's gaze, but nodded in grudging assent.

'Of course you want your mom to stop drinking,' Marvin said. 'So do I. Staying in jail overnight might be just what she needs in the long run. Jail isn't a long-term solution – she'll have to go to rehab next, but we'll sort that piece out tomorrow.'

I was irritated at the incongruity of Marvin caring about Mom after he had thrown her off the back deck and given his heart to Ellie Tillerman, but it was slowly dawning on me that while I inhabited a black and white world, adults lived in a world of grey.

'Where's rehab?' I asked, hoping it would be somewhere very nearby.

'Rehab is short for rehabilitation, so it's not exactly a place of its own,' Marvin explained. 'Rehab is where you learn how to recover from alcoholism. There are rehab centres scattered here and there. Your mother will probably go to Brattleboro.'

'How long will she have to stay?'

'I don't know, Beth Anne, but I'll be leaving when she comes back,' Marvin added, as if I hadn't coped with enough for one night.

'What do you mean, leaving?' The thought struck me that maybe there was rehab for all manner of character flaws – maybe in addition to alcoholics, abusers could also end up in rehab. That must be where Marvin would be going: Mom and Marvin were just taking turns. 'Are you going to rehab after Mom?'

Marvin laughed outright. 'I'm not the one with the drinking problem, Beth Anne. No, I'll be leaving your mother. We shouldn't have ever gotten married, really, but I just couldn't resist her.'

A numbness crept over first my body, then my mind. I felt like I had been sucked into a black hole – all the edges of my world were lost, everything flattened out, and there was only emptiness. Except there wasn't. Every young child who first learns about black holes believes that they are what they say on the box – holes, containing nothing; every older child who has done their physics homework, however, knows that black holes are the exact opposite of nothing

– that, instead, their destructive power lies in the denseness of their mass. The black hole I disappeared into after my mother vanished and we were left in the care of the man who had broken her body was immeasurably heavy, and the mass at its centre was pain.

Just as in space, my personal black hole stopped time, because the only time that mattered any more was the moment at which Mom's airborne body had begun its descent. My mind replayed that evening for me, over and over, from the instant Marvin had lifted Mom – in what could have been an embrace, but instead became an assault – to the moment when my mother lay broken on the ground below him. I rewound the evening further countless times, searching for the chink where I might have used my own weapons, such as they were, to alter the outcome. Maybe if I had risked Mom's wrath and courageously poured out the contents of every green bottle Mom wouldn't have ended up out of control that night. Maybe if I had brought my brother and sister into the room where the argument was taking place, protesting with our mere presence, the grown-ups might have been shamed into something closer to appropriate behaviour. Maybe if it had been me that tackled Mom and wrested the knife from her hands, Mom would still be with us and Marvin would have no plans to leave – that was the most redemptive, although the least realistic, alternate ending of all.

* * *

My actual redemption came from an unexpected source. The day after school ended, a motorhome lumbered into our driveway and Grandma Lenore stepped out.

'Hi, kids,' Grandma Lenore said in her bird-like warble, 'so good to see you. Now, there's someone I want you to meet – Beau, come here for a minute.'

The driver's side door of the motorhome opened and a big man who looked for all the world like Santa Claus without the beard appeared. 'Well, hello there!' he boomed. 'Haven't I heard all about you three!'

The man – Beau – had a belt buckle inlaid with turquoise the size of three silver dollars over which his sizeable belly protruded. A smaller but matching piece of turquoise hung on his chest on a funny sort of necklace more like a shoestring of black leather; below the stone, the tails of the leather separated, each ending in a shiny silver tube.

'This is my husband, Beauregard. We were married a few months ago – did your dad tell you? You can call him Grandpa Morin,' Grandma Lenore explained.

As if on cue, Grandpa Morin opened his arms out wide. 'Come to Grandpa!' he shouted.

Andy, Alice and I stayed firmly in position, befuddled by this stranger who was now apparently family.

'What, do I look like I'm gonna bite?' Grandpa Morin said, feigning hurt. 'I just wanna give my new grandchildren a great big bear hug! I might be fat, but I promise I didn't get that way from eating children! Ha ha ha!'

I took a couple of tentative steps in Grandpa Morin's direction.

'That's the spirit! You're Beth Anne, aren't you? What a lovely name – Beth Anne! I have a daughter of my own called Mary Anne, and I always call her Mary Anne, never just Mary. I hope everyone calls you Beth Anne?'

'We call her Beth sometimes,' Andy informed our new grandfather.

Grandpa Morin raised his eyebrows in mock horror. 'Oh, that's gotta stop! You'll always be Beth Anne to me, little missy! Now come here, I've been kneeling for ages waiting for my hug, and I'm beginning to feel it on my knees! You three are the slowest huggers on the planet – don't make me stay down here any longer, or I might not ever be able to get back up again!'

'Go ahead, kids, give your grandpa a hug. He won't hurt you,' Grandma Lenore said, looking at her new husband indulgently.

The last thing in the world I wanted was to be the reason an adult remained on the ground. I skipped over to this man with his loud exclamations and his unusual accessories and he wrapped one beefy arm around me, leaving the other one extended to welcome my brother and sister, who soon followed. Soon we were all enclosed in our new grandfather's bountiful embrace.

'That's the spirit,' Grandpa Morin said, at a volume somewhat more suitable to our proximity. 'I like bear hugs, and I especially like bear hugs with my grandkids. Now I've heard from your Grandma Lenore that you three have been through a bit of a tough time, and I want you to know that for the next week, you have nothing to worry about except trying to sleep while I'm snoring next door! Ha ha ha!'

At this, Grandpa Morin gave us all an extra squeeze, and he held us there – in a sort of football huddle – for longer than we had ever been held as a group before.

Grandma Lenore, meanwhile, spoke to Marvin. 'From what I understand, you've been on your own with our grandchildren this past week.'

Marvin nodded.

'Well, I know something about being a single parent – it's not easy, whatever the circumstances. God bless you,' Grandma Lenore said, patting Marvin maternally on the shoulder. Marvin, normally unruffled, reddened. 'Now, Beau,' Grandma Lenore trilled, 'we should be getting on – we've got a long drive ahead of us.'

It was indeed a long drive. Grandma Lenore and Grandpa Morin drove us all the way to Swallow Falls State Park, in the westernmost part of Maryland, where Lenore's sister Margaret and her husband Lenny had decked the awning outside their motorhome with what looked like Christmas lights, even though it was the middle of June.

311

Andy and I were relegated to a tent outside our grandparents' camper van, while Alice, because she was the youngest, was given the spare berth in the van itself. Andy and I considered ourselves the lottery winners, because not only did we get a tent all to ourselves, but we were also that much further from Grandpa Morin's earth-shaking snores. Grandpa Morin's sleep symphony wasn't limited to night-time either; several days after lunch, when Grandma Lenore wanted to take us out adventuring, Grandpa Morin volunteered himself to look after the campsite. When we returned and Grandpa Morin was napping, we could hear him from several pitches away; as we inched closer, giggling, we could see the entire camper van shuddering with each of Grandpa Morin's exhalations.

We were welcomed back to the campsite one afternoon by a still more extraordinary sound. New campers had taken up residence on the site next to that of our grandparents; they were eating lunch in the company of their jet-black mynah bird, who was holding court.

'Ritz crackers! You're pretty!' the mynah bird warbled when we came within earshot.

'Would you listen to that?' Grandpa Beau boomed. 'Lenore, these wonderful folks are from your old stomping grounds – they've come all the way up from Georgia! And kids, you'd better hold on to your Ritz crackers – Peaches here can't get enough of them.'

'Ritz crackers!' the bird echoed.

Grandpa Morin threw his head back in hysterics. When he'd recovered sufficiently, Beau asked the silver-haired couple from Georgia, 'So what else can Peaches say?'

'She says "Hello", don't you, Peaches?' the man said, while the woman refilled their plastic glasses with iced tea.

Peaches cooperated. 'Hello,' the mynah bird called out. 'Hello! Don't be scared! Hello!'

Andy, Alice and I all laughed. Alice ventured towards the bird, holding her hand out tentatively.

'You can come closer,' the woman from Georgia said. 'Peaches won't hurt you, especially if you offer her a Ritz cracker,' she added, winking at her husband.

'Why is the bird talking?' I asked.

'You're pretty! Ritz crackers!' Peaches said, which didn't seem like an answer.

'She's a mynah bird,' the man explained, in a southern drawl even thicker than my dad's. 'They imitate what they hear, like parrots. Peaches tends to repeat herself,' the man said, stroking the back of the bird's neck. The man handed Alice a couple of bird food pellets. 'We call these Ritz crackers, but they're really bird food. Now hold out your hand flat, like this, little miss,' the man said, prying Alice's fingers open and flattening them out, 'and after you give Peaches the "cracker", she'll have something special to say to you.'

Alice did as instructed. Peaches hopped over and pecked the bird food out of her palm.

'Peace be with you,' Peaches cackled, after gulping the pellets down her throat.

Alice widened her eyes in amazement and delight.

Grandpa Beau's belly shook with laughter, cementing my theory that our new grandfather, if not Santa Claus himself, was closely related to the great man. 'Doesn't that just figure, a Catholic mynah bird? I'm Catholic too – imagine if Peaches went along to Communion! What a hit she'd be!'

'That's what we were thinking,' the woman from Georgia said. 'We thought our priest might need a break. He hasn't taken us up on our offer of Peaches as an officiant yet though.'

'Ha ha ha!' Grandpa Morin chortled. 'Give her another "wafer", Alice!'

The man poured a few more pellets into Alice's cupped hand.

'Don't be scared!' Peaches said in anticipation. 'Hello!'

Alice offered Peaches the new pellets, with the same result. The bird gobbled down the food, then blessed my little sister. 'Peace be with you! Ritz crackers!'

'Would you listen to that! I think she's fond of you, Alice,' Grandpa Beau said.

Alice puffed up with pride. I liked Grandpa Morin.

My favourite trail in the park next to the campground, and the trail we returned to the most, was the Swallow Falls Canyon Trail. The trail officially began under the wide arc of a dark brown wooden sign bearing its name; it then wound along beside the Youghiogheny River – along paths strewn with wood, over rocks and up steps built into the hillsides – all under a canopy of ancient trees. The roar of Muddy Creek Falls, the first of four waterfalls on the Canyon Trail, made it hard to hear Grandma Lenore when she expounded – in well-formed sentences containing many scientific words – on the formation of waterfalls in general, and on the geology of the area in particular. Grandma Lenore was well educated, and her amassed knowledge coloured her interpretation of her entire world. I was going on a pretty walk through the woods next to a river, but Grandma Lenore was appreciating the mountain laurels at eye level and the towering eastern hemlocks and white pines above, while simultaneously inspecting the path the Youghiogheny had cut through the rock formations formed millions of years ago. It was the age of our surroundings that Grandma Lenore most wanted us to fathom.

'You're well acquainted with the dinosaurs, aren't you?' Grandma Lenore asked.

'Yes. My favourite is stegosaurus, but Andy's favourite is T. rex and Alice likes brontosaurus,' I replied.

Grandma Lenore's eyes twinkled. 'That's fantastic. Isn't it just like a boy to choose T. rex? Personally, I find the herbivorous dinosaurs

314

far more fascinating. Be that as it may, the rocks here are older even than the dinosaurs. Can you believe that, Beth Anne?'

'Was there no life on Earth when these rocks were made?'

'Heavens – what do they teach third-graders nowadays? Earth was teeming with life long before the dinosaurs entered the picture, Beth Anne, but the creatures that existed then looked nothing like the creatures of today. The climate was drastically different, and we would have found it most inhospitable indeed. These rocks formed in the Pennsylvanian period during the late Carboniferous era.'

'Like Pennsylvania where the Evans' farm is?' I asked, to indicate that I was paying attention.

Grandma Lenore's eyes darkened. 'Yes, that Pennsylvania.'

We gazed at the waterfall in silence for a moment until Grandma Lenore's eyes brightened again.

'Do you know how long ago the Carboniferous era was, Beth Anne?' my grandmother asked me.

I chanced an answer. 'A million years?'

'Longer. Almost three hundred million years ago. These rocks, Beth Anne, have been here for not just thousands, but hundreds of millions of years, and they may well be here for hundreds of millions of years more. These rocks were here long before we were, and they'll be here long after we're gone. Isn't the world amazing?'

Grandma Lenore's enthusiasm was infectious, but at night, as I lay in the tent listening to Andy's quiet breathing beside me and Grandpa Morin's noisy snoring through the flimsy walls of the camper van, the cold hands of panic would take hold of me. I'd altered my by now habitual prayer, giving my mother pride of place – 'Please God, bring Mom and Shiva home to me' – and I'd rattle that prayer off to myself in a whisper, over and over and over again, until finally sleep overpowered fear.

31

Fireworks

W hether because I'd bumped Shiva down the prayer list or because God's ways are inscrutable, when we came back from Maryland ten days later, Mom was at the house on Braintree Hill, but Shiva was not. Neither for that matter was Marvin, nor any of his possessions. It was as though he had merely been a figment of our collective imagination, and as though the rest of us were well on our way towards a similar fate, because anything of ours that would fit in a box was out of sight. The rooms echoed, and the only source of recorded music was a small transistor radio, because the turntable had been Marvin's, as well as most of the records. Like the house, Mom was changed too, most visibly by the seven-inch foam collar around her neck, but also in a far more important, albeit invisible way – Mom, at least for the moment, had stopped drinking. She told us as much over dinner that first night of our new lives with her.

'I'm sober now, kids. To stay that way, I'll be going to AA meetings once a week for at least the next three months. And guess what, we're moving to our very own house on Saturday! It's tiny – almost like a doll's house – but we're going to own it, thanks to my parents, so we won't be relying on any man to keep the roof over our heads, like we had to with your father, Michael and Marvin. That'll be such a blessed relief.'

'Why do you need the funny collar?' Alice asked. 'Can I try it?'

'Alice, you wouldn't be able to see a thing if you put this collar on. It's made for grown-ups – it would cover your whole face. And besides, it's for me, because I'm still recovering from the injuries of the night before I went away for a while. Marvin broke two of my ribs,' Mom added.

'Did you have them in casts while you were gone?' I asked.

'You can't put ribs in a cast very easily, Beth Anne.'

'Why didn't Marvin want to say goodbye? And what about Shiva?' I inquired, although I knew I shouldn't.

Mom might have been sober, but she still minced no words. 'Marvin didn't want to say goodbye because he's a bastard, that's why, and Shiva was his dog, Beth Anne, not ours.'

My not yet nine-year-old emotional hardware was not programmed to cope with this amount of loss; my system began an unexpected shutdown, but Mom – perhaps because she was sober – intervened.

'When we move to our new house, Beth Anne, we can get a puppy of our own. How would that be? Maybe a Labrador mix or something. A friendly mutt. Any dog would be better than that bloodthirsty white shepherd.'

It stung that Mom had badmouthed the friend whose return I had longed for and prayed for almost as much as her own, but the promise of a puppy outweighed my indignation. I knew just what to call our future family member. 'Can we name her Fawn? After the calf from the Masons' farm?'

'That's a bit macabre, don't you think? But if that's what you want, we could put it to a vote. Speaking of macabre,' Mom continued, 'I should let you know that our new home is right next to the town cemetery. It's also very tiny. We'll be building an extension, because right now my bedroom will also serve as the living room, and two of you will need to share a room. But none of that matters, because it will be ours.'

'Will the house be haunted by ghosts from the graveyard?' Andy asked.

'I'd prefer to think of them as friendly spirits of the dearly departed,' Mom said. 'People believe in ghosts because they're afraid of death, Andrew, but death is nothing to be afraid of. It happens to all of us, sooner or later. Ghosts are a figment of the imagination, created by humans to help them cope. Like mythology. People make up stories to explain what they can't understand.'

Andy, with his brain that already gravitated towards the rational and scientific, nodded in agreement. Alice latched on to "ghost" - possibly the only word she had managed to pick out of Mom's response.

'I want to be a ghost for Halloween,' Alice announced.

'Halloween's months away,' Mom pointed out.

Alice stood firm. 'I still want to be a ghost.'

We each said something vaguely affirming to Alice, but I was not ready to let go of the previous subject. 'I don't want death to happen soon,' I said. 'Not for me. Not for any of us.'

Mom waved her hand dismissively. 'You don't have to worry about death for many, many years, Beth Anne. You have long-lived genes on both sides, my side and your father's side. Except for your dad's father of course, who died young of a heart attack.'

'I thought he died in a helicopter accident?'

My question caught Mom off guard; her eyes widened and she looked straight at me. 'Do you mean Frank Evans?'

'Yes, Dad's dad,' I confirmed.

'Frank Evans wasn't your dad's birth father, Beth Anne, remember? Your dad's birth father was Arthur Lynskey, the writer, who left your grandmother before your father could even walk.'

'But Frank Evans was still Dad's father, just like Marvin was our father,' I insisted.

'Marvin was not your father. He was your stepfather. And look what good that did.'

We accompanied Mom to an Alcoholics Anonymous meeting for the first time that Thursday evening. The meetings were held in the basement of the local branch of the United Church of Christ, a white clapboard church with black shutters, coincidentally christened Bethany.

The similarity to my name had not escaped Mom. 'Doesn't it just figure, Beth Anne, that the meetings meant to keep me sober would be held in a church named after you? We may even have to try out the church service on Sunday, as I can't help but think this is all a sign from above.'

Mom, I sensed, was mostly, but not completely joking on both counts; for lack of a suitable response, I kept silent and clasped Alice's hand harder. I wasn't sure what to expect from a meeting of people who drank too much, and I feared the worst.

The doors down to the church basement were exceptionally wide, designed as they were to allow through several parishioners at once on their way to post-service refreshments, but while the doors were noteworthy, the stairs were even more remarkable – they spanned from one end of the hall nearly to the other, as if the parishioners, once through those doors, would then fan out in every direction. The stairs were considerately fitted with commercial-grade black no-slip strips – very like sandpaper to the touch, and with the same hint of sparkle – meant to keep parishioners safe in their hurry to reach the after-church coffee and cake on a Sunday.

Inside the room, a seemingly random collection of perhaps sixteen people sitting on grey metal folding chairs had arranged themselves in a loose circle. Some were chatting in twos or threes, some sat – arms crossed over beer bellies – stoically alone, others had pulled up extra chairs especially for their ashtrays and puffed intently on their cigarettes as small clouds of smoke formed above them. The attendees came in all shapes, sizes and ages, but – as this was a small town in Vermont in 1976 – in only one colour, except for the more devoted sun-worshippers among them, who leaned towards brown. Normally Mom would have been among the ranks of the tanned, but given her weeks of inpatient rehab and the weeks spent mostly indoors with the Brothers Gallo prior to admittance, Mom's melanin had some catching up to do.

Mom had forewarned the secretary of the meeting that her children would be attending; when the meeting was called to order, the secretary welcomed us by directing an additional procedural note to the floor.

'As you can all see, Elizabeth has her kids with her. Elizabeth can't afford babysitting at the moment, so I told her the kids would be welcome to play here, as long as they behave themselves. Don't let the kids stop you from saying what you need to say – Elizabeth assured me there's no language any of you can use that the kids haven't heard before.' The secretary turned to us. 'You three can pull up chairs behind your mom, but you can also play on the stage or on the stairs, as long as you're quiet. And remember, kids, for you – just like for everyone else in this room – what you hear here, stays here. That means you don't talk about it with your friends at school.'

It had been a rhetorical statement, but Andy commented anyway. 'We're not in school right now. School starts in September.'

The secretary peered over her reading glasses at Andy. 'Well, don't talk about what you've heard here when school starts back up then, young man,' she said.

She then led the assembly through a recitation of the Lord's Prayer, during which all the adults in the circle lowered their heads and two-thirds of them closed their eyes. Next, she passed around a laminated sheet with large print and asked those who were willing to introduce themselves and read aloud one of the Twelve Steps.

'Hi, my name is Samantha and I'm an alcoholic,' began a gaunt, wizened woman with layered silver hair. ' "Step One: We admitted we were powerless over alcohol – that our lives had become unmanageable." '

As the sheet made its way around the circle, a couple of people skipped their turns. One man with a thick neck and a red face was so choked up already that he couldn't even introduce himself. One woman in a twinset who looked like a librarian made it through 'I'm Jenny and I'm an alcoholic' before her voice caught and she had to pass reading a step on to the next person. As Mom's moment in the spotlight drew nearer, I paid closer and closer attention. Part of me wished that Mom wouldn't say the words everyone else had said, because it was clear to me that to be an alcoholic was some sort of failure, but part of me desperately hoped she would, because it was also evident that everyone sitting in that church basement wanted nothing more than to right that wrong and be rid of their addiction. Some of the people in that circle scared me – the woman with the wayward eye and the straggly hair, the man with the mechanical voice – but if they could help my mother relinquish the yoke that alcohol had laid on her, then they were friends of mine, and I would be proud of Mom if she publicly joined their motley crew.

When the wayward-eye woman handed Mom the sheet, I held my breath. Mom scanned to the Step that had fallen to her, sucked in a breath, and said, 'Hi, my name is Elizabeth – or Liza, if it's easier – and I'm an alcoholic. "Step Eleven: Sought through prayer and meditation to improve our conscious contact with God as we understood Him, praying only for knowledge of His will for us and the power to carry that out." '

I breathed out, rejoicing inwardly at Mom's bravery, then went to join Andy and Alice's game on the wide and welcoming stairs.

We moved house two days later and a bunch of Mom's new AA friends came to help. My only job was to occupy Andy and Alice and keep myself and my siblings out of the way. I accomplished this by starting a long game of hide-and-seek among the gravestones that would be our new neighbours. By dinnertime Mom was tired but elated.

'So how about that – here we are in our very own house!' Mom announced as we sat down to a meal of TV dinners. I had been granted my favourite: Swanson's *Salisbury Steak*, complete with chicken noodle soup appetizer and peach cobbler dessert. It was exciting to be in our very own home, but it was more immediately exciting to watch the steam rise up out of the peach cobbler when I broke open the top with my spoon so the peaches would cool down enough to eat by the time I'd finished the rest of the meal. The house, just as Mom had warned us, was indeed cosy, but the piano was downstairs in what would be both the living room and Mom's bedroom until the extension was built, my white iron bedframe was already assembled in the smaller bedroom upstairs, and my books were in a box at the foot of my bed, so I had everything I needed, except for someone to tell me the continuation of the story of Lulela and her flying horse. Still, I was more than capable of making that up myself.

Mom was true to her word: the morning after the move, although we were still surrounded by boxes, Mom told us to get dressed up for church. This time, instead of heading straight down the stairs into the basement, we ascended to the Bethany sanctuary. An usher led us to a pew towards the back, and we filed in while a woman with flaming hair and a white robe played an unfamiliar but beautiful tune on the piano. Rails on the back of the pew in front of us held copies of the church hymnal, which I noticed was not the *Moravian Youth Hymnal*; there was also a small wooden shelf with three half-dollar-sized holes between the hymnal rails.

'What are the holes for?' I whispered to Mom.

'They're for the Communion glasses,' Mom answered.

This meant nothing to me, but I didn't have time to follow up, because the woman with the red hair, who had left the piano and was now standing facing us at the edge of the staircase leading to the altar, had opened her arms wide and was reciting Psalm 100 in a rich and resonant voice. The sleeves of the minister's robe hung down, making her look like the imprint of a snow angel come to life; she smiled broadly when she announced that we should now turn to the hymn 'Morning Has Broken'.

I elbowed Mom and hissed, 'That's not a hymn! That's a Cat Stevens song!'

'It was a hymn first, Beth Anne. Now stop talking and start singing,' Mom said, leading by example with her soft and breathy but pitch-perfect alto.

I did my best to join in, but was distracted by the children in the choir at the front of the sanctuary. They too were wearing white robes and while most of them looked like they'd been tapped by the same angel who'd visited the minister, some of them looked nervous, and a few looked like they would rather be at home watching TV. In other words, they looked like nice, normal kids, and although I couldn't jump rope, I could sing.

I nudged Mom again. I could tell she was vaguely irritated by my continued interruptions, but now that she wasn't drinking, her boundaries of acceptable interaction had expanded and her irritation gave way to affection.

'What is it now?' she asked in a low voice.

'I want to join the choir,' I whispered back.

Andy shushed me, giving me the evil eye and putting his finger to his pursed lips. 'Shut up, Beth Anne,' Andy hissed. 'I like this song.'

'It'd be better to have you up there with the choir than back here disturbing your brother,' Mom said, grinning. 'I'll ask the minister if they could use any more singers.'

We weren't the only ones celebrating our independence that summer. On the Fourth of July, the United States of America would celebrate her bicentennial, marking two hundred years since the Declaration of Independence was adopted by the Founding Fathers on the same date in 1776. I didn't have the slightest inkling at the time that there was any ambiguity to the Bicentennial – that my country, draped in the Stars and Stripes, had stolen land from the Native Americans, who had called it home for so many thousands of years that it was impossible to assign ages to their nations, never mind pin down actual birthdays. Yes, I was aware there had been some fighting between the Native Americans and the Pilgrims, but after the fighting, according to my sources, they had shared Thanksgiving together - when the men with the feather headdresses and the men with the black hats with golden buckles made up and became friends again. I knew all about fighting and making up, having fought and made up with my brother and sister countless times, so I guessed that if the two warring factions could sit at a table sharing turkey and pumpkin pie, then the Native Americans and the Pilgrims wouldn't later leave the table to do each other serious harm. Not so with the mean British and their infuriating Tea Tax. I had a love/hate relationship with the British: while I treasured certain British storytellers and felt a kinship with my transatlantic cousins thanks to my own distant British background, as an American – and particularly as an American child during the American Bicentennial – I also regarded the British as our historic enemy. How could the British presume to control our feisty young nation from the other side of the ocean? How could they stand in the way of our independence? I hero-worshipped Paul Revere, who had famously ridden to Lexington in time to warn the colonial militia of an impending British attack. I pictured him in his dashing uniform, somehow swinging two lanterns while galloping at breakneck speed, and I longed to have been the one to perform that feat of unspeakable valour.

It hadn't always been certain that the United States of America would still be united in 1976. There had been the Civil War, fought by the North against the South because the South wanted to keep slaves and the North believed the slaves should be freed. I had never properly met a black person, but as my mom and my little sister became toasted marshmallow brown and coffee brown respectively by the end of each summer, I saw absolutely no reason why the colour of somebody's skin should lead to their enslavement, so I was pleased to live in the North, as it had been on the sensible side of that particular conflict. After what had apparently been a bitter and bloody war, the South had come around to the North's way of thinking, slavery was abolished and the North and the South were again unified.

American flags were everywhere during the summer of 1976. I wished Vermont could have laid claim to the first star rather than the fourteenth on the square of Old Glory Blue, but fourteen was still quite good, far better than poor California, at thirty-one, or worse yet, Hawaii, at fifty. I had only to hear the opening descending minor thirds of 'The Star-Spangled Banner' to throw my shoulders back, clutch my right hand over my heart and gaze proudly at the Stars and Stripes.

Mom took us to the town fireworks the night before the Fourth of July. We joined the long line of cars inching towards the grassy field repurposed for the night as both parking lot and picnic lawn. Mom's window was already rolled down, so nothing prevented the man collecting money from leaning his forearms on the black rubber window seal.

'This yer first time at the Randolph fireworks?' the man asked. He was wearing a green baseball cap bearing the John Deere logo that looked as if it had seen him through several harvests already and would be made to see him through several more.

'It is, in fact,' Mom admitted, opening her tawny leather saddlebag and handing over her crumpled five-dollar bill.

The man smiled. 'I thought as much. I took the money last year too, and I don't recall seeing a woman as beautiful as you here then. And I see you got some mighty cute kiddos with you too. This yer first time at the Randolph fireworks, kids?'

'Yes,' we all answered.

'This is our first time seeing any fireworks,' I specified.

'Really? You ain't seen fireworks 'fore now?'

'No,' I said, and my brother and sister both shook their heads from side to side in confirmation.

'Well, ain't you in fer a treat! This here is gonna be an extra special display 'cause of the Bicentennial, and there ain't a cloud in the sky nor any wind to speak of. Perfect weather for settin' 'em off. Just follow my buddy down thataway, and he'll show you where to park yer car, then you can take yer blanket and move to the front, ma'am, so the kiddos here can get a good view.'

We did as the man suggested and traipsed through the rows of already-parked cars until we reached the crowd of picnic blankets. Mom spotted a space suitable for our plaid woollen blanket and spread it on the longish grass now damp from the night-time dew.

We heard the whistle first, then the bang, then the sky erupted with colours: long strands of red, orange and yellow arced out from the bright star of the fireworks' centres, fizzling at their ends into blackness, only to be replaced by new wonders. The real stars, arranged in constellations far beyond where the fireworks could hope to reach, formed a backdrop to the controlled explosions below, like a set especially designed for this very human show of beautiful chemistry skillfully engineered. My mouth hung open in amazement from the first boom and didn't shut until after the finale.

The following morning, Mom took us to the village Fourth of July parade. The insistent rhythm of the marching band's cadence drove the Rotary Club and 4H floats forward, and there were flags, flags and more flags. I was fit to explode with patriotic pride. My motherland was a great country – one nation under God, with liberty and justice for all. We had shown those pesky Brits what for, transforming ourselves from a lowly colony into the land of the free and the home of the brave, demonstrating once and for all that anything was possible in America the beautiful. And if my country was proof of that triumph on a national level, then my most immediate family was proof of a similar triumph on a personal level, because just like the United States of America, we too had thrown off our oppressors, we were reunited after battle and we too were finally free.

Acknowledgements

Thank you to my friend Monica Byles, editor extraordinaire, without whom this book would be suffocating under the weight of hundreds of superfluous semicolons. Monica's offer to read any book I managed to complete - an offer I'm not sure she realised I would take so seriously - was like a light at the end of the tunnel while I worked on this manuscript.

Thank you to all those who read, commented on, and liked my blog and social media posts during the ten years it took me to become skilled enough as a writer to attempt a book-length work.

Thank you to Helene Parry who successfully submitted two of my poems to Fitzrovia News prior to the commencement of the writing of this novel; seeing my poetry in print in a column in a newspaper made me hungry to see my prose in print in the pages of a book.

Thank you to my first readers, Suzanne Gilbey, Lauren Harris, and Laura Lennuyeux-Comnene, for both their enthusiastic praise and their constructive criticism. Thank you to Tracey Mullins for writerly support. Thanks to my second wave of readers whose feedback kept me motivated to pursue publication.

Thank you to the many establishments that didn't kick me out although my tea cup was empty.

Thank you to BBC 6 Music for their company during this long and solitary journey. Particular thanks to Mary Anne Hobbs for her inspiring *Three-Minute Epiphany* interviews with a wide range of artists and to Chris Hawkins who, unbeknownst to him, provided me with the title of this book through his *Five Before Six* feature.

Thank you to my sisters, whose support for this work means a great deal to me, to my brothers, just for being my brothers, and to my Boston parents for - perhaps unintentionally - teaching me that "artist" is a bona fide job title. Thanks to my Vermont parents, especially to my mother, without whose unwavering belief in and encouragement of my writing habit this book would not have been possible.

Thank you to my husband, Håkan, who always believed I was capable of writing a book and only wondered why it had to take me so long.

Thank you to our two children, Sam and Nina, who were my best cheerleaders and who tolerated frequent late dinners during the writing process without complaining.

Finally, thank you for reading.

Permissions and Suggestions

***

If you are currently affected by any of the issues raised in this story, please know that there are individuals and organisations ready, willing, and able to help you. I encourage you to seek them out.

If you instead find yourself wondering how you might help real children whose every days are darker than Beth Anne Evans' worst day, I hope you will consider how you might be a firefly.

About the Author

Bess Linnet grew up in the United States but has lived in the United Kingdom for many years. Despite rejection by every MFA in Creative Writing programme she applied to in her twenties, Bess never gave up on her dream of becoming an author. Bess began writing *Three Before Nine* just after her fiftieth birthday, and this is her debut novel.

Bess lives with her Swedish husband, their two children and Harry the Jack Russell in southwest London. She usually writes at cafés because at home she is easily distracted by housework, family administration, and social media.

If writing doesn't pan out, Bess is considering taking up full-time busking. She will have the distinction of being the only guitar-playing busker to use a music stand, as while Bess loves to write words, she has a dreadful time committing lyrics to memory. Look for her covering David Bowie next time you're in the capital.

Lightning Source UK Ltd.
Milton Keynes UK
UKHW011831210221
379146UK00001B/21